Wicked Academia
LOST STARS

Jasmine Jenkins & Sophie Suliman

LUNA FOX
PRESS

WICKED ACADEMIA

LOST STARS

Jasmine Jenkins & Sophie Suliman

Published by Luna Fox Press

First Edition published April 2022

Map Design © 2022 by Jasmine Jenkins

Cover Design and Illustration © 2022 by Jasmine Jenkins

Identifiers

ISBN: 978-1-7780319-1-5 (eBook)

ISBN: 978-1-7780319-2-2 (paperback)

ISBN: 978-1-7780319-0-8 (hardcover)

To Mom and Dad, with love
and
To anyone who has ever believed in the magic of a falling star

Wicked Academia is an adult fantasy book. It contains mature themes and is intended for audiences 18+. For a complete list of content warnings, please go to www.wickedacademia.com

THE
CELESTIAL ACADEMY
FOR FALLEN STARS

MEADOW OF SHATTERED STARS

ENCHANTED FOREST

POND OF GALAXIES

THE GLASS CATHEDRAL

FARMS

THE ACADEMY

SELENE CRESCENT

ISLE OF
ARGOS

The Isle of Argos

KIRRINTSOVA

Mount Laeto

Fort Exoligus

Ever Ash Grove

Balthazar's Fangs

Fort Allistar

Balthazar's Fangs

Zaremara

Corpse Marshes

Naberiysk

Novagrad

Tariq Cay

Qusen

As Above

Thraina

So Below

Singing Harvest Moon

A time of change and prosperity. The days grow colder, but orange light still lingers to glow over the bountiful harvests, where farmers reap the hard work of the warmer moons. Workers sing legends of Rhaemyria's great fires that blazed with the same colors as the leaves.

It is also a time of celebration as the Celestial Academy for Fallen Stars welcomes potential recruits to the floating Isle of Argos. These hopeful students will see if they are blessed by a falling star and will wield the magic of the gods.

1
IN WHICH VIVIAN GETS A VERY PECULIAR CUSTOMER

VIVIAN GREYWICK WISHED she could fly. But in the land of Thraina, wishes weren't granted from falling stars. They were granted by those who caught them. And Vivian knew better than to place her wishes in a Starling's hand.

So, she couldn't fly over the massive crowd blocking her path. Couldn't even wish for it. She was going to be *so* late and in *so* much trouble.

"Excuse me!" Her words were lost to the noise of the streets. If only she'd left the apartment when Marion had. Her sister, younger by several minutes, had no difficulty pushing her way through a throng.

The sun had barely risen, golden rays cresting between the tall turrets of the castle, melting the frost on the town's roofs and windowsills. Already the warmth of summer had faded, and autumn had fully encapsulated Wolfhelm. The morning cold prickled her cheeks and ungloved hands.

The crowd was meandering, looking into foggy shoppe windows, pausing at every statue, marveling at the blue and gold flags strung between houses. There were so many visitors from out of town, all here for Unification Day. *All here to catch a glimpse of the Prince.*

Her sister Marion said festivals were self-indulgent nonsense. Vivian wouldn't go that far, but they certainly were a nuisance. It really was all Prince Darius's fault for having Unification Day in the first place.

And all these visitors were potential customers; another reason Mrs. Meryladon wouldn't tolerate her being so late. Vivian dodged horses, carriages, and people alike, her worn boots slipping over the slick cobblestone. As she ran, she swept her chestnut hair up on her head with a blue ribbon.

She turned the last corner. Lanterns shone halos through the lingering mist. There was the Wondrous Wick, the candle shoppe in which she worked. They did not sell the dull candles that provided light in the dark, or the strange narrow kind alchemists melted over their creations. These candles were purely for smelling, or as Vivian liked to think of it, to escape. To capture a whiff of the sea or feel the chill of a crisp autumn day. Shoppers bought these to relive their most fantastic memories with absolutely no magic at all—because, for an ordinary person, magic was forbidden.

And today everyone seemed to want a bit of that magic. A line curved around the shoppe.

"No, no, no." Vivian pushed through the crowd, mud splashing up her hem as she didn't bother dodging the puddles.

Orange buttery light spilled onto the damp cobblestone from inside the shoppe. Silhouettes shifted within. So busy already. *Maybe I can slip in and avoid Mrs. Meryladon...*

Darkness crept along the path beside her, and she skidded to a stop in front of the shoppe door. An enormous shadow slithered over the buildings, causing street lanterns to bloom as if it were night. Her heart beat wildly in her chest. Gasps of awe sounded from the crowd, townsfolk straining their necks to look up.

A curtain of clouds split and out soared a floating island, so great it eclipsed the rising sun as it sailed across the grey-blue sky.

She could only see the bottom: jagged brown rocks, like the tip of an upside-down mountain. Waterfalls cascaded off and disappeared into the mist surrounding the massive island. Through the clouds, Vivian swore she caught a gleam of white towers.

The floating Isle of Argos.

Upon which lay an enchanted forest, the Glass Cathedral, the Pond of Galaxies, and... "The Celestial Academy for Fallen Stars." Vivian heard herself whisper the name along with the rest of the swelling crowd, who rejoiced as the school floated above.

"Are the Starlings looking down on us?" the people wondered, laughing and clapping. Already the sky was full of hot air balloons and sky skiffs as students flew down to Wolfhelm for the Unification Day Festival. Students who had swallowed a falling star, who had discovered their magic.

But Vivian could not smile. Her father's voice roared in her head: "Get inside. Never let its shadow touch you." Though her heart still beat with the same fear, she couldn't make herself move.

This was as close as she would ever be—to the clouds, to the school, to the stars themselves.

Something hard hit her in the back, and she stumbled, smacking into a customer exiting the shoppe. There was a clatter and a smash. Vivian looked up to see the distraught face of a woman, a child wrapped in her arms, and a candle shattered on the ground. The child started to cry.

"I'm so sorr—"

Mrs. Meryladon herself stalked out of the candle shoppe at the sound. She may have been pretty if not for the twisted scowl, and her permanently squinted eyes from counting every verdallion.

"Greywick! There you are, and late as usual." Mrs. Meryladon's bird-like gaze swept from the broken candle to the crying child, up to the Isle of Argos, floating beyond the horizon.

"I was on my way in," Vivian tried to explain, "but the crowd, and the school, and I–"

"Always with your head in the clouds." She smacked Vivian on the back of her skull. "You should have saved me the grief and gone up with the rest of those hopefuls earlier this moon. That magic would have burned you from the inside out, and I'd have hired a decent worker to replace you."

"I-I'm..." Vivian stuttered. "I didn't mean—"

Mrs. Meryladon narrowed her eyes even more. "This is your last chance, Greywick. See if anyone else will hire a moon-headed spinster like you."

Vivian wanted to protest she should hardly be considered a spinster at nineteen, but she was shaking, and tears threatened to fall. Mrs. Meryladon had yelled at her before, but never in front of such a crowd. She deserved it, always being so late, for spending more time daydreaming than dusting...

"Clean this up, girl." Mrs. Meryladon shoved a broom and dustpan into her hands, and turned to the customer, voice dripping in remorse. "Now, let's get you a new candle. My clumsy worker will pay for the replacement."

Vivian's heart tightened. Candles were a luxury. Compensating for one would mean another night her siblings went hungry. She wanted to fight her case, tell Mrs. Meryladon it wasn't fair. But what was the point? She dropped to her knees, broom in hand.

"Excuse me," a deep voice said, and suddenly there were shining black boots in front of her. "Let me pay for the candle. It was my party that knocked the girl."

Vivian's face burned; she didn't need some stranger's pity. She already got enough of that from her siblings.

Mrs. Meryladon clucked like a proud hen and happily accepted the coins. She went back inside to replace the broken candle.

"Of course he did that," a female voice sighed behind Vivian.

"What did you expect, Mills?" A male laughed. "He sees a pretty girl in need and must save the day."

"I needn't interfere if you hadn't been so clumsy, friend," the first man said.

Vivian's face grew hotter, but she kept her gaze down, concentrating on carefully sweeping every shard of glass into the dustpan. The last thing she needed was for someone to cut themselves.

"You dropped this." The man kneeled before her.

She flicked her eyes up. The man wasn't much older than she was. His eyes were deep blue, the color of the sky on a stormy day. He wore a fine cloak over his hair, fabric joined at his neck by a golden clasp: a crescent moon. He looked familiar, but she was sure they'd never met.

In his outstretched hand, he held a blue ribbon. It must have fallen from her hair.

"Thank you..." She reached for the ribbon, her fingers brushing against his. A tingling shock jolted through her.

His breath hitched, and he smiled. It was suddenly like she was staring at the clouds again, lost and wondering.

She shook her head and tied her chestnut brown hair back with the ribbon before picking up her dustpan and standing. "You didn't need to do that."

"No one should be punished for watching the wonders of the sky." He rose too. By the Three, he was tall. "It wasn't your fault."

"And it wasn't yours." She sighed. "We can blame the ruddy Prince and his stupid festival for drawing the crowds."

Laughter erupted from behind them, where the young man's two friends stood. The girl muttered, "It *is* a stupid festival, isn't it?"

The man in front of her laughed but seized her gaze as he said, "Don't the people love it, though? Exciting games and food and music? The sweep of a dance?"

Despite herself, Vivian smiled and held up her broom. "Well, first I'll sweep the candle shoppe, then I'll surely owe the Prince a dance for all the loveliness he has brought me today." She gestured to the long line outside the shoppe. There would be no enjoying the festival for her. And it wasn't as if she could go after work. Not with it being a moonless night and all.

The man didn't answer, and she turned, regretfully, pushing her way back into the shoppe. There was wax to melt, and oil to boil, candles to sell, and no time to dwell about princes and boys with storm-filled eyes.

The day's bustle of activity had no end. Mrs. Meryladon left as soon as Vivian came in, lamenting that Vivian had given her such a headache she must rest. With Mrs. Meryladon gone, Detvar Gibbons took off at the noon bell, complaining of a weak constitution. Shortly after, Kendra Ohlsen contracted a case of the chills. But Vivian knew they all wanted to attend the festival, to experience what the boy with the stormy eyes had spoken of: the games and food and music and dancing.

She didn't mind. The shoppe kept her busy, and it wasn't like she would attend the festival anyhow.

As the light turned from gold to red, customers trickled in slower and slower. Everyone was heading to the town square for the main ceremony. It was unusual for an event to occur at night.

The night was for magic. And monsters.

But the Prince was now a Starling, a student at the Celestial Academy for Fallen Stars, so she'd heard. No doubt they wanted a show of his abilities.

Finally, she could breathe. Vivian wiped the sweat from her brow and loosely tied her matted brown hair up in a knotted nest with her blue ribbon. It was a gift from her brother, Timothée. She was glad she hadn't lost it.

Vivian padded over to the entrance and was halfway through flipping the sign to closed when the door burst open.

She stumbled back. It wasn't a group of tourists.

"Oh, we'll only be a moment," a girl said. Vivian's age, but with ashen hair perfectly coiled around her rosy cheeks, and a hat trimmed with cherries made of shining baubles and lace. "You don't mind, do you, Viv?"

Tilda Dovetail and her friends were locals of Wolfhelm. She delighted in talking loudly about her trips and her studies at the Royal Drunning Academy. Success meant little unless you had someone to show it to.

Vivian would be twenty soon, and she tried not to think about it, how other girls her age traveled to far-off schools. To learn about the world, the people, and places.

The door opened again, and a man walked in. *The* man in the fine blue cloak she'd met this morning. Why was he back? Had he regretted his choice to pay for the candle and wanted his money? Or perhaps he was some royal zealot and had taken offense to her jeer of the Prince? Perhaps he'd set the Celestial Knights on her. She almost laughed. It sounded like a story her brother Timothée would make up.

The young man still wore the cloak over his head, but she felt his gaze on her. She took a deep breath and flipped the sign over. At least that would prevent anyone new from coming in.

First deal with Tilda, then the boy. Once she finished serving them, she'd be out of here well before sunset.

"Oh, must have been quite busy today." Tilda furrowed her brow as she looked across the shoppe at the near-empty shelves and her heels crunching over the brown and yellow leaves that had blown in. "I'd hate to see you stuck here all night."

Vivian sucked in a tight breath and busied her hands folding tissue that didn't need folding. Words didn't come easily to her; they hardly ever did. While her sister, Marion, made words her weapon, Vivian was often at a loss for them entirely.

"Everyone left to get ready for the festival," Vivian said. But Tilda and her friends had already turned away.

Vivian was once again reminded Tilda wasn't her friend. She had no friends besides her brother and sister. Marion hated Tilda. But Vivian didn't. She enjoyed watching her. Not when she was busy gossiping in the shoppe, but other moments when she and her friends were sharing crumb cakes in the town square or laughing at a local theater troupe.

Tilda swished over, carrying a dyed blue candle. "Will we see you at the festival tonight, Vivian?" Tilda's voice was as squeaky as the mice that burrowed around Vivian's apartment. She leaned far over the counter, the veins in her thin white neck visibly pulsing.

Vivian took an involuntary breath. The blueberry candle's scent was mercifully potent.

"I-I'll be with my sister and brother." Vivian busied herself wrapping the candle.

Tilda gave a clucking noise, partly between a snort and a laugh. "Of course. Why did I ask? You three are always boarded up inside that sad little apartment of yours." She looked around for her friends. "Can you imagine the stench? You, stinking of cheap candle, and your sister reeking of those putrid leeches!"

Vivian's hands wavered on the tissue paper as the laughter of Tilda's friends echoed in the shoppe.

"Their brother works in a bakery," one of the other girls said as she waltzed over to the counter. "He must smell of fresh cookies."

Tilda pretended to plug her nose. "He's worse! Stinking of horse from always rolling in the hay with the boy from the stables. But Jenny knows, doesn't she?"

Tilda poked the short girl beside her. Jenny Cotswood twirled one of her silky black curls around her finger. "All I remember was he was slobbery, like a dog." She giggled, then added, "He has those big puppy dog eyes, though."

Squawking laughter filled the shoppe.

Vivian's lips tightened over her teeth. Her vision blurred, only able to see Tilda's white throat bobbing up and down.

"Please don't talk about my brother that way." Her voice was barely a whisper over their never-ending cackles. Vivian chanced a look at the boy, but he didn't seem to be paying attention, his back to them, inspecting a candle. For the best.

"Oh, are you jealous of how *popular* your brother is around town?" Tilda worried her lip. "If you weren't stuck here all night, you could come with us. Catch a man of your own."

"I—" Words caught in her throat. It was an empty offer. She would never be welcome to spend time with Tilda and her friends. Vivian hated the tiny flicker of excitement that sparked inside her. *To be a normal girl.*

"Of course, Tilda's going to go right up to the stage to see the Prince," Jenny said. "They say he's more handsome than the gods."

"He's just a man." Tilda laughed deviously before turning to Vivian. "But I've heard the ward from Medihsa is quite the scoundrel. Perhaps he'll be the one to first take poor little candle girl's—"

"Your candle." Vivian placed it in front of Tilda with more force than necessary, a perfect bow completed on top of the tissue. "One verdallion."

Tilda wrinkled her nose, clearly irritated with being interrupted. She slammed the gold coin down on the counter. "It's for your house. To get rid of the leech odor."

Silence echoed through the shoppe. Vivian kept her eyes down, feeling Tilda's gaze burrow into her.

The sound of boots broke the hush, the steps so heavy it made the candles tremble and chime together. It was the man. Vivian had nearly forgotten he was still in the shoppe.

"Excuse me," he said, his voice like steel. He stepped in front of Tilda and her friends, who gave an indignant look at being pushed back.

The man put his hands on the counter. "What time shall I return to pick you up for the festival this evening?"

Vivian was so taken aback, she looked behind her, as if there were someone else he was talking to. "Pardon?"

The man's hood dropped. Golden strands of hair fell across his storm blue eyes.

There was murmuring, a low rumble like thunder. But she couldn't concentrate on anything except the boy standing before her.

He was familiar because she had seen him in paintings, in statues, etched into the coins she counted in the shoppe every day.

Because he was not just a man at all. He was a prince.

"I do recall," he smiled, leaning on the counter, "you owe me a dance."

Darius Störmberg, Starling of the Celestial Academy, and heir to Andúrigard, was in her candle shoppe.

Marion would not be happy about this.

2
IN WHICH MARION IS STRUCK BY FATE

MARION GREYWICK WAS known in Wolfhelm as the leech girl.

It wasn't a lovely nickname in the slightest. She'd much rather be known as the kind girl, or the beautiful girl, or even 'one of the triplets' would have been just fine. Who would want to be associated with fat, slimy critters found at the bottom of swamps?

Though it wasn't a lovely nickname, it was accurate. She was, in fact, the leech girl, and she was quite good at it, thank you very much.

Marion watched with perfectly hidden impatience as the slinking black slugs slithered up Mrs. Sigrud's wrinkled legs. Mrs. Sigrud suffered from a distressing case of gout and had been one of Marion's best customers. Not because of the leeches, Marion was certain. It'd been three years since she'd started renting the shoppe from the last bloodletter, and she still wasn't halfway convinced the darned things did anything but leave nasty little crosses in your skin. No, Mrs. Sigrud was here for the conversation. Because that was the other part of being the leech girl. You had to listen.

And there was oh so much to listen about today. Mrs. Sigrud was old, past seventy, and being so old, a festival was nothing but a disturbance.

"Gaudy, isn't it?" Mrs. Sigrud sighed, totally unbothered by the fat black leeches gobbling at her paper-thin skin. They had a form of anesthetic. They numbed the spot where they bit, then sucked the blood up. "In my time, death was never celebrated but *lamented.*"

Marion looked over her shoulder, out the window. Crowds of people jostled past, carrying flags with Andúrigard's crest, and shouting the name of the late king.

"It's not just a memorial. It's Unification Day. It fills the people with hope," Marion responded, if only to contradict Mrs. Sigrud. She had to get her fun where she could. "You should treat yourself to one of those sugar sticks the vendors are selling and tuck yourself into bed and forget all about it."

"Sugar sticks?" Mrs. Sigrud scoffed. "You young things. All you know is dancing and games and sugar sticks. Not like us old goats. Those of us who are old enough to remember the *war.*"

Yes, yes, Marion knew all about the war. Mrs. Sigrud had droned on through countless leeching sessions. And they weren't quick, mind you. The leeches or Mrs. Sigrud's stories. Marion stared at her leeches intensely, watching their bellies swell and their color darken as they drank more blood. Normally, she was of the utmost patience, but not today. Not when dusk neared, and it was a moonless night.

Tonight, she wanted to grab her siblings and run to their little apartment on Enola Avenue and shutter the windows tight. They'd huddle beneath a blanket and she and Timothée would split a loaf of bread and a block of cheese while Vivian cracked open her old drawing notebook, filled with sketches of the lavender farm.

Marion was pushing it even now, taking a customer to almost dusk. But there were no days off for the leech girl.

Not when Vivian was so sick.

Finally, when the leeches were full to the bursting, Marion plucked them off Mrs. Sigrud and stuck them in a bowl. "I agree with you,

Mrs. Sigrud. Everyone throws themselves into such a fuss to get a sight of the Prince. I'm not bothered in the least. You know us Greywicks though. We're a practical sort."

Mrs. Sigrud gave a rumbling laugh. "I wouldn't say that of your brother! But your sister and you, good heads on your shoulders. Won't find you running off into some silly celebration."

Marion popped the leeches off, slapping their fat black bodies thick with blood, into the bowl, wiped Mrs. Sigrud down roughly, and pulled her to her feet. The old lady gave a small sound of indignation but still left a gold verdallion on the counter before scuttling outside.

A girl like Marion really had no business going to a festival. As she had told Mrs. Sigrud, she was a practical sort. The sun hung low in the grey sky. It wouldn't be long before dusk fell and shadows crept over the city.

The leech shoppe was small, a tiny front room and an even tinier back workspace. The front had a lounge chair with a covering of vinyl over it to easily wipe up the spilled blood. A collection of cobwebs decorated the corners, but Marion never swept them down. It'd seemed fitting for spiders to make a home in a leech shoppe. The floorboards squeaked, and there was some form of plant life growing on the windowsill; it was always so damp and cold in Wolfhelm, and the window wasn't sealed properly.

Perhaps the most distinct feature of the shoppe was the smell: the sickly sweetness of mold from the rotten wood, with the swampy, wet odor of the leech tank in the back room, all mixed with the coppery tang of blood.

No wonder Vivian could never visit here.

Marion rushed her bowl of leeches to the back and separated them into two jars: five leeches bound for the icebox, where they would freeze and keep nicely with her other jars of frozen, blood-filled leeches. Three leeches were left alive. She placed those in a short jar that she stuck in the small, quilted bag she used as a purse. Vivian would need them tonight, and fresh was better than frozen.

She took a worried glance out the window as she quickly wiped the counters. Then she took a worried peek at her leech tank, only ten or so left swimming through the murky water. The triplets would have to make the journey to the lake soon, wearing their thickest clothes, and wading through the water with nets. Other bloodletters reused their leeches, but Marion's were one-and-done. Wasn't like she was the leech girl for the money (poor) or because she genuinely believed in the power of leeching (a hoax). The only thing that mattered was how much blood her little black slugs could suck up.

She shook her head and took a worried glance—goodness, did everything have to be such a worry? Had she always been like this? Certainly not. At the lavender farm, there was nothing at all to worry about. Back then, Father had done the worrying and she, Vivian, and Tim had done the laughing and the eating and the playing.

But that was three long years ago. Her childhood had ended at sixteen and in Father's absence, it was up to her to keep the family together. Vivian was too ill for it despite being the eldest, and Timothée was... well, *hopeless* wouldn't be an unfair thing to call him.

With the shoppe clean enough for closing, Marion took off her blood-stained apron. Beneath, she had only a plain grey dress with buttons all down the front. At the farm, she'd had splendid dresses, light shifts brocaded with flowers, hats with lace, even a petticoat. Whatever became of them?

All she had now was a blue ribbon, a gift from her brother Timothée, tied into her golden curls. No one would see, of course, not when she swung her dark cloak over her shoulders and pulled the hood up over her hair. It wasn't quite dusk yet, let alone night, but she'd fully embraced being the fuss of the family.

With her cloak firmly wrapped around her, and her purse with the jar of leeches slung over her shoulder, Marion locked up the shoppe, ready to head home.

"Good evening, Marion."

At the sound of the mopish voice, Marion stiffened. *Oh bother.* Just what she needed, on today of all days. She forced a deep inhale of the cold air and turned, unable to muster any semblance of a smile. "Huxley. You're here. At my shoppe."

Huxley Macgregor stood before her, a gangly stick of a boy, resembling one of the ceiling spiders with his too-long legs. He had a shock of red hair and wide eyes that always dashed around like he was waiting for something to leap out at him.

Huxley reached for Marion's hand. She turned and pretended to preen in the window reflection. It was so dirty, she could barely see herself. At least it kept her hands occupied.

"Of course I'm here, Mare. It's the festival." He offered a nervous smile. He was dressed well, for him, wearing a dark brown frock coat about a size too big, and what appeared to be a new necktie. With his meager salary as the tanner's assistant, it must have cost him a week's wages, at least.

Oh bother. Marion knew where this was going. There could only be so many times she took him into the back of the leech shoppe before he either left or started pushing for more.

"I thought you and I could… Well, I thought we could go. I'll buy you one of those pretty blue flags and we can have a dance."

Marion snorted. Forced herself to cross her arms and look him up and down with disdain. There would be no dancing with the tanner's assistant. No handholding or promenading or whispering sweet nothings.

Huxley Macgregor had proven himself an adequate distraction, a convenient outlet for the annoyance of base need. Once in a moon, she bid him come at closing, where she would slip off her blood-soaked dress and stand naked before him.

There would be no ripping of clothes or declaration of desire. No hands dragged through hair or swollen lips from rough kisses, the way she'd read about in the scandalous books her clients devoured as they were leeched.

She would simply let him bury himself deep within her, her skin still wet with lake water from the leech tank, and his hands brown with dried blood from the cattle he skinned for their hides. There was no romance in the work, and no romance in the act. All she felt was the rough counter on her thighs, as her mind went blissfully numb.

"You know I do not attend festivals," Marion said with as much dignity as a leech girl could muster. "I'm quite busy tonight, but please enjoy yourself. Alone."

She turned away from him, but he caught her arm. She looked down at it scornfully. He did not touch her outside of the leech shoppe.

"Come on, Marion." Huxley's face was pleading. "It'll be fun. You never do anything but go to work and go home. It'd be good for you."

That was the problem. It would be fun. In a different life, she would have loved the chance to get glossed up with Vivian and *tsk* over Timothée's hair. She and Viv would parade down the street, while Timothée and Father would sell the lavender and use the earnings to buy big balloons in yellow and purple and blue. They would stay out under a moonless sky and marvel, rather than fear, the falling stars.

Father wouldn't have allowed that, even if he had been alive.

Father was dead. Vivian was sick. And if Marion did not get her siblings back into the apartment by nightfall, it would rip away whatever semblance of a life they had created here in Wolfhelm over the last three years.

"Only I know what is good for me," Marion snapped and tore her arm aside. "Good evening, Huxley."

At his fallen face, Marion's cheeks heated.

There were some times when they'd lie together on the vinyl-covered leeching chair, when she'd let him wrap her in his arms. When she'd nestle her face in the crook of his neck and inhale something besides the butchered cow or tanning chemicals. She'd smell wood smoke or coffee or a pleasant musk. Huxley would wrap one of her golden curls round and round his finger and his body was warm against the chill. In those moments, Marion wondered if Huxley wasn't such an impish, sop of a boy but actually a kind man, with a steady job, and a delicate heart that hadn't been frozen by Wolfhelm's ways.

But those moments passed as quickly as they came. Because to be married would be to leave Vivian and Timothée. And Vivian was sick with an illness no one could know about, and Timothée was clueless as a rock.

It was much safer to think of all the ways Huxley annoyed her than all the ways he could make her smile.

She sighed and plunged into the crowd so she couldn't tempt herself by looking back. It was such a bother to be the responsible one.

Vendors and tourists and citizens of Wolfhelm crowded the streets. Such a fuss, all for some overblown holiday and the chance to see the Prince. Ahead, people were pushing to the courtyard before the castle; they'd been setting up a stage there all yesterday. It must be where the Prince and his wards were going to make their appearance.

Marion moved against the crowd. People shrunk away as she walked. Maybe it was the deep scowl she kept etched on her face. Maybe it was because she didn't mind using a little elbow to make it through. Maybe it was because she smelled and would always smell of blood and lake water and she was the damned leech girl instead of the lavender girl, and Father should *be* here, and today was three years since everything had gone straight to pot—

Slam!

Marion ran into something and fell hard on her rump, hood flung back, and purse fallen beside her. No, she hadn't run into something, but *someone*. A person, a *rude* person had stepped right out in front of her when she was clearly in a hurry. All she could see was a shaggy brown cloak.

"Excuse me!" she said most indignantly. What else could go wrong on this horrid day?

The cloaked figure turned and pulled down his hood. A young man stood before her, eyes flashing green as a meadow. He had brown skin and black hair tousled over his brow, with one piece that looked too perfectly askew. A small golden ring hung in a single ear. A smirk slithered up his face, an expression that seemed all too comfortable for him.

And for a moment, Marion forgot her worries. Every single one of them. The night could fall, and she would sit here like a wobbling calf as long as she lit up enough to see those green eyes flashing in the dark.

What was wrong with her? Ogling was the equivalent of daydreaming, and Vivian and Timothée lost enough time with that sort of thing. There was no good to be wasted dreaming about princes and getting swept off by green-eyed cavaliers.

And yet… here she was… struck. By this stranger.

The young man's smirk turned to a grin, and he said, "You are excused."

Her moment passed, and every worry rushed back into her with a healthy amount of annoyance. The stupid O her mouth had formed turned into a scowl. "Excuse *me?*"

"I already said it," the boy said. His voice was light, teasing. "You are excused. Perhaps watch your step next time?"

A series of sputtering sounds sprung from her mouth. There were many things she wanted to tell this extremely rude fellow who had stepped in front of *her*, but words escaped her. What a fool she must look, sprawled in the dirt. Her cheeks burned.

She had been *struck*, in body and in heart. What a ridiculous notion. And it was this boy's fault. He had made her look a fool and was blaming her for it.

He held out his hand. "Let me help you up." His smile struck deep as an arrow, and she couldn't imagine being more irritated if she'd actually been hit by one.

"No thank you," she finally managed and angrily gathered herself from the ground.

"Come on, let me help you." He picked up her purse. "You're so clumsy you're likely to hurt yourself just standing up."

"I'm clumsy? You ran into me! And I am in an awful hurry!"

He clutched his heart as if she had seriously offended him. "I merely stepped out into the street to be struck upon by you, fair maiden! And I too am in an awful hurry and terribly late for an appointment."

Was it possible his voice had gotten higher, mocking? Whatever the case, Marion felt quite ready to wipe that ridiculous smirk off his face. Instead, she forced herself to take a deep breath in through her nose and out through her mouth.

Yes, she still smelled like leeches.

"I don't have time for this," she said. "Good day to you, sir." And because she couldn't help herself: "And good riddance!" She turned her nose straight to the sky and walked around him.

Who was he? Some street rat, based on his old cloak. But the earring had shone like actual gold… Perhaps he'd murdered someone in a dark alley and stolen it straight off their ear. Regardless, she would never see him or his distracting green eyes ever—

"That's it? No name? For all the inconvenience you've caused me, you could at least give me your name."

By the gods, he was back! Walking in step with her! With that absolutely stupid, irritating, all too careless smirk of his!

Marion kept her nose to the sky. "I don't talk to strangers."

He darted ahead of her and swept down in an elegant bow. "Then allow me to introduce myself. Khalid Ali Bagheeri, son of the prime ministers of Medihsa, and ward of Prince Darius Störmberg, at your service."

Marion rolled her eyes so hard they nearly touched the back of her skull. She gave a mocking smile and curtseyed. "Ah, Lord Khalid, there you are! I, Lady Carmilla Vladimirovna, heir to the fallen empire of Kirrintsova, and also a ward of Prince Darius Störmberg, have been looking all over for you. Don't you know the annual swearing of allegiance is about to start? We are most late!"

The foolish boy blinked. "You're right. That is about to start."

Marion pushed past him with an unladylike "Ugh."

This time, the boy stayed where he was. A strange compulsion forced Marion to turn her head.

He stood staring rather dumbly into space, but as soon as he caught her eye, his expression took on that smirking mask. Wind seized the tousled strands of his hair, whispering them across his brow. Marion had the irritating pull to stomp back there and push them off his face.

"Are you going to the stage?" he called.

Marion flung around. "Maybe!"

There was a beat of silence. Then his voice trailed after her: "What's your real name?"

The word had wings of its own and sailed from her lips onto the breeze. "Marion."

Then she threw her hood over her golden curls and scurried ahead to lose herself in the crowd.

Dreams and longing were better left to fools. Fools like her brother Timothée.

3

IN WHICH TIMOTHÉE FORGETS SOMETHING IMPORTANT

TIMOTHÉE THOUGHT HIS sister Marion might have told him something important this morning, in between his frantic bites of soggy oats and Vivian trying to push down his wayward hair (pointless, honestly). It was just he really didn't want to think about his sisters right now, not with Carim Lingrint's mouth slowly working its way down his unbuttoned shirt.

Timothée squeezed his eyes shut and tilted his head back. Dimming lamplight flickered off the ceiling. Bags of flour and tins of sugar, oil, chocolate pieces, and preserved berries surrounded him. "I think I've forgotten something."

Lingrint gave a long sigh. He was never much for talking during this sort of thing, or any other time, really. "And you need to remember it right now?"

"No, I—" The sensation of Lingrint's calloused fingers on his hips cut off his words. Timothée threw a hand behind him, clasping the splintering shelf.

He wished he could dig his hands through Lingrint's hair, but it was shorn so short there wasn't anything to grab onto.

Lingrint's slimy tongue slid across his stomach. Timothée felt his blood rush lower and lower. Lingrint sat back on his haunches when he reached Timothée's belt. Except Timothée didn't have a belt. The buckle had broken last week. In its place, he had tied an old rope around his loose pants.

Lingrint was the son of the baker who owned this shoppe. Timothée knew it was a bad idea to disappear into the back room with him so often. It was common knowledge the baker wanted Lingrint to marry the wainwright's son, Alson Towers. The Towers were well off, and Alson would inherit the thriving carriage repair business soon enough. But Alson chose to wait until marriage to do *anything*.

So, it was obvious why Lingrint pulled Timothée into the back room before closing, why he stuck his hands down Timothée's pants and grinned at him like they had a secret. And it *was* a secret though they never said it. *Who would I even tell?*

Lingrint chose him because he had no friends, because no one spoke to the messy-haired boy who lived in the decrepit apartment on Enola Avenue.

Despite the guilt, despite the strange gross sensation that constantly crept through Timothée's chest as he buttoned up his shirt and pants, the few minutes of pleasure in the backroom were worth it.

At least Lingrint knew he existed.

Now, Lingrint cursed, impatient as ever, as his sausage-thick fingers fumbled over the rope tied around Timothée's pants.

"Here." Timothée reached for it himself.

Lingrint stood and undid his own trousers. "Don't bother."

He roughly pulled Timothée toward him. Timothée couldn't help it. He tilted his chin in Lingrint's direction. Maybe Lingrint wasn't the most handsome person in Wolfhelm, but it would be nice to kiss someone during all this.

He tried once, a few moons ago, and Lingrint had shoved him away and laughed. "Jenny Cotswood was right, baker boy. You *are* a bad kisser."

Lingrint ignored Timothée's upturned face and pushed him to his knees. But Timothée stumbled over his own legs, arms flailing, and smacked against a shelf. There was a splintering crack, and the shelf tilted on its axis. Off slid a tin of sugar, a glass container of chocolate, jars of jam, and an enormous bag of flour.

Timothée held up his hands to stop it, and Lingrint stepped out of the way. The bag exploded into a puff of white dust, falling over Timothée's head like snow.

Lingrint's face turned more red than usual. "Look what you did! Who's going to pay for all this waste?"

Timothée sat up, blowing flour from his hair.

"That is going to take hours to clean." Lingrint was already buttoning up his pants. "I'm leaving for the festival. I won't be stuck here with you all night, baker boy."

He didn't look back as he strode out of the shoppe, door slamming on his way out. Timothée stood and looked around at the smashed jars, and spilled sugar, and red jam puddling on the ground like blood. Lingrint was right—this would take forever to clean. If he had the power of the god Xydrious and swallowed an Evening Star, he could fix the broken jars with a wave of his hand. Or if he swallowed a Morning Star with Rhaemyria's power, he could summon water to wash the floors and blow all the flour away with wind.

But he wasn't a Starling.

He wasn't anything.

Just an orphan who worked at a bakery without a single real friend.

There was a sudden yowl, and Timothée turned to Yvaine, sitting in the doorway. The little black cat had a snarl on her face as if she had read his mind.

"Except you," Timothée said.

That seemed to satisfy her, and she walked in, paw prints adorning the spilled flour. He scooped her into his arms and stroked her scruffy fur. No matter how much he tried to smooth it down, it always stuck up.

He named her Yvaine after the evening sky, but she belonged to the witch who owned the shoppe next door, who called her Cat. Being called Cat was no better than being called "baker boy".

The witch next door wasn't actually magical, of course. She cured ailments by mixing orris root with lavender oil, and she had an evil enough glare, and he supposed Yvaine helped with the look, so no one questioned her. But everybody knew she didn't have *real* magic. Only Starlings could use starcraft. Only those who attended the Celestial Academy for Fallen Stars.

Timothée had adored Yvaine from the first moment he'd seen her. No, she wasn't the most beautiful cat. The fur around her ears was tufted in a weird way, and her tail had an odd kink to it. People avoided her, moving to the other side of the shoppe, or if she looked too formidable in the window with her big blue eyes, they would walk right past.

People avoided him too.

He never quite knew why. He smiled, he was polite, he attempted to be helpful. But… no matter how hard he tried, he'd never had a friend.

Besides Yvaine. And his sisters. But that changed too, exactly three years ago today. Vivian was too sick to daydream about stories and heroes and adventures. She used to draw his favorite scenes from books, but he couldn't remember the last time she'd picked up her pencils.

And now Marion was more of a parent than a sister, and not in the fun way, the way Father had been. Timothée shook his head and grabbed the broom. He was being ungrateful again. He knew Marion held everything together. Without her, they'd be a lot worse off.

But sometimes he wondered how much worse things could get.

By the time he finished sweeping and mopping the floor and hiding all the broken jars, the sun was red as roses. A nagging feeling plucked at his chest.

Was it the festival? He'd tried not to think too much about it. His heart would ache with longing if he did. Delicious food, dancing, music, a display of magic—real starcraft, from none other than the Prince himself.

But of course, they couldn't go. Tonight was—

Marion's face flashed in his mind, her blond curls frizzy, hand on her hip, grey eyes stern. "You come straight home after work today, Timothée. No dawdling while you clean, no visits to the library, don't even think about chatting with that witch, no stopping to look at the Unification Day Festival, and absolutely no dallying with any of your," she said the words with bitterness, as if he didn't know how often Huxley Macgregor *visited* the leech shoppe, "acquaintances. Tonight is a moonless night."

A moonless night. *That's* what he had forgotten. Well, the sun hadn't set yet. And he wasn't far from their apartment if he hurried. He might still beat her home and save himself a scolding.

He sighed, quickly closing the rest of the shoppe. Yvaine had fallen asleep on the counter, so he picked her up and wrapped her around his neck like a scarf, where she continued to sleep peacefully. He took her home with him every night and the witch hadn't ever said a thing.

Outside, there was an icy chill in the air. The last remnants of summer were finally leaving, and bright orange and red leaves scattered the streets. There was an urgent energy to the crowd, an excited tone to their voices.

It would take him forever to push his way through. He darted his gaze to an empty alley. It was well known in the capital to avoid the narrow labyrinth of backstreets that cut through the city. But if he didn't get home before dark...

Timothée ducked into the nearest alley, and immediately the chaos and swell of the crowd drifted away. Bags of garbage and crumbling wood, shuttered windows, and skittering rats spread before him.

Timothée could deal with all of that.

"This isn't so bad," he muttered to Yvaine. Puddles of what he hoped was water seeped into his old boots. "Nothing to worry about—"

He stumbled to a stop. In front of him lay a pile of discarded old cloth. But it was moving. No, not just moving.

Breathing.

Timothée lurched back, and Yvaine hissed, digging her claws into his shoulder. He needed to move, to turn around, but it was like roots had tangled around his feet.

This was why you didn't cut through the alleys. This is why everyone in Wolfhelm stayed away from the shadows. This is why people hardly ever went out after dark.

The fabric shifted. No, not fabric, but wings. Great membranous wings, tattered and holed as a moth-eaten blanket. A head lifted from in between. A face barren of all color, hair merely a few oily strands. Eyes a blind white.

Timothée's stomach roiled, and he stumbled back as it opened its mouth. Two long fangs shone in the dim light.

Wolfhelm was better than most cities at keeping them at bay, making it seem like they weren't a problem at all. But even the capital city of Andúrigard couldn't destroy them completely. For these creatures were born in the dark and lived in the shadows.

Vampires.

Living wasn't the right term for this thing. This creature was wasting away. It was what happened to them when they couldn't feed. They became barren husks.

Properly fed vampires appeared just like humans. Well, not *just* like humans. They were faster, stronger, damaged by the sun, and lived off blood. That's why they were so hard to eradicate. You could never know who was your neighbor and who was pretending in order to get close to your neck.

A low, pitiful moan escaped the creature, and it extended a shaking white hand toward him.

He had some old crust and stale cookies in his bag. Though he knew the creature longed for neither, he tossed them at it.

Just keeping its attention off me, he told himself. Deep down there was a sick part of him that wanted to help it. But he could barely think the thought. It felt like a betrayal. Especially on this day. After all the vampires had done to this city, to his family...

The bread and cookies wouldn't help it. Sure, normal vampires could eat human food, but this creature was beyond it all. He knew the one thing that would save the monster was something he wouldn't give.

How could he hate this thing so much, and yet his heart hurt for it?

He squeezed his eyes shut and hurried out of the alley. *Marion won't let that happen,* he repeated in his mind until he reached their apartment. She'd be mad he brought none of the stale bread home.

At least Vivian wouldn't care.

He knew she only pretended to taste it anyway.

4
IN WHICH VIVIAN CONVERSES WITH ROYALTY

A PRINCE WAS STANDING in her candle shoppe. It was so bizarre Vivian could hardly enjoy the look of utter confusion on Tilda's face.

"What did you say?" Vivian whispered.

"I'm escorting you to the festival." The Prince flashed her a grin. "Don't you recall? You promised me a dance."

She had mockingly said she owed the Prince a dance earlier this morning. Oh stars, she wished the floor would open and swallow her whole. That's why his friends had laughed. She had been conversing with royalty and not even known it.

Yet, he was staring at her with no cynicism on his face. As if he, a prince, a Starling, was really here to dance with a candle girl.

"I can't dance," Vivian mustered.

"I'll teach you."

There was a sound like a horse whinnying: Tilda Dovetail, *delicately* clearing her throat.

"Viv, darling, I couldn't have possibly heard that right. Are you hosting the *Prince of Andúrigard?*" Tilda pranced over beside Vivian and laced an arm through hers as if they were best friends.

But Vivian barely felt Tilda's lace-gloved fingers pinching at her elbow. Barely heard Tilda's squeaky little breaths. There was only the space between her and the Prince.

"Get out," Vivian said. "Leave my shoppe. We're closed."

Tilda gave a startled inhale and dropped her arm. "But Viv—"

"The lady asked you to go," Prince Darius said, not dropping Vivian's gaze. "My guards are outside. They'd be happy to escort you if needed."

Tilda made a blubbering noise all the way out. The door chimed mercifully as she and her friends left.

And then Vivian was alone with the Prince.

"Thank you for staying open for me. I won't be long." Finally, he broke their stare and looked around the shoppe. "I returned for more than just taking you up on your offer. I'm of a mind to purchase two gifts, and something for myself." His words had a distinguished edge to them that made her conscious of the cobwebs that drooped from the ceiling like banners and the speckles of dust suspended in the dying sunbeams.

She swallowed and turned, taking down a few different wares. "The selection is slim. We were very busy today with the festival, Your Highness."

"You mean the stupid festival?" There was laughter in his words. "Please, call me Darius."

"Darius," she echoed the word. The name was made to be formed by her lips, and she was seized with the urge to say it again, scream it, whisper it, yell it, moan it—

Her thoughts cut off with a shake of her head and she realized she was staring at the curved angle of his jaw, the broadness of his shoulders, the intensity of his storm blue eyes. He was giving her the most peculiar look.

"I'm Vivian," she said finally.

"Vivian."

And now it was her turn to give him a peculiar look, because she wasn't sure how, but they had somehow exchanged more than names.

"Is it true what you said?" she asked. "There are guards outside?"

"Princes don't have the luxury of going anywhere alone." He inclined his head to the window.

Through the dusted glass, Vivian saw the silhouette of two Celestial Knights, soldiers of both the Church and kingdom. Adorned in golden armor, they wore colored sashes around their waists, one yellow, the other blue. That meant they were Starlings, graduates of the Celestial Academy for Fallen Stars, capable of wielding untold magic. But only when the sun hid, and the stars appeared.

"They didn't feel the need to accompany you in here?"

"Are you dangerous?" Prince Darius asked with a smile.

"Very." It wasn't a lie.

He chuckled, and she busied herself by laying out a spread of candles on the wooden counter. Prince Darius had seen such horror in his life, not much could frighten him now. At only nineteen, he was a renowned hero, beloved by his people, championed by the Church.

Apparently, Unification Day had been a dull holiday prior to the events of three years ago. A day to celebrate the surrender of Kirrintsova and Medihsa and their swearing of loyalty to Andúrigard. Every year, there was a dreary fealty renewal in Wolfhelm, where the young wards from Kirrintsova and Medihsa bent the knee once again.

But three years ago, tragedy struck the capital. A long-banished cult led by their leader, the Dark Prophet, attacked the royal family. This cult meddled in the forbidden Dark Star magic.

And vampirism.

Vivian's vision blurred and her breathing turned shallow. She gripped the counter.

"Are you alright?" Darius caught her arm with a rough hand.

"Quite," she managed. "Just a dizzy spell."

It was a testimony to his honor he could still find warmth. He had been the only survivor of the Störmberg family massacre. And not only had he avenged them by single-handedly striking down the Dark Prophet that night, but he also drove the cult away and led his citizens in peace for the last three years.

He truly was the hero the people believed.

Now, Darius had turned dull Unification Day into a grand festival of both memorial for his family and celebration over his defeat of the Dark Prophet. As if the smell of sugar sticks could blot out the stench of blood that had soaked the streets, or the troubadours' singing could silence the screams that had rung from dusk to dawn.

She wondered if the festival helped Darius forget the memories of that night.

It certainly doesn't dull them for me.

"You've managed to hold on to your ribbon," Darius said.

It didn't sound like a question, but she answered him, nevertheless. "My brother gave it to me last week. He traded a poor boy a loaf of bread for it. My sister, oh, she was so cross! Told him he had bread for brains. Timothée can be, well," she shook her head, a blush crossing her features. "Above all things, he's kind."

"It looks lovely on you," the Prince said. "Brings out the blue in your eyes."

"My eyes are grey."

Darius gave her one last look, then uncorked a candle, bringing it up to his nose.

"That one's Honey Maple. The syrup is imported from Ashwell Grove."

"I'll take it. I know someone who needs a little sweetness in her life."

He popped the wooden cork out of several more candles, smelling them. As he did so, Vivian found herself telling stories about the candles, how they were made, the type of people who purchased them. And she told him the tales she imagined when they lit the candles in the shoppe. Somewhere between the stories, she forgot finding words was hard. They strung together more easily moment after moment, and for every one of her stories, Darius had one to match. As the wicks burned down, the stories started to resemble something very much like conversation.

The light turned from buttery copper to the deep red only an autumn sunset could bring.

Darius followed her gaze and sighed. "I should pick a candle and stop taking up all of your time."

She wanted to tell him he had taken nothing, she'd gifted it to him, and gladly would do so again. But instead, she held up one of her most popular candles. "Try this."

He bent his head. "Ahh." He inhaled. "Vanilla. I'll take it for myself."

She tried for a word, but somehow only exhaled.

He tilted his chin up at her. A storm raged in those eyes. He was like that, all of him, rippling with static that could strike into lightning at any moment.

He straightened. "And last, one for my friend. Do you have a candle that smells of the sea?"

"Yes." Vivian dug for only a bit before she found what she was looking for. The wax was dyed a startling blue. "It's quite accurate. I used to live by the ocean."

She smelled it before handing it to him, and saw dark waves, heard gulls overhead, and tasted salt on her tongue.

As he reached for it, his heavy cloak fell loose, revealing the shine of silver brocade. He wore an elegant outfit of fine navy fabric, constellations woven by shining thread.

The uniform of a student who attended the Celestial Academy for Fallen Stars.

Stay hidden until the shadow passes. The school is evil. Do you understand, my children?

She felt like she was falling.

"Another dizzy spell?" Suddenly, his hand was on her arm.

She pulled away. "I... thought I saw a shadow." There was no reason to be afraid of the Prince. He was only here to buy a candle. It had nothing to do with her at all. "You really caught one?" she asked, even though she knew she shouldn't. "You're a *Starling*?"

"Yes, I swallowed my star earlier this moon. Have you ever seen the star showers, Vivian?"

It was a rhetorical question. Stars fell as often as rain over Thraina. She offered him her truth. "Only glimpses."

Glimpses through frosted windows.

He studied her for a moment, and shifted uncomfortably, as if he wanted to say something more, but politeness held him back. Finally, he asked, "Have you ever thought of attending?"

At the beginning of the Singing Harvest Moon, hundreds of young people gathered in the town square, waiting as sky skiffs fluttered them up to the Isle of Argos. All for the annual ceremony where a potential student could claim their magic. Although stars often fell across Thraina, there was only one place you were permitted to catch them.

Only one place you could catch them and not be hanged for it.

The Meadow of Shattered Stars, on the Isle of Argos, right beside the Academy. Many claimed the stars were more potent up there, but Vivian wasn't sure she believed that. She wasn't sure what she believed.

She laughed. "How did you know I wasn't there? One of the hundreds of hopefuls with no star to fall unto waiting hands, who flew down in shame to a life without starcraft, to work in a dreary place like a candle shoppe?"

The Prince didn't break her gaze. "If you were there, I would have seen you."

The idea was prosperous. She believed him.

"And," he admitted, "I overheard that shrill of a woman talking to you. She was wrong, though. The magic would not burn you. It would ignite you. The stars would line up in the sky for the grace of your lips."

The way he spoke of it... It didn't sound dangerous or wicked as Father had said. It sounded *miraculous*.

But she summoned some of her sister's common sense. "You'll never see me there."

"Why not? Contrary to what people believe, the school isn't just for nobles. Many commoners—" He coughed, stumbling over his words. "Not that you're... What I mean is—"

He broke off and ran a hand through his blond hair, a red flush from cheek to cheek.

"It's alright. I am what the world made me," Vivian whispered. "The sky is for Starlings, and the ground is for girls who work in candle shoppes."

"Well, it is a wonderful candle shoppe. I thank you for letting me stay." He placed a handful of verdallions on the counter. "In truth, this is the first time I've felt like I could breathe all day."

"I hate crowds too," she admitted. "It's been busy since we opened."

"Thanks to the ruddy Prince." He grinned.

"He's not so bad after all." And for the first time in a very long time, a true smile spread across Vivian's face.

She finished wrapping his candles and handed him a paper bag. This was the part where she told the customers to be safe, never to burn their candle too long or leave it unattended. But there wasn't any space for words between them.

He turned to go, opening the door but a crack. Music wafted in, the troubadours singing tales of heroes and loss and courage.

Then Prince Darius dropped his bag and said, "I believe you still owe me a dance."

"N-now?"

His mouth curved in a half-smile. "It'll be practice. I think I can slip away after my barrage of duties to properly escort you around the festival."

There were a million excuses on her lips, but she stepped from behind the counter, and walked in front of him. Vivian was tall compared to Tilda and the other girls in town, but Darius was so much taller than her.

"One dance," she whispered. "Until the end of the song."

"Then we better begin." His heartbeat was so loud it nearly blocked out the music. It thrummed between her ears as if it were her own. Was it possible? Could it even be? Was the Prince of Andúrigard nervous?

He placed one hand on her waist, then twined his other through her fingers.

"Until the music ends," he whispered lowly.

And then they were moving about the candle shoppe. It wasn't really true, what she had said before, about not being able to dance. It had just been so long. Her father used to bring out his old music box, and they'd waltz around their cabin in Seagrass. Father was the best, placing her small feet on top of his. Marion always had to be the leader, and Timothée, well, he was hopeless as he was with most things.

Darius's hair had fallen askew over his brows. She clasped his hand tighter when the music outside stopped, but he kept moving, and so did she. Maybe she'd gotten her wish after all, and she was flying right now.

He twirled her around once more before she fell against his chest, and they stumbled to a stop, clattering the candles on the walls.

"I told you," she laughed, "I can't dance."

"I don't know about that. Perhaps you just need more practice."

"Indeed." She stepped back but felt his hesitation to release her hand. Outside, the sky was darkening. If she didn't get home soon…

Darius stared out the window. "I've been to every Unification Day since I was born, but never tried the sugar sticks."

"They are highly regarded as the very best part of it all."

"Why do you think I'm so upset about it?" His smile was the glimpse of sunlight through clouds.

She took a step closer.

"I'd love to escort you to the festival," he said.

She could almost hear herself saying the words: *Give me a moment to clean up. We can go together. And eat sugar sticks until our fingers and lips are sticky.*

Words like that were for girls with destinies. Not sick girls like her.

She looked down. "I have to get home."

Sadness flashed across his face. "I cannot say I am not disappointed. If you were there, it might make the whole arduous affair more bearable."

"I'm truly sorry," she said, each word more difficult than the last.

"Do not say this is goodbye then."

"You can stop in for a candle the next time you're in town." There was a heaviness to her heart. If she told Marion about this meeting, no doubt her sister's fear would grow wild.

She tugged at the ribbon in her hair until it came loose, then clasped his arm. *Of all the days to be bold, today you decide to touch a prince.*

But Darius let her guide him forward, and for a moment, the only feeling was the frantic fluttering of his pulse beneath her fingers.

She carefully tied the ribbon around his wrist, knotting it into a bow.

"There," she whispered. "Now you can't forget me."

She should drop his hand. She didn't.

"You know that won't happen."

It wouldn't. She felt it in the shift of the air. She flicked her head up at him and wished there weren't tears in her eyes.

His expression mirrored her own.

The door jingled and the two Celestial Knights stepped inside. "Your Highness, the hour of the ceremony approaches."

They ushered him out, and suddenly she couldn't remember if she said goodbye. Or if it even mattered. But the candle shoppe was so quiet she heard the ringing of their words between the wooden walls.

She stared at the bells, still jingling back and forth. And Vivian knew if she stayed here, she would never see Prince Darius again. She'd remain in the shadows of the candle shoppe until she burned away like the wicks and wax.

Her breath hitched in her throat. She pushed outside, blinking frantically in the crimson light. The streets were frenzied. Hiking up her skirts, she sped through the swarm until she caught the golden glint of his hair.

"Darius," she called.

He kept moving forward, surrounded by his knights.

"Darius!"

Finally, he turned and the smile on his face was so spectacular, her heart fluttered. "Vivian?"

She would wear a cloak, stick to the dark awnings. She would figure out a way. There *had* to be a way.

"I'll come," she yelled, willing the wind to carry her words. "I'll come to the festival!"

"I'll find you!" he called back.

"There will be thousands of people."

The crowd swept between them like a current.

"It does not matter." He waved his hand, the blue ribbon fluttering. "I'll find you."

And Vivian Greywick, who had not believed in anything in a long, long time, believed in that.

5

IN WHICH MARION IS REMINDED WHY HER SIBLINGS SHOULD NEVER ATTEND A FESTIVAL

ℰLECTRIC ENERGY HAD taken over the streets of Wolfhelm; people waved gold streamers and danced to live music. Girls had woven blue lilies through their hair in remembrance of the late King and Queen. Many clutched burning lanterns, believing the fire would ward off any unsavory individuals.

Marion hustled through the crowd, impatient to get home and reunite with her siblings in the safety of their apartment. For a girl who grew up on a farm with only her family, she had little issue shoving past the slow-moving celebrators. They were like a herd of sheep; if they needed a bite on their heels, so be it.

Worst of all were the many young people in uniforms of blue and gold and purple, eagerly awaiting night to fall when their magic came alive. The regalia meant they were students from that cursed school. Though Marion longed to push them the hardest, she kept her distance. Her fear surpassed her loathing.

Besides, the sky had turned from orange to red. Time was running short. She needed to see Timothée and Vivian safe in their apartment with the boarded-up windows. Only then could she put the whole day, including that obnoxious boy with the green eyes, behind her.

It had been a horrid interaction, all in all. How he'd knocked her to the ground, her purse flying off, and then teased her—

Wait. She reached for her purse with the jar of leeches.

Gone. It was gone!

She had dropped it. Dropped it when she bumped into that *boy*. Had he stolen it from her? Knocked into her on purpose as a pickpocketing ruse?

She stormed in the opposite direction. No, not back to the leech shoppe to grab her frozen reserves, which would have been the sensible thing to do.

That boy had stolen both her senses and her leeches. And she was determined to get them back.

The pickpocket had asked her if she would be at the festival. He was probably in the main square, trying to swindle more citizens. Well, she would have none of it. How hard could it be to find one green-eyed boy in a crowd of hundreds?

She chanced a look at the reddening sky. It wouldn't be so bad, just going into a crowded festival, stealing back her purse, and returning home, all before the sun set.

Marion shoved into the main courtyard. She had never seen it so busy. Wolfhelm Castle towered ahead, protected by a high stone wall and wooden gate. People traveled from all over Thraina to look upon the stone wall. It was painted with glorious murals, depicting legends of the gods, fantastical mythical beasts, and the creation of Thraina. She often caught Vivian walking past the murals on her way home from work, staring transfixed at the flourishes of shape and bursts of color. Perhaps one day Viv would pick up her paints and pencils again.

Now, offerings to the gods lined the stone wall: flowers and fruits and feathers and even urns containing ashes of the dead mixed with burnt-up star matter. Father had not been a holy man, and the triplets had never attended a day of church. Come to think of it, Seagrass didn't even have a church.

Marion didn't know why the people left offerings, or what they prayed for. Maybe that's why the Greywicks' life had been so full of sorrow the last three years: the gods were sick of being ignored.

Or maybe it was all a lot of pig dung and life was just cruel and you couldn't count on anyone or anything to save you. Especially some sentient constellation that sat their arse on a star and never bothered to help the people they apparently created.

Marion gritted her teeth and scanned the crowd for the pickpocket. Yet, her eyes kept going back to the murals. The largest was of a woman in robes of pure white, hair golden as the sun. She stood with arms outstretched, rays of light bursting from all around her.

Rhaemyria, the Sun Mother. The First Being and Grand Creator. Marion's heart stalled, chest tightening.

A conversation leapt into her mind: Mrs. Sigrud sitting in her leeching chair. "Tell me about yourself, girl," the old lady had said, legs covered in leeches. "You're a young thing. Where are your parents?"

"Dead. I'm an orphan," Marion had responded proudly as if saying she had gotten top marks at school. For if she wore her tragedy with pride, no one could battle her with pity.

"Aye, is that so?" Mrs. Sigrud nestled deep into the chair. "Your mother must have been a pretty thing like yourself."

"Wouldn't know. Never met her. Died when I was a babe."

"Well, take heart. We've all got a mother. Rhaemyria watches over us. She loves us all. Even a lowly leech girl."

The words ringing in her ears, Marion stared at the mural of Rhaemyria. Behind the goddess's image was Xydrious, the Moon Father. At their feet were three babes. The Lost Star Children.

Legend had it, Rhaemyria and Xydrious gave birth to a son named Noctis. But Noctis had not been gifted in the act of creation like his mother, or the will of change like his father. Noctis could only destroy. In his greed for his parents' power, he corrupted humans into vampires. Rhaemyria was forced to wage a great war and destroy her own son. That was thousands of years ago, and she'd hid in the stars forever after.

Well, not forever after. The Church had made a big announcement, something like two decades ago. Rhaemyria had sent three children down to Thraina to save the world from the vampires her first son had created. But the children vanished, never to be seen or heard from again.

Marion scowled at the painting. Mrs. Sigrud might have said Rhaemyria was mother to all, but she wasn't Marion's mother. Marion didn't need a mother, especially one that killed her son then *lost* three of her children. Maybe if she'd been a better mother, Noctis wouldn't have gone mad and created a cult of blood-sucking demons.

Marion rolled her eyes. It was nothing but bedtime stories for the elderly. Real problems needed solving.

Like finding that damned pickpocket.

A wooden stage with a cream tent boasting the flag of Andúrigard lay in the center of the square. Hanging blue tassels and golden string decorated the edges of the stage. Lipstick on a pig: that 'stage' was the gallows, where at least once a moon some poor sob with a taste for the forbidden found himself with a short drop and a sudden stop. Marion didn't understand why commoners were so keen to hunt down stars when they knew a hint of magic without a badge from the Celestial Academy would find them at the end of a rope, but people did a lot of things she didn't understand.

It seemed since she'd left her beloved fields of lavender three years ago, everything had stopped making sense.

Knights wearing both the sigil of the kingdom and the Celestial Church patrolled the crowd, some standing by the many vendors along the courtyard's walls, some up on the stage where a green-haired man ran hitherto, rearranging the blue bouquets.

The crowd buzzed like thousands of flies. The annual swearing of allegiance ceremony would begin soon—and the Prince would make his appearance.

Marion made note of the exits from the square. If she took the east exit and skirted down the side streets past Taliesin Avenue, she would be home before the sky turned purple. Vivian and Timothée would be waiting for her—

Except it wasn't true.

Because Vivian was not waiting for her at home.

Vivian was here. At the festival.

What in the bloody stars?

At the front of the stage, a sheet of chestnut hair blew freely in the wind. Vivian was so tall she was easily seen among the masses. Marion's heart thrummed. No, no, no. Everything was going so terribly, dangerously wrong.

What possessed Vivian to come to the festival? Marion put her elbows out on either side and shoved her way through the crowd.

To anyone around them, Marion appeared a model sister, graciously grabbing her sister's arm and greeting her with a smile. They did not see the way her fingers clawed into Vivian's skin or hear the angry whisper: "What in the Three do you think you're doing here?"

For her credit, Viv didn't flinch. Her eyes were trained on the stage. "Didn't you get my note? I left it on the apartment door. I want to see a little of the ceremony. What's the problem?"

"What's the problem?" Marion cast her eyes to the heavens as if one of the Three would offer reassurance she hadn't gone completely mad. "It's a moonless night, *that's* the problem. And the sun has nearly set. Besides," she glanced at the stage where the green-haired man paced, "you don't have to be here for this. Let's go home and pretend it never happened."

Vivian didn't blink. "I can never forget it happened."

Curse her loose tongue. A hot wave of shame flooded Marion's cheeks. Of course, Vivian couldn't. She looked especially pale—she always did, of course, but she was almost translucent in the dimming sun. Her brilliant grey eyes sunk deep into dark circles as if she had not slept in days. She was still beautiful… but unwell. And every day a little piece of her seemed to slip further away.

"You should at least eat something," Marion said crossly. That was the problem with worry. It always made her cross.

She needed to find her bag, then Vivian could duck down, have something to eat and be more reasonable. She peered through the crowd. Cured of her initial rage, she realized she had as much chance of finding one boy here as she did of finding a unicorn in the woods. Those legendary beasts had disappeared when the gods did.

Damn that green-eyed boy and his scheme!

"I've lost my bag," Marion admitted. "It was foolish to think I could get it back. Let's go now. We'll stop at the shoppe and pick up a frozen jar. There's still time—"

But Vivian didn't move, even when Marion tugged on her thin wrist. She stared as if seeing a ghost. Or a god.

The crowd erupted into cheers. Clapping, crying, screaming—all in fervent reverence.

For out of the tent on the top of the stage walked Darius Störmberg, Crown Prince of Andúrigard.

Marion stifled an eye roll. She cared little of princes and even less for the crowds they drew. She had never thought Vivian had any interest in the Prince either. Yet today, it was like a fever had taken her.

Gods, she had eaten yesterday, hadn't she?

"All hail Prince Darius!" the green-haired man said. He seemed a nervous sort. Marion recognized him from other ceremonies held in the capital: the loremaster of the Celestial Academy, Setviren.

Prince Darius walked out and waved. Marion allowed herself to hesitate a moment. He *was* handsome, as handsome as all the ladies who came in for their leechings loved to gush about. He was so close she could see how his hair shimmered like golden thread in the dusk, his eyes flashing like shards of glass. He wore a dark blue uniform with silver embellishments.

Beside him stood a massive soldier, standing over a head taller than the already tall Prince. Based on the sigil across his exceedingly large chest—a wolf's claw—and the way he stood so close to Darius, he must be the Prince's loyal guard, Ser Remont. The ladies loved to talk about him in their leechings too, about how he was an undisputed warrior, the prized jewel of the kingdom. Ser Remont had served the royal line for generations, the starcraft keeping him young and strong.

Marion tugged on Vivian's wrist again. "Now can we go?"

Her sister acted as if Marion were a breeze tugging on a curl. "I want to watch a moment more." Vivian's voice was breathy like she'd stepped out of a dream.

"As above," the green-haired man, Setviren, called to the crowd. He touched three fingers to each eyelid.

"So below," the citizens chanted back, and copied his movement. The customary opening to any ceremony.

Setviren cleared his throat and stepped forward. He wore robes of white and a sash around his neck embroidered with both the sigil of Andúrigard and the Church. "Today is the twelfth Unification Day, a celebration of the integration of the three nations and the ending of the Trinity War."

Another calamity overcame the crowd as they cheered and screamed. Marion knew all about the Trinity War; though it had happened over a decade ago, no one here could *let it go*.

"King Halvor and Queen Elise squashed the rebellions of Kirrintsova and Medihsa. The traitors from Medihsa were welcomed back into Andúrigard, and the Kirrintsovan Empire was absorbed into the greater territory. We became one nation under the Three. And since then, Thraina has thrived!"

Cue another uproarious cheer. Yes, yes, Andúrigard good, rebellions bad. Marion never had much interest in history or politics at the lavender farm and she had less interest in it now, even though they lived in the Andúrigardian capital. Every day was about survival: was there enough food? Enough money? Enough leeches?

She was about to be very cross indeed that Vivian was still staring moon-eyed up at the stage when a commotion clattered in the crowd beside them.

"Watch it, kid!"

"We're standing here!"

"Ah-CHOO!"

"Ow, my foot!"

Out of a cloud of flour erupted an ugly black cat and a gangly boy.

The tornado of chaos skidded to a stop in a flurry of, "Sorry! Pardon me! Oh, was that your foot? Sorry!" and finally a sigh of relief. "Hello, sisters."

Marion wasn't surprised. How could this day get any worse than all three of the Greywick siblings being out in a public festival with no moon to dim the light of the stars?

Marion snatched Timothée's skinny arm. "Do I even want to know why you are here and not at the apartment?"

He shrugged haplessly. "I saw Viv's note about going to the festival. At first, I couldn't believe it, but then I thought it would be nice to have a lick of fun—"

"Looks like you had more than a lick of fun," Marion snapped. "Your *pants*." Timothée looked down and quickly began retying the rope he used as a belt. Marion forced a deep breath. Vivian had barely acknowledged their brother, her eyes still locked on the Prince. He wasn't *that* handsome.

"Look at you. Cover up at the very least," she grumbled and set upon Timothée. She snatched the hat from his pocket and stuffed it on his head. Then grabbed the scarf from around Vivian's neck and wound it tightly over Timothée's face. "You know better than to be exposed tonight."

Timothée swatted her away and his scrawny cat yowled, jumping from Timothée's shoulder to his arms. Let them both complain. She was right.

For triplets, they were all quite different. Vivian's hair was warm brown, like roasted chestnuts, Timothée's dark as wood, and Marion's golden as the dawn. Vivian always preferred to bundle her hair up in a knot on the top of her head, despite Marion's pleading it would look beautiful if she left it down. Which she had done today, another oddity. Timothée, on the other hand, never bothered with one thought of his hair, his dark waves always perpetually bound to get in his eyes.

All three were tall, with Timothée being the tallest though he was the youngest by twenty minutes. He was thin as a rail, a boy in a man's gangly body. Marion had no idea how one could work in a bakery and never seem to have any meat on them; she would die to be surrounded by white cakes and macaroons in every shade of pastel, and cream puffs with swirls of vanilla icing. Instead, she had leeches as company. But Timothée was not as enchanted by sugar as she was; he'd so often lose himself in his work or a book or his own misty head he wouldn't think of eating or drinking until Marion reminded him to.

Vivian had always been strong, with lean muscle. She'd been the one most likely to do the harvest with Father. But Marion had seen her coming out of the bath the other day. Gone were the muscles in her legs and arms. Instead, her skin seemed too small, stretched over the bone until Marion could count her ribs. She needed to eat more. Marion should keep the leech shoppe open later. Maybe Timothée could write some pamphlets to get more customers, and if Vivian was up to it, she could draw her wonderful pictures on the front.

"Guess you're right, Mare," Timothée said. "It's late. Do you suppose—"

"Yes, I suppose," Marion snapped, though she was grateful at least one sibling of hers had any sense.

"One more moment," Vivian said.

The loremaster had been droning on all this time about the annual swearing of allegiance in a few minutes where the wards from Kirrintsova and Medihsa would re-swear their fealty to the Prince. How dull. Besides, Marion wanted to leave before they started talking about the other anniversary today.

Before she was forced to remember.

"Today," Setviren said, "we also honor another anniversary. Today marks three years since the loss of our beloved King, Queen, and Princess."

Too late.

"Three years ago, our capital was viciously and mercilessly attacked by a cult led by a zealot known as the Dark Prophet." Setviren's voice took on a maniacal fervor and his hands shook. "This cult not only wielded the unlawful and disgusting abomination of dark magic," the crowd gave a horrified gasp as if they had not heard this story thousands of times before, "but was also made up entirely of..." Setviren's eyes narrowed and his thin mouth resembled a snake's, "vampires."

The crowd gave another horrified gasp. One woman screamed.

"Come on," Marion urged, pinching Vivian's arm. "We don't want to hear this."

"I need to stay," Vivian whispered.

No one had more reason to hate vampires than the Greywick children. Well, perhaps Prince Darius did. He had lost his father, mother, and younger sister to them.

But had he loved his father the way Marion had loved hers?

Had his father cooked him eggs with butter every morning? Taken him on walks through fields of purple flowers? Played him lullabies upon the dulcimer? Had his father protected him from every danger of the world?

Marion stared at the Prince, bound to be king once he graduated from that awful school in the sky. Darius stood listening as Setviren recalled the tale to the crowd. Listening to the truth turned legend of how his family was massacred.

For once, Marion quieted her nagging. She must have looked just like Vivian and all the other citizens, staring entranced at their tragic prince. He was still, his body taut as a bowstring. There were depths beyond depths in those eyes... of grief, of resolve, of something else.

A bitter flash of anger flickered through her chest. *The royal family were not the only ones to pay the price that night.*

"Though that night is bathed in sorrow," Setviren drawled, "one thing is clear: the strength and bravery of our future king. That very night, Prince Darius slew the Dark Prophet."

A chorus of cheers and chants burst from the crowd.

"Prince Darius continues to protect the kingdom and live in divine servitude to the Three!" Setviren roared piously. "All hail the future king!"

Despite the fanatic reverence of the crowd, Prince Darius still stood cold as his ice shard eyes.

No one knew much else of the Dark Prophet and his cult of vampires. Some thought they were supporters of Kirrintsova, fighting to reclaim their freedom. Others believed they were disciples of the fallen god, Noctis.

But there was one thing all the citizens agreed upon: if Prince Darius had not slain the Dark Prophet, scattering his vampire followers into chaos, they could be living in a very different Wolfhelm.

"It's getting dark. The stars will be out soon. We should go." Marion turned, preparing to push through the crowd. She had just about enough of princes, and festivals, and Setviren's nasally voice.

Then she saw it. She saw him.

By *it*, she meant her jar of leeches glinting in the fading sun. By *him*, she meant the green-eyed street rat. Slung over his shoulder was her woven bag. He leaned against the side of the stage, unbothered by the guards standing watch. The slippery bastard *had* stolen her purse!

As if he had known where she was all along, he turned to face her. His piercing gaze shot through her, an arrow to the lungs, forcing out all her breath.

And then he winked.

Winked.

Marion stopped. Her hands formed fists, nails digging into her palms. Her lip curled back into a cat's snarl. He'd stolen her leeches. And worse than that, he'd tricked her.

No. Absolutely not. No one would take advantage of her or her family.

Marion headed for the stage.

"Mare?" Timothée called. "I thought we were leaving."

"One moment," she growled. "I'm taking back something that belongs to me."

Marion ignored the grumbles of "Quit shoving!" and "Watch it!" as she pushed through the crowd while Timothée and Vivian apologized profusely behind her.

The boy didn't move as she approached. In fact, he stared at her the whole time, grin widening. He was baiting her, and she was walking straight into his trap.

Well, this boy didn't know he'd set a crab trap for a shark.

Marion reached the side of the stage. If she looked up, she could see the back of Prince Darius and Setviren, still rambling about the night of the massacre.

The boy straightened as she approached. That one lock of hair still fell between his eyebrows, touching his nose. Marion grabbed her skirts in her hands and stomped right up to him, about to tell him just what she thought of thieves—

He bowed low and held out her purse on one gloved finger, the jar of leeches peeking out from the flap. "Your purse, Miss Marion," he said, voice smooth as leech skin. "You ran off in such a hurry, I didn't notice I'd picked it up until you were long gone. But fate has brought us back together, hmm?"

She snatched the purse. "H-How dare—"

He straightened and smiled. "Are these your siblings?"

Only now did she realize Vivian and Timothée flanking her. Her face grew more flushed.

"Triplets," the boy said. "That's rare. A unique blessing." He stared at each of them like an artist deciding which kind of paint to use.

"Well, you have returned what you have stolen, so we'll be leaving now," Marion finally managed.

He laughed. "I am many things, but I am no thief. Won't you stay and watch the rest of the ceremony? The best part is coming up." His smile was as mesmerizing as his voice and Marion found herself blinking owlishly at him.

"No, we can't." Timothée tugged on her arm. "We have to be going."

The boy went back to leaning against the stage. "Suit yourself."

The three turned, facing back to the crowd. "Who was that?" Vivian whispered.

Marion closed her eyes and inhaled deeply. *What a disaster.* She wanted nothing but to leave this place and never—

"Oh, Marion?"

At the sound of his voice, she whipped around. The wind caught her long golden curls and pushed them off her face. She thought she was leveling him with a glare. Or maybe she was staring at him the same way he was staring at her. As if the crowd had melted away like dying rays of sun and the two of them were alone.

"Why do you have a jar of leeches in your purse?" he called.

"I'm the leech girl," she responded. "What else do you expect?"

His smile broadened, full of unasked questions. "Oh, I expect a lot."

A flash of red caught her eye. A girl poked her head out of the cream tent on the stage. She wore the purple uniform of the Celestial Academy, and her hair was crimson as the blood the leeches greedily sucked out of Mrs. Sigrud. She had the most unusual necklace, tight around her throat. Small gems dangled from it as she looked left and right and then down.

"What in the Three are you doing down there?" the red-haired girl hissed at the boy. "Get up here now!"

The boy sighed. "It's nothing but work with you." Then he turned back to Marion. "That's my cue. See you around." With a smile and a wink, he threw off his brown robe and jumped up on the stage beside the girl.

And at the same time, Setviren's nasally voice called out to the people: "We shall begin the annual re-swearing of allegiance!

Please welcome Princess Carmilla Vladimirovna, ward from Kirrintsova, and His Right Honorable Khalid Ali Bagheeri, ward from Medihsa!"

The crowd erupted into a mixture of cheers and boos as the red-haired girl walked out from behind the tent to stand beside Prince Darius. And following her was the boy. The boy who was wearing the gold uniform of the Celestial Academy, which he had hidden beneath brown robes. The boy who was not a thief at all, and also not a liar because he had told the truth. He really was Khalid Ali Bagheeri, child to the traitors from the rebellion of Medihsa.

How could she have been so stupid?

Khalid looked so nonchalant up there beside the Prince of Andúrigard and the former Crown Princess of the Empire. All three were dressed in their Celestial Academy uniforms, though in different colors: Darius's being blue, Carmilla's purple, and Khalid's gold. She knew the colors signified different starcraft, but Father had forbidden any questions of the Academy. Setviren was now going off about how the three had begun their first year at the Celestial Academy for Fallen Stars earlier this moon.

Not only was Khalid one of the most important political figures in Thraina but he was a Starling. That made him dangerous. More dangerous than any common ruffian in a back alley. How many times had Father warned them of the Celestial Academy? Hid them inside the house when the great shadow crept over the farm as the Isle of Argos floated by?

Father had called them villains. And Marion had let herself fall straight into one's lap.

She had to be better than this. Her siblings were counting on her. It was no good for someone like her to get caught up in green eyes and ruses.

"Alright," Marion sighed. "Let's go home."

"I'm not," Vivian said.

Marion glanced at the sky then at her sister. "The sun is about to set."

"I'll wear my cloak, shade my face and—" Vivian looked so desperate, her eyes watering, her hair wild around her face, Marion almost pitied her.

Almost.

But pity wouldn't keep her alive. Only the truth would do that.

"None of us can hide what we are." Marion bared her teeth. "Especially *you*."

Her sister's face blanched, lips trembling.

"Marion." Timothée reached toward Vivian, but she backed away from him. Even his cat perked up, blinking her sleepy blue eyes.

"Darius came into the candle shoppe," Vivian said, and soft tears fell down her cheeks. "He told me to meet him here. I wanted to be a girl who could."

Marion wasn't sure if she should laugh or squeal or cry or scream. Vivian had met the Prince of Andúrigard? There was no one in Thraina more dangerous.

And she would do anything to keep her sister safe.

"You'll never be that girl," Marion hissed.

Vivian wiped her eyes with the heel of her palm. "And I'll always have you to remind me of it."

Vivian turned from the stage, from the Prince.

There should have been a sense of relief. But two things happened at once.

First, Timothée's cat let out a horrible yowl, such an awful sound it caused Setviren's odious speech to stutter to a stop.

The cat leapt from her brother's arms onto the stage, and ran straight for the Prince of Andúrigard, all matted fur and claws lunging at his polished boots.

"Yvaine!" Timothée cried, reaching out his hand.

"Timothée!" Vivian yelled, clasping his arm.

"Vivian," Prince Darius breathed, trying to shake off the wild cat on his leg.

"Order! Order!" Setviren bellowed frantically.

Behind him, Khalid just smiled, as if the whole thing were an elaborate play, and Carmilla pinched the bridge of her nose.

But Marion was hardly concerned with any of it. Because in that same moment the shadows came to life.

Dark shapes crept out from behind vendor stalls, from the alleyways. Not dark shapes: hooded figures. Creatures clothed in blackness slithered one after another out of every dark corner and took post around the perimeter of the square.

"What's going on?" Timothée cried, reaching his arm far enough on stage to grip his cat by the tail and tug her back.

Prince Darius was shouting commands to his guards. He cast a frantic look down. "Protect them," he ordered.

It was too late.

The dark creatures completely barricaded the courtyard. And one by one, white flashed within the darkness of their hoods: fangs.

They had come three years ago. And now on the anniversary of their first massacre, they had returned.

The vampires.

6

IN WHICH TIMOTHÉE WITNESSES A GREAT DEAL OF MAGIC

TIMOTHÉE SHOULD HAVE listened to his sister. He said that a lot. But this time he really, *really* should have listened to his sister. It was just being surrounded by vampires usually wasn't the consequence of not listening.

A platoon of guards formed a perimeter around the makeshift stage. And thanks to Prince Darius's orders to keep them safe, the Greywicks were within that protection.

Timothée clutched Yvaine tight to his chest. He'd never seen her act like that. Jumping up and attacking the Prince's boot—what in the stars had gotten into her?

"Y'know," Timothée ventured, "maybe we shouldn't have gone to the festival."

Marion sent him a withering glare.

Vampires never came out during the day, for their skin was so easily scorched by sunlight. And if they were out in the sun long enough, they turned completely to ash. At least, that's what Timothée had read. But like Marion had been saying, it wasn't day. Not anymore. Dusky purple rays spilled over the square. The vampires wore heavy cloaks to protect them from the lingering light.

Soon they wouldn't need them at all.

Panic tore through the crowd like a living thing. Timothée barely heard the shouts of the guards over the rising cries.

"We have to get out of here," Marion said.

"How?" Vivian asked. Guards surrounded the platform, and beyond them was the panicked crowd and a dozen cloaked vampires.

These weren't the usual vampires that slunk around Wolfhelm: hunched and weak, bodies broken with protruding bones, more monster than person like the one he'd seen earlier today. These vampires were different, all elegant features and sharp fangs peering from beneath their hoods. Their movements were purposeful. Like they weren't even hungry.

They were here for a reason.

Panic laced Vivian's words. "Is it going to be like three years ago?"

Three years ago had been a full-out attack, a slaughter. These vampires hadn't hurt anyone yet. They closed around the edges of the crowd, blocking the alleys and the streets. The guards had their swords drawn, waiting for the command to strike.

"Hold," Prince Darius growled at his guards. Once blood was drawn, there would be nothing to stop these monsters.

"We have to go," Marion whispered over and over again, her eyes flicking from the vampires to the ever-darkening sky.

There is no moon tonight.

Stillness trembled over the crowd, and it felt as if the air snapped from autumn to winter in an instant.

And then Timothée saw him. The one who had sucked the warmth from the courtyard, rendered the crowd speechless with fear.

Timothée's lips moved against the coarse fabric of his scarf as he whispered: "The Dark Prophet."

"It's impossible. He's dead," Vivian said. She gazed up at the Prince of Andúrigard, who, by the look on his face, had believed the same thing.

Darius pushed aside his guards. "You," the Prince said.

The Dark Prophet only stepped forward in response. His black cape, which appeared made of torn shadows, flowed behind him. He wore armor of black obsidian with sharp pointed edges. A helmet covered his entire face, adorned with bat wings along the side, and painted purple fangs. The vampires herded the crowd back, forming a path straight to the stage. Straight to the Prince.

And unfortunately, straight to Timothée.

He clutched Yvaine tighter. "Is it too late to say you were right, Mare?"

"Shut up." Her voice shook.

It was as if the entire world was holding its breath to see what the Dark Prophet would do. The guards started to draw closer, but the Prince stopped them with a flash of his hand. He too must have sensed what the vampires wanted. A show, not a massacre, and he'd play along to protect his people.

Or maybe he didn't want anyone to touch the Dark Prophet before he could.

The loremaster, Setviren, looked as if he would expire on the stage. His face turned ghastly white, a sickly contrast to the green of his hair. "It cannot be so," he muttered, eyes as wide as an animal's at slaughter. "It cannot be so."

The Dark Prophet paused when he reached the bottom of the platform.

"It cannot be so!" Setviren shrieked and bolted down the stairs.

To escape, to attack… Whatever his plan, it was futile. The Dark Prophet whipped out his arm and snatched the frail man around the neck. He held him up until his feet kicked and dangled like a petulant child.

"It's been a long time, Darius." The Dark Prophet spoke casually, as if addressing an old friend. As if he didn't have his hand around a church official's neck.

"Let him go," Darius snarled. "You can't be real—"

"Did you really think, in all your golden arrogance, you could have killed me?" The Dark Prophet's voice was edged with the bitter taste of night, a metallic sound that rattled beneath his obsidian helmet. "One as weak as you, one who cannot defend his own family?"

Three years ago, the Dark Prophet's cult of vampires had stormed Wolfhelm. He had slain the King, Queen, and Princess before Darius defeated him.

The crowd quivered, a palpable fear flooding through them. They pressed together, their hushed cries getting lost to the night. Still there was the sense of desperate hope. Darius had saved them once. Couldn't he do so again?

Darius roared and surged forward but the Medihsan ward, Khalid, pushed him back. "We're Darius's family too," Khalid called, "but I'm assuming based on your ensemble you don't get invited to many family gatherings, so maybe you're a little fuzzy on the details?"

Marion managed a groan.

The Dark Prophet turned to the fearful loremaster in his grip. "This man claims to speak for the gods. He only tells you what that *woman* wants you to hear. Lies for sheep."

With unnatural strength, the Dark Prophet whipped Setviren across the courtyard. He skidded, bouncing, bouncing, bouncing on the cobblestone, until he landed near the feet of some citizens. His eyes fluttered and his chest rose slowly up and down, but he did not rise.

"Setviren!" Darius called, then turned with a snarl to the Dark Prophet. "Begone from my sight, vermin of darkness!"

Somehow, Timothée got the distinct feeling the Dark Prophet was smiling beneath his helmet. "I am here to deliver a message. One granted from the stars above, for I have had a vision."

For I have had a vision.

Timothée knew those words, words printed in forbidden books he'd pilfered from the library. They were ancient words spoken by the lieutenant of the fallen god Noctis. The lieutenant was known as the Prophet of Stars. It was said in the ancient wars, he foresaw the battles, and his prophecies always came true.

Timothée didn't really believe this creature who called himself the Dark Prophet was the Prophet of Stars reborn, but it was evident Darius hadn't finished off this impersonator three years ago. The murderer's words had chilled the crowd so thoroughly, one could hear their collective breath.

"The night sky has shown me the future," the Dark Prophet said. "He will return."

There was no questioning who *he* was.

Noctis, the fallen god.

A rumble erupted through the crowd at those words, and the Dark Prophet leaned back on his heels, as if the scared whispers were honey to his ears. "In the space between the stars I saw him," he continued. "Soon, the God of Shadows will return to Thraina. Mountains will crumble, rivers run red, and the sky will weep."

"You spread lies!" Darius yelled down at him. "Noctis is dead, and you will join him forthcoming."

"You have dubbed me a prophet because I can see the future in the stars." The Dark Prophet laughed. "I saw Noctis and I, side by side, as we were at the start of his world. We stood on the Isle of Argos as his shadows devoured your precious school. The Celestial Academy will fall and anyone who does not bend the knee to the One True God of Above and Below will feel our wrath."

The crowd quaked, and Timothée shivered along with them. What he was saying, the crazy ravings of a zealot… It couldn't be true. A god hadn't been seen by commonfolk in over a thousand years, and to foretell the return of a fallen one—it was madness.

A tremor flickered on Darius's face but before he moved, a Celestial Knight stepped out. "Get His Highness to safety," he said sternly.

Murmurs sounded through the crowd: "Ser Remont, the Blade Breaker."

He was a soldier of legends, taller and wider than any man Timothée had ever seen. The Prince roared as Remont pushed him away, and the other soldiers shoved him and the two wards into the tent on the stage.

Remont thudded down the stairs and drew his great axe. He cast a look to the sky. "The stars have not yet awoken," he boomed. "But it is no matter. I will dispose of this vile interloper with might alone."

The people, frightened and trapped, gave a weak cheer.

"Magic is fun and all," the Dark Prophet sneered, "but if you think I need it, you haven't been paying attention."

The Dark Prophet drew a sword that seemed longer than himself. At first glance, it looked to be made of the same obsidian as his armor. But shadows crept within the blade, curling like smoke. *It cannot be.* Timothée knew from his many late nights in the library there could be only one way to forge a blade of smoke and shadow. Gravastarium, forged from dead stars. The forbidden metal.

The crowd stopped cheering.

Remont roared and swung his great axe, bringing it down upon the Dark Prophet. The murderer stepped out of the way without a flinch, and Remont's axe cleaved open the cobblestone. The Dark Prophet whirled around the bigger man. He was as fluid as a dancer, but as quick as a viper. His sword struck Remont's side, slicing through armor.

"We won't be able to escape," Timothée said. "At least not right now. It's too organized. The Dark Prophet is making a spectacle. We have to hide and—"

"Wait for a little chaos," Marion finished.

"Exactly. We can escape then."

"What about the night?" Marion glanced at the sky.

"I think the people have bigger problems to worry about." Timothée forced himself to breathe as Remont barely countered a series of lightning-fast slashes.

"There's nowhere to hide," Vivian whispered, eyes wide, hands wrapped tight around her throat.

He grabbed his sister's hand and squeezed it three times. "I have an idea."

"What about Darius?" Fear etched Vivian's face. "We can't leave him. We can't!"

"Yes, we can," Marion said urgently. "It will be easy. He won't even notice you're gone."

"But—" Vivian protested.

Timothée felt a pang of pity for her. This very well might have been the first thing she'd ever asked for in the last three years. Granted, saving the Prince of Andúrigard from a homicidal zealot dressed in creepy armor was *quite* the ask.

He set his jaw. "I've got an idea for that too. Get down."

The Greywicks crouched to their knees and Timothée motioned to the stage. They began to crawl, the perimeter of guards shielding them from view. Yvaine padded along beside him.

"I thought we would hide away from the *target*," Marion hissed.

Timothée sighed. She really couldn't let anyone else do *anything*. He ignored her and continued crawling until they reached the stage. Dangling ribbons of blue fabric decorated the base of the platform. He pushed them aside and motioned for his sisters to crawl underneath.

Marion's mouth twitched with anger before her bottom was even under cover.

"Yes?" he sighed.

"This is your hiding spot? The Dark Prophet is literally right outside!" She gestured, and through the ribbons of fabric, they could see the Dark Prophet and Remont fighting, feet stirring the earth, back and forth, back and forth.

"The closer we are to danger, the further we are from harm." Timothée smiled.

"That doesn't make any sense." Marion grabbed her hair. He was surprised she hadn't ripped it out by this point.

"What about Darius?" Vivian urged.

"Oh right," Timothée stammered. "About that."

He knew this square; he'd walked by it every day for the last three years. This stage wasn't built for the festival. It was always here, just with a different purpose. Because the only thing the people of Wolfhelm loved more than celebrating royalty with magic was hanging common-folk with magic.

The tall beam in the center, from which usually hung a rope, today had a tent strung up from it. The tent the Prince and his wards were in. And if Timothée had it lined up right in his head, which he thought he did, then... then this might work.

He quickly sketched something in the dirt with his finger, then picked up Yvaine and showed her the plan. "Listen! No more silliness, Yvaine. See this? Push here with your paws."

Marion pulled on her hair harder. "You're speaking to a *cat*."

"Yes," Timothée answered. "A witch's cat. She's special." He placed Yvaine down on the ground. "Do this and I swear I'll give you all the fish you can eat. But we have to save the Prince."

"Timothée," Marion growled.

He looked down at Yvaine and sighed. "It's not your fault she prefers blood-sucking bugs."

Yvaine meowed and pranced out from the blue cloth.

"Of all the fates!" Marion threw herself to the ground. "Trusting my life to an ugly cat! You best not come crying to me when your stupid cat gets its blood sucked out."

Vivian recoiled.

"Hey—" Timothée started, but there was no time for arguing. A large creak sounded and tumbling through the open trapdoor was Prince Darius and his two wards.

"Darius!" Vivian cried and crawled to the heap of three Celestial Academy students.

"What in the Three above?" Khalid Ali Bagheeri rubbed his head. He looked up as the trapdoor closed, shrouding them in darkness again.

"What is going on?" Prince Darius sat up. "Vivian?"

She blinked at him, but before she spoke, Marion answered: "Okay, we've got your prince. *Now* can we escape?"

"Escape?" the girl from Kirrintsova said. Carmilla Vladi—Vladi*something*. She sat up, parting her red hair, and scowled. "Is this some sort of deranged rescue mission? Who are you three?"

"We're nobody," Marion said. "We just want to survive, and I'm assuming you three do as well."

Darius took a long look at Vivian, and she stared back at him. To Timothée, it felt like a lot of words without any words at all.

"And how do you propose that?" Carmilla scoffed. "You don't think those monsters are going to find us as soon as they realize we're not in the tent anymore?"

"We wait for movement in the crowd," Vivian said. "You three could make for the castle walls. You must know a way inside."

"Of course," Khalid said. "I can sneak inside that place with my eyes closed. The problem is a pack of bloodsuckers blocks our path. And not the kind your sister likes to keep in her bag."

"Shut up," Marion said. "We have to wait for our moment."

Khalid turned to fully look at her and a smile curved up his face. "Trust me. I'm always waiting for my moment."

For once, Marion had no reply.

A yell shattered the night, and all eyes peered out through the flaps of fabric. Remont had collapsed to his knees, fingers grasping for his axe, as the Dark Prophet circled him.

Darius gritted his teeth. "I have to help him."

"Darius." Khalid grabbed him by the shoulders. It was strange seeing someone touch the future king so carelessly. But a look of familiarity passed between the Prince and his ward. "Listen to me," Khalid said. "If the Dark Prophet kills Remont, he kills a knight. If he kills you, he kills all of Andúrigard."

Darius balled his hands into fists but did not move.

"Is this all you have to offer?" the Dark Prophet drawled. He held out his arms, his shadow blade like a living tendril of smoke. He didn't seem human, his face entirely hidden by that horrible fanged helmet. "Is this the best defense Andúrigard has?"

Ser Remont struggled to his knees. Blood covered his face, and he couldn't get a grip on his massive axe.

Timothée's throat closed. *He's a royal guard. He can't fall!*

The Dark Prophet turned away, exposing his back to the knight. An arrogant show. But if Remont could just grab his axe...

"What a bore." The Dark Prophet swung out his sword, and without even making eye contact, removed Ser Remont's head.

A horrid thunk reverberated through the night. Then the silence was replaced with screams.

The Dark Prophet had killed Andúrigard's best knight, and he hadn't even needed magic to do it.

Darius shot up, Remont's name upon his lips, but Khalid was faster. He snatched his hand around the Prince's mouth. "Don't do it, Dare."

"You couldn't even offer me a challenge." A laugh echoed from the Dark Prophet. "I don't remember you being so frightened last time we met, little prince."

Darius thrashed against Khalid's hold, breaking free. But Carmilla placed a hand on Darius's arm like it belonged there. "You will have your chance to fight him. But wait for the right time. You've done it before."

Timothée felt the space between him and the golden prince spread miles, though their shoulders were close enough to touch.

"You *have* done it before." Khalid jerked Darius to meet his gaze. "Remember that night, Dare?"

"I grow tired of these guards," the Dark Prophet said.

Then there wasn't just one thunk—there were several as all around them bodies fell. Blood began to leak beneath the platform and pool by Timothée's knees. The vampires were striking.

And they weren't even stopping to feed.

Vivian let out a shuddering breath and her eyes rolled to white.

Marion wrapped her arms around her sister, not in a hug but a hold. "We have to find a way out. *Now.*"

But there was no movement beyond the thud of bodies.

The crowd was paralyzed with fear. The panic, the chaos they had predicted—it wasn't happening. Timothée felt it too. Fear so cold it froze. Vivian drew her knees to her chest, hands gripping Marion's chain-tight arms hard enough to leave marks. Timothée crept his head out from under the stage and looked to the sky. The stars were blinking awake.

Shit. Shit. Shit.

The wooden stage groaned as the Dark Prophet stepped onto the stairs. Shadows swept down from the night and gathered around them. The ground trembled and began to churn.

Darkness leeched its way from the dirt between the cobblestones, sprouting up in the form of inky spiders, and long cockroaches, and spiraled worms. They crawled to the surface, drawn to something.

Drawn to the Dark Prophet?

There was the swooshing of fabric and the light fall of it. The Dark Prophet stepping into the tent above them. Then amused laughter. "Think you can hide?"

A large spider with eight hairy legs crawled its way up Carmilla's boot. Her breath hitched.

Khalid locked eyes with her and slowly shook his head.

Carmilla bit her lip, trembling. The spider was still on her leg.

The platform creaked. The Dark Prophet was right above them.

Marion slowly released Vivian and inched forward. She snatched the spider by its thorax and unceremoniously dropped it to the ground. Her eyes shot daggers of warning at the Kirrintsovan girl.

Timothée let out a breath. Carmilla gave a weak smile and leaned back. Her hand landed on a long centipede. It coiled, tiny legs shivering up her arm.

Carmilla screamed.

Khalid clapped a hand over her mouth, but it was too late. There was the rush of boots then a crisp chill, and Timothée saw it: shadows with marbled purple veins curling around the legs of the platform.

"Shadowcraft," Khalid gasped.

Marion looked from Timothée to Vivian. "Night has fallen."

The stage rose. The Dark Prophet's purple shadows lifted the entire wooden platform off the ground. Any semblance of protection they had was gone.

Time seemed to slow, and for a moment, all Timothée could see was the Dark Prophet, hard angled edges of metal and magic. And the crowd was still there, trapped by the vampires, forced to watch this horror.

Then the stage crashed down behind them, wood splintering across the ground.

Darius and his two wards crouched in front of them. And Marion yanked her siblings back toward the wreckage of the stage, hiding them underneath the cover of the ripped tent, just as Timothée felt the warm brush of starlight on his skin.

Night had fallen and they could not let the light of the stars touch them. If they followed one rule of their late father, it was that one. *Never go outside on a moonless night.*

What was there to do but hide under this ripped cloth? The Dark Prophet would kill the Prince first, and then maybe the wards, and after that... After that, he'd probably let his vampires do what they did best.

It would be like three years ago all over again, when the streets ran red with blood. Only this time there would be no golden prince to save Wolfhelm.

"We're going to die," Marion whispered.

But Timothée peered out from the cloth, watching Darius.

"I've killed you before," Darius snarled to the Dark Prophet.

"Dare, remember what happened last time." Khalid grabbed his shoulder, but Darius shrugged him off and stood.

"Last time," Darius drew a small shining cube of metal from his pocket, "I wasn't a Starling."

Khalid sighed and looked behind him where the triplets hid. "He's only been a Starling for a moon, so it's really not as impressive as he makes it sound in that heroic voice of his."

But Darius *did* look heroic, more heroic than Timothée and his sisters, who huddled against the ruined wood. More heroic than Carmilla and Khalid standing idle in front of them. More heroic than the remaining guards, whose spears shook in their hands. More heroic than the Celestial Academy students, scattered in the crowd, too afraid to move.

Darius stepped past the fallen guards, past the shallow breathing body of Setviren, past the corpse of Remont, and the vampires who eyed him. The Dark Prophet simply waved his creatures down.

The cube of metal Darius held was pure stellarite: a rare metal used by Starlings. The stars seemed to crackle, and light shone around the Prince. A soft blue glow surrounded him and the stellarite molded in his hands. It swirled and stretched until it formed a gleaming sword.

Darius turned around. "Don't follow me." He was only speaking to one person.

Vivian's eyes glistened; her lips trembled.

Darius ran, stellarite sword drawn. The Dark Prophet raised his cursed blade. A sound like ice breaking rang across the night as their swords clashed. The magic of starlight against darkness, like in the tales of old.

Maybe there's hope after all.

Darius moved like lightning, a flash of gold and blue. And if he had been battling someone else, *anyone* else, Timothée thought this fight would have ended as quick as all that: a flash of lightning. But he was crossing blades with something akin to a shadow. The Prince may have been taller than the Prophet, but he couldn't land a hit.

And how could anyone fight that?

"He's going to get himself killed," Khalid hissed.

"No one fights like Darius," Carmilla said.

"And no one will die like him either." Khalid eyed the crowd, their faces a mixture of hope and fear. "If he's killed, it's going to be a bloodbath."

Carmilla glared at him. "If you spent more time training and less time scheming, then perhaps you could actually be a help to *our* Prince."

"Oh, love," Khalid said. "You know as well as I do, I'd only be in the way up there. The Dark Prophet would cut through me like warm butter."

The battle raged on, with neither side gaining an advantage. Though Timothée couldn't help but feel, through some sick sense he couldn't explain, the Dark Prophet was simply toying with the Prince.

"When—*if* the Prince falls," Marion pulled Timothée's scarf higher on his face and his hat so low it almost blocked his vision, "we run. It's our only hope. Vivian, hood up."

Vivian stared at Darius, a gasp upon her lips as the Dark Prophet cut a red line across the young prince's chest.

"We *tried*, Vivian," Marion said. "There's nothing more we can do. This is so much bigger than us."

The surrounding vampires wavered eagerly, hoods flown back as night had fallen. It was so eerie; their faces looked human, except for the hunger lingering beneath their eyes and the glint of white fangs.

The Dark Prophet surged so fast the Prince fell off-kilter and landed on the ground at the murderer's feet.

This was it. Marion rose to a crouch, still clutching the tent fabric tight around them. She was ready to bolt. The vampires pulled their lips back, fangs glittering white. Vivian turned to her siblings. "Not this time," she whispered. "I cannot go with you."

She ran into the square.

7
IN WHICH VIVIAN EMBRACES THE STARLIGHT

VIVIAN SPRANG TO her feet and ran out of the protection of the tent fabric, past Carmilla and Khalid, and right into the middle of the square. She ignored her siblings' cries behind her.

Three years ago, when she'd left the safety of their cart to look for their father, she'd arguably made the worst decision of her life.

But she didn't regret it. She didn't regret trying to save her father. She would keep making terrible choices.

Again, and again, and again. If it meant a chance.

A chance for someone she loved.

"Darius!"

He whirled to face her, then rolled, barely dodging the Dark Prophet's sword which embedded hard into the earth.

A sickening sensation itched its way along her skin as she felt the gaze of the vampires that surrounded the square.

Not just the vampires. The people too.

Because it was a moonless night, when the light of the stars was the strongest.

A soft glow emitted around her. She knew it was spreading from her eyes, which glowed as bright and radiant as the stars themselves.

Darius scrambled to his feet and ran toward her. He made a motion with his hand, and she felt the stars obey. The earth rose, cobblestone forming a circular barrier around them. Darius pulled her against his chest.

She blinked up at him, and he quickly wiped away the tears from her glowing eyes. "Well, that's something, isn't it? You shine as bright as the candles."

"I don't know what I'm doing, just that I have to do something." She tangled her fingers in his shirt. Outside the world raged on, but here, shielded by the rock wall, she had a moment, a breath, maybe two.

"Something binds us together. A thread—"

"A ribbon." Vivian clasped his wrists, fingers tightening around the blue fluttering fabric.

"A ribbon." Darius leaned down, pressing their foreheads together. "And nothing can ever cut it. I am tied to you, and you to me. I will keep you safe, through this moment and whatever comes after."

Lashes of shadow broke apart the rock barrier. Darius pushed Vivian back and rose his sword to clash against the Dark Prophet.

"Deal with her," the Dark Prophet snarled as he whirled an attack on the Prince.

A vampire rushed toward Vivian and grabbed her arm. Memories hurled at her like swords—running through the streets of Wolfhelm, trying to

scream her father's name when her throat was clogged with blood. That had been the last time she'd faced vampires.

And she'd lost.

But she wasn't the same girl anymore. The vampires had made sure of that.

She turned to it, prepared to face it down with any means necessary.

But the vampire screamed. Red blossomed around its face and down its neck, and great boils formed along its body—like it was burning.

But that wasn't right. Vampires only burned in sunlight. The stars were too far away to hurt them.

The vampire dropped her arm and fell to its knees, clutching its scalding face.

It had burned when the light of her eyes cast upon it.

A flash of movement and two more vampires stalked toward her. How could she look so many places at once?

Someone knocked into her. "Timothée!"

Timothée yanked off his gloves. Beneath it, his skin glowed. On moonless nights, when her eyes were lit with celestial light, the same came from her brother's skin.

He held his hands up toward the vampires. They shrieked, skin burning away in strips of ashen flesh.

"It's hurting them!" Timothée gasped.

"I know." She nodded. "We can help." She grabbed his hand, and the soft glow of his skin spread across hers. Something of her passed to him as well, lighting Timothée's eyes up like diamonds.

"Remember?" Timothée said.

She did. "Marion," she yelled to her sister's huddled form beneath the tent fabric. "We *need* you."

Be brave for me, sister.

Slowly, Marion crept from her hiding spot. Her gaze was wary, watching the Dark Prophet and the Prince locked in battle.

Marion pulled her hood down and glowing curls spilled out. She grabbed Timothée's other hand.

Brighter together.

Something they had discovered deep in the cellar of the lavender cabin. When they held hands on a moonless night, the light encircled all of them. As if they had become their own sun, their own star. They were light in a darkened world.

It happened on nights like this—when the moon hid, and the light of the stars were at their brightest.

On nights like this, they shone.

And if they touched, they were all light, not just her eyes, or Marion's hair, or Timothée's skin—but every part of them.

Vivian squeezed Timothée and Marion's hands and the light—their light—spread from them, over the ground, over the pools of blood, over the vampires. There was a horrible cry of agony, of burning and pain.

Some of the vampires dropped to the ground, screeching, unable to move. Others turned, fleeing into the streets. Finally, there was the chaos they'd been waiting for. The crowd began cheering. And when Vivian closed her eyes, she saw herself in the sky, a star herself, and the lights of the world swirled around her, so many broken pieces.

Through the din of screams and cheers, the Dark Prophet let out a deep breath. "And that is quite enough of that."

The Dark Prophet rose his hand, palm facing the sky, and the air trembled. Shadows swirled around his feet, inky and flowing like spilled oil. The shadows rose, curling around his body, higher and higher until they shot upward. Darkness spilled over them, so thick it blocked out the light of the stars.

Darius's sword crumbled upon itself, reducing to the cube of stellarite and falling hard to the ground. The blue glow around him faded.

Without starlight, a Starling couldn't use their magic. Darius was defenseless.

But the Greywicks were no Starlings. And the light around them didn't fade. They grew brighter.

The Dark Prophet turned his attention to them. "Now that's annoying." As he passed Darius, he threw out his arm. A sweep of darkness struck the Prince in the chest, flinging him backward. He hit a stall and crashed to the ground.

"Darius!" Vivian shouted and lunged forward, but Timothée gripped her tighter.

"Don't let go," Marion ordered. "This is the only thing we have right now."

Her heart hammered in her chest as she stared at Darius's crumbled form, but she made herself clutch her siblings' hands tighter. Marion was right.

The Dark Prophet looked from Darius to her. "Worried about him?" he asked. "How quaint."

There was something bitter in his words. Mocking.

"He's getting closer," Timothée whimpered. "I don't think he cares about the glowing as much as the vampires."

"Can you do anything besides *glow?*" Khalid crept up behind them. Carmilla was there too, red hair stuck to her forehead with sweat and blood.

"Can *you* do anything at all?" Marion glared at him. "Except be completely useless, which is *all* you've done since the first moment I met you? Aren't you a Starling?"

He shrugged toward the hovering dark above them—clouds of inky blackness. "No stars. No magic."

"Three years ago," the Dark Prophet mused, "I thought I'd taken everyone you ever cared about."

Blood dripped from Darius's head, coating his blond hair.

"Your father. Your mother. Your little sister."

Darius clutched his chest, fine clothes torn and ragged. With great effort, he struggled to his feet.

The Dark Prophet stopped only feet away from Vivian and her siblings. "So, who is she?"

"Stay away from her," Darius growled.

"That's what I thought." The Dark Prophet flicked his wrist and shadows whipped at them like lashes.

Timothée and Marion flew away from her, hitting hard against the broken stage.

But she stayed, blackness clouding around her. It coiled like a snake, barbs of shadow sinking into her skin. She screamed as the Dark Prophet's shadows suspended her in the air above him.

8

IN WHICH TIMOTHÉE TOPPLES THE STARS

TIMOTHÉE'S HAT FELL to the ground, soaked in blood. Marion was collapsed at the edge of the crowd.

He lay in the broken remains of the stage. Slowly, the world came back into focus.

The chaos of the crowd had been stunned still again as soon as the Dark Prophet had called forth his shadows. Darius was on his feet, but his sword was gone. His magic was gone. He reached into his boot and yanked out a small dagger. Three years ago, the Prince had defeated the Dark Prophet, and he'd had no magic then—but now Timothée couldn't imagine how that feat had ever been possible.

"Do you remember how I did it, little prince?" the Dark Prophet asked. He sent a lash of magic toward Darius. The Prince went flying, losing grip of his dagger. It skidded on the ground and landed in front of Carmilla and Khalid.

Khalid looked down at the dagger. "If this is a sign from above, I am choosing to ignore it."

Darius did not move.

"A pity," the Dark Prophet said, as if it weren't really a pity at all. "I wanted you to be conscious when I killed her. I suppose you'll have to weep over her dead and broken body."

"Vivian!" Marion screamed, and she struggled to her feet. Her hair still glowed, but her clothes were streaked with blood.

Khalid sprinted over to her, the first sense of urgency Timothée had ever seen from the ward. He laced his arms around her. "Stop, Marion! You'll get yourself killed."

She struggled in his grip. "Get off of me!"

Vivian was still suspended in the Dark Prophet's hold, shadows lacing up her neck. She screamed with raw terror.

"Tell me what type of starcraft you wield," the Dark Prophet snarled. "What god blessed you with that infernal glow?"

Vivian screamed, clawing at the shadows that wrapped around her body.

Yvaine darted out of the rubble toward Timothée. She pawed at his legs, mewling.

"I know!" he gasped. "I know. I know."

He had to do something. He was still glowing, but little good that would do. He didn't have any star magic—and even if he did, the Dark Prophet had blocked out the sky.

All he had was his glowing skin and his stupid scarf.

He looked down at Yvaine sadly. "It will have to do," he murmured. Yvaine gave what could only be a disappointed look.

Timothée rushed forward, on the opposite side of where Prince Darius lay. On the opposite side of where the Dark Prophet's attention was focused.

He heard Marion and Khalid shouting behind him. And why wouldn't they? He was quite possibly the most stupid person in the entire kingdom. But he could not—would not—let his sister die for him.

Not again.

As he ran, he unhooked his stupid scarf from his stupid neck. Then he was behind the Dark Prophet, and somehow the Dark Prophet didn't notice him. Not yet. The murderer extended his hand, fingers closing, black magic tightening around Vivian.

Yvaine dashed out, a black shadow herself, across the Dark Prophet's gaze. He looked at her, just for a moment, but a moment was all Timothée needed. Timothée dropped low, wrapped his scarf around the Dark Prophet's feet and pulled.

And… and it worked.

The Dark Prophet tilted, falling off-kilter, and crashed to the ground. The shadows dropped from Vivian, and she fell in a heap. Marion broke out of Khalid's grip and rushed to her.

And Timothée was so astounded, he forgot to move. The Dark Prophet rose, fury coiling off him in black waves of magic.

"So, you want to dance, huh?" The Dark Prophet drew his sword, that glittering black blade made of dead stars.

This was how Timothée Greywick would die, lying on the ground, stunned and stupid. The Dark Prophet turned, his sword raised to strike—and he stopped.

Hesitating wasn't the right word because he wasn't even moving. He was utterly and completely still.

He was staring at him, and Timothée wasn't sure how you could know someone was staring at you through a closed helmet. It was the oddest feeling. The Dark Prophet was *staring* at him.

"How?" the Dark Prophet asked, and even his words stumbled. "How are you here? Noctis?"

The Dark Prophet pitched forward, and there was a flash of red, and Carmilla was in front of him. She wielded Darius's dagger and struck it through the armor of the Dark Prophet. He clattered to the ground.

"Leave this place!" she snarled, her body on top of his, digging her dagger deeper between the plates. Her head was bent low, gaze furious. Shadows rose around them, encasing the Dark Prophet.

Then a shimmering black portal manifested in the ground below the Dark Prophet, and he fell through. Vanished in an instant. Carmilla kneeled alone on the ground, the bloody dagger in her hand.

Panting, she turned to Timothée. "Really," she gasped, "who *are* you?"

Timothée looked at his glowing hands and had no answer.

9
IN WHICH MARION LEARNS THE TRUTH OF THEIR FATHER

ARION GREYWICK BELIEVED the habit of wishing for things to be a very poor habit indeed. At the farm, Timothée languished his days reading stories and dreaming of adventures with far-off places and daring sword fights. Vivian took walks by herself down by the water, head as far in the clouds as the floating school.

Meanwhile, Marion was quite content with what she had. It was easy. She had fields of sweet-smelling flowers, fulfilling work helping Father build the bouquets and transforming buds into perfumes and candles and even icing sugar for cupcakes. And best of all, she had her family. Vivian, Timothée, Father. They were all so happy together.

Wishing became an even stupider thing when they came to the capital three years ago. Wishing wouldn't bring Father back. It wouldn't cure Vivian. They were not heroes in one of Timothée's stories.

To wish was to play the fool.

And yet, Marion wished for a great many things in a single instant.

She wished they'd never come to Wolfhelm. She wished she did not know what a vampire was or what they were capable of. She wished her siblings would listen to her.

And most of all, she wished her hair didn't glow on moonless nights.

Marion's legs were too shaky to run, so she scrambled over the cold cobblestone toward her sister. The Dark Prophet's shadows had disappeared with him, and now great rumbling clouds moved in. A few fat raindrops smacked against the ground and sloshed in the puddles of blood.

Everything around them reflected white light; it glistened in the strangest way, brighter than torchlight, and without the comfortable flicker of fire. She should have chopped her hair all off, if only she hadn't been so vain. But they were so careful not to be out on a moonless night… normally so careful.

Marion flung herself over her sister. "Vivian! Viv, are you alright?"

Vivian opened her eyes. They were lit with the same glowing white light as Marion's hair.

"Mar—" Vivian began. Marion shot forward and covered Vivian's mouth with her hand.

"Lips closed," she hissed. "They can't see."

Vivian's starlight eyes were wide and frightened. Rightfully so. The vampires might be gone but there were still foxes in the chicken pen. Marion just wasn't sure if she and her siblings were the foxes or the chickens.

Her senses returned to her: icy rain creeping down her spine, the pain in her hands and knees from falling, the shouts of the guards and the calamity of the remaining crowd. *Not yet.* She needed to stay numb, stay in control, for a few minutes longer. Get Vivian up. Find Timothée.

Run.

She was grateful for the rain—it would wash away the blood. That would make things slightly easier for Vivian at least. Her sister trembled in her arms as she forced her to stand. The ground glowed brighter as Timothée staggered closer.

He was a vision.

Everyone in the capital loved to talk of their gods, praise them, and honor them. Marion had seen no miracles in her life. If there were majestic gods in the sky, they certainly would do well to come down to Thraina and improve it a mite. But if there was to be a god who walked the earth, it would look like Timothée. He shone like starlight itself, his very skin lit up in a twinkling glimmer.

"Mare! Viv!" Timothée rushed forward, then stopped suddenly, bringing a hand to his temple. A large laceration cut across his left brow. His hair was matted with blood.

"We have to get out of here," Marion said hurriedly. "While everyone's distracted, we have to go—"

But as Marion looked for a way to escape, her heart stuttered to a stop. Every single person—from the terrified citizens, to the royal guards, to the waking loremaster, to Carmilla Vladimirovna who had saved Timothée's life and chased away the Dark Prophet, to Khalid Ali Bagheeri and his flickering green eyes, to the future ruler of Andúrigard—was staring at them.

"Oh bother," Marion said.

Timothée scooped up his ragged black cat. "Why's everyone looking at us?"

"We're glowing, Tim," Vivian rasped.

They had broken the one cardinal rule their father had set for them: *never* go out on a moonless night.

It was no stranger than vampires who drank blood to survive, or a school floating in the clouds, or students who swallowed stars. All the Greywicks did was glow. But Marion knew in Thraina, different meant dangerous.

Yet, no one was wondering where that monster, the Dark Prophet, had run off to. No one was cheering for the Kirrintsovan ward who had stabbed him and chased him away. They were all so focused on their bloody *glowing*.

But Marion didn't blame the guards for not immediately searching for the Dark Prophet. The way his magic had sucked the warmth from the air, commanded shadow... If all Starlings were dangerous, then that kind of magic was pure evil. There was no defense against such reckless power.

The Prince took a staggering step forward. "Vivian—"

Marion had no time to wonder what Vivian could have possibly done in one simple afternoon to have this prince so enthralled with her. They needed to run. Her heart pounded against her chest. There had to be a way to escape...

Her eyes caught on Khalid. His arms were crossed, gaze focused on her, the hint of a smile on his face. Not a kind smile, but a curious one. He leaned over to Loremaster Setviren who was regaining consciousness. Whispered something without ever taking his eyes off Marion.

The loremaster looked at Khalid, eyes wide, and mouth dropping to an O. Then he looked back at the triplets.

Marion was about to drag her siblings through the circle of guards and take their chances in the crowd when Prince Darius spoke: "You're glowing..."

Marion pushed her sister behind her and laid a glower on Darius. Prince or no prince, he would not take her sister. He was an affiliate of the Celestial Academy. To their core, Starlings were wicked. She would fight to the death—

Khalid placed a hand on Darius's shoulder. "Dare, if there ever was a message from the gods, this is it! You found them. Of course, Xydrious would send them to you. The Lost Stars. You found them."

Darius looked around without focusing. "I found them..."

"They're here," Khalid said, looking from the Prince back to the glowing triplets. "Rhaemyria and Xydrious have blessed your kingdom with their children."

Marion's throat went dry. She didn't like the way Prince Darius looked at them, how the guards shifted from foot to foot. And she certainly didn't like how fast Khalid was moving as he rushed back to the loremaster and put his lips to his ear. Only Carmilla was still, hands crossed in front of her chest, watching and waiting.

The loremaster looked like he'd lost his words. He hadn't taken his eyes off them to even blink. Tears streamed down his face, mixing with the blood from his head wound. He looked to the sky, hands held wide. Like a crack of thunder, his voice boomed across the courtyard, louder and stronger than any mortal man's voice should be. "Blessed be the citizens of Andúrigard! Though the Fallen Darkness sends his demons, Rhaemyria protects us! The Sun Mother has sent us her greatest gift in our greatest need! Blessed be the future King, for he has found our saviors!" Setviren turned to the three of them, back to back, circling and staring out at the silent crowd. "The Lost Star Children have been found!"

"Now," Khalid was behind them, voice low, "would be a good time to join hands."

Marion looked to her siblings. Timothée shrugged. Vivian's eyes were locked on Darius. "Oh bother," Marion snarled, but she was out of ideas. So, she took her siblings' hands.

Together, they glowed like all the falling stars across Thraina. The faces of every citizen lit up. A gasp rippled through the people. A few cried out.

They stared at the Greywick children like they were the brightest stars in the sky. And maybe they were.

Marion had the strangest feeling she would never be the same. That she never could.

Once a star falls, it cannot be hung back in the sky.

"Rhaemyria and Xydrious's three lost children!" Setviren cried out. "The Lost Stars have been returned!"

Darius stepped into a beam of white light. It suited him, this light. He looked every bit the holy king he would someday be, covered in rain and blood and starlight.

The Prince of Andúrigard dropped to his knee in front of them.

Carmilla was next, walking out into the glow with her head held high. "What a spectacle," she said as she dropped to one knee beside the Prince.

Khalid's smile seemed even stranger in this light. "So, the little leech girl is actually a wishing star," he said. Then he fell to his knee on the other side of Darius.

Marion knew as she looked out at the crowd, all fallen to their knees around her siblings, she was no wishing star. Because her wishes never came true.

RAIN POUNDED THE roof of the carriage. It was strangely comforting, staring out the window, watching the streets of Wolfhelm rush by. Marion had never traveled in anything that went so fast; the closest was riding in the back of Father's wagon as his old donkey, Murdie, pulled them along. Murdie had disappeared the same night Father had died. She wondered which vampire had feasted on donkey blood.

The capital looked beautiful in its wet dark flashes of light. And the seat of the carriage was fine scarlet velvet, luxuriously soft beneath her hands. And it was warm in here, despite her soaking wet hair and clothes.

But even the finest carriage was no better than a prison.

Her siblings sat beside her. Vivian was in the middle, nervously twiddling her thumbs. Timothée stared out the window with a glassy gaze, Yvaine, the ugly cat, on his lap. And Loremaster Setviren sat across from them taking tiny wispy breaths in through his nostrils. He was awash in the white light of their glowing.

They were being taken to the castle, but she did not know why. It had all happened so fast—the vampires, the glowing, the bowing. They'd been ushered into a carriage and driven through the city toward the castle.

"Are we prisoners?" Her voice sounded like breaking glass.

Setviren's little breaths stopped but his nostrils stayed flared. "P-Prisoners? Gracious no! What say do mere mortals have over the children of the gods?" He laughed to himself as if it were the funniest thing he'd heard all night.

The triplets looked at each other. Unspoken words flew between them. This man had obviously not recovered from his incident with the Dark Prophet. And yet…

The Lost Star Children have been found!

Everyone had bowed. Even the bloody Prince of Andúrigard had bowed.

Marion wondered how much it would hurt to fling herself from the carriage.

"Sir, I think you've made a mistake," Vivian said politely. Enough time had passed she could open her mouth safely again. "We are not children of the g-g—" She struggled to get the word out and ended up blurting, "We're just the Greywick children."

"Oh my dears," Setviren said, watery eyes wide. He clutched Vivian's hands. It would not be so strange if he thought them icy cold, for they had been out in the rain and shock would keep the warmth from your fingers too. "Twenty years we've searched for you. High and low, across Thraina, across Andúrigard, from Kirrintsova to Medihsa. All this time, you've been right under our noses." He searched their faces. "And you do not even know…"

Marion crossed her arms and blew a wet curl out of her face. Of all the bothersome ploys to get themselves caught up in—

Timothée sat forward. "Who's been looking for us?"

Setviren blinked. "Archpriestess Kassandra, of course."

The name sent shivers up Marion's spine.

Why must we hide, Father?

Yes, Father, why? I want to see the floating school!

Children, it may be called a school, but it is a hive, run by a priestess of wickedness.

"Archpriestess Kassandra," Marion repeated. "The Archpriestess of the Celestial Church."

Setviren closed his eyes as if simply hearing her name was a soothing balm. "Indeed."

"Why would she be looking for us?" Vivian asked.

Setviren opened one eye. "Why, she's your adoptive mother, of course."

Every time the loremaster opened his slimy mouth, it was like a dart, tearing at her skin. Marion's lip curled back. "We have no mother but the one that died in childbirth nineteen years ago."

The loremaster wrinkled his thin nose. "Who told you all these things?"

Vivian said, "Our father, Henry Greywick."

Setviren stared at her, the hollows of his eyes purple and cavernous. The bandage around his head had already bled through. He reached into his robes and held up a cube of stellarite, like the one Prince Darius had shaped into a sword.

The air felt like it was crackling into glitter and a blue glow surrounded Setviren. *He's using starcraft!* Marion flung herself back against the seat. She'd never been this close to anyone using this heinous power—

The cube of stellarite took shape. Setviren held it aloft in one hand, and with the other he molded the air, like an artist with clay. The cube responded to the precise movements of his fingers, changing, altering.

Until it formed the bust of a man.

Tears sprung to Marion's eyes. How did this church minion know? The shape of the eyebrows, the scar across the bottom lip, the depth of the eyes reflected in the shining navy metal… Her fingers dug into Vivian's knee, a silent plea: *Don't say anything.*

But it was not Vivian who needed the reminder.

"Father!" Timothée cried, lurching forward so hard, his cat yowled.

The loremaster kept his face steady. "You recognize this figure?"

Marion snarled, "Never seen him!" but was interrupted by her brother reaching for the bust.

"It's Father." Timothée's long fingers ran across the bust's chiseled jaw. "How do you know what he looked like?"

Setviren took the bust and, with a snap of his fingers, dissolved it back into a cube. Marion's body tightened as her father's face disappeared. The loremaster gave a pitying smile. "My dears, all this time you've been deceived. No wonder you know nothing of your true nature."

"True nature?" Marion spat. "All I know is we were cajoled into this carriage only to be told about legends and fairy tales from a stranger claiming to know our father!"

The Lost Star Children were a favorite myth among the pious of the kingdom, which was everyone. They were kept in daily prayer, celebrated during starlight showers, painted into murals on the stone wall outside the castle. Marion cared for it as much as she cared for any legends of the gods, which was not at all.

"It's no story, dear one," Setviren said calmly. "Your father... Where is he now?"

"Dead," Marion said.

"Hmmm." Setviren's nostrils flared. "And he lived in the capital with you?"

"No," Timothée said. "We lived on a farm on the coast. When he died three years ago, we came out to the capital ourselves."

Marion didn't want to tell this man anything about her father or their home before. It felt like each word was seizing away the precious few fragments of her life, and she'd never get them back.

"And all that time at the farm, did he ever tell you of the gods? Of the Lost Star Children?"

We had more important things to learn about than fables made to keep the people in line, Marion thought bitterly, but had enough sense not to say it aloud. Everyone in the kingdom loved the Three, because if you didn't, you best love swinging at the end of a rope.

"He told us of the Celestial Academy," Vivian chimed in. That was true of course. He told them of its wickedness, how it converted people into pawns for the Church. How the floating school would turn and twist you until there was nothing left—

"Ah, I suppose he would," Setviren said. "He was once the headmaster."

"What?" the triplets said at once.

Setviren sighed. "Your father, *Mr. Greywick,* can only be Bram Cavald, the greatest Evening Star professor the Celestial Academy has ever seen." He folded his hands on his lap. "And your kidnapper."

"Lies," Marion snarled. She turned appealingly to her siblings. "We do not have to listen to this. We're not under arrest. They can't force us to go to the castle."

But Timothée stared at Setviren as if he could find answers in those damp eyes. "He did know an awful lot about the school, Mare."

"It should be Archpriestess Kassandra telling you this story," Setviren said. "But alas, all you have is me. So, I shall do my best to tell you. As you know, the Mother Goddess Rhaemyria lives among the stars with her husband, Xydrious. After the fall of their first child," Setviren flashed a strange look at Timothée, "Rhaemyria was determined to send a new savior, a new child, to Thraina to right the wrongs of her first. She spoke to Archpriestess Kassandra and told her it was so."

Convenient, Marion thought.

"Twenty years ago, Rhaemyria sent her and Xydrious's gift to Thraina. But instead of one savior, she sent three. Three babies given to Kassandra to raise until they were old enough to enact the will of the Sun Mother and save Thraina. It was said the day you arrived, the stars were as bright as the sun, and all the lesser gods danced in celebration." Setviren's voice rose and fell in an erratic cadence. He had one of those faces that was finely wrinkled but with the foolishness of a young man, so one could not be certain how old he was.

"But only days after the children arrived on Thraina, they were stolen. The headmaster and trusted confidante of Archpriestess Kassandra, Bram Cavald, spirited the children away in the night. They were never seen again. Until now." A smile grew on Setviren's face. "Rhaemyria has saved you from your kidnapper and deemed it time for you to rise and—"

"By saved us from our kidnapper, do you mean killed our father?" Hot anger rushed through Marion's chest. None of this was true. She was no child of a god sent to save Thraina. That was too preposterous to consider. Her father couldn't have been the headmaster at the Celestial Academy. He hated the place, hated the Archpriestess.

But could that have been why he stole them away?

"I know this must all be overwhelming. Especially after everything you've been through. Rest tonight. Tomorrow we will make the arrangements." Setviren leaned against the seat of the carriage and closed his eyes.

"Arrangements for what?" Vivian asked.

"To travel to the school and meet Archpriestess Kassandra, of course." He didn't even open his eyes. "It is imperative you begin your studies right away."

"Us?" Timothée gasped. "Study at the school?"

"Of course," he said. "It is the Celestial Academy for Fallen Stars, after all. It is meant for you."

The rain continued to pound and the wheels clatter and the horse trot, and Marion's heart thumped heavy against her chest. And just as she could not stop the rain from falling or the carriage from moving toward the towering castle in the distance, she could not stop the school from twisting her heart already.

And finally, she understood why Father had always been so afraid.

10
IN WHICH VIVIAN EATS COOKIES WITH AN EMPRESS

VIVIAN WAS HOT. The stone walls of the castle felt like the inside of an oven. Maybe that was because she'd only ever known a cabin that was always damp with salt spray from the stormy sea or a dripping apartment with permanently frosted windows.

Now, she wore a long-sleeved wool dress and stood in a lavish room with not one, but *two*, roaring fires.

The Greywicks had been ushered straight from the carriage, surrounded by a tight line of guards, and through huge doors and the long hallways of the castle. It had happened so quickly, Vivian couldn't stop to wonder at the splendor of it all.

After that, they had been stuck in the castle infirmary. A palace physician, a graduate from the Celestial Academy for Fallen Stars, had come to examine them. Marion had thrown up the fuss of all fusses. Finally, the green-haired man, Setviren, brought in a non-magical doctor. Marion had still grumbled at that, but less so.

Vivian had to thank her sister in those moments. The physician had wanted to poke and prod them all night, but Marion had adamantly refused. Thank the stars. She didn't want anyone looking too closely at her.

Then they'd be stuck in what looked like a drawing room. Outside, they'd overheard a great deal of arguing between Setviren and some others. She swore she'd heard Darius's voice.

The last time she saw him, he was bowing to her. The Prince of Andúrigard had *bowed* to her. This was all some fantastical dream. Or nightmare. She hadn't decided which yet.

Finally, the door had opened. Setviren, as well as a host of guards, led them down more twisted halls until they were ushered into a new set of rooms.

And now, she, Marion, and Timothée were all alone. Yards and yards of silken curtains hung from the towering windows. Plush rugs covered the floors, and the room had three beds heaped with blankets and feather pillows. Gilding covered every inch of the place, from the doorframes to the fireplace mantle to the posts of the bed.

A single pillow from this room could pay for everything in her little candle shoppe thrice over.

Vivian sat down on the edge of the bed and sunk deep within it. Everything in the room seemed too soft and clean compared to the world outside. Compared to the Greywicks.

It was the first thing Marion had done when they were alone in the room. Shut the drapes tight, as if she were ashamed someone would see Vivian's glowing eyes, her hair, Timothée's skin. As if hiding their glow from the world could protect them.

Father had tried that.

But no matter the thick velvet curtains covering the windows, they still glowed. Marion's hair shone like dawn rays, and Timothée's freckles were distinct against his starshine skin.

Nothing could hide what they were, what they'd done.

Setviren had called them the children of the gods.

How could that be possible?

Marion shoved a cold jar into her lap. "Here," she said. "Eat."

"Are these Sigrud leeches?"

"What of it?" Marion dismissed the question with a wave of her hand.

Vivian wrinkled her nose but sucked one between her lips. Blood exploded in her mouth as she chomped the wriggling creature in half. She hated Mrs. Sigrud's leeches; they always tasted like stale roses.

When she was done, Marion tucked the jar back in her bag, then handed her a dried mint leaf. Vivian chewed it thoroughly, lest her siblings endure her leech breath. *They should try eating one,* she thought bitterly as the taste of mint filled her mouth. Only after she ate leeches could she taste anything but blood.

Marion's eyes were heavy upon her.

"We don't have to, you know," Vivian said.

"Have to what?" Marion asked. "You don't know what I was going to say."

"We don't have to run away. We could—"

"Go see the Archpriestess?" Marion's lip curled. "At that school? Father wouldn't even let us look at it when it flew over Seagrass! What would he say if he knew—"

"He can't say anything." Timothée scooped Yvaine off the ground. "He can't ever know because he's dead. And now we'll never figure out why he hated that school so much. Why he was so afraid of it."

"Why he was so afraid of *us*," Vivian said. "Setviren knew who we were right away. That's more answers than Father ever told us."

Marion scoffed. "Setviren's a fool. People like him will believe in anything. I know there's magic in this world. There's lots of strange stuff. And we're part of it. Because we fit some line in an ancient text doesn't mean we're the Lost Star Children."

"Haven't you ever wondered why we're like this?" Vivian asked.

"Of course." Marion flashed her steely gaze from Timothée to Vivian. "But when did we stop trusting Father? He said *never* go out on a moonless night. *Never* look up at the school. And now you're ready to go there, all because some fanatic with green hair says so? Or is this about the Prince?"

It was and it wasn't. Vivian walked to the pitcher of water, poured some into a crystal glass. She swirled the cold liquid around her mouth, washing away the last taste of the leeches and mint, then spit it back into the cup. Darius had come into her life like a flash of lightning. But she couldn't go back to how it was before. None of them could.

"I want to go to the Academy," she said softly, knowing the words were a betrayal. "I want to know what's above the clouds."

"I believe Father wanted to keep us safe," Timothée said. "But we haven't been safe. Not for the last three years. And Vivian is getting, uh…"

Is getting worse. They never said it. Never voiced it outright. But it was true. She was too skinny, too pale. She touched the protruding bones of her shoulders. And if she dared let her siblings know about…

Marion gave Timothée a sharp look. He'd almost talked about it. Maybe they all lived with a secret sort of hope that if they didn't mention it, it wasn't true.

Vivian couldn't stand when Timothée and Marion looked at her like that, dissecting her with their eyes. Searching for the most wrong, most monstrous parts of her. As if they could identify and hide those, then the rest of her would be normal.

"I'm just saying," Timothée continued, "no matter what, things are bad. At least at the Academy, we could find answers about ourselves. About Father."

"What, are you planning on *enrolling* now?" Marion crossed her arms.

"Why not me?" Timothée said. "Why not face this danger head-on instead of hiding? I could do it."

Marion let out a haughty breath. "Noble and brave Timothée doing something he's dreamt about for years and masquerading it as heroism."

"I haven't—"

Marion rounded on him. "You don't think I haven't noticed the stories you're always reading, of Starlings and wars and the gods? How when Argos flies over, you still peek at it?"

"I—" Timothée ran a hand through his hair. "I'm trying to help. If that weird green-haired man was right, we were born at that school. I can't go on like this anymore."

"On like what?" Marion put her hands on her hips.

"Surviving! Slithering in the dark." Timothée was shouting. He never shouted. Yvaine jumped from his arms. "Father was hiding something from us."

"Enough," Vivian yelled. They both looked at her.

Marion rubbed the bridge of her nose. "You're right. This is enough. Enough of silly dreams and fairy tales. Tonight, we sneak out of this terrible place."

And that was that.

There would be no talking her out of this one. Because her sister still had the fear of it all, the fear their father had laid brick by brick. And no matter what Vivian wanted, she had the fear too. Layered so many times, all she could do was follow her sister.

"Marion," Timothée said, then looked pleadingly at Vivian. "Viv?"

Vivian couldn't meet his hurt gaze. "You're both hungry. Let me find you some food. Setviren said we can ask the staff for anything. We can discuss this later."

"I can do it," Marion started. "You should rest—"

"I'll be fine," she assured, not wanting another lecture. Between the heat of the fire and her siblings' tempers, she needed a moment to herself. She popped out the door, closed it quickly behind her, and let loose a shuddering breath.

She hated when it was like this. When they were fighting. If she had never gotten sick, at least she would feel united in their pleas. But now she was different, and all their arguments always circled back to her.

Vivian looked up and down the hall. No one to ask for help. When Setviren and a host of other very official-looking people had brought them to their room, they hadn't been explicit with the instructions. Setviren had brought them dry clothes and said they were to rest and recover. She hadn't been told to stay in…

Something soft brushed her ankles. Yvaine. "You best be careful," Vivian whispered. "We don't belong in a place like this."

The little black cat, bearing more appearance to rat than feline, blinked her blue eyes.

"Now to find some food for those cranky pants."

Yvaine padded off down the gilded hallway, and Vivian figured it was as good of a direction as any.

The halls were long, with towering ceilings. She craned her neck to see they were all painted with constellations. If she had gone to school in the capital, she would have learned all about Rhaemyria and Xydrious, their fallen son, and all the lesser gods that ruled below the Three. But while her father had taught them to read and write and the history of Thraina, he had never told them stories of the gods.

Why had that been?

They rounded a corner and Yvaine let out a startled hiss, darting back around Vivian's legs. There was someone standing in the hall.

"Hello," Vivian said.

Carmilla Vladimirovna turned her attention from one of the many oil paintings on the wall. She had changed from the regal attire she'd appeared in earlier, and now wore a simple grey shirt, a long red scarf, and... trousers.

"I'm surprised Setviren let you out of his sight," Carmilla said. Her words were thick with the cold Kirrintsovan accent. "I've never seen him in such a state."

"I think my sister scared him off for a little while," Vivian said, a surprising smile to her words.

"Right. The girl with the glowing hair. Quite fascinating. All three of you are." Carmilla stepped toward Vivian. "Why are you wandering the halls?"

"I'm looking for food."

"Follow me."

Vivian and Yvaine trailed after the former heir to the Kirrintsovan Empire. She was quite a bit shorter and smaller than Vivian yet held so much more confidence and authority. Vivian had caught a glimpse of it, how Carmilla had stabbed the Dark Prophet. She had saved them all with her bravery.

"There's a huge gathering of nobles in the royal meeting room," Carmilla explained as they walked. "If you thank Setviren for anything, it's that he's keeping that horde away from you. He insists the first person you talk to be Kassandra."

"Kassandra," Vivian echoed. "Archpriestess Kassandra of the Celestial Academy?"

"Archpriestess *and* headmistress," Carmilla said. "Been so for about twenty years now."

Twenty years. According to Setviren, that was when the last headmaster, Bram Cavald, stole the Lost Stars away. Could he and their father truly be one in the same? Regardless, Archpriestess Kassandra must have taken the mantle of headmistress after he disappeared.

Carmilla stopped in front of a plain wooden door and threw it open. An array of mingling smells wafted out from the kitchen, and none were appealing. "Skoog," she called. There was the banging of pots and a series of foul exasperations. "Wait here." She ducked into the kitchen, and a moment later emerged with the hint of a smile. Strands of blood-red hair had come loose from the pinned braid atop her head and now hung in sharp plates on the side of her face.

"I was too young to remember much of the Trinity War," Carmilla said, "but I cannot imagine it being more chaotic than Skoog's kitchen. Here."

She handed Vivian a cookie. It was big and round as the ones Timothée made at the bakery, the ones they could never afford.

"Some trays will be sent up to your room," Carmilla continued. "I hope you're hungry. I told him he was cooking for gods."

If Vivian had consumed any more leeches, she may have blushed. Not knowing what to say, she bit into the cookie. It was soft and fluffy and tasted like ash in her mouth. "Delicious."

"Khalid and I used to steal platefuls from the kitchen," Carmilla said. "We'd bring them back to Darius's room, and he'd always pretend to be so mad, then eat more than both of us combined."

Vivian realized Carmilla wasn't wearing shoes. But why would she? This was her home. She had grown up in the palace with Darius and Khalid. They were family.

Carmilla walked past her, munching on her own cookie. Vivian became aware it was her time to say something. She wanted to tell Carmilla of the lavender cupcakes she used to make. How Timothée would lick the bowl, and one time she found him covered from head to toe in icing, and she and Marion had dragged him down to the ocean to wash. They had ended up swimming, even though the water was so cold.

But that was a silly memory, of a simple life and a simple family, and not something the ward of Andúrigard would care about.

Here, in this castle, everyone thought Vivian was something more than a simple girl. And anything she said could shatter that illusion.

They made it back to the hall where she'd first encountered Carmilla.

"Think you can make it back from here?"

"I'll be fine," Vivian said, then noticed the painting Carmilla had been looking at. It was huge, adorned in an elegant golden frame. The portrait was of a tall man, a beautiful woman beside him, wearing a sapphire crown. In front were two children: a young girl with a sly smile and golden curls, and... Darius. A few years younger, but undisputedly him. There was a lightness to his expression.

Yvaine meowed, clearly ready to keep exploring.

Carmilla stood beside Vivian, eyes trained on the painting. "Darius has more reason than most to be devastated by the Dark Prophet's reappearance."

"I thought he'd been killed."

"So did everyone," Carmilla said. "So did Darius. It was the Dark Prophet who led the attack that night three years ago when the vampires invaded Wolfhelm."

"Did you..." Vivian asked slowly, "did you kill him tonight?"

Carmilla gave a low laugh. "It will take more than a dagger to kill the Dark Prophet. I suspect he ran because he was frightened. Frightened by you."

Vivian grabbed her elbows. "I don't even..."

Carmilla put her hand on Vivian's arm. "If you don't believe in yourself, no one else will. Doesn't matter whether you glow under the stars or not." She turned and walked down the hall. "Get some rest, little star. You'll need it."

Vivian stood there a moment longer staring up at the painting. The royal family was all gone. All gone except him.

"I suppose we should head back," she said to Yvaine. She would have to face Marion and Timothée eventually. Hopefully, the food would help.

Yvaine gave a little meow that sounded more like a snarl, then trotted off in the other direction.

"Hey, come back!" With her luck, some servant would come across Yvaine and mistake her for a rodent. "Yvaine!"

Yvaine began to sprint, taking turns Vivian would never remember. She dashed around a corner, finding herself in a large hallway, decorated with silver suits of armor and grand vases brimming with blue and yellow roses.

A door was cracked open. And Yvaine sat in front of it, looking back as if she was waiting for Vivian.

Voices carried from the room.

Khalid and Darius.

Darius.

Vivian crept closer. She shouldn't listen but looked down at the cat. *You're a bad influence.*

"You can't blame me for being worried," Khalid was saying.

"Well, you're worrying in vain, my friend," Darius said. "I am fine."

The two boys seemed to be in the middle of an argument or skirting around the edge of one.

"Wolfhelm gets ambushed, Ser Remont falls, at least twenty guards were killed, the Dark Prophet returns, and you're *fine*."

There was movement. "It is not ideal. But those guards died for what they believed in. I will avenge Ser Remont, as I will all those who fell to the vampires' terror. We secured Wolfhelm, and we found—"

"Yes, the Lost Stars. But the Dark Prophet—"

"It is a shame he lives," Darius replied, "and a greater one that he escaped. But you and Carmilla were not harmed. I will continue my training and the next time I meet him, he will fall."

"That simple, huh?"

"Why are you looking at me like that?"

Vivian couldn't see them from behind the door, and she wondered exactly what expression Khalid was giving the Prince.

"Dare," Khalid's tone edged on frantic, "you *know* why. I don't want—"

"I told you I'm fine." Darius's voice silenced everything.

Vivian gasped, pressing herself against the wall. And Yvaine must have taken her motion as a signal because she darted into the room.

Stupid cat!

"Khalid, wait," Darius said. "You don't have to leave."

"I need some air," Khalid said. "Besides, there's someone that wants to see you. Hey, kitty."

Vivian gritted her teeth and cursed under her breath. Stupid, *stupid* cat.

Before Vivian figured out an escape plan, Khalid walked through the door. He too had changed, wearing a loose white tunic and trousers.

"Vivian Greywick." Khalid leaned against the doorway. "You certainly are magical, and you don't even need to glow to do it."

"What are you..." she started.

"Nothing," Khalid said, then: "He'll be happy to see you."

She peered through the doorway. She couldn't see Darius, only the red glow of a fire as its light licked across a plush rug.

"Hey, Vivian," Khalid called back, already halfway down the hall.

"Yes?"

"On a scale from one to getting my head lobbed off, how happy do you think your sister would be to see me tonight?"

Vivian looked at the mischievous glint in his green eyes. "Imagine the one thing worse than getting your head lobbed off, and *that's* your scale."

His eyes widened, and he laughed. "Point taken. Good night!"

When he'd disappeared around the corner, Vivian took a deep breath and walked into the Prince's room.

11

IN WHICH MARION HAPPENS UPON SCHEMERS, RABBITS, AND BROKEN HEARTS

CASTLES WERE NOT so different from alleyways. Both were dark and seemingly endless. Both hid shadowy dangers. Though in an alley, it was most likely to be a ruffian robbing you for the verdallion in your purse, while in a castle it was a deranged loremaster forcing you to go to some wicked cult in the sky.

But if Marion thought of the castle just like the alleys around their little apartment on Enola Avenue, it was easier to keep her wits about her. Even though she wanted to hide in bed. Even though she wanted to cry.

But she couldn't. Not while her family counted on her.

One of the servants had taken Marion's soaking wet cloak when they arrived at the castle. Now she wore one of the fine down blankets around her like a shawl, her hair wrapped up in a silken pillowcase. The castle was still quiet, though dawn loomed on the horizon. At least the rain had stopped.

Marion crept through the corridors of the castle, doing her best to avoid servants. She needed to get out of the castle and back into town without notice. They didn't have much, but they had a stash of verdallions hidden under their mattress at the apartment, and she'd need to grab the frozen leeches. Those jars would last a few moons, but she'd have to think of something else after.

They couldn't stay in the capital any longer. Now that the loremaster had labeled them some fictitious Lost Stars, they would be forced up to the Academy. Father had told them enough for her to know the Celestial Academy for Fallen Stars was a place of evil.

Vivian and Timothée wanted to go. Wanted answers. But there were no answers in that place. If there had been, Father would have told them. Marion was sure of it.

She'd decided to return to the apartment on her own. It would be less noticeable than the three of them together. A part of her felt guilty for leaving while Vivian was out of the room, but she couldn't stand the pained look on her sister's face.

Vivian and Timothée thought her unbending. Cruel, even. But it had been her unbending self that had kept the Greywicks alive. When Father died and all that was left was his blood splattered on wet stone… When Vivian had been attacked, and the sickness came, and she spent a moon screeching and clawing at them like a feral animal… It was Marion who forged a spine of iron so as not to break. The life they had, pathetic and dreary it may be, was possible because she had made it so. Not once in the last three years had she let herself shed a single tear.

So, she would be the villain. A coward even, if that's what they needed to call her. As long as it kept them safe.

Her plan was simple. She would return undetected to their apartment, collect their valuables, and wait in front of the leech shoppe. Timothée and Vivian would meet her there after dawn, when all the Starlings in the castle should be fast asleep. Then the Greywicks would make their escape. Maybe they'd go north to the mining town of Miskunnland. Or south, to the islands of Medihsa. She'd always wanted to see the Sea of Flowers, said to blow in the wind like rainbow waves.

Finally, after trailing a mousey-looking scullery maid for an obnoxiously long time, Marion found the servants' entrance and snuck outside the castle. The air was cold and damp and grey, typical of Wolfhelm. Next moon, the snows would come, and the idea of anything green or growing would become a distant memory.

There were a few guards posted along the servants' trail that led out of the castle grounds and toward town. But with the blanket wrapped tight around her like a shawl, and her hair swept up in a dark pillowcase, she looked nothing more than every other bent-headed serving girl leaving the night shift.

A fine mist hung in the air like gauze above a wound. The sun, hidden behind the thick clouds, shrouded the city in grey light. The streets were empty. Everyone was still asleep, warm in bed with their families.

She avoided the town square, not wanting to know if the rain had washed the blood away or not. The streets were thick with shadows, and as she approached the avenue leading to the apartment, there was a peculiar shadow leaning against the wall.

A man in a dirty brown cloak.

"Well, well," the young man flung back his hood, "my wishing star is so fickle. Always trying to make me catch her."

Marion stood before Khalid. Immediately, her back teeth began to grind; her body grew tense. She could run, but likely he was faster. She wasn't much good at running, and didn't have the clothes for it, besides. "What are you doing here?"

He flashed her a charming smile. "If you're running away, I thought I'd come with you. I do love a good adventure."

"I'm not running away!" Marion's face flushed. He'd seen right through her plan. "How are you always by yourself? Shouldn't you have guards? Or does the Prince not care if you get murdered?"

He laughed. "The Prince does in fact care if I get murdered which is why he insists I take guards wherever I go. But I like my privacy.

So, I know if I keep Ser Henrietta supplied with Medihsan wine, she gets sloppy. And Feridan and I have an agreement. I go where I like, and he gets to keep lying to his wife about his late nights." Khalid gave an exaggerated wink. "The secret is knowing everything about everyone."

"You're despicable."

"We're getting personal now, are we?" He straightened to his full height, forcing Marion to look up at him. She didn't like that and took a large step backward. "Why did you leave the castle?"

"I'm getting my affects," Marion said, which was not entirely untrue.

"Wonderful," he said. "I shall accompany you."

Marion sighed. She didn't bother asking how he'd found her. She'd come to accept Khalid was a stasher of secrets.

"How delightfully wonderful," she said. "Follow me."

He walked in step beside her, hands in the pockets of his dirty cloak. She kept sneaking glances up at him as they walked. It annoyed her, the consistent smirk, the shimmering eyes. She wondered what he looked like behind that nonchalant mask.

It was silly though, to wish to see him in the raw. She'd have to lose him eventually, then never intended to see him again.

They walked down the avenue, grey mist parting before them like a carpet rolled out. What would Father think of her walking with a Starling? *Of all the dangerous, no good, foolish ideas, Timothée Greywick!* It was Father saying Timothée's name in her head, of course. She was always well-behaved.

But she didn't feel afraid. It was almost nice to have company on her last walk to the apartment.

"Here we are," she said. The door was made of decaying wood, the lock sticky. Khalid held the door for her and gave a little bow as she passed through. The narrow stairs creaked as she walked up. She threw a pointed glare behind her. "Don't dare stare at my bottom."

"I wouldn't dream," he said with a gleaming smile.

There were four separate apartments at the top of the stairs. It was easy enough to tell which belonged to the Greywicks. It was the one with a sprig of dried lavender hanging from the handle. Vivian's note was still hung to the door, the one saying she was going to the festival. Marion scrunched it in her hand and dropped it to the ground.

A flush of embarrassment hovered over Marion as she unlocked the door. Khalid had grown up in a castle. Here, he would be lucky to avoid falling through a decayed floorboard. Marion and her siblings had done their best to make the apartment homey by finding things that reminded them of Seagrass: a misshapen candle that smelled of salt air, a garland of dried lavender above the window.

But it was no Seagrass. And certainly no palace.

"Make yourself comfortable." Marion gestured vaguely. "I'd offer you refreshments, but I'm not inclined to host my kidnapper."

Khalid flung himself down on a moth-eaten chair. "Kidnapper? Is that what you think I am? I like it. Makes me sound daring."

"Taking us from our home without a choice. What else am I to call you?" She didn't miss the way Khalid's eyes searched the room, taking in every detail, every piece of her. She busied herself with dragging out the dusty houndstooth bag from under the bed and throwing clothes into it.

"Like I said, I came to escort you. Though I'm surprised to hear a night in the palace and an invitation to join the Celestial Academy is akin to kidnapping." He raised a brow. "Anyone else would cheat, steal, or murder for one of those things."

Marion chucked one of Timothée's bed shirts into the bag. "I'm not anyone else."

"I'm fully aware," Khalid said without humor.

Silence settled over the room. The back of Marion's neck tingled from Khalid's eyes on her. She'd never been in this room with anyone but her siblings. She felt vulnerable, like she was on display.

Finally, Khalid said, "You don't intend to go." His voice was matter-of-fact, without blame or emotion.

She looked over her shoulder. He sat forward in the chair now. Was it only her imagination that his eyes looked kind? "What does it matter what I say, Mr. Ali Bagheeri? If I tell you we don't intend to go, you'll send the guards after me. If I tell you I do," she sighed, "we'll both know I'm lying."

He stood. Crossed the room with slow, light-footed steps. Grey light filtered through the window, making his single gold earring gleam. He rose his hand to the wrap around her hair and pulled. Her golden tresses fell over her shoulders in a shimmering wave.

"They say you are the daughter of the gods," he murmured. He caressed a strand of her hair, gently wound it round his fingers. Marion was perfectly still, scarcely able to breathe. "They say you are a blessing sent to save us."

"Is that what you believe?" she whispered.

He closed his eyes, brought the strand of hair to his lips. Then in an instant, it trailed out of his hand, and he smiled that infuriatingly hidden smile. "That's the thing, wishing star. It doesn't matter what I believe. It all matters what they believe."

He looked toward the window. People were starting their day; the streets were filling with vendors and workers.

"I don't want anyone's love," Marion whispered.

"And what of their fear?"

She realized heatedly that she didn't mind so much how he seemed to look straight inside her. It felt good to be seen to the bone.

Marion darted her gaze to his hand. "Is it true?" she whispered. "You have caught a falling star and can do m-m-m—"

"Magic?" Khalid said. "Miracles? Whatever you prefer to call it, yes. I couldn't be a student at the Celestial Academy if I hadn't been able to catch a star of my own." He looked to the window. "Though you'll have to wait to see my tricks. Dawn is upon us."

So that was true. Starlings *could* only do magic at night.

Khalid stepped back. "You're not tempted? Not even a little? Setviren has offered you a place at the school. You know what that means, don't you? You'd get to catch and swallow a star of your own! You could have magic, Marion Greywick."

"There's enough strangeness in the world without me adding to it," Marion said matter-of-factly and returned to packing.

"It's a shame you feel that way." His voice was silk over bare skin. He came up behind her, and she felt the warmth of his body, the shiver of his breath on the back of her neck. "I'm quite inclined to strangeness. Stasis is the true evil. And there's one thing I believe above all else."

Marion tried in inhale, couldn't. Swung around to look at him. He was so close, a breath away. Her legs bumped the bed. She stuck her nose in the air and tried to make her voice calm. "And what is that?"

A thousand thoughts and memories and feelings flashed in his green eyes. "The world is not enough."

A sad smile crept over her face. "Then your world must be very small indeed."

She thought he may pull away or laugh or decide it was time to call the guards after all. But instead, he cupped her cheek, his hands smooth and warm, and leaned down a breath away from her mouth. "Come with me," he whispered. "To the stars."

Maybe Timothée was right all this time. Maybe there was something in forgetting yourself, pretending you were in a story where a noble would sweep you off to starlight and castles in the sky. She leaned in so close her nose brushed Khalid's, and her hand drifted to the back of his neck.

She grazed her lips over his and whispered, "No."

Marion was not Timothée. She did not lose herself in games of pretend, no matter how good smelling they were. Because as wonderful as it was to forget everything for a moment, it also filled her with surging guilt. Father had said the school was evil, and so it was.

She shoved him away. "If you excuse me, Mr. Ali Bagheeri, I need to pack."

Khalid put his arm behind his head. "You sure know how to hurt a guy."

"You'll recover."

Marion worked in silence, throwing the last of their meager belongings into the bag. Two changes of clothes each, a pouch of coins, a pot and pan, a few utensils, Timothée's beloved books, a drawing notebook and pencil for Vivian just in case, and a single bunch of dried lavender.

She sighed and stared at the room. There had been happy memories here, through the grief.

"Where to now?" Khalid asked as he followed her out of the building.

"I have to go to the leech shoppe."

"Then I shall—"

"Escort me. I got it." Marion heaved the heavy bag higher on her shoulder and stormed through the foggy streets. She walked quickly, although she was hindered by Khalid trying to carry her bag (which she vehemently refused) and him endlessly trying to change her mind about the Academy.

"And the food! The food, you'll never taste anything like it. Peach sorbet anytime you want. And apparently at Yuletide, they have an endless fountain of mashed potatoes with gravy. A fountain!"

Marion ignored him, though she did like the sound of endless peach sorbet.

"It's a *castle in the sky*, Marion. It flies over everything." He grabbed her arm so she looked back at him. "You can see the world."

He didn't suit this, the foggy grey of Wolfhelm. Even in his dirty cloaked disguise, Khalid appeared to her like a spot of sunshine. It made her angry. She'd spent the last three years trying to be as unnoticed as possible. Being with him felt like being forced into the light.

"I like the world fine from what I've seen."

"Then you've never seen Medihsa." His gaze drifted upward. "Beaches of white sand and rose-gold cliffs. The biggest museums and libraries you could ever imagine! And of course, we have the Sea of Flowers. You would like that, having grown up on a lavender farm and all."

Marion didn't remember telling Khalid that, but maybe she had. Or maybe he'd seen all the lavender in the apartment.

"Enough!" Her bag slipped off her shoulder and splashed in a puddle at her feet. Khalid dove to get it and she smacked his hand away. "Why do you care if we go to this school? You don't seem to particularly believe we're some god children like the other zealots. What's the point?"

Khalid widened his eyes then laughed. "Zealots? Watch your mouth, wishing star. That kind of talk will find you at the end of a rope." He winked salaciously. "Don't worry. It will be our little secret."

Khalid seemed like the type of person who was good at keeping secrets in the very worst way.

"I don't understand you." Marion kicked her now soaking bag. "Why does it matter to you what I do? You have everything you could want in the world."

"Everything I could want?" His smile dropped. "Is that what you think?"

"You live in a castle. Eat the best food. Wear the finest clothes." Marion waved her hand flittingly. "Your best friend is a *prince*."

He caught her wrist, pulled her so she stared straight at him. "My *captor* is a prince. Don't you know your history, wishing star? No one else forgets who I am. You shouldn't either."

Marion inhaled. His hand was warm around her wrist. He pulled her so close they were chest to chest, his breath hot on her face, smelling deliciously of mint and orange. The mist drifted around them. There were people through the fog, going about their day, but they seemed no more real than ghosts.

She thought of the waves breaking upon the shore at their home in Seagrass. She was caught up in his current and very close to smashing against the rocks.

She pulled away from him and made a show of massaging her wrist and pouting. "I know my history." Father had played the role of teacher too. It was called the Trinity War. Sixteen years ago, Medihsa had tried to reclaim its independence from Andúrigard and organized a rebellion, with the aid of the Kirrintsovan Empire. After four years of violence, Andúrigard prevailed. The kingdom took the son of Medihsa's prime ministers as a ward to ensure their compliance. They did the same to Kirrintsova, claiming the emperor's daughter as ward as well.

Khalid said nothing, his eyes intense. Though Marion kept her face dour, there was the slightest flicker of satisfaction in her belly. She'd gotten a rise out of Khalid. So it *was* possible.

"It's over there." She heaved the soaking bag over her shoulder.

"The little leech girl," Khalid murmured, looking ahead to the shoppe. "Who would have thought you'd be the one?"

"Not me, and I still don't." Marion dug in her bag for the key. *Little leech girl.* Well, he'd looked at that little leech girl with a fire in his eyes, so what did that make him? She sighed. It was all pretend anyway. Best for this whole morning to fade away to a distant memory, more dream than truth.

But if this were a dream, surely it was a nightmare. For leaning against the door of the leech shoppe was Huxley Macgregor.

He wore his usual leather apron, cracked with dried blood from his work at the tanner's. His eyes were red and swollen, like he hadn't slept a wink. His thatch of red hair, usually slicked back with sweat

and leather oil, was mussy. He wrapped his pale hands tight around the leash of his pet rabbit, Bill. Why he insisted on dragging the poor thing everywhere...

"What is he doing here?" Marion growled under her breath.

"A client?" Khalid asked.

"Worse," Marion said. "A friend."

Friend wasn't exactly the right word for Huxley, because to be friends with someone, you had to enjoy their company.

"Marion!" Huxley called when he saw her approach. "Y-you're here! I wasn't sure if you were alright or not. I saw you at the festival. You... you... you were—"

"Glowing? Yes, yes, she was." To her horror, Khalid draped an arm around her shoulder as if they were old schoolyard chums. "Wasn't she ravishing? A vision that rivals Rhaemyria, if it's not heresy to say. Even if it was, I'd say it! I'd scream it from the rooftops. Marion Greywick, you are positively the most enchanting creature to ever walk Thraina—"

Her face flushed so hot, she was surprised steam wasn't coming from her ears. "Say one more word and I will make the Dark Prophet look like a nursemaid."

Khalid whistled through his teeth but unhanded her.

Huxley looked from Marion to Khalid back to Marion again. "Is... is this a client?"

She supposed in his dirty cloak, Khalid could be mistaken for a commoner. She had done it herself yesterday. But now she couldn't understand it, how anyone could look at Khalid and see just another citizen of Wolfhelm. Everything from the calculated tilt of his head to the suspicious raise of his dark brows gave him away as something more. In a town of grim frost, he radiated.

What a bother.

Khalid stuck his hands in his pockets. "A client? Sure, I'll be your client. Was that why you wanted to bring me here? Shall I undress for you, Marion?"

She weighed the key in her hand and wondered how hard it would be to lodge it in someone's throat. She wasn't sure what Khalid's game was, trying to embarrass her so, but she wouldn't take the bait. Ignoring both of them, she unlocked the door. "I have work to do."

"W-wait!" Huxley grabbed her arm. He had touched her many times, yet only in the confines of the leech shoppe. In the daylight, it felt too intimate.

She wanted to pull away, but Huxley's eyes were wide, desperate. "Marion, are you okay? What about Vivian and Timothée? Is everyone alright?"

He was worried about her. The idea of someone other than her siblings wondering over her... It made Marion's stomach curl. It wasn't that she hadn't enjoyed their trysts. They'd been a needed distraction from the pressures of keeping Vivian alive. But she couldn't care for Huxley Macgregor, no matter how many times he left a daisy on her doorstep or let her pet his stupid cute rabbit.

She had no more room in her heart to care for someone else.

But as she stared into his watery brown eyes, she wished she could tell him many things. *Yes, yes, don't worry, everything is okay. I'll be fine. I have a little work to do, but why don't you meet me this evening? No, not at the shoppe. At that café you always talk about. I'll finally let you buy me a sweetcake. Everything's going to be alright.*

But all she managed was: "I'm going to be fine." Because that was the truth. She would be.

Khalid looked between the two of them and began whistling a tune.

Huxley scooped Bill into his arms, clutching it like a child would a teddy bear. His gaze settled on Khalid. "Wait. I recognize you from the ceremony. You're... you're the Medihsan ward, Khalid Ali Bagheeri." He stumbled into a bow. "My lord!"

Some citizens of Wolfhelm regarded the wards as pseudo-royalty. Others considered them criminals dressed in fancy clothes. Thankfully, Huxley appeared to be the former.

Khalid, for all his smugness, merely ran a hand through his thick black hair.

116

The damp interior of the leech shoppe had never been so inviting. Marion needed to escape this conversation. She turned the door handle. "If you excuse me—"

"Why have you packed such a big bag?" Huxley's voice was soft. "You're traveling with a member of the royal party. The loremaster called you a *Star Child*. You're leaving, aren't you?"

Marion's mouth went dry. *What do I say? I can't tell him the truth.*

"She's coming with me." Khalid grinned. "She's going to be the newest student at the Celestial Academy for Fallen Stars and change the world. What's your name?"

"H-Huxley."

"Just you wait, Mucksley! Marion Greywick is heading to the stars—"

Marion shoved the door open and grabbed Khalid's hand. "I have to get going." She pushed Khalid inside, then looked out the crack of the door for a last moment. Huxley's eyes seemed redder than before, and his hands shook in Bill's fur. She looked down at the wet cobblestone. "I-I'm sorry, Huxley. Your friendship was a kindness. Goodbye."

"I'll find you there!" Huxley cried. "I'll find you in the st—"

But Marion shut the door, blocking out the last of his cries.

She leaned her head against the cold wood and took a few deep breaths.

Khalid was already squirming around, running a finger along the leeching chair, staring up at her spider friends in their webs. "Lovely establishment you have here. What's that smell? Is that lilac with a hint of sandalwood, perhaps? Absolutely luxurious. Reminds me of evenings sailing down the Harrine River—"

"*You.*" The word was a snarl. Then she was standing right below his nose, finger dug into his chest. "Humiliate me all you want. Laugh at me. Ridicule me. Whatever you try, it's pointless. I will *never* go to your school."

Khalid's face softened, his smile dropping. His full lips pressed to a tight line. "I wasn't trying to embarrass you, Marion."

She sneered at him. "Sure. That's why you were saying all those things in front of Huxley. *Ravishing and enchanting.*"

"The best way to lie is to tell the truth." He grabbed her hand, gently removing the finger that dug deep into his chest. "You *are* ravishing. And not just when you're emitting a light powerful enough to turn vampires into kindling. You're beautiful, and I'm obviously not the only one who thinks so."

Heat curled its way up her belly. "But why did you say I was going—"

"You want to run away, don't you?" Khalid began to massage her hand. "Now everyone will assume you're at the Academy. If the Celestial Knights come looking for you, no one will be able to give them any clues of where you've gone."

"You were helping me."

"Outlandish, I know." His fingers were so warm against her. "Help from your kidnapper."

"I don't need anyone's aid."

"You don't." Somehow, he had managed to step closer to her, their joined hands the only thing separating them. "But what can I say? I was jealous."

"Jealous?" She didn't smell the leech shoppe anymore, so engrossed was she in the orange and mint of his brown skin.

"I saw the way he looked at you. Were you lovers? Did he bring you flowers and whisper sweet nothings?" Khalid's own voice sounded both sweet and bitter.

"It's none of your business."

"You know by now, Marion, everyone's business is my business."

A wicked part of her heart flickered. *I want to be your business.* Instead, she held his gaze, said: "I have work to do."

His eyes flashed with his own wicked desire. "So do I."

He dropped her hand and laced his fingers through her hair, pulling her flush against him. Khalid closed his eyes, and his lips moved down toward her.

12

IN WHICH VIVIAN REALIZES SHE'S IN LOVE

HOW WAS VIVIAN Greywick going to explain to the Prince of Andúrigard why she was in his bedroom? It was all Timothée's cat's fault. Marion was right. They should have cooked her up with some butter.

"I'm sorry." Vivian kept her eyes on her feet, skirting over the marbled floors. "It's my brother's cat, and she doesn't listen to me and—"

Darius put his hand under her chin and drew her face upward. He wore a loose beige tunic, untied at the neck, that revealed a muscled, bandaged-wrapped chest. He still had the blue ribbon tied around his wrist, though the edges were splattered with blood. *His* blood, by the smell.

"Darius."

"Vivian."

As if in a spring's breeze, all her worries drifted away, and she fell into him, and he into her.

Somehow, her hands knotted in his shirt, and he pulled her tighter against him. And she hated this—hated that since the moment he'd come into the candle shoppe, she hadn't stopped thinking about him. She'd gone to a festival on a moonless night just to catch a glimpse. And when he'd been in danger, she had found some sort of bravery in her blood.

Marion resented her for it.

But she couldn't regret it. If the Greywicks hadn't been there, glowing...

They had shown the world who they were. But more importantly, they had saved lives. They had saved Darius.

"I was hoping to see you before dawn." His lips were against her temple.

"Me too."

He pulled away slightly, his forehead resting upon hers. His arms still held her body close enough to feel the hard panes of him against her jagged edges.

"There are so many things I want to ask you," he murmured, and her stomach tightened. "But from what Setviren has told me, you may have more questions than anyone."

"I had no idea," she stammered, "that we were... that our father—"

"Worry not." The stormy waters in his eyes calmed. "We don't have to talk about it now. I'm just happy you're safe. That you're here with me."

She hoped he saw the gratefulness in her expression.

"I feel... protective over you," Darius murmured. "When the Dark Prophet had you, I felt a sense of helplessness I haven't experienced in a long time."

"Helpless to save a girl you just met?" She smoothed a crease in his thin shirt.

"Perhaps the same feeling that had you running into the middle of the square surrounded by those vile vampires?"

She sucked in a breath. *Vile vampires indeed.*

She leaned her head against his chest. As she listened to the steady beat of his heart, she wondered if he could feel the unnatural beat of her own.

"I do have a little complaint." He smirked.

"A complaint?"

He pulled away from her and walked to a huge four-poster bed. With him out of her arms, she finally found herself able to take in the room: fine decorations, paintings of dreamlike landscapes, grand settees with billowing pillows, the reassuring crackle of flame from a huge fireplace. She really was in the room of a prince.

She may have fainted at that notion alone, but her horror continued. Yvaine—Timothée's scraggly, matted, fake witch's cat—jumped up on Darius's bed as if she belonged there. She certainly didn't suffer from any imposter syndrome of being in a castle.

Vivian scampered over to his bed and scooped Yvaine up, hoping she hadn't left muddy paw prints on the fine linen.

The Prince looked down at the cat. "Is that—"

"The cat that attacked you during the ceremony? Yes."

"Well, it was better than the other interruption." Darkness clouded his eyes.

"She doesn't like anyone besides my brother," Vivian said, surprised as Yvaine started purring in her arms.

Darius gave a little smirk and held out a candle. The vanilla one he'd bought from her shoppe earlier. "I think you sold me the wrong candle."

She clutched Yvaine tighter. "I take my job very seriously. I never sell the wrong candle."

"I distinctly remember the smell of lavender." He brought the candle to his nose. "But this smells nothing like that."

Her face threatened to flush. "That was probably me."

"You?" He stepped closer.

She stumbled back, bumped into the edge of his bed. Thank goodness Marion made her eat those leeches. "I used to live on a lavender farm. I still put dried flowers in my hair."

"Is that so?" He grabbed a lock of her hair and brought it to his nose. "Then accept my deepest apologies for doubting you."

"Apology accepted." Her voice was a breath.

Golden hair fell across his brow. He was so close, gazing down at her like there was nothing else in the world.

A shrieking howl filled the air as Darius's body pressed against Yvaine. She leapt from Vivian's arms, hissing and spitting the whole way down.

Nothing in the world except them *and* an annoying cat.

"She is a disaster." Vivian sighed. "Just like my brother."

"Khalid and Carmilla used to say the same thing about my little sister." Darius laughed and didn't look bothered in the slightest. He grabbed Vivian's hand. "Come on, it's almost sunrise. You'll want to see this."

Their fingers twined together as he pulled her through his chambers and out two glass doors to a sprawling balcony.

Her wool skirt dusted the damp ground; the air smelled of cold rain. Below the balcony lay the small roofs of Wolfhelm, where billowing grey smoke rose as people began their day. Beyond the walls of the capital, sprawling green fields led to tall and mighty mountains.

Vivian knew if she traveled over the fields and along the coast, she would eventually make it to a small village by the sea. And upon a hill would be a lavender farm.

She wondered if anyone was there, or if the flowers had grown wild and free. "This is beautiful."

Dim light flickered on Darius's face. Her eyes must still be glowing faintly from the lingering stars.

Darius led her to the edge where they leaned against the balcony railing.

"For most people," Darius said, "a sunrise is a beginning. For me, it's the end."

Starlings could only use magic at night, and thus they slept with the sun and rose with the stars.

Darius yawned and, in that moment, did not look a grand prince, but a boy. He was nearing twenty, she knew, but seemed like a sleepy child, barely able to keep eyes afloat. "I would be crawling into bed right now."

"Do you ever miss the sun?" she asked, running her thumb along his wrist, feeling his pulse.

"I've come to appreciate the wonders of the night. Speaking of..." Slowly, he reached his hand toward her chin and guided her to look out at the horizon.

A great shadow swept across the fields, but it was not caused by any cloud.

"When we were young, Khalid, Carmilla, my little sister Celeste, and I all used to wait out here for it to pass above. We dreamt of attending, and if we would become Morning or Evening Stars."

When it passed over when I was a child, Vivian thought, *my father used to shove us in crates filled with so much lavender I thought I was going to suffocate.*

And there was a part of her still, that wild frantic beating of her heart, that wanted to run and hide.

But Yvaine gave a soft meow as the shadow drew closer, and Darius's hand was still in hers and she realized, with him here, at least for right now, that fear her father had given her felt a little smaller.

"What star did you catch?"

"An Evening Star, the magic of change." He held out his hand. "A Morning Star can create water, but I can turn it to ice or steam."

He touched the dewdrops gathered on the balcony railing. They crystalized into a little pile of snow. He blew, the new snow dusting around Vivian's face. She laughed, feeling the tickle of magic on her.

"There are some who are unable to catch a falling star," Vivian said, thinking of all the hopeful students that waited to be flown up to the school at the beginning of the Singing Harvest Moon. "Why is that?"

"From what I've come to understand at the Academy, some people are born with magic inside them. Starlings are like a candle; we have a wick inside of us. And think of the match as—"

"The star," Vivian finished.

"Yes." Darius smiled, then continued: "You're the candle, the wick is the magic inside you, but it doesn't really do anything until you catch a star, swallow it—"

"And ignite the magic within."

"Precisely."

"Do you like studying at the Academy?" she asked. Regret stirred in her chest. No matter what he said, it would hurt. If he said it was terrible, it would confirm Father and Marion's belief. But if he said he loved it...

"When I'm learning starcraft alongside my best friends," Darius said, "it's the only place in the world I feel more like a man than a prince."

With sickening agony, she realized that with him was the only time she felt more girl than monster.

The broad shadow drew closer until it covered the tiny houses, and the wafting smoke turned from grey to black. "The Isle of Argos."

The last time it had passed overhead, it had seemed nothing but a faraway speck in the sky. Now, it felt even further away. As far away from her as the stars themselves.

This was as close as she would ever get to the clouds, to the school. Soon, Marion would spirit them away, somewhere no starlight could touch them again.

"You'll love it." Darius's smile was maddening. "There's the Glass Cathedral, and a forest that glows, and of course the enormous library."

The dark blue shadow cast over them, as the last star winked out along with her eyes.

"It's waiting for us." He moved closer to her. "It's waiting for you."

Would it be so wrong to pretend? Just for a moment?

Vivian stared across the sweeping horizon, Darius's hand tight in hers. The sunrise washed them in pink and red and orange. And as the night faded away, she remembered this wasn't how the world worked. Princes didn't walk into shoppes and become enchanted with candle girls. This was the ending of a story, not the beginning of one. Dread crept into the shadows where the sun couldn't reach.

He turned to her, glowing gold in the sunrise, and pressed a hand against her face.

"I don't belong there," she whispered.

"Vivian," he tilted her chin so she'd look up at him, "you are a star. You belong in the sky."

She gripped his wrist, hands closing over the blue ribbon.

She felt like she was flying.

She felt like she was dying.

This was truly as close as she would ever get to the clouds, and the sky, and the stars above. And maybe on a sun-washed balcony, with a prince as gentle and heroic as in the stories, this was high enough for a girl like her.

But she couldn't help, as she always did, but want a little more. And maybe it was because soon enough, she'd be gone from his life. Maybe all the life and death of the past evening had made her reckless.

His hair blew across his face like threads of gold, his mouth fixed in a smile. Their breath, clouds of fog in the chilly autumn morning, mingled together. She took a deep breath and pressed her lips against his.

His body stilled in surprise, and for one horrible moment, she feared she'd made a mistake. Then, his arms closed around her.

She truly felt like a star, tumbling down and crashing straight into a prince. His lips were soft, and her fingers knotted in his hair. When she finally pulled away, she was shivering.

His breath was heavy in his throat, matching her own. The clouds of darkness in his eyes had dissipated; he looked so happy. She wanted to smile back at him but kept her lips closed, running her tongue along a sharpening tooth. It wasn't just the smell and sight of blood that could give her away.

"The gods have already given me one star." Darius placed a kiss on her jaw. "But now another has fallen to me. I will keep you safe."

She could have wept at the words. For a girl who had been hiding for so long, it was all she wanted. Something—be it the gods, destiny, a love of candles, a ribbon—had woven their stories together. And if it were the gods, then it was as she had suspected all along. They were truly wicked.

Because, as Darius Störmberg held her in his arms, she knew she loved him with every unnatural beat of her heart.

And as someone who knew great misfortune well, then falling in love was the wickedest curse of them all.

He would never love her back.

How could the Prince of Andúrigard, who had lost everything to darkness, ever fall in love with her?

Ever fall in love with a vampire?

13
IN WHICH MARION FINDS HER SENSE OF ADVENTURE

I N THE LAST day, Marion Greywick had faced vampires, shadowcraft, and a nasally religious loremaster. Yet, none of that was as strange as Khalid Ali Bagheeri leaning down to kiss her.

She placed her finger against his lips. They were oh-so-soft. He opened his eyes, blinking. "I told you," she said, "I have work to do."

She whirled out of his grip, trying to ignore the regret settling in her chest.

"You're quite the enigma, Marion Greywick." Khalid picked an invisible piece of lint off his sleeve. The usual cockiness had left his tone. Marion wondered if she'd finally hurt his feelings.

"There's nothing mysterious about me at all, Mr. Ali Bagheeri," she assured. "I'm merely practical. Wait at the front, please." It wouldn't be any good to have him see her sticking frozen leeches in her bag.

"As you wish."

She walked to the back, glad to hide her heating cheeks. *What was that?* Had Khalid Ali Bagheeri, ward of Prince Darius, son of the ministers of Medihsa, truly been about to kiss her?

Or was it just another one of his tricks?

She busied herself in the back of the shoppe. She didn't *have* to tidy it—she didn't give a rat's left ass cheek what happened to the shoppe after she left. But once she did leave, that was it. She'd stick to her word. She'd get her siblings and run, as was the necessity. Green-eyed, silver spoon-fed boys had no place in her plan.

She wiped the countertop, scrubbing at a splotch of dried blood, and stared past the dirty curtain that separated the front of the shoppe from the back. Khalid had his hands in his pockets and whistled a tune through his plush lips. They had been so close to hers; she could still feel the warmth of his breath against her finger. If she hadn't stopped him, would he truly have…

Heat spread through her body and she clutched the countertop as if it would pass. But as she thought of the soft wetness of his mouth against her finger, the press of his body so close to hers, the warmth curled lower.

It was utter foolery. She had never thought of Huxley in such a desperate manner. Huxley hadn't been *unattractive,* and he was kind and considerate. *And quick,* she thought bitterly.

They'd spent many cold nights upon the reclined leeching chair. Huxley always turned red as his hair when she undressed, eyes averting her body. She had been thankful for it at the time, not wanting any sappy compliments or awkward innuendo.

But now as Khalid wandered over to the chair and ran a hand over the covering, she wondered what it would be like to stand bare before him. He had a way of looking at her like he saw all the way beneath the skin. What would he make of his wishing star then?

"Maybe I'll take a nap while you work. I hate to work, and I love to nap, so it seems like a good choice."

Marion's eyes darted like a shot to where Khalid was now lying on the leeching chair. He'd thrown off his dark cloak. Without it, she observed the litheness of his body, how long he was stretched out, boots hanging over the edge of the reclining chair. He was no longer wearing the golden uniform of the Celestial Academy, but

rather a loose white top. It was too thin for the weather, fitted only at the cuffs. The shirt's deep V revealed toned brown skin, a hint of elegant clavicle.

She wanted to throw the cloak back on him. She wanted to throw herself on top of him.

The curtain was not pulled all the way, and he was staring at her staring at him.

He smiled wickedly. "This is actually very comfortable. Would you care to join me?"

Yes, she wanted to join him. She wanted to push his shirt over his head and stare greedily at his body, to see something hidden and vulnerable about Khalid Ali Bagheeri. She wanted to forget about how her siblings hated her, how her family was in danger. She wanted to lose herself for a moment, to forget her name and all the terrible things that came with it.

But what she wanted didn't matter.

Couldn't matter.

Marion busied herself to put Khalid out of her mind. She went to the freezer box and stuck every frozen jar in the bag. It was enough for three moons, maybe. Three moons to get situated somewhere and find a way to manage Vivian's illness.

Marion took a deep breath in and shut her stinging eyes. She could do this. She *had* to do this.

She motioned for them to leave, then locked up the shoppe for the last time.

Khalid stared up at the brightening sky. "It's past my bedtime."

Right. Starlings slept during the day and woke under the stars when their magic was alive.

"I'm all done," she said.

"Are you wanting to leave now? I can get your siblings for you if you like. Or cause a distraction." He winked. "I'm very good at distractions."

"You would help me leave?"

He held out his arm for her to take. "As much as I would love your company at the Academy, I would never trap anyone. What is life without freedom? And what is freedom without choice?"

She took his arm. It seemed at the perfect height. "That's surprisingly gentlemanly of you."

"I want you to be happy, Marion. I want your family to be happy." He looked down at her. "That's why I have to tell you: you will never find what you're looking for by running away."

"However could you know what I'm looking for?" she asked.

His face was soft, eyes seeing through hers. A wolf in the finest sheep's clothing. "You want a cure for your sister's vampirism. And you'll only find one at the Academy."

Her heart stuttered once then surged. Marion dropped the bag, snatched Khalid by his dirty robe, and slammed him against the leech shoppe door. "Never say that word! Ever!" she growled. "Who told you? Answer me!"

Khalid did not seem bothered by being manhandled. He placed his hands over hers. "Easy, wishing star. I won't tell anyone. I promise."

Marion drew back her teeth and tightened her grip. Then released him. She didn't trust anyone beyond her family, especially the ward of the kingdom. But did she have a choice? "How do you know?"

"When you dance with kings and demons, you're only worth what you know." He smiled shrewdly. "I take it upon myself to know everything."

"Is this blackmail? I do what you want, or you'll tell the Prince?"

Anger flared across his face. "How many times do I have to tell you? I won't trap you, Marion. If you want to leave, fine. Do it. I'll take Vivian's secret to the grave. But I couldn't in good conscience let you run away without telling you there's hope." He grabbed her wrist. "There is a magic hidden within the school powerful enough to cure your sister. Powerful enough to change the course of the future. And if we work together, we can find it."

A beat passed between them. His words filled her with hope. Hope was poisonous.

A mask fell hard over him, and a huge smile crossed his face. He closed his eyes and threw his hands behind his head. "It's up to you if you want to change your fate, Marion Greywick!"

The skies cracked open, and the rain began again.

A cure. Vivian could finally be free from the illness that had torn their family open three years ago. But it was at the Academy. The one place Father had told them never to go. It would be a betrayal to him.

But it was a betrayal to Vivian not to try to find it.

"I told you, Marion," Khalid said. "Your world isn't enough either. You're a Lost Star!" He held out his hand. "Let's change the world."

"A cure," Marion whispered, "hidden in a castle in the sky."

"We're on the edge of an adventure," Khalid said, hand still extended. "Isn't it exciting?"

"I don't much like adventure."

Go to the Academy.

Find the cure.

None of this changing the world business.

She took Khalid's hand, knowing something quite unsettling.

Adventure liked her.

14
IN WHICH TIMOTHÉE
TOUCHES THE CLOUDS

MARION HAD CALLED it a special skill, his ability to fall asleep anywhere: whether splayed out in the lavender field, squished between his sisters in their giant bed on the farm, or on the ratty couch at their apartment on Enola Avenue, nothing posed a problem for him. He'd even fallen asleep in the bakery from time to time. That has caused Lingrint a great deal of grief.

But now, in this soft plush bed, with the roar of the fire, the light of the flames dancing across the white sheets… Timothée didn't think he would ever sleep.

Something had crept into his mind and refused to leave. A vine of darkness had taken root since the square. He'd pushed it back as soon as the rain plopped over his blood-streaked hair.

But now, alone in the darkness, he couldn't forget anymore.

A terrible awareness crept over him. It was such a feeling he knew his life would never be the same. A terrible destiny had claimed him when he and his sisters glowed in the square, when the Dark Prophet gazed at him. He knew it was a gaze, even behind the sharp angled obsidian mask. And that monster had spoken a word that broke flesh and bone and descended to Timothée's wicked core.

Noctis.

The way he'd spoken the name, a splintered sort of sound… It was the sound of utter agony, though Timothée couldn't explain why he thought that.

The night replayed over and over in his mind's eye. Some parts sharpened to focus so clear it was as if he were there now. The fluid way the Dark Prophet had moved, the deep richness of his black sword made of gravastarium which swallowed light instead of reflecting it.

And he thought of the prophecy the Dark Prophet had foretold. The words echoed in his head.

The God of Shadows will return.

Mountains will crumble, rivers run red, and the sky will weep.

Timothée rolled over and covered his head with a pillow, but the voice grew louder and louder and louder.

Noctis and I, side by side, as we were at the start of his world.

Twice the Dark Prophet had said that name. The first time, it was spoken with such reverence. But the second time, when the Dark Prophet had looked down at him… the word was agony. Reverence and agony. What did it mean?

Noctis.

Reverence and agony.

He had called Timothée, Noctis.

Why?

Noctis.

Noctis was the son of the gods. And Setviren and the people were calling the Greywicks the children of the gods.

Was Timothée really the brother of a god? The son of them? Hot tears streamed down his cheeks. It made him question his own belief. He realized he'd never truly tried to make sense of it all: the making of the world, the cosmos, the magic, and the stars that fell…

He'd spent the last nineteen years dreaming of destiny, and now that it had befallen him, he found himself drowning under the vast awareness of what it could mean. A part of him understood Marion's desire to shuttle them away to a simple life. And he knew she had felt it too, that dark purpose. That's what she was running from: the unimaginable spread of the universe before them.

His fingernails dug bloody crescents into his palms. Another part of him—that deep dark seed—knew there was no place in all of Thraina they could run to now.

Laughter sounded in the hallway and Timothée bolted up. His body and limbs were heavy, like the shadows of his waking dream were pulling him back down to the bed.

Slowly, he stepped out of bed and padded across the floor. Slivers of sunlight crept from underneath the long curtains. It was day then. But this was when stars slept. *This is when you sleep.*

Another laugh, and this time he recognized it at Vivian's. *How long has it been since I heard your laugh, sister?*

He pushed the door open a crack and peered into the hallway. Vivian stood against the wall as the Prince leaned over her. Yvaine sat happily in his arms.

Traitor. He'd thought himself a special sort, with Yvaine taking a liking to only him and tolerating his sisters. But he couldn't blame her for liking the Prince. He was handsome and brave—braver than anyone! He had stood against the Dark Prophet and survived.

"I really should let you rest," the Prince said. He ran a thumb over Vivian's cheek.

Something tightened in Timothée's stomach. He had been with *many* more people than his sister. It wasn't hard because she'd never kissed anyone. But no one had ever looked at him the way the Prince was looking at her.

And no one ever will. He couldn't stop the dark clouds of his mind. *Not when you've got such a wicked heart.*

Then the Prince pulled Vivian up against him, kissing her. Timothée began to shut the door when he caught Vivian's closed mouth smile as she pulled away.

She's happy, he thought. *Happy but scared.*

He hated to interrupt, but this was for her own good. *I sound an awful lot like Marion.*

Timothée stepped back from the door, then started to call loudly for Yvaine. A moment later, he heard a little meow, a scuffle, and Vivian—Yvaine clutched in her arms—crept through the door.

"She followed me through the castle and..." Vivian trailed off and narrowed her eyes at him. "But you already knew that. You were watching me."

Timothée skipped over and Yvaine immediately jumped to his shoulder. "I had to save you."

"Save me—"

"Your fangs are out, aren't they?" He reached for her mouth and pulled back her cheeks. Sure enough, he saw two white fangs. "But you're not hungry, *are you?*"

"Stop it—" She swatted his hand away. "You only know that because of all those terrible banned books you charmed Jenny Cotswood into giving you."

Timothée laughed. This felt like the best revenge for all the times she'd teased him about the boys and girls he saw around town. "Hey, those books were packed full of information that has helped us along the way. Like if you get enough blood, you can eat real food and—"

Vivian crossed her arms. "Yes, that's why you read them. To help me."

Timothée shrugged. Vivian was in a good mood. It had been a long time since he'd been able to joke around with her like this. This was how the two of them dealt with what she was, through jests. But when Marion was around, not a word was uttered about Vivian's *illness.* For her, it became too real, the terribleness of it brought forth in stark color.

With his sister here, hearing the lightness in her voice, the dark thoughts from earlier felt further away. *Or deeper down.*

"But the fang thing," Timothée smirked, "that's true, huh? You also get them when you feel *desire?*"

She smacked his arm. "I'm not talking to *you* about this."

"Come on, I know you want to tell me. He kissed you?"

"I kissed him." Vivian looked down. "I needed to know what it was like before..." She shook her head. "Where's Marion?"

Timothée felt it, the necessary hard conversation, lingering on the edge of their laughter. With great reluctance, he told her Marion's plan. Now, he and Vivian would have to sneak out and meet Marion. From there, the future was uncertain.

"It's for the best," Vivian said sadly.

"No, it's not." A great unfairness was occurring to his eldest sister, an unfairness from this whole world. "He loves you and you love him."

"Timothée."

"I've read hundreds of books, and none of them ever came close to describing how Darius looked when the Dark Prophet had you." He ran a hand through his hair. "And when you ran out to him, you were like the hero from the stories. You can't just *leave* him."

Vivian took his hand, squeezed it three times. "Even if that's true, he doesn't truly love me. He can't. He doesn't know me."

Timothée gave his sister a sidelong glance.

She smiled sadly. "Fangs, remember?"

"But what if love is enough for him to—"

He broke off as they heard a commotion at the door, a great deal of squawking and bickering.

"I am perfectly fine making it to my quarters on my own." Marion's voice carried through the door.

"What is she doing back?" Vivian looked over at Timothée who shrugged.

"I was trying to be a gentleman." Timothée recognized the smooth-talking cadence of the Medihsan ward, Khalid Ali Bagheeri.

"You being a gentleman is like a rat calling itself a wolf," Marion said.

"I'm wounded! That's the third time this moon I've been compared to a rat, but never so viciously as you've delivered."

"Good night, Mr. Ali Bagheeri," Marion said firmly.

"Good day, actually."

"Well," Marion's voice suddenly got lower, breathier, "good day, then."

The door flew open and Timothée caught a single glance of Khalid striding away before Marion slipped inside.

Marion studied them and dropped her large bag. "What are you two doing?"

"What are *you* doing?" Vivian said. Her fangs had retracted, so at least she wouldn't have to explain anything to Marion right away. "We didn't expect you to come back."

"And with the Medihsan ward." Timothée crossed his arms.

"What?" Marion snapped, shuffling over to the chairs by the fire. She slumped down as if carrying a great weight. "I ran into Khalid in town. I was getting information out of him."

"Everyone's having a good time with the royalty, and I've been stuck here in the room!" Timothée lamented. "Should I try to seduce Carmilla? She frightens me."

"Good luck." Marion snorted. "Besides, Khalid isn't royalty. He's..." She shook her head. "Doesn't matter. The situation has changed."

Timothée and Vivian exchanged a glance before sitting on the long couch across from her. She looked them both square in the face and gave a long sigh. "I think we should attempt to enroll at the Academy."

Timothée's heart leapt in his chest. But he forced his face to remain neutral. "Why do you think that?"

Marion took a deep, shuddering breath. "Khalid knows about Vivian's illness. I don't know how, but he does. And he says there's a great power at the Celestial Academy. And we could use it to create a cure."

"He knows what I am?" Vivian started shaking. "And you still want us to go there?"

"I do," Marion said, though it sounded like the words were hard for her to say.

"You must really trust him, huh?" Timothée placed Yvaine down.

"No," Marion said. She grabbed Vivian's hands. "But I trust in us. And if there's a chance to cure Viv, no matter how small, we have to take it."

"What if Khalid tells Darius?" Vivian said.

"He won't."

"You're so sure?"

Marion looked down. "I'm not sure about anything. But you were right earlier. We can't go on like this. I need to get you better, Viv. And I don't know any other way." Her eyes were shiny but her back straightened like a rod.

She is truly desperate. Timothée thought of the vampire he'd seen in the streets, with his paper-thin wings and ashen skin. *Maybe we have to be desperate. For Vivian.*

Timothée and Vivian squeezed into the chair with Marion, wrapping their arms around her.

"We won't just be students there," Marion said, voice fighting for some bit of control. "Our purpose will be to find a cure."

"To find answers about Father," Timothée added.

"Yes," Marion agreed. "We can't get caught up in all this Lost Star nonsense. These people love their legends. If we can use the story to our advantage, fine. But until proven otherwise, it's just that. A story."

"Right," Vivian said. "Eyes and ears open. We do this together."

"Together," Marion said.

And as she said it, as it became final, something coiled inside Timothée, like a key sliding into place, unlocking a door that should not be opened. And he saw the smile of the Dark Prophet, though he did not know how a mask could smile. Some ancient instinctual memory took over his mind, hurtling images at him in sharp flashes: the Celestial Academy devoured in shadows, great lances of darkness cutting through the trees and shattering the Glass Cathedral, and the Dark Prophet was with him hand-in-hand—

"Timothée!" Vivian was shaking him.

"You look like you're about to be sick," Marion said.

Timothée shook his head, realized both his sisters were staring at him, and he was wavering in place. He ran his hands through his wayward hair and took a couple deep breaths. "I'm alright. Just tired."

He was just tired, and still scared from the events earlier. That's why those images wouldn't stop replaying in his mind.

"By the way," Marion looked between them, "what were you two doing when I came in, looking so suspicious?"

Timothée shrugged and said, "Vivian kissed the Prince."

Marion let out a long sigh. "Oh bother."

THE WAXING CRESCENT moon hung like a lantern in the sky, backed by thousands of stars. The night air had the crispness of autumn, and brittle leaves crunched under Timothée's feet. Fog thick as soup wound its way around the castle grounds, turning statues into gargoyles, and branches into monster's limbs.

Timothée bundled the heavy wool jacket he'd been given tighter around himself and followed closely behind his sisters, the Prince, and the wards of the kingdom.

Setviren, the loremaster, held an oil lantern. The warm orange glow barely cut through the murk.

Timothée had thankfully fallen into a dreamless sleep, comforted by the presence of his sisters. He tried to leave no room in his mind for the Dark Prophet, or prescience, or Noctis.

They'd been awoken in the early evening with a tray of breakfast outside their door. "Breakfast in the evening. I'll never get used to this," Marion had complained, while shoving an entire piece of jam toast in her mouth.

"It's when the Starlings wake up." Vivian sucked on a frozen leech. If she ate three a day, they had discovered, it was enough for her to keep her fangs down and eat bites of normal food.

Well, it had been enough for a while. She hadn't eaten normal food in ages, and Timothée knew she wasn't sleeping well.

That's why we're going to the Academy, he had reminded himself. *For Vivian.*

The rest of the evening had been a flurry as they prepared for their departure to the Isle of Argos. They would fly up at midnight to the Celestial Academy for Fallen Stars.

Now, they passed through a maze of hedges and flowers that all looked black and grey and thorned in the gloom. They came upon a large open lawn within the palace walls.

Lined up were many metal contraptions. They reminded Timothée of thick canoes, made of shimmering sheet metal. At the front of each was a hub with thin blades attached. Wings stretched out on both sides of each contraption, making them look like chubby silver birds. A Celestial Knight leapt into one and a moment later, the hub began to rotate, the blades swinging around and around in a deadly whirl.

Sky skiffs. Timothée had seen them dot the sky over Wolfhelm and always wondered what it would be like to fly in one.

Beside the skiffs was a large wicker basket, and something attached to it by thick ropes. A huge sheet of canvas…

"Is that," Timothée gasped, "a hot air balloon?"

The Prince grinned at him. Well, he was probably grinning at Vivian beside him.

Setviren gave a long sigh. "In case anyone wants a more practical, time-efficient experience, you may ride in a sky skiff with me. Why the Prince chooses to fly on that boorish contraption is a wonder."

"Oh, come on, you old kook," Khalid jeered, slapping him on the back. "The Star Children are riding with us."

Setviren winced, his lantern swinging back and forth. "So be it. If I was in charge, you'd all be riding in sky skiffs." He gave a long sigh. "Alas, until we return to the Academy, I defer to you, Your Highness."

Darius was barely listening to him, his concentration on the large canvas sheet. "Khalid," he called, "I could use some light over here."

Khalid shrugged. "Duty calls."

Something tickled the back of Timothée's mind when he looked at Khalid. Something in the keen glint of his green eyes. He was sure he had never met the Medihsan before and yet...

"Is that really how we get up there?" Marion said warily.

The words shook Timothée from his thoughts. "It's in the sky. Did you think we were going to walk?" He gave Yvaine a reassuring pat as she lay coiled around his neck. Setviren had begrudgingly allowed Timothée to keep her. One animal companion was allowed per student. Setviren had pleaded to let him find Timothée a more aesthetically pleasing pet, but of course, Timothée had refused.

A warm glow emitted from where Khalid and Darius set up the balloon, though Timothée didn't remember Khalid having a lantern.

Carmilla grabbed his arm. "Come on, kids. The boys want to show off."

Timothée was glad the cover of night hid his burning cheeks. Carmilla was so beautiful... and frightening. They walked over to the wicker basket, which lay on its side. Thick rope attached the balloon to the basket, and there was a strange metal contraption affixed to it.

"Good. You're here." Darius straightened. "Stand close to the basket and get ready."

"They're acting like they haven't done this before." Carmilla leaned closer to Timothée. "I think your pretty sisters make them nervous."

"Alright, Khalid." Darius threw back his hood, running a hand through his blond hair. "Ready?"

"Always, Your Highness." Khalid cracked his knuckles. "Timothée, hold on to Marion. I don't want her swooning."

Timothée stepped closer to Marion, who groaned and shoved him away.

"These children used powers strong enough to chase away a coven of vampires," Carmilla drawled. "I doubt your party tricks will impress them."

"But did they do it looking quite so dashing as me?" Khalid affected an expression of genuine hurt. He flicked his gloved fingers. An orange flame sprouted from his hand. It caught on the metal piece attached to the balloon and hissed into a ball of fire.

"Morning Star," Marion whispered. "The power of creation."

That must have been the glow Timothée had seen. Khalid could *create* fire.

The light of Khalid's flame bounced off Darius and his hair looked like burnished gold. He drifted his hands in the air, and the flames grew bigger. The balloon expanded as warm air rushed into it. The night pricked with magic.

Khalid walked backwards toward them, then tipped the basket up as the balloon started to rise into the sky.

"All aboard." He grinned and held out his hand. "Next stop: the stars."

Marion purposely walked past him, but he caught her hand. They ended up in an awkward sort of tussle as they maneuvered into the balloon.

Timothée tightened his grip on his bag. Marion had packed him a couple outfits, and his beloved books. He'd had little else. There was nothing left for him in Wolfhelm.

As Timothée stepped into the basket, he knew his feet would not touch the ground for a very long time.

Khalid closed the small swinging door behind them. It was crowded, and with Marion refusing to be in the same vicinity as Khalid, Timothée was squeezed up against the Medihsan ward and Carmilla.

The balloon grew and grew, revealing a colorful pattern. Blue and gold with the silhouette of a snarling wolf beneath three stars: the sigil of Andúrigard.

Darius stood outside the basket. Magic crackled around him as the flame grew bigger and bigger.

Khalid and Carmilla started moving the ropes, then Khalid threw something over the edge of the basket and Timothée's stomach dropped as they lifted off the ground.

"You're going to miss the ride, Your Highness!" Khalid called.

"Right!" Darius danced back across the field and leapt over the side. The balloon pitched, and he fell forward, reaching for Vivian and wrapping his arms around her waist. Timothée was pushed tighter against Khalid.

The balloon swayed back and forth, as if tossed on stormy ocean waves. Below, the tops of the trees and hedges grew smaller and smaller.

A *wrrr* sounded beside them as Setviren's sky skiff fluttered past. Setviren gave a sharp angled look through ridiculously thick goggles, then disappeared into the clouds.

"He'll make sure the cavalry is there to greet us," Khalid said. "Or rather, greet *you*."

"Do not fret." Darius waved a hand, and the flame shrank. "Enjoy the ride."

"You're an… an Evening Star." Timothée tried to sound confident in front of the Prince. He'd suspected as much after watching Darius fight the Dark Prophet, but this all but confirmed it.

"Right," Darius said. "I'm changing the composition of the gases in the air to make Khalid's fire grow larger or smaller."

"Can't Khalid change the shape of his fire?" Timothée asked.

"Hey, I only caught my star earlier this moon! Don't expect miracles." Khalid laughed.

"Once Khalid practices his abilities, he'll be able to control the elements he creates," Darius said. "But we're still first years. I'm learning the basics of change, like ice to water to vapor. But those truly blessed by Xydrious could theoretically shape the world around them to their will."

Timothée's heart flipped in his chest. Was he really going to learn all this, to be like the Prince?

"We got it, Dare," Khalid groaned, tugging on the rigging. "Evening Stars can change, Morning Stars create. I thought we escaped Professor Kunuk's lessons for a little while."

Clouds gathered around them as they rose higher. Timothée could barely see his own hand. A black, heavy mist hung in the air.

"Morning Stars can create any natural element: water, air, earth, and fire," Carmilla said. "Some Morning Stars can even create aether, the celestial matter. It allows them to control what they create."

"And Evening Stars can change matter," Vivian said. "What do you excel at, Darius?"

Carmilla and Khalid exchanged a look then burst into laughter.

"What?" Marion asked.

"Darius excels at everything," Carmilla said coolly. The glow from the flames powering the balloon licked at her smile.

A pink flush crossed Darius's face. "Now, that's not true."

"Whatever you say, your royal perfectness." Khalid's voice dripped with mock sweetness.

But Timothée remembered how Darius had fought against the Dark Prophet, created the sword out of stellarite. Perhaps the Prince was being too modest.

"I have much to learn," Darius continued. "There are many ways you can specialize your magic. Some Evening Stars become physicians by learning the art of healing. They can mend broken bones or seal wounds. Many others become craftspeople. It's very common for Morning Stars to focus on perfecting the summon of a specific element. Our navy would not be as strong as it is without the aircrafters who ensure there is always a wind."

"Or the Medihsan sailors," Khalid said through his teeth.

"Absolutely!" Darius clapped him on the shoulder. "During our first year at the Academy, we learn the basics. Second years are given a chance to test out many specialities. Third and fourth year are used to hone your particular talents."

"So, you really caught a falling star," Timothée said, then, "What star did you catch, Carmilla?"

There was a beat of silence and stiffness. Carmilla touched the black choker at her neck.

"Look," Darius interrupted. "We're almost out of the clouds."

Carmilla weaved closer to Timothée. "Remember, there are three types of stars, Greywick."

"There!" Darius pointed.

The clouds parted as they rose into a sapphire sky, which sparkled with the sliver of the moon. And there, in the center of it all was the floating Isle of Argos.

It had always seemed so large in the sky, at times blocking the sun and covering the horizon. But now he realized how wrong he had been.

It was not large—it was immense. Land and forest and water: a castle in the sky. The bottom of it was sheer cliffs, tapered like an upside-down mountain. Waterfalls fell off the edges, tails disappearing into a great skirt of mist. They floated higher, and he saw a shadowy forest, and a huge sprawling field, and a sapphire pond. A glittering cathedral made of glass reflected every sparkling star. And there... The moon-washed stone of the Academy.

Their balloon drew closer, and he saw the tiny movements of people, students. Starlings. They ran across the field, waving. A sea of blue and gold uniforms. Setviren's sky skiff had landed, and he stood beside it, all white robes and green hair.

"The Celestial Academy for Fallen Stars," Timothée whispered.

"Children of the gods," Darius said, "welcome home."

15
IN WHICH MARION ENTERS THE CELESTIAL ACADEMY FOR FALLEN STARS

HE COULDN'T DO it. She couldn't get out of the balloon. Marion Greywick's foot hovered over the grass, but she couldn't take the step. Vivian and Timothée had already exited the hot air balloon and were looking around wonderstruck as Setviren preened over them like a mother hen. Marion was the last one in the basket. All she had to do was step out.

It was impossible.

A castle in the sky… More like a kingdom in the sky. She had seen it from below, how it had blocked out the sun when it passed over and shrouded the land in shadow. But to see the massive land-form so close…

It didn't matter that a great green field stretched out before them. It didn't matter the basket sat on this grass, or her siblings were walking around.

If Marion placed her foot on the Isle of Argos, she was quite certain she would fall through.

"If you find the grass so fascinating, wait until you see the cobble-stone." It was Khalid, of course, bowing low before her, hand extended. It felt like mockery, a ward of the Prince stooping to her. She looked up long enough to glare at him before returning to her hovering foot.

She had nearly let herself feel something for Khalid back in the leech shoppe of Wolfhelm. But she had seen what he was firsthand on the trip here. He had lit the balloon with fire made from nothing.

No. Not nothing.

Made from starcraft.

"Are you alright?" Khalid tried to grab her hand and Marion slapped it away.

Her siblings walked ahead with Setviren, Darius, and Carmilla. Of all the humiliating, shameful things to be afraid of. Marion gritted her teeth. "I-I can't do it. I can't get out of the basket."

Khalid looked from her to the ground. "Why not?"

"I don't know!" Marion snarled in a harsh whisper.

Khalid stroked his chin. "This is a thorny situation, isn't it? Well, not to worry. I, Khalid Ali Bagheeri, am at your service." With that, Khalid swept Marion into his arms.

She was so shocked, she didn't even protest. At least until Khalid stumbled away from the basket, musical laugh chiming into the night, arms full of skirts and girl.

"Let me down!" She wrapped tight around his neck.

"I'll carry you for your entire time at the Academy, if that's what you need," Khalid said despite the bead of sweat forming on his brow.

"You fool!" Marion broke out of his grip. Damp grass squished underneath her thin slippers.

But she didn't fall through. She was still here.

Still fighting.

Khalid's smile was brighter than the stars in the sky. Marion sighed. Curse the Three for making Khalid Ali Bagheeri so hand-some. It was distracting.

"Quickly now!" Setviren called from ahead. "We don't want to keep the Archpriestess waiting."

Khalid tugged her forward. A strong breeze whipped at her skirts and hair, blowing the crisp scent of the night. The sky was a blanket above them, quilted with inky tendrils. And the stars...

Marion reached up, swearing she could pluck them from the sky like juicy peaches.

Khalid smiled at her. "Beautiful."

She dropped her hand, blushing. The way he looked at her suggested he wasn't talking about the stars.

Ahead, the field melted into a courtyard of shimmering, moon-frosted stone. Towering lamps lit by multifaceted crystals scattered rainbows of soft light over the ground. A massive ivory fountain spouted water in every shade of yellow, blue, and purple, and each gush was a different creature: this one a fish, the next a whale, the other a dolphin.

Great fir trees decorated the courtyard in between the lampposts, casting shadows through the colored lights. The courtyard itself was caged in by buildings with painted windows and bright doorways bursting with music. Marion caught sight of one sign: *Crescent Cakes, Lunar Lattes, and Fengari Tea.*

"This is Selene Crescent," Khalid said.

A little town upon the island. What a strange place this was.

Movement flittered under the soft lamplight: shapes coming out of the buildings.

"Are those...?" Timothée asked.

"Starling students," Setviren confirmed. "Yes, of course. You'll have time to meet them later. Hurry now."

Marion pulled her hand from Khalid's and stepped in front of her siblings, as if to shield them. But there was no way to escape the stares. They were mice to owls. She pulled her hair over her shoulder, trying to hide herself as much as possible; ribbons of colored light made her hair shine blue and red and purple.

The students clustered together, staring, whispering. Some had little lights floating around them, others carried candles or lanterns. Most looked like young adults, though some were older. There was a mix of blue and yellow uniforms, though none were quite the same: long dresses, trousers with belted tunics and woven stars, capes, and felt hats and gauzy veils. The only consistency were the colors: gold or blue. Marion knew from the balloon it differentiated the Morning Star students from the Evening Star.

But there was a third house, Carmilla had said. The former imperial princess wore a purple uniform and a black choker around her neck. Where were those students?

"Back to class!" Setviren called, shooing away the students. But it did no good. More gathered, their eyes curious and questioning as the siblings shuffled through them like livestock heading for the slaughter.

Khalid threw his arm around Marion. "Guess word has already spread of the Lost Stars."

Marion didn't miss how bug-eyed and feverish the students got when Khalid casually touched her. She shrugged him off.

They left Selene Crescent and walked over a railed pathway along the edge of the Isle.

"Look ahead," Vivian murmured. "Is that where Father lived?"

Ahead lay a grand castle of white stone. Two massive mahogany doors, rich as blood, marked the entrance. The doors were carved with intricate runes and strange animals. Each immense tower and turret had gaping windows, where soft white light radiated outward. Glass made up portions of each roof.

"To let the starlight in," Marion murmured to herself.

The Celestial Academy for Fallen Stars.

Their new home.

No, Marion thought. *Not my home. Never my home. I don't belong here.*

Setviren looked up at the position of the moon then turned to the Prince and his wards. "Look at the time. You'll all be late for class."

The three let out a collective sigh of disbelief. "You've got to be kidding, Professor!" Khalid cried. "We almost got assassinated last night and we still have to go to lectures?"

"We've only just arrived." Carmilla kept her voice calmer than Khalid's. "Surely, there can be an exception—"

"There are no exceptions for members of the courtly house or even princes." The loremaster gave an adoring look at Darius. "Hurry now. Your instructors are waiting."

"Come on." Darius laughed and placed a hand on each of his friends' shoulders. "We have to set a good example for the new students."

"I'm always a shining example." Khalid winked.

Marion didn't miss the way the Prince grabbed Vivian's hand, the lowered pitch of his voice as he said to her, "Setviren will take good care of you. Enjoy your first night at the Academy. There's truly nothing like it."

"This place is so…"

"You'll be fine." Darius unclasped his heavy blue cloak and draped it around Vivian's shoulders. "Although the wind can bring quite a chill this high up."

"Will I see you soon?" Vivian touched the cloak's clasp.

"I'll find you after class." He held up his wrist, exposing a ribbon of blue. "I always do."

Marion jumped as a warm voice caressed her ear, shocking her out of her eavesdropping: "Would you like a romantic send-off as well?"

Marion merely rolled her eyes at Khalid.

"I'd give you *my* cloak, but my Medihsan blood can't handle a chill." He placed a hand on her waist and swung in front of her. His jade eyes twinkled beneath the colored lights. "If anyone gives you trouble, remember," he leaned close, his lips upon her ear, "you belong among the stars."

Marion's heart stuttered. He was gone as quick as he had appeared, throwing his arms over Darius and Carmilla's shoulders. "Be good, little Greywicks!" Khalid called as they melded into the night.

Marion touched the side of her face, where his warm breath had been a moment ago.

She suddenly felt exposed without Khalid and his friends. Even though they were dangerous. Even though Darius was the damned *prince* of the entire kingdom. Even though Carmilla looked at her like she was evaluating her every movement. Even though Khalid made her want to simultaneously smack him and ask him what his favorite food was. She couldn't deny there had been something comforting about their presence.

Now, the siblings were out in the open, where Setviren could shred them apart and lay out their pieces to examine.

A huge bridge spanning over cascading water led the way to the castle. "This way," Setviren said. "The headmistress awaits."

The massive doors opened with a wave of Setviren's hand. "You will meet with Kassandra, the Archpriestess of the Celestial Church and the headmistress of the Celestial Academy for Fallen Stars."

He walked swiftly ahead of them, but the triplets stopped all together in a line. As if they all had the same feeling.

"You may refer to her as 'Your Holiness', 'Holy Mother', 'Your Eminence', 'Your Grace', or 'my lady'. Is that under—?" His voice echoed as he stepped into the entrance atrium. Setviren turned, noticed the triplets weren't following him. "Whatever is the problem?"

The triplets held hands, their toes reaching where the white brick of the bridge became the black floor of the Academy. The feeling sung in Marion's heart, and she knew it sung in her siblings', too.

A terrible destiny.

To take one more step, to enter the Celestial Academy for Fallen Stars, would ignite a change within them that could never be undone. It would be to accept this terrible destiny, to give way to whatever wickedness sat dormant within their hearts. It would be to leave the earth for the constellations, never knowing if they would come down again.

With one hand, she held tight to Timothée, and with the other, Vivian.

A breeze rustled through their hair, slowly playing with the strands, and wafting through their clasped fingers. The breeze…

"Is that…?" Timothée asked.

"Lavender," Vivian confirmed. "And salt air."

For Father. For Vivian. Marion squeezed her siblings' hands three times. They would face their terrible destiny together.

The Greywicks stepped through the doorway.

It was like stepping into a dream. The atrium was immense. Opulent navy rugs covered dark stone. Grand staircases led this way and that, leading up, up, up. Starlight shimmered in from the glass roof. It danced on her skin.

Setviren paused in front of a wall decorated with shimmering constellations in the shape of winged horses, and giant bats, and flame-shrouded phoenixes.

"There are three orders of magic studied at the Academy," Setviren said. He pointed to the winged horse, the phoenix, then the bat. "Evening Star, Morning Star, and Dark Star."

With a wave of his hand, the light shining upon the mural changed to blue. "Evening Stars are disciples of the god Xydrious. They wield the magic of change. We Evening Stars tend to be quite imaginative, determined, and resourceful." Setviren looked chuffed. Then with another wave, the light turned gold. "The goddess Rhaemyria blesses Morning Stars. They're curious, clever, and serene, like the Sun Mother." He sighed as if thinking of a long-lost love. "They brandish the magic of creation. Now, hurry along—"

"Wait!" Timothée said. "What about the other house?"

Setviren sighed. "The Dark Stars? Oh, there's nothing to fear from them anymore. They may be acolytes of Noctis, but we don't allow anyone to wield shadowcraft. The Academy takes the safety of its students seriously. They have their magic bound and instead study the noble art of potion making."

Timothée's nose scrunched up and Marion thought of the black choker Carmilla wore around her neck.

"Chop chop!" Setviren had a renewed confidence upon entering the Academy. "The Archpriestess has been waiting a long time to meet you."

They followed dutifully behind the green-haired loremaster. "Archpriestess Kassandra is a disciple of the goddess Rhaemyria. That

makes her a Morning Star, and the most powerful one in Thraina. You'll mind your manners around her. Don't speak unless spoken to. If she offers you her staff, kiss it. Oh, and of course, *genuflect!*"

"What does genuflect mean?" Timothée whispered.

Marion shrugged.

Setviren led them down a dark blue carpeted hallway until they came upon two mahogany doors with no handles. They slid apart with a *whish* of his hand. Marion's skin pricked with the magic.

"Please enter." He motioned them through the doors. It led to a small room, slightly bigger than a closet, carpeted in the same night blue.

"There's nothing here—" Marion began when Setviren stepped in with them. The doors whooshed shut with another flourish. "Wait, are you locking us—"

The loremaster rose his arms upward, white sleeves waving like an albatross's wings. And the room moved. Upward! The triplets shrieked and held on to one another.

"Heavens me, I wouldn't ask you to walk all the way up on your first night," Setviren said as if the *moving room* were the most normal thing in the world.

Setviren was doing this. Marion concentrated on his rising hands. Somehow, he was using starcraft to move them.

"Steady now. Here we are." With a jolt, Setviren lowered his hands, and the room shuddered to a stop. The triplets were nearly on top of one another.

"Somehow, that was worse than the hot air balloon." Vivian touched her forehead.

"Prepare yourself." The doors slid open at Setviren's command. "This is her office."

The triplets stepped out of the moving closet. The office was a circular room made entirely of glass. It was like standing in a great orb. They were so high up, so close to the stars. Marion imagined she was sitting in the heavens upon a moon-carved throne, or swimming in a sea of starlight.

The floor gleamed beneath a large ivory desk inlaid with gold leaf. The legs of the desk were two golden wyvern claws. White wooden easels held up strange maps of places Marion didn't recognize. Crescent moon bookshelves held tomes with runes instead of letters on the spines. A massive pearl statue of a phoenix, wings outstretched, body ensconced with fire, glittered with nearby candlelight. And everywhere, everywhere, the stars watched, and waited, and—

From behind the phoenix statue, stepped out a creature.

Calling her a woman seemed an injustice, for her beauty was so immense. Marion's heart stuttered in her chest.

"My lady," Setviren rasped and the reverence in his voice made Marion's spine tingle.

This woman looked like one of the elven princesses from Timothée's favorite fairytales. Her hair was white-gold, her skin an alabaster that shimmered as she walked. Her eyes were pale, two diamonds twinkling. She wore great white robes with golden trim, heavy and billowing enough to hide her figure. Hundreds of tiny bells adorned her robes, so she tinkled as she moved. In one hand, she held a black staff.

Setviren fell to a knee and bowed his head. He looked back at the triplets, standing dumbfounded. *"Genuflect,"* he snarled under his breath.

Clumsily, they all knelt. Marion was thankful to look down.

"My dearest Setviren." The woman's voice was like an orchestra of every harp, every sweet bird song, every lullaby. "Is it true? Have you brought me this mighty gift?"

Marion peered through her golden sheath of hair to watch the woman extend a hand to Setviren. He looked up at her with a feverous gaze. Something wilder than love, deeper than reverence. Complete and utter loyalty.

He accepted her hand and stood. "Yes, yes, Your Holiness. I have brought them. It is true. I saw it with mine own eyes."

The Archpriestess walked over to them. Quickly, Marion looked down again. Her heart leapt like a rabbit.

"Look at me."

Marion obeyed.

"Who is the eldest?"

Vivian's voice rang strong: "I am."

Kassandra walked before her. "What do you call yourself, child?"

"Vivian. Vivian Greywick."

Eternity seemed to pass before Archpriestess Kassandra held out her staff to Vivian. Behind the Archpriestess, Setviren mouthed: *"Kiss the staff!"*

It was the strangest thing, long and straight, but made of a curious black metal. It appeared as if the metal was moving. Trapped shadows, misting up and down its length. And at the tip, caged in by metallic tendrils, was a large black gem. It certainly wasn't any gem Marion would have chosen to adorn a special staff; this was lumpy, and the color of coal except for a few veins of purple. The whole thing seemed entirely out of place for the Archpriestess's starlight-white office.

Vivian looked anxiously from Setviren to the staff then placed a tentative kiss upon the gem. When she removed her lips, her eyes were wide and questioning.

"You wear the Prince's cloak," the Archpriestess said.

"He placed it over her shoulders himself." Setviren scurried forward before Vivian answered. "And he protected her during the Dark Prophet's attack."

Marion had to stop herself from rolling her eyes. How about when Vivian had saved *him?*

"As your report stated," the Archpriestess said.

"He met her *before* the festival, Your Grace," Setviren continued. "It seems fate had already led him to a child of the stars. Perhaps it's as we've discussed. The young prince may be the one—"

"I am well aware of your thoughts on the heir to Andúrigard, loremaster. Now," the Archpriestess turned back to them, her robes filling the air with a musical chime, "who is the second eldest?"

Marion took a deep breath, wishing she could smell the lavender and sea spray from earlier. It had given her courage. She met the priestess's diamond eyes. "I am."

"What do you call yourself?"

"Marion Greywick."

Then the gem was before her, that hideous rock, like smoke trapped in hardened soot.

"*Kiss it!*" Setviren hissed.

The room spun. The rock and starlight, mixing together in terrible destiny. All she needed to do was place her lips upon it and the sky would stop swirling and she wanted to, desperately wanted to—

A shadowy writhing in her heart yearned for the rock and she had an image of yanking the whole staff out of Archpriestess Kassandra's hands—

"KISS IT!" Setviren's shrill voice cut through the image.

Marion placed a kiss upon the gem.

A voice hissed inside her mind, *Marion.*

She looked up, startled. Who had said her name?

Archpriestess Kassandra had already moved on to Timothée. She stood above him while he quivered. Marion longed to rush to him, but fear held her still.

"What is your name?" Archpriestess Kassandra asked.

"T-Timothée."

"Timothée." The Archpriestess said it like a winter's wind. "Child, tell me. Do you glow during the moonless nights? Like your sisters?"

Marion saw the fear and courage warring in her brother's eyes. "Yes, ma'am—Your Holiness."

Archpriestess Kassandra looked at her staff but did not offer it to Timothée for a kiss. "Very well." She returned to her desk and placed the staff down. "Rise, Greywick children."

With shaking legs, Marion obeyed. The siblings huddled together, cowed beneath the Archpriestess's presence.

The stoic expression upon Archpriestess Kassandra's face melted, and she offered a strange smile. "It is true. My children have returned to me. After nineteen years, my children have returned."

The triplets looked at each other.

"This must be so strange for you," Archpriestess Kassandra murmured. "All your life, not knowing who you are."

"We know who we are," Marion said. "We're the Greywick children."

"*Your Holiness*," Setviren said under a cough.

"Y-your Holiness," Marion added.

"Of course you are." She dropped her hand and stepped back. "Do you know who I am?"

Timothée said, "Y-you're Archpriestess Kassandra, the Archpriestess and headmistress here, My H-Holy Graceness."

Setviren slapped a palm against his forehead.

Archpriestess Kassandra smiled graciously. "Yes, my child. I am charged with the wellbeing of all the students of the Celestial Academy for Fallen Stars. But my greatest blessing is the three of you."

A hollow pit opened in Marion's stomach. Archpriestess Kassandra had an odd, longing expression on her face. And she kept raising and dropping her hands, as if she wanted to touch them but couldn't. Marion crossed her arms over her chest.

Archpriestess Kassandra turned away, a hand to her heart. "I was given life in this land to be a messenger for Rhaemyria, to pass on her teachings, and lead the flock in celestial righteousness. For this mission, I serve as Archpriestess and headmistress. But no role is so important as the one Rhaemyria gifted me nineteen years ago." She turned back to them, jewel eyes flashing. "The role of mother."

Setviren let out a reverent sob.

The head of the whole bloody Church believes this nonsense, Marion thought. *Will this help us find Vivian's cure or hinder us?*

"Rhaemyria sent you to me, so I may raise you in her stead. But I failed. You were stolen." Kassandra gripped her desk, knuckles turning as white as the marble. "What has returned to me? Are you still the blessed born?"

"My lady," Vivian said quietly, "we have no power. We just glow. And only on moonless nights, at that."

Kassandra stiffened. "If your powers remain, they lie dormant within you. We must ignite them." She turned to her desk and snapped a finger. "Setviren!"

Like a flapping bird, he was behind her. "Y-yes, Your Eminence!"

"There is no doubt these are the children of Rhaemyria and Xydrious. But they have grown in the arms of a traitor. We must see if their hearts are strong enough to wield starcraft." She sat behind her desk in a flourish of white robes. "There is to be a star shower. Begin the arrangement immediately. Tomorrow, the Greywicks will attend the Celestial Rite."

Marion stumbled back. Of course, swallowing a star would be a requirement of attending the school. It was for *Starlings*, after all. But that meant having magic inside of you forever. And Father had said...

"No." The word was out of her mouth before she could stop it.

Setviren gasped and nearly swallowed his lip. Even Vivian and Timothée gaped at her. But Archpriestess Kassandra's only betrayal of emotion was the barest quiver of her shoulders.

Marion stuck her chin in the air. "If we are the children of the gods, as you so claim, then why should we need to swallow a star to wield magic? We glow all on our own just fine."

Slowly, Archpriestess Kassandra rose. "Dear one, how do you think your mother Rhaemyria got her power?"

From the legends of desperate fanatics, Marion thought.

"Even the gods get their powers from the celestial bodies." Archpriestess Kassandra smiled as if she were explaining how to button a coat to a child. "It is what can be ignited within that marks the power."

Fear and rage blazed through Marion. "And what if it burns us from the inside out? Don't lie to us! We know it can happen!"

An unspoken horror: every year hundreds of hopefuls attempted to catch a star upon the Isle of Argos. To swallow a star meant attendance at the school, prestige, wealth, and years of servitude to the Church as a Starling. To fail to catch a star at all, as would happen to most, meant returning home to whatever dull vocation you could acquire.

But to catch a star, to swallow it, and welcome the celestial flame into your body only for your heart to be too weak…

Marion had seen the bodies returned from the Isle of Argos. The charred corpses. The screams imprinted upon the scorched skin.

Kassandra held her in an icy gaze. "It can happen. And it does. If there is nothing to ignite, the star will feast instead." She walked over to Marion. Ran a hand down her golden hair. "A star will fall to each of you, of this I am certain. But whether you are blessed or cursed is to be determined. You were made to be ignited."

No, no, she wasn't made. She was a Greywick, born in Seagrass, a farmer's daughter. "But Father said—"

Kassandra's face shifted. Such loveliness changed into a vicious snarl. "The man you call Father was a thief and a traitor. He has filled you with fear and poison. It is my greatest regret he smuggled you away from me." Her hand tightened painfully in Marion's hair. "Only Rhaemyria herself will take you from me again."

Then in an instant, her hand was lovingly petting Marion, and she smiled a soft and sunlight-bright smile. "Now, you must be tired. Setviren, have them stay in the sanatorium until we determine their houses and proper rooms can be prepared." She turned. "Children, I'm so very glad you're home. I pray for the strength of your hearts."

16

IN WHICH VIVIAN IS INTERVIEWED ON BEING A VAMPIRE

ETVIREN HAD LEFT them to rest in the sanatorium. There were no patients currently, just empty beds with crisp white sheets. Enormous windows revealed the clear starlit sky.

With plush beds, a twinkling chandelier, and a beautifully painted ceiling of celestial bodies, it could have easily been mistaken for a luxurious spa. Strange crystals in fixtures along the walls cast pastel pink, purple, and teal light.

Vivian's brother wandered around the room, going over to a cart filled with small bottles. He picked up a vial. Vivian came up behind him and spied over his shoulder. The vial was filled with a vibrant liquid and a fading parchment label, which written in elegant handwriting read: *Vitality with the essence of bergamot and hibiscus–V. Sun–1ˢᵗ year.*

"Timothée!" Marion snapped. "Don't touch that."

He fumbled, barely catching the potion, and set it down. Vivian stifled a giggle before grabbing her brother's hand and leading him over to the bed across from Marion's. Yvaine was curled up at the bottom, flicking her tail.

"I thought Setviren would never leave." Marion crossed her arms and blew a curl out of her eyes. "We need to focus."

Vivian straightened a wrinkle in her skirt. "The Archpriestess said the Celestial Rite will happen tomorrow night."

"I don't think she liked me very much," Timothée murmured.

Vivian blinked at him. "Why do you say that?"

"She didn't let me kiss her staff."

The sisters eyed him curiously.

"Archpriestess Kassandra let you both kiss her staff. But she didn't offer it to me."

"Think nothing of it." Marion fluffed a pillow on her bed. "That lady's a kook, like the rest of them. Probably the kookiest."

Vivian looked down nervously and rubbed her arm. "I'm sure you're right, Mare, but…"

"But what?"

Vivian's eyes shone. "I swear when I kissed the staff, it said my name."

Marion's hands stilled on the pillow. Her body tensed. Then she returned to fluffing, more aggressively this time. "I'm sure it was nothing. We're all over-tired and overwhelmed. We'll play the priestess's little game, but she's no mother of ours."

Something sat wrong in Vivian's belly, a twisting and turning. A memory that could only be felt, not recalled. "There was something odd about that staff. I just know it."

Timothée's eyes widened. "It was made of gravastarium. The forbidden metal. Like the Dark Prophet's sword."

"Another reason not to trust this place," Marion said. "That lady outlaws a metal then hoards an entire staff of the stuff? And she called Father a thief and traitor. What a bother!"

Vivian wandered over to the window, looked over the Isle. "A bother it may be, but tomorrow we become a part of it. If we're going to go through with this, we'll have to swallow a star."

"And what if our hearts aren't strong enough?"

"What are you worried about, Mare?" Timothée leapt up and wrapped his arms around her shoulders. "You're not going to get all burnt up. You've got the strongest heart I know!"

"It's not just that," Marion snapped. "Didn't you notice on our way in? Gold and blue uniforms only. And haven't you been listening to Setviren? Morning Star this, Evening Star that. There's another house, you know. And they treat them like lepers."

Vivian thought of Carmilla in her purple uniform, the black choker tight around her neck. "The Dark Stars."

"You worry too much!" Timothée said. "Jenny Cotswood told me it's very rare to swallow a Dark Star."

"Well, I have rotten luck," Marion mumbled.

"Aren't Dark Stars supposed to wield the magic of Noctis?" Vivian whispered. "The same magic he was killed for centuries ago?"

Something haunting passed across Timothée's face. "The Dark Prophet... He looked at me and called me Noctis."

Marion clicked her tongue. "Are you sure he was calling you Noctis? He's a raving cultist. He was blathering on and on about Noctis before he tried to murder Vivian's prince."

"But what if Noctis really is our brother?" Timothée urged.

Marion patted his hand. "I have one brother, and he is right beside me."

"Let us focus on the task at hand and do what we've always done," Vivian said decidedly. "Take one step at a time. Whatever happens, we'll get through it together."

"Sure," Marion grumbled, "unless one of us catches the evil star or burns up."

Marion and Timothée began to argue, but Vivian could only hear the rapid racing of her siblings' blood through their veins. Vivian knew what her sister meant. What if the monstrous part of her drew a Dark Star down from the sky? What if she was too weak to wield starcraft?

Vivian placed a hand upon the irregular beat of her heart. How tired she was. Her siblings knew it. Maybe it would be a mercy to float away into the cosmos, the pieces of her drifting into stardust.

She tilted her head and looked up at the mural adorning the ceiling. Pinpricks of painted starlight formed shapes: a howling wolf, a woman in flowing garb, a sword with a winged hilt. How could a monster like her possibly belong here?

As if in answer, a chill sparked up her arms. A cold voice drifted between the beats of her heart: *I made the maker of your maker. All have failed me. What of you? Will you ignite or combust?*

Vivian jumped. Had she imagined the voice?

She squeezed her eyes shut. Marion and Timothée were too loud, talking about her like she wasn't there, deciding her fate for her.

"Stop." She stood. Her siblings blinked their matching grey eyes. "I may not survive the Celestial Rite. But I'm not going to survive without it either."

Marion closed her eyes as if in resignation.

"We can't stay here without a star," Vivian said. "And if we want answers, this is the only place we'll find them."

Together they would do the very thing their Father had feared the most.

They would attempt to be students at the Celestial Academy for Fallen Stars.

THE LAST HOURS of night passed quickly. An Evening Star student named Safiya brought them clean clothes and trays of delicious food: spinach pie, buttered bread, roasted carrots, and bowls of kheer.

After they ate, the triplets took turns freshening up in the washroom attached to the sanatorium. They hadn't had hot water at their apartment in Enola Avenue, and Vivian wanted to stay under the stream of steaming water forever.

A thin line of sunlight sparkled on the horizon, and they began closing the curtains to attempt some sleep. They were at the Celestial Academy, so they would do as the Starlings did: sleep with the sun and rise with the stars.

Just as they were tucking into their beds, the door to the sanatorium opened, letting in a burst of light from the hallway.

"How are my favorite triplets doing?" came the sing-song voice of Khalid Ali Bagheeri.

Vivian took a deep breath at his approach. They had been so careful for three years, but this person, one of the most important political figures in Thraina, had figured out her secret.

Whatever he had said to Marion had been enough to convince her to come here. And Vivian knew how difficult it was to convince Marion of anything.

"What are you doing here?" Marion stood and put her hands on her hips.

"Think of me as your personal welcoming committee." He flashed a too-perfect grin. With his mop of wavy black hair, green eyes, and warm brown skin, Khalid was incredibly handsome. Vivian wondered if that had anything to do with her sister's willingness to listen to him. But based on Marion's scowl, she would not be swayed, even by a charming noble.

Khalid strolled in and placed a hand on Timothée's shoulder as if they were old pals. Her brother blushed. "I thought I'd make sure you're being taken care of."

"It's good you've come," Marion said sternly. "There's no time like the present."

Khalid ran a hand through his dark hair. "For what? A tour? A recount of my life? A date, perhaps?"

Marion forced him to sit on a bed. "For a cure. You told me if we came to the Academy, you would help us. So, talk. What do you know, Mr. Ali Bagheeri?"

All three Greywicks sat down on the bed across from the Medihsan ward.

Khalid's eyes widened. "What *I* know? Practically nothing. Only there's no more magical a place in all of Thraina. The answers are here. I told you I make it my business to know everything about everyone. And the more information I have on Vivian's condition, the better a researcher I'll be." He smiled dangerously at the Greywicks. "So, in that case, *you* talk."

Vivian looked at her siblings. She might be cosmic dust in a few hours. Might as well keep being reckless.

"Here's what we know," Vivian began. "I've been like this for three years. But I'm not entirely the same as other v-v—" She forced herself to say the word to him. "Vampires."

Khalid crossed his legs and leaned his chin on his fist. "Oh?"

"She can go out in the sun," Timothée said. "It doesn't hurt her one bit."

Vivian took a breath. She hated remembering how they'd found out that particular piece of knowledge.

It had been one moon, maybe two, since she had gotten sick. Hunger crawled through her entire body. She remembered nothing but the aching pain. Except that wasn't true. She remembered the tired look in Marion's eyes. She remembered Timothée's tear-stained face. She remembered knowing she was tearing her family apart.

That it would have better if she had stayed dead.

And she remembered screaming and clawing as Marion tried to force a cup of goat's blood down her throat. How they'd thrashed, how it'd spilled over Marion's only dress, and seeped into the rotten wood floorboards. She'd run for the door, thrown it open, and flung herself into the streets as dawn broke.

She'd seen the sun cresting over the shambled apartments of Wolfhelm, the pink-grey light. And then she'd known fear.

Because something sparked within her. She wanted this life, even the broken pieces of one. But it was too late for her to get back inside.

Timothée tackled her to the ground, covering her body with his. Then Marion was on top of them with a giant cloak. And none of them said anything as the warmth of the sun trailed over them. They stayed huddled together, intertwined as one.

Until she'd said: "I'm okay." Because her hand was poking out from under the cloak, and a sunbeam was hitting her arm. She only felt warmth.

Slowly, she'd extended her full arm, and when nothing happened, Marion and Timothée crawled off her. And they'd laid, covered in goat's blood, on the dirty streets of Wolfhelm, and watched the sunrise together.

"Hmm." Khalid's voice chased her from her memories. "That is strange. Usually, a little sun will turn a vampire to kindling. I wonder if it has anything to do with your god's blood."

Marion snorted. "God's blood. Don't tell me you believe that nonsense."

"That *nonsense* has made you three the most important people in Thraina. Even if you don't believe it, I'd advise you to let others think what they will." Khalid turned to Vivian. "What have you been eating the last three years?"

"Leeches filled with human blood," Vivian said.

"Only that?"

"We've tried other things," Timothée said. "Rat blood. A goat. It made her hungrier."

Khalid nodded as if they were telling him the answers to a math quiz. "And you haven't tried to feed on one of your siblings?"

The starkness of the question made her eyes widen. "N-No—"

Timothée rubbed his wrist. "We tried putting our blood in a cup, but it made her sick."

If Vivian had enough blood to flush, she would have. The memory filled her with shame. She'd tried to drink each of her siblings' blood, and both times it had wrecked her body, caused her insides to feel like they were crawling outside.

"What about feeding from them directly?"

"We don't know how a vampire is made," Marion said matter-of-factly. "So we couldn't chance her biting one of us and—"

"Her turning you," Khalid finished.

Vivian ran a finger along her flat teeth. It was almost a relief to have someone else know her truth. And Khalid wasn't running away. He didn't seem the least bit afraid of her.

He stretched, his shirt riding up and revealing a sliver of toned skin. "You were turned into a vampire three years ago. Don't you remember how it was to be made?"

Her breathing quickened. A searing pain flashed in her neck, and she rubbed it. "No, I d-don't remember."

Being made was like being undone. There was only the pain, the cold rain pounding on her skull, and a yellow eye. The yellow eye she remembered most of all.

Immediately, Marion's arms were around her. "That's enough! You can't interrogate her like this."

"I'm only collecting data." Khalid shrugged.

"I-It's okay," Vivian whispered. "We need all the help we can get."

"That's the spirit!" Khalid stood up and strode around the sanatorium. Pastel light from the crystals shone over his black hair. "So, we don't know how vampires are made. We know you can only survive on human blood, and you got sick when you drank it from a cup, but it was okay in the leech. Have—"

"Enough of your questions. Time for one of mine." Marion stood, an indomitable force of curly locks and skirts, and stormed over to Khalid. "How did you know? How *could* you know?"

Khalid smiled with self-satisfaction. "You know what's lost these days? The subtle art of observation. Everyone's so busy, only paying attention to themselves. But if you stop and look around," he wandered over to Vivian, trailed a hand up her jaw, "you see things others miss."

"My fangs," Vivian whispered.

"The vampire left a lot of bleeding bodies around the courtyard." Khalid smirked. "When does that little party trick happen? Only when you smell blood or—?"

Vivian exchanged a look with Timothée. Her little brother could never keep his mouth shut. "Uh, I read in a book once they can also appear when a vampire feels desire."

Khalid crossed his arms. "Interesting. Not that I'm making any plans, but out of curiosity: do you three know what kills a vampire? Besides sunlight and your little glowing trick."

The siblings exchanged looks. Maybe if they'd known, they'd have been able to protect Father. Maybe Vivian could have protected herself.

When they didn't answer, Khalid said, "*Very* interesting." He sighed and tilted his head. "They say vampires are immortal."

"I don't think that's true." Timothée looked down. "There were some really old, sick vampires around Wolfhelm. Maybe if a vampire is eating, sure. But when they're not…"

"They turn into monsters," Vivian said. *They. Me.*

Khalid peered at her. "You don't look any younger than your siblings. Maybe you're aging because your diet has been so poor. Really, this is all so fascinating. If we run some tests—"

"You're not turning her into a science experiment," Marion snarled. "We're curing her."

Khalid straightened his golden jacket, embroidered with silver thread in the design of suns. "Believe it or not, Greywicks, I meant what I said. I swear I'll do everything in my power to help."

There was something in the flicker of his green eyes that made Vivian believe him.

"In fact, my sticky fingers found themselves in the restricted section of the library the other day," he said. "I have a book in my room about the Blood War and Noctis's vampire army. Maybe it can help us."

"Can you bring it here?" Marion asked excitedly.

"I barely pilfered it out of there without getting caught." A smile curved up his face. "But you can come to my room if you want to look."

Marion's haughty retort faded into the background as Vivian retreated into her thoughts. Khalid had lived in the palace during the massacre three years ago. And with the incident last night, that meant he had lived through two horrific vampire attacks. Yet, he wanted to help her. He wasn't afraid.

If Khalid accepted her, why not Darius?

"Sound good, Viv?"

She shook her head. "Huh?"

Marion crossed her arms. "I'm going to go peek at this book. I'll be back in a bit. Don't do anything without me, okay?"

Vivian nodded. Timothée gave a reassuring squeeze as Marion and Khalid turned away.

Taking a deep breath, Vivian shot up. "Khalid?"

"Yeah?" He turned around.

"Do you think Darius would understand? What I am?"

Khalid scratched the back of his head. "Vivian… Darius lost his whole family to vampires. His hatred was the only thing that got him past his grief."

Marion drifted over to Vivian. "Keep your distance from the Prince. There are dangers all around us. Don't tempt fate, Viv." She kissed the top of her head and left the room.

TIMOTHÉE SETTLED DOWN in his bed, and Vivian excused herself to the adjacent washroom.

She stripped out of the new warm cotton dress they'd given her and looked in the mirror: skin pulled tight over protruding ribs, knobby elbows. The word god had been thrown around so many times, but it didn't suit her at all.

Why would a star ever choose me?

A slow trickle of blood slid down her back and onto the floor.

She had felt it, but it was so much worse than she suspected.

Two wounds slashed either side of her shoulders, though no one had ever hurt her there.

No, these wounds were coming from the inside.

Tentatively, she reached up and touched the pus-filled and broken skin. The lesions were yellow and green and purple. Curved bones jutted from the torn flesh. Or maybe it was hard cartilage. She wasn't sure.

Vivian scrambled on the floor until she found the black belt from her new dress and placed the leather strap between her teeth. Bit down. Then stood and braced her hands against the wall.

This was always the hardest part.

Eyes squeezed shut, she gave a muffled scream into the strap.

She had to be quiet. Even her siblings didn't know this monstrous part of her.

She willed the bones or whatever they were back into her body. They were a part of her after all, and she had learned to control this.

Pain lanced down her spine, and her toes curled, and she bit down hard, tasting the leather in her mouth. And then finally—a crack and release, and she straightened, spitting the leather to the floor.

She didn't let herself rest and searched the cabinets until she found a bottle of spirits and a cloth.

Another spasm of pain rippled through her as she poured the liquid over her wounds. She carefully wiped her back as best she could, the wounds already scabbing over. After that, she wiped the blood from the floor with the cloth and tossed it in the bin. Then put her clothes back on piece by piece.

One more day of pretending to be human.

17
IN WHICH MARION TEMPTS TROUBLE

MARION WALKED IN silence beside Khalid. If she was not a pragmatic sort, she might believe she was walking through a dream. How else would she be strolling down a blue velvet lined hallway with painted walls of mythical creatures and massive windows that looked out to a star-swept sky? How else would she be step-in-step with a disarmingly handsome young noble who whistled as he walked?

But Marion was the pragmatic sort. And she knew this was not a dream, but a nightmare. One that told her even if she and her siblings survived the Celestial Rite tomorrow, they would be infected with magic and surrounded by people who would rather see her sister tortured than taught.

"You seem nervous." Khalid looked to her. Smiled. "Am I making you nervous?"

He was always smiling! Of all the loathsome things to do! There was no reason for any one person to smile so much. "I'm not nervous."

Marion's shoulders tensed. Why bother lying? She knew he saw through it. "Fine. A little. About the Celestial Rite tomorrow."

"That's fair. I was a wreck before mine earlier this moon."

Somehow, she couldn't imagine Khalid ever being worried.

He glanced at her through his peripheral. "What are you more afraid of? Burning up or not catching a star at all?"

"Both. And catching one too. Then triple that fear for my siblings."

Khalid ran a hand over a windowsill. Golden dawn light kissed his skin. "I understand. I felt that way about Darius. Though I shouldn't have worried. He was the first one to catch his star the night of our Celestial Rite. It came straight to him as soon as he stepped out onto the meadow. Always a show-off."

There was a sense of both brotherly affection and annoyance in his voice. *It makes you seem a little more human.*

"At your Rite, did anyone," Marion whispered, "burn up?"

"There was one chap. A carriage driver from Wolfhelm." Khalid shivered. "Took all of five seconds for his flesh to sizzle off."

Marion placed a hand on her breast.

Khalid grabbed her hand and led her up a staircase carpeted in gold velvet. The hallways were painted with colorful birds flitting through sunbeams. "You're worried about your sister. That she won't survive the Rite."

Ah, so Khalid didn't know everything about her. On the outside, Vivian may appear the weakest. But if a star only cared about the strength of one's heart, Vivian would be fine. Timothée would be fine.

They weren't cowards like her.

"We're here," Khalid said.

Before them was a set of iridescent pearl double doors, guarded by two golden statues of phoenixes, reminiscent of the one in Archpriestess Kassandra's office. Etched words above the doorway read: *From the Ashes.*

"Welcome to the Morning Star House." Khalid pushed open the doors.

"Really, I don't think I should be in here. I don't have a house or a star or a clue—" Marion cut her words off. Gasped.

It was as if she had stepped out onto a dawn-lit cloud. Soft light drifted through massive floor to ceiling windows, dusting everything in gold. Ethereal paintings of gods and goddesses adorned the ceiling. Marion blinked. There was too much to take in. A massive fireplace blazed with bright orange flame. A rolling ladder leaned against one of the towering bookshelves. On the edge of each bookshelf were glass cases displaying sparkling geodes, crystals, and ancient tomes. Plants hung from the walls, sprawled over the bookshelves, and flourished in pots in every corner.

"This," Khalid said, "is the Nest."

Marion gulped. "I shouldn't be here."

"No one will know. It's dawn. All the good little Starlings are tucked into bed by now."

"Guess we're not good little Starlings."

Marion turned to the voice. Two students dressed in the gold and silver uniform of House Morning Star lounged on a cabriole sofa. A deck of cards was strewn across the coffee table in front of them.

"Looks like we have a visitor," one of the boys said, pushing back his dark brown hair.

"Is that allowed?" the other said, speaking with a thick Medihsan accent.

"Good morning, Hamza. Calcifer." Khalid threw an arm over Marion, an oddly protective gesture. "I won't tell your secrets if you won't tell mine."

He led Marion toward a staircase leading up. Marion gulped, feeling the eyes of the two Morning Star boys on her. Khalid's hand was a reassuring pressure.

They passed by a set of open glass doors leading out to a massive balcony. Marion stopped, eyes drawn to the rising sun, spilling orange light over the veranda. Never had she seen a sunrise like this, so vast, so powerful. Not even in Seagrass. She took a step toward it.

Someone sat cross-legged on the balcony. Her eyes were closed, hands on her knees, face serene.

She blinked her eyes open and let loose a screech.

Marion jumped, but the girl was upon them in an instant, sprinting inside the Nest and rocking back and forth on her heels. Whatever serenity she'd achieved on the balcony appeared to have stayed out there.

"Oh my Three! Khalid, what do you think you're doing? Is that Marion Greywick? Are you Marion Greywick? Stars, you *are*. You're not supposed to be in here! Khalid, she's not supposed to be in here. But you are here! A Lost Star!" She closed her eyes and scrunched up her nose in glee. "This is *so* fun!"

Khalid took a deep breath. "Marion, meet my cousin, Rayna Ang."

Rayna did a perfect curtsey. "It's so nice to meet you! Khalid's a bad influence. Or a good one, depending on if you've got a wild side." She gave an exaggerated wink. "You know what they say. Never trust a Medihsan!"

Marion was at a loss for words. Who were these people, playing cards, meditating? It all seemed so... normal. But they were Starlings. Dangerous.

Though Rayna didn't *look* dangerous. She had short hair, blue as a robin's egg, and searching brown eyes. She wore a short-sleeved yellow shirt, revealing thin brown arms. Marion wondered how she'd stayed warm out on the balcony.

"Thank you, Rayna," Khalid said, voice rough. "I'm taking Marion on a little behind-the-scenes tour so if you excuse us—"

"Is it true you have your Celestial Rite tomorrow?" Rayna walked in step with them. "There's never been more than one held in a single year!"

Marion swallowed in a dry throat. "How did you hear about that?"

"Oh, I've got my ways."

They are cousins, indeed.

Khalid led Marion up another stairwell, his arm still firmly around her shoulders. "I think Marion has enough on her mind right now—"

"My Celestial Rite was amazing," Rayna crooned. "That feeling when you first taste starlight is like coming back to a home you didn't realize you'd forgotten. How would you describe it, Khalid?"

He gave a tight-lipped smile. "I'm unable to put it into words."

"I was a little worried about you, cousin." Rayna grabbed Khalid's arm. "You were wandering the meadow until dawn! I thought you'd never get your star."

"You should know to never underestimate me."

Rayna stopped walking. "I'll let you continue your little tour. Marion Greywick, you're a rule-breaker before you're even a student. I hope this is a trend." With a wave of her hand, Rayna disappeared down the stairwell.

"Look at you." Khalid nudged Marion. "Making friends already."

"I haven't made a single friend beyond my siblings in nineteen years. I don't intend to start now."

Khalid laughed and stopped in front of a mahogany door. "Don't make promises you can't keep. We might just be becoming friends."

He opened the door and pulled her inside.

If this was a dorm room, she could barely imagine the headmistress's suite. She should have expected nothing less after seeing the common area of the Nest. The bed looked ridiculously soft, piled with plush pillows and blankets. There was a stately desk stacked with messy papers, and a bunch of clothes thrown on the floor.

Marion gulped. She certainly shouldn't have been in the Nest. But she *most* certainly shouldn't be in Khalid Ali Bagheeri's room. It felt too personal, seeing his bedsheets a mess, and what might be his knickers on the floor.

"I'm here to look at the book," she told herself out loud.

"I know." He pushed her into the chair by the desk and slammed a massive tome down. A cloud of dust made her cough.

"There was a chapter in here you might want to read about the making of the first vampire." He leaned over her to flip the pages.

She held her breath. He was much too close. Close enough she could smell the citrus on his skin.

"I would start reading from this chapter." His lips were right by her ear. Was he doing it on purpose?

"Thank you, Mr. Ali Bagheeri," she said. "I can take it from here."

He stretched. "Suit yourself."

She needed to concentrate on the book. There was something about Noctis and a sickly Andúrigardian prince, but she couldn't focus on the words. In her peripheral, she saw Khalid shed his golden uniform jacket and strip off the black shirt underneath.

"Must you do that here?" she huffed.

He slipped on a loose white top. "Well, this is *my* room. And it's morning. I'm going to sleep after you leave."

Marion's face flushed. Why did thinking of Khalid slipping into bed make her heat from the tips of her toes to the top of her head?

Khalid gave an exaggerated yawn. "Need any help?"

"No."

"Alright." Khalid collapsed to his mattress.

"Are you always napping?"

"You should try it sometime."

She blew out an annoyed breath. "I have work to do." Like Rhaemyria, who ripped the top off Mount Argos and made it float in the sky, a safe place for Starlings to learn magic after the Blood War.

At least, she thought that was what the page said. It was hard to concentrate.

"You're always saying that, little leech girl."

She was always saying it because it was *true*. And right now, she needed to re-read this paragraph for the fourth time about Rhaemyria and the eruption of Mount Laeto and an ashen forest—

"I mean, there's a chance you might die tomorrow, right? Maybe you should, I don't know, enjoy yourself."

"Shut up."

"Come on! What if you burn to ash? Do you want your last thought to be 'Drat, I really wish I'd read more of that boring ancient text'?"

She spun around in her chair. Khalid was leaning back on his elbows, long body lounged across the bed. His shirt was unabashedly low-cut. "What should I do instead?"

His eyes flashed. "Take a nap."

Marion's chest tightened. He was teasing her... and he wasn't. He was wrong... and he wasn't.

She could die tomorrow.

And Khalid Ali Bagheeri, in all his gorgeousness, was laid out upon the comfiest looking bed she'd ever seen. For this moment, her siblings were safe. She could read the tome when her mind was clearer.

But if her coward's heart was going to burn to ash tomorrow night, shouldn't she at least try to be brave now?

She stood.

Khalid's eyes widened and his smile fell. He hadn't expected her to act on his words. Was it only her then, that had felt the heat between them? Had he just been trying to get a rise out of her this whole time?

What a fool. He was the *ward of Andúrigard*. He'd probably been with a thousand women all more beautiful than the last. They probably had dresses made of spun gold, and smelled of the finest perfumes, and weren't so prickly as the leech girl.

Khalid was sitting up now. For the first time since she'd met him, he looked nervous.

It electrified her.

"What did it for you? My love of napping?" He held her gaze, but his words were jilted. "That's the angle I should have gone for from the st—"

She shoved his legs apart with her knees. Stars, he was handsome, his green eyes like chips of jade, his cheekbones sharp as daggers. She dragged a hand through his black hair. Her fingernails scraped the nape of his neck.

"Is this all I have to do to get you to shut up?" Her voice was husky.

His hands grabbed her thick hips with surprising force. "No promises if you keep that up."

She stared down at him, ran a finger down his long nose. Traced the line of his lips. "I'm not going to fall in love with you, you know."

He nipped at her finger, catching it with his teeth. He pressed his lips over it, as soft and warm as she remembered. "Well," he murmured against her skin, "I can't promise that either."

A raspy laugh escaped her. "You're asking for a lot of trouble, Mr. Ali Bagheeri."

He grabbed her tight against him, hands digging into her hips. "Come on, Marion. I love trouble." Then with a single smooth motion, he flipped her onto the bed. It was as soft as it looked. Suddenly, she was the one trembling and nervous. His smile was lascivious, green eyes roaming over her.

Seen to the bone.

"Besides," his voice was a growl, "no one calls me *Mr. Ali Bagheeri*. What do you think this is, *Ms. Greywick*? High tea?" He gripped her calf. His hands were big and strong, and she marveled at the way they stroked her skin.

"Then what is this, Kh—Kh—"

"Say my name."

She pursed her lips and gave him her best attempt at a sneer. But his hands roamed higher on her legs, stroking over her knees, up her thick thighs, bunching her dress up to her belly, revealing her thin cotton undergarments.

"Say my name, Marion," he ordered. His fingers were long and calloused, a tinkerer's fingers. They wandered over her soft stomach, then one dragged through her golden curls. He collapsed more of his body on top of hers, wedging a leg into the apex of her thighs. Desperate need shot through her chest, and she barely stopped a frantic cry.

His lips whispered over her throat, and she wondered if he felt the fast trembling of her pulse.

She took a ragged breath, struggling to regain the ability to form words. But how could she? He pressed his hardness against her hips and stomach. She needed more of him. Her hands dragged underneath his shirt, feeling the smooth skin of his back.

He gave a dark chuckle. "Did you like that? You can have more. Just say my name. Say it."

She wanted to obey him. She'd get down on her knees and crawl if he asked her to. But her thoughts were fragmented as drops of starlight.

He ground his knee against her, a punishing pleasure against her throbbing wetness. Pulse after pulse of need thrummed through her as Khalid drove his hips against hers. His hardness pressed into her like a delicious promise.

Khalid. That's what he wanted her to say. And she wanted to scream it at the top of her lungs, wanted to hear him moan her name in return. But she could barely catch her breath as his teeth dragged down her throat, dipping lower to her breasts.

The thrum of his hardness against her was too much. She reached down, feeling the shape of him through his pants. He groaned into her skin. Stars, he was rigid and hard as iron, the outline of him long and pressed tight against his straining pants. Her palm worked up and down, urging him as her fingers traced the outline of his hard cock.

It was *marvelous.* She could tell already. There were so many things she needed from this cock—to see it and feel the silken smoothness against her palm, to take him in her mouth and taste him, to feel him erupt inside her—

This was not how things had been with Huxley, a matter-of-fact arrangement. He was soft and gentle and nice and did as she asked.

She had the feeling Khalid would do as she asked, but only if she was on her knees and begging. The thought made her grip his cock through his pants harder. He panted and bucked against her hand.

Khalid's soft mouth licked and kissed over the spillage of her breasts until his teeth found the buttons. He looked up at her with a wicked smile.

With the deft nip of his teeth, he undid the first button. Then the second. Then the third.

With the fourth button unsheathed, her copious breasts sprung out of the dress. Khalid sat up, staring down at her with a look of shock. The cool air sung over her naked chest, pebbling her nipples.

Khalid wiped his disbelieving face then looked up to the sky, touching three fingers to each eyelid.

Marion sat up on her elbows. "Whatever are you doing? Is something wrong?"

He shook his head. "I'm giving thanks to the goddess. I have no idea what I did to deserve *this*," his eyes were trained on her breasts, "but I need to send up a prayer of thanks."

She threw her head back and laughed at his dramatics. Laughter. What a strange idea during this sort of activity.

"Now, if you excuse me," he gave a wolfish grin, "I've got work to do."

He buried his face in the mounds of her breasts. He looked up at her with a delighted glint in his eye. "The work, by the way, is getting you to say my name."

"Won't happen, Mr. Ali—" she began, but her words were stolen as Khalid sucked her breast into his mouth.

Her eyes squeezed shut. It was all she could do to hold on to the soft black strands of his hair as he worked her; mouth sucking and nipping one breast, the other being squeezed and massaged by his long fingers. His other hand he pressed between her legs, stroking the outside of her wet undergarments.

Each press of his hand and flick of his tongue sent waves of pleasure pouring over her. *This* is what she'd read about in the silly books the old women devoured as they were leeched. All this time, she'd thought it was a stupid fantasy. No, it was real with him. This stranger who made the impossible possible.

He pulled his mouth from her breast and stared at her. Stared at her with those green fire eyes. She couldn't breathe beneath his gaze. The way he looked at her, brows knotted together, mouth in a perfect O...

Seen to the bone.

"Marion," he whispered.

And he stroked up her center, fingers circling at the apex of her legs. A rush of fire surged through her body, building and building, a release like a lightning strike within grasp—

Her words found wings. "Khalid!" she cried out. "Khalid, Khalid—"

He moaned at the sound, ravenous and feral. His hand kept circling, urging her release onward, while his other stroked her flushed cheek. "Kiss me."

He lunged for her mouth, his beautiful lips searching for hers.

But Marion twisted her face out of his reach, a mite of sanity finding its way back into her molten mind.

Kissing was for lovers.

His hand stopped stroking her. Her release, simmering through her body like embers ready to spring into flame, began to cool. She grabbed his hand, urging him to continue, but he sat up.

Was that hurt on his face? Because she hadn't kissed him?

She sat up on her elbows. Goosebumps prickled over her breasts and arms without his warm body overtop of her.

Khalid swung off the bed. He turned his back to her and adjusted himself in his pants. Then he walked to the desk and closed the book.

Marion's breath was too fast. She had been so close to experiencing a release unlike anything she had felt before. And she would have reciprocated for him, whatever he wanted. Her hand, her mouth, her whole body—

But when Khalid turned back to her, fingers dragging through his mussed hair, his mask was firmly in place. The nonchalant grin, eyes half-closed like everything was a big joke.

Anger made her cheeks burn. That's probably all this was to him. Teasing the leech girl. He'd go laugh about it with his friends. Then find a better girl to fuck, a girl befitting his station.

Her fingers trembled as she redid her buttons. The memory of his skin against her skin ached like an old wound.

He held out his hand to help her off the bed. She sneered and swatted his hand away.

"Come on now, Mare, don't look so grumpy. I'll walk you back to the sanatorium."

She hated the way he said her nickname, as if they were old friends. She stalked to the door. "No thank you. I'll ask Rayna."

He pushed ahead of her and blocked her path. Black tendrils of hair fell into his eyes, making him look deliciously disheveled. She hated that she loved how mussed he was because of her.

"I was doing you a favor."

"Oh, yes? And what was that?"

He grabbed her chin. It felt like the room was on fire, her skin alight beneath his. "If I had finished what I was doing, you would have fallen in love with me."

Her breath escaped in a rush. "I would—"

"Don't deny it. It's true." His gaze was scorching. "And it wouldn't do for you to fall in love with me, wishing star. So say thank you."

She couldn't help herself. Her chest heaved and her legs went weak beneath her. "Thank you. Khalid."

A muscle in his jaw throbbed. "You're welcome." He dropped her chin and opened the door for her.

She stepped out, took a shuddering breath. Before he closed the door, he said, "But know this. I don't like to leave things half-finished. One day, you'll scream my name so loud, the clouds will weep with starlight. And you'll fall in love with me, Marion. Don't say I didn't warn you."

18
IN WHICH TIMOTHÉE MEETS VAL

IF TIMOTHÉE COMPARED himself to the heroes of all the stories he'd read (which of course he wouldn't, because that would get him laughed at by his sisters), then he was on track with some of his favorite legends. He had the pleasant childhood (lavender farm), the deep sadness (dead father), a fateful encounter with an archenemy (Dark Prophet), and a pathway to destiny (the Celestial Academy). All he needed now was to fall in love and overcome a great evil.

Maybe things were finally looking up for Timothée Greywick.

Timothée and Vivian prepared to sleep in the sanatorium beds. Marion hadn't returned from her escapade with Khalid, and he wondered what was taking so long.

Timothée kissed Vivian on the head and settled into his own soft bed. He'd closed thick curtains over the windows to keep out the approaching light. They'd have to get used to sleeping during the day, like Starlings.

The pale glowing crystals had dimmed as soon as they'd laid down to sleep. As if the room had been waiting for them. He squeezed his eyes shut. He was exhausted, thoughts heavy.

Something slithered into his mind: a whisper, someone's breath brushing the curls from his forehead. He shot up, throwing his hands out, but there was no one there.

Vivian slept peacefully beside him.

He rubbed his ear; he swore he'd heard someone whispering to him. He lay back down, eyes wide on the ceiling.

A cold chill slithered from one end of his mind to the other: *This way.*

The voice was coming from the other side of the door.

"Hello?" Timothée whispered.

The crystal lights on the walls blinked in response.

He carefully looked over at Vivian. If he were to wake her, she'd say he feared being in a new place and tell him to go back to sleep. But he *had* heard something.

He swung his legs over the bed, and Yvaine, who had been sleeping, gave an angry growl and hopped over to Vivian's bed.

"Fine," Timothée whispered. "I'll go alone."

He wore his new light long-sleeve shirt and pants. The sleeves were a little short, and the cuffs of the pants hung over his ankles. He tugged on his new boots, laces undone, and shuffled out the door.

A frigid breeze traveled through the room, strong enough to make him stumble. He swore the breeze carried words: *This way.* Except, there could be no breeze. All the windows were closed.

It was cold without a blanket, and the halls had a silence that hadn't been there earlier. But it was almost dawn, and the Starlings would be asleep. *So, who is whispering?*

Timothée turned corner after corner, looking for any source of the voice. The Academy was built with huge, polished stones, and each hallway was lit by those crystal light fixtures. He past suits of armor holding flags of the Celestial Church and Andúrigard. Regal doors were closed along his path. Some had small scrolls hung outside listing the names of different classes: *History of Thraina, Study of Celestial Bodies, Astronomical Arithmetic.*

This way, this way. Now it felt like the voice was demanding from between his ears. It sounded familiar but he couldn't place who the voice belonged to.

There was something unsettling about the only sound being the echo of his footsteps. *And that voice in my head.*

He came to a huge hallway, one he recognized from earlier when Setviren had ushered them in. It must be one of the main corridors through the school.

Giant portraits covered this hall, all the way to the ceiling. He had to crane his neck to take them in. He wanted to examine them, but the whisper in his mind became more insistent: *This way. This way. This way.* He caught glimpses of the landscapes of Thraina, but most were paintings of the night sky.

He passed by a small alcove. A shadow tremored from within. *There's someone in there.* Timothée slowed his steps, then turned back. *This way,* the voice in his mind hissed.

But he was curious and peered into the shadowy alcove. It was lined with more paintings, and suits of armor, and someone stood at the end staring up at a huge portrait the light didn't reach.

Turn around, the whisper said.

Timothée began to obey the voice, carefully turning around so as not to disturb the figure. But he stepped on his boot lace and stumbled. Reaching out to steady himself, he grabbed onto a suit of armor. It clanged loudly as he crashed to the floor, amidst the steel chest plate and gauntlets. The helmet rolled loudly, very loudly, down the alcove.

The person at the end didn't flinch. *They must have known I was there, even before I made any noise.*

They turned as the helmet clanged its way toward them and stomped their boot down upon it.

A crystal light fixture flared to life, revealing the figure in a fuchsia shimmer. It was a boy, a student... a Starling. He wore the broken parts of a uniform, the dark purple cloak inlaid with silver stars thrown over one shoulder, a grey shirt partly buttoned, dark violet pants rolled up above his pale ankles, and low-cut boots.

"It isn't wise to wander the halls once the sun rises." The boy walked closer to Timothée.

He was beautiful.

Beautiful in the way a lightning storm was beautiful: deadly, striking, enchanting.

His hair was light, rippling with lilac shadows. His eyes were that color as well, as bright as the lavender flowers on their old farm.

And Timothée was sitting in a pile of broken armor, looking like a complete idiot. He felt annoyed about it. "Well, it's hard to sleep when someone's whispering outside my door." He stumbled to his feet, clattering the armor some more. "Was that you? Were you using magic?"

The boy stared at Timothée, the way one would study the most fascinating book. Timothée would gladly lay his pages out to be read. "I was wondering when our paths would cross, Morbris." He spoke his words slowly, in a cunning, distinguished voice, rasping slightly at the edges, like a brittle winter tree. Then he turned from the alcove and started down the hallway.

Morbris? Timothée was pretty sure he didn't even want to know what that meant. "Hey, wait." Timothée trailed after him, his annoyance shifting to curiosity. "Was it you doing starcraft?"

"How could I do starcraft?" The boy laughed darkly and touched something at his neck. A choker, like Carmilla wore.

"Don't tell me you're like all the other first years," the Dark Star boy continued, "saying the castle is haunted." He cast a discerning glance back. "Come on now. I expected more from you, Timothée Greywick."

Timothée stumbled. "How do you—"

"Know your name? All the Celestial Academy knows who you are. Everyone's enthralled with the Lost Stars. Information spreads as fast as light here." The boy turned, hair falling across his face. "We all have stars after all."

Timothée was so struck by him—the bright spark of his eyes, the knife-edge curve of his smile, the effortless elegance in which he

moved—that he couldn't think of anything to say, didn't even realize it *was* his turn to say something.

The boy scrunched his nose. "Hearing ghosts again?"

"You know my name," Timothée said. "What's yours?"

"Valentine Sun." His long, elegant fingers stroked the violet stone on his thick black choker.

Timothée hadn't expected the boy to offer his name so freely. He mouthed the word silently. It sounded as strange as it did familiar.

Valentine.

The whisper in his mind echoed him, the voice the same but different all at once.

Val.

Timothée, startled, grabbed Valentine's wrist. And Timothée didn't think Valentine could look more displeased if he'd seen a big fat rat crawling up his arm.

"I heard the whisper again, Val." He dropped his hand.

"What did you call me?"

"Val."

Crystals flickered along another hallway. Timothée was sure that hall had been dark before. He stepped toward it.

"That way, huh?" Valentine said, mirroring his steps.

"You heard the whisper too?"

"Maybe this school *is* haunted. Stars know I wouldn't be able to go in search of the mystery if I wasn't following behind *the* Timothée Greywick."

The Timothée Greywick. His cheeks burned. For once, he was glad the halls were so dark.

Timothée followed the pulsing crystal lights, and the whispers in his mind dulled to an encouraging murmur.

He wasn't imagining it. Val heard it too.

He gave the boy beside him a quick glance. A Starling. Someone he would take classes with, and eat with in the dining hall, and walk around the grounds with. If Dark Stars were even allowed to do that sort of thing. It would be a shame if they couldn't spend time together because they were in different houses.

"Why do you need me?" Timothée asked.

"You're a Star Child, aren't you?" Val replied. "So you must be brave. Setviren recounted great tales of you three from the events in Wolfhelm."

Did scaring vampires away with glowing skin count as bravery? He certainly hadn't felt brave, flat on his back with the Dark Prophet's sword about to impale him.

Val didn't know that. It didn't sound like he had been among the Starlings who watched the ceremony.

"Well," Timothée said, running a hand through his hair. It fell and flopped over his eyes. "There *were* a lot of vampires there."

"How many?"

"At least fifty. Led by the, y'know," he lowered his voice, "the Dark Prophet."

"Oh, the Dark Prophet." Valentine arched a brow. "I did hear he returned. Everyone assumed the little prince got him years ago. I'd love to hear your firsthand account."

Timothée couldn't remember the last time someone was interested in anything he had to say. Certainly not his sisters, nor the customers at the bakery, or Lingrint, or Jenny Cotswood, or the fake witch from next door. Occasionally Yvaine, but she didn't count because she was a cat.

Valentine seemed genuinely interested. The crystal lights on the wall played off his sharp cheekbones and flashed in the lavender shine of his piercing eyes. The mint and turquoise and pink light painted his pale face and hair in every color.

"Well, Prince Darius was lying defeated on the ground, and my sister was in trouble, and I saved her and," he captured Val's gaze, "the Dark Prophet came after me."

"He did?"

"I knocked him to the ground and—" Timothée lowered his voice, took a step closer, "the Dark Prophet ran away."

"Ran away from you?" Val's eyes widened.

Timothée shrugged. "You could say that." It would be a lie, but you *could* say it. He may have left out a couple details.

"It would be a pity if *I* crossed you, then." Val's voice dropped in a way that made a shiver course through Timothée's body.

They were standing close now, whispering alone in the hallway. Uneven strands of lavender hair fell on either side of Val's face. His hair was cut shorter in the back. It looked soft as it draped across the delicate planes of his cheekbones.

And Timothée realized he hadn't replied. He wasn't sure how much time had passed. It might have been a second or a thousand years.

"Your freckles have a pattern." Valentine's voice was pitched so low Timothée wasn't sure the words were meant for him. "A very distinct part of the night sky."

Even the darkness couldn't hide his red cheeks.

"Why are you awake?" Timothée swallowed in a dry throat. "Don't Starlings usually go to bed around this time?"

"Couldn't sleep," Val said simply, and Timothée sensed there was more behind his words.

"I know what you mean."

Val turned sharply. "Did you hear that?"

Timothée blinked. He hadn't heard anything that time, but he had been... distracted.

Val took off down the twisting hallways until they came to a wooden door with a rounded top and brass handle. Val tore it open. A stone staircase spiraled downward.

Val stepped down a few steps then looked back over his shoulder. "Are you coming?"

Timothée's heart beat painfully in his chest.

"Yes," he said and followed Val into the dark.

19
IN WHICH MARION VISITS THE GLASS CATHEDRAL

THE LAST THING Marion Greywick needed was to lose her brother. But that's exactly what had happened. Rayna had been kind enough to walk her back to the sanatorium, and when she arrived, Vivian was in a state. Her sister had woken up and Timothée was gone.

They'd searched the hallways, the atrium, and even found their way to the dining hall, but no Timothée. Rayna, who had quite a loud voice for such a small person, had ordered Vivian to keep looking inside, Marion to check the cathedral, and she would go alert Loremaster Setviren.

Marion walked the cobblestone path across the bridge and through Selene Crescent. *Check the Glass Cathedral.* She wouldn't put it past her brother to go off exploring, and a massive glass building might be just the thing to excite him.

She and Timothée were both fools. Him for running off, and her for messing around with the ward of Andúrigard. And a *Starling*, nonetheless. Perhaps it was a blessing they had not gone any further than they did. She had denied Khalid a kiss; he had denied her the completion of her pleasure.

She shook her head angrily. Not kissing him had *definitely* been a good idea.

Otherwise, she might have proven him right. She might have fallen in love with him.

Marion took a deep breath of cold air and focused on the task at hand. Walking in the moments of early morning was like walking in the space between worlds. The people on the Isle of Argos were drifting to sleep, tucked away in their dorms. But the rest of the Isle was awakening. Birds fluttered between the trees, frost melted off the flower petals, and the Glass Cathedral glowed.

Marion walked up to the massive crystal structure like one condemned. It loomed before her a thing of immense beauty and immense power. It was strange a structure made almost entirely of glass would exhibit such strength. As if it dared the world to attempt to break it.

The structure was oak and stone, but the walls were made of a mixture of clear and stained glass. Great crystal murals told legends of the gods and mythical beasts. The spire atop the cathedral was a masterpiece of colored glass, sparkling like a crystalized rainbow in the early dawn rays.

Marion's heavy footsteps echoed as she walked up the stairs and stood on the veranda before the doors. Her heart thundered in her chest, too hard and too loud for the peace of daybreak.

Setting her jaw, Marion heaved open the huge doors and entered the cathedral. *You better be in here, you little shit.*

A great weight fell upon her as she walked between the pews. The air was cold, not much warmer than outside. The vastness of the windows made the sky feel like it pressed down upon her. There was something in the echo of her footsteps that made her feel like she wasn't alone.

Like everything that happened within this sacred space was watched from the stars.

If Marion were not so preoccupied with the pounding of her heart, the nausea in her belly, she may have better appreciated the beauty of the cathedral: the ornate designs on the flooring, the crystal pews, the statues that stood guard on the ends of the aisle and shimmered like pearls. But even with her nervousness, she thought the whole thing garish. A cathedral was a place for prayer. Did the gods listen better if you kneeled on a marble floor?

"Timothée?" Marion called. This place was empty, save her and the gods.

A tinkle sounded from the dais at the end of the aisle.

"Hello?" Marion whispered.

From behind the backdrop of gauzy curtains stepped Archpriestess Kassandra.

Marion stopped. Couldn't breathe. She was too beautiful to take in. Beautiful in a way that was painful to look at, disturbing in its perfection. *What is she doing here?*

The Archpriestess walked forward, staff hitting the ground like a third footstep. Little bells and ornaments were sewed over the robes, making her tinkle with each step.

Tinkle, tinkle, tinkle.

"Marion Greywick. I did not expect to see you here. Did you come to pray?" Her voice echoed as if it were coming from many places at once.

Marion knew her manners, instantly couldn't remember them. Managed an awkward curtsey. "I'm, ah, looking for my brother. He wandered off."

"I'm sorry to say he's not here. Do you believe he would come here to seek wisdom from the gods?" Her face remained stoic. "Or forgiveness?"

"Oh, well, uh, Timothée loves the gods, so I thought he might come this way." Marion dug a toe into the floor. "But he's not here, so I won't interrupt you any longer. Goodbye—"

"Come, sweet one. Stand here with me." Kassandra held out her hand.

Oh bother. Marion walked with heavy steps toward the dais. Why had she lied to the Archpriestess about Timothée's love of the gods? Would her execution take place here in private, or would the Archpriestess arrange a spectacle? As Marion stepped beside her, eyes low, the Archpriestess touched her back in greeting. Marion shivered.

"Look here upon the apse. Do you know who that is?" Kassandra gestured to the semicircular vault in the ceiling. The mosaic of a woman made from pieces of colored glass. Her eyes were closed, arms outstretched. Rays of sun radiated from her hands down to a field filled with workers below.

"It's Rhaemyria," Marion managed, voice rusty.

"Yes. She is called the First Phoenix, because like the legendary firebird, from nothingness does greatness emerge." Kassandra smiled, though it did not reach her ice-chip eyes. "She is your mother."

Marion looked down. What was one to say to that? *Oh yes, my mumsy took a few years off the whole parenting thing to lounge around the cosmos.* Best she kept her mouth shut.

Kassandra inhaled. "Daughter of Rhaemyria and Xydrious. Sister to Noctis."

An image flashed in Marion's vision. She cried out, clutching her head. A forest of ashen skeletons. Something thumping in her hand, hot and wet. Screams and pain, oh, the pain in her chest as she clenched that thing in her hands, willing it to cease beating...

"Shush, my darling." Archpriestess Kassandra whirled upon her like a torrent of tinkling bells and white robes. She grabbed Marion's hand with her free one. "Do not let his name spark fear in your heart. Noctis is gone. Forever."

Marion yanked her hand back. "I do not fear Noctis's memory."

The rising sun trickled through the glass walls, causing the Archpriestess's staff to glitter. She stared at Marion with a cold gaze. "You should. The God of Shadows wielded his magic without restraint. You do not know the evil that is Noctis's creations."

Noctis's creations. Vampires.

"I do know that evil," Marion snarled. "That evil killed my father."

Kassandra turned away, bells clattering. "Bram was a dear friend of mine, before his betrayal. I carry fond memories of him. Tell me, dear, if you can. What became of your father?"

20
IN WHICH VIVIAN FINDS HER WINGS

FIND TIMOTHÉE. WELL, that wasn't anything new. Vivian and Marion had spent more than one night in Wolfhelm scouring the streets for their little brother, only to find him in the strangest places. They'd found him buried in books at the library, feeding a family of racoons, and she didn't even want to think about the time at the stables.

And now Timothée had got himself lost at the Celestial Academy for Fallen Stars. Typical. Hopefully, they'd find him smiling and laughing in a peculiar corner, mumbling: "Oh, I couldn't sleep. Just wanted to explore a tad."

The alternative was too terrible to imagine.

Her father's warnings still raged in her mind.

The Celestial Academy is dangerous.

But it was so at odds from what she saw as she walked through the halls. The sun was rising, and pink light filtered through the glass windows and ceilings. The last few students drifted to their dorms. They looked so elegant in their uniforms, edges sparkling

202

with silver thread, and arms full of books and parchment and vials of glowing liquid.

Vivian's chest tightened. It was absurd. How could Archpriestess Kassandra and Loremaster Setviren believe she and her siblings might be like these students, these Starlings?

Marion could be, Timothée could be…

But she? A vampire?

Never.

Vivian tugged Darius's cloak closer, shielding the plain white shift she wore. She must look so foolish walking these halls. She wanted to find Timothée and sprint back to the privacy of the sanatorium.

A door opened, and Vivian startled to a stop. A young woman walked out, arms full of thick tomes. Vivian glanced behind the girl: towering shelves of books. That must be the library.

"Hello?" The girl stopped in front of her. There was a falcon perched on her shoulder, the ends of its wings tipped with blue. "Are you lost? You look lost."

She *was* lost. Soon, Marion would search for both her and Timothée. "I'm trying to find my brother. Is there a boy in there? Tall, freckles on his face, probably staring off into the sky?"

The girl scrunched up her nose. She was pretty, with dark black hair and brown skin. Her eyes widened. "*You're* Vivian Greywick, the Lost Star. I was so mad I didn't get to see you when your balloon landed! I was dealing with a huge headache in the Den. I'm the Evening Star house leader, by the way, which you might think is strange because I'm only a second year. But you can't argue with the votes, can you? Oh, my name's Tafieri. But everyone calls me Taf." She released her hand from the stack of books and held it out. "And this is Minerva."

"Nice to meet you both." Vivian shook Taf's hand and eyed the Falcon warily. "My brother?"

"Follow me." Taf hiked up the books in her arms. "Just need to drop these off at the Den, then I'll help you look for him."

Panic flared in Vivian's mind. "I don't want to trouble you. I know it's late—uh, I mean early, for Starlings."

"Nonsense." Taf let out a big breath, blowing hair out of her eyes. She wore a long blue tunic, the edges trimmed with silver constellations, thick navy leggings, and tall black boots.

Vivian trailed after Taf. They headed up a wide marble staircase, and when Vivian peeked out the window, there was nothing but clouds below. "What's the Den?"

"It's the Evening Star common room. Each house has an area near our dorms where we can relax and study. The Morning Star common room is the Nest, and the Dark Stars…" Taf stopped on the stair landing next to the tall window and pointed outside to a dark tower. That part of the castle didn't have any of the glass windows Vivian was used to seeing. "That's the Cauldron, where the Dark Stars live."

Vivian felt an icy shiver as she stared at the tower, remembering how the Dark Prophet's magic had bound her. Did all of his followers wield shadowcraft or could they have any type of magic?

She didn't know what would be worse come nightfall: no star coming to her, or a dark one.

"Don't be frightened," Taf said, continuing up the stairs. "The Dark Stars can't use their magic; they just practice their weird potions. The professors developed these enchanted chokers. It binds their magic, so they can't accidentally hurt anyone. Or themselves."

The black necklace around Carmilla's throat… It was binding her magic. Her shadowcraft.

Vivian took one last lingering glance at the tower then followed Taf. Eventually, the Evening Star stopped in front of a set of grand double doors. They were a brilliant blue, with silver embossed designs of stars and constellations. The door handles were brilliant white wings. Arched over the top of the doors were the words: *Forged on the Wings of Starlight*

"Wait here." Taf threw them open.

Vivian glimpsed blue hanging lights shaped like geometric stars, a low couch, smelled fresh pine and—the door shut.

She gathered her hair over her shoulder. Students actually lived here, where the walls weren't soggy with rot, where there were endless books to read, where the ceiling didn't leak, and windows didn't frost.

She hadn't thought about how wonderful their home had been in Seagrass, with the crackling fire, and Father's warm turnip stew, and the pile of quilts. They'd only lived in Wolfhelm for three years, but she didn't think she would ever take a dry home for granted again.

The door to the Den swooped open. "Vivian."

Prince Darius Störmberg stood before her. His hair was mussed, and he wore a simple white shirt and loose trousers that were hastily tucked into shiny black boots.

Keep your distance from the Prince, Marion had told her. *There are dangers all around us. Don't tempt fate, Viv.*

But it felt like fate was always putting him in front of her. They were tied together, if by nothing but a blue ribbon.

A blue ribbon that was still around his wrist.

"Taf just informed me Timothée is missing."

The Evening Star girl popped out behind him. "He jumped up from lounging on the sofa the moment he heard who I'd met in the hall."

Darius ran a hand through his hair, smoothing it down. "I, uh…"

"And if you're wondering how I knew exactly who you are," Taf looked Vivian up and down, "it's because our resident royal didn't shut up about you *all* night."

Darius flushed. "I was merely explaining the events of Wolfhelm to my friends."

"If you mean describing the *starlight* color of her eyes, then yes, you did a fantastic job, Your Highness." Taf rolled her eyes and punched him in the arm. "Anyway, there's a crisis because Lando has accused Olivier of spilling paint over his essay, so I'll join your hunt for the missing Greywick as soon as I settle it."

"Oh." Vivian said. "Well, it's okay. Maybe Marion has already found him."

"I'll help you look," Darius said.

Vivian nodded and walked in front of him. As hard as it was, Marion was right. It was best for everyone if she kept her distance from Darius. He'd help her find Timothée, then she'd have to stay away.

21

IN WHICH MARION IS TOLD SHE MUST GUIDE THE GODS HOME

"**W**HAT BECAME OF your father?"

The memory was three years long buried, but with that single question, Marion could feel the cold wet night in Wolfhelm. Smell the rain and the lavender from their cart. Hear her father's voice say her name one last time.

Why had they ever wanted to leave Seagrass? Life in their little village was sweet with lavender and salty with ocean air. There was always a cool breeze, whether summer or winter, and the screech of seabirds rang day and night.

Down the hill from their cabin was the small village. Marion could still hear the cries of Mr. Pierce peddling his fresh-grown cabbages, or see the children running down to the ocean, playing in the foamy waves. There was a little library, market stalls, a woodcutter, and blacksmith. When they were hungry, they ate soft bread from the bakery, or when they needed new clothes, Nanny Zell would make them dresses.

But it hadn't been enough for three wicked triplets.

Father made his living selling lavender in Wolfhelm. He'd take the horse and the cart filled with dried flowers and disappear over the rolling hills to the capital where he'd sell their treasures at the markets.

He never let the triplets come. Said Wolfhelm was smelly. Busy. Dirty. The people were tricksters, scoundrels. Marion would later learn all of this was true. But at that time, sixteen years of age, the triplets had desperately wished to go.

And Marion, being the cleverest, had devised a plan to make it so.

Father prepared for weeks for the market on Unification Day. They canned lavender jam, dried bushels, made oil and sweet perfumes. Father loaded up their biggest cart and hitched the horse.

He was to leave the morning of the festival and stay the night so he could sell in the next day's market as well. His beard tickled their faces as he kissed each of their foreheads. "I'll be back by dusk tomorrow."

But he was never back at all.

As soon as his cart crested the first rolling hill on the road to Wolfhelm, the triplets sprung to action. They'd take the smaller cart, and the old donkey. Everyone said the road led straight to Wolfhelm—how could they get lost? And the city was supposedly huge. They'd stay clear of the market, and Father would never be the wiser. They'd travel back home under the light of the moon, long before Father even left the city.

The plan, hatched among dreamy stories of colorful flags and grand music and sightings of the Prince and Princess, was perfect. Marion had taken care of every detail. Her siblings were so excited. She only wanted them to have a good time.

This was before Marion learned that all good things came with consequences.

She remembered the exhilarated rush of her heart on that ride to Wolfhelm. Timothée lay amongst the canvas cover in the back of the cart, reading the books he'd brought. Marion and Vivian sat up front, their carefully chosen festival outfits hidden under Father's old riding cloaks. They'd curled their hair that morning but wore straw-brimmed hats so as not to draw attention on the road. But it was a baseless fear. An hour outside of Seagrass and the road became crowded with commuters to the festival. And the Greywicks were a giggling, trembling mess of rebellious anticipation.

If this memory wasn't so painful, Marion would relive the joy of that Unification Day forever. The people! The music! The smells! The city of Wolfhelm was alive in a way that Seagrass had never been. And Marion had been unafraid. She delighted in talking to the hostler as they boarded their cart and donkey at the city stable, took flowers from a stranger and offered a curtsey in return, and danced in the streets with wild abandon.

The city was alive, and so was she.

That day, time spread before her as a horizon of possibilities. There was so much to do, to see, to experience, and it all seemed endless. And Timothée and Vivian were so happy.

And Seagrass would be waiting for them when they were ready to go home.

The bright day turned to dusk. They caught a glimpse of the ceremony, of the blue-eyed, blond-haired Prince and Princess, and ate raspberry pie for dinner.

"Think we'll ever come back?" Timothée had asked as he licked red filling off his fingers.

"Of course we will," Marion had insisted. "Now that we know how wrong Father is, we have to."

Vivian nodded enthusiastically. "Maybe we can convince him to take us to market."

"Yes, but we have to do it carefully," Marion said. "I know how Father works. Once we're home safe and sound, we can tell him of our adventure. How everything worked out just fine!"

Dusk turned to night, and the triplets treasured every moment of music and merrymaking. Even as the moon rose high, the party continued.

Timothée sighed deeply as they collected their donkey and cart from the stable. "I wish we didn't have to go."

"Right now the moon is bright," Vivian said. "We don't want to travel the road in darkness."

Marion's throat felt thick with sorrow. She wished she could extend this night forever. "What about one last sugar stick?"

Her siblings looked at each other. Smiled. And they weaved the donkey and cart through the streets to the stall.

That's when the screams began.

At first, the sounds blended in with the laughter and chatter. Then more voices joined the chorus.

And chaos. Chaos. Chaos. The memories of that moment swirled together, a hideous kaleidoscope of panicked faces, whinnying horses, the rush of bodies past her own. With a crack of lightning, the storm came when the sky had been clear moments ago. The only light was the streetlamps, revealing the sheets of rain.

"What's happening?" one of them cried. Which one? Marion couldn't remember. They were all clutching each other, looking this way and that, trying to figure out why everyone was running and screaming.

The smell of blood assaulted her nose. Had she ever smelled blood at that point? Marion couldn't remember. After three years in the leech shoppe, it was familiar as her own skin. But had she known what that thick, coppery smell was at the time?

She did know that the puddles shining in the lamplight now ran red.

A blaze of light appeared on the horizon: the castle on fire. Where were the knights? The guards? Anyone but screaming, fleeing citizens?

And the monsters.

They appeared like moving shadows, drifting through the crowd. Icebergs floating amid a cacophonous sea. Black robes, a glint of white fangs, then a citizen's throat ripped open, blood spurting to the sky. Vampires in the capital.

Marion held back a scream.

"What do we do?" Vivian cried.

There were so many people pushing around them. Bodies fell as black shadows emerged and teeth ripped and tore. Marion looked to their donkey and cart. The old beast bucked, breaking free, and charged through the crowd.

"Let's hide!" Marion cried. "Into the cart!"

The triplets sprinted into the back of their old beat-up cart, threw the canvas cover over themselves. Rain pounded over their heads, fast as their hearts.

Minutes passed as they lay there trembling. Screams and trampling feet sounded outside. Cruel laughter. Marion squeezed her eyes shut and counted the pulse of blood in her veins.

Finally, the sounds dulled.

"Are they gone?" Vivian whispered.

The three moved in unison, peering over the edge of the cart. The rain-slick cobblestone gleamed in the dim light. The streets were empty, and the screams distant.

Then one scream was heard over them all.

Father.

His voice, so familiar in songs and bedtime stories and wise musings on the way of life, was now an anguished cry. Coming from above them.

Marion peered through the murk. Released a scream of her own.

Timothée cut it off with a hand to her mouth, pulling her flush against the cart. The canvas fell off. Marion managed a shaky finger up to the clouds.

A great animal flew through the night: a giant bat. Its membranous wings cut through the storm, long snout like a fox, glinting eyes. And clutched in its feet was Father.

A crash of lightning illuminated the sky. And that single moment became burned in Marion's mind. Her dear father, trapped in the grip of that monster. Blood gushed from her father's body. His dull eyes flashed open, trained on her, and he reached a hand toward them. "Vivian. Marion. Timothée."

The great animal swooped down and dropped their Father behind a building. With a screech, the beast flew toward the castle.

Amidst the heavy rain: silence. Then Vivian said, "I must find Father."

Of course. Of course they had to find Father. They couldn't leave him. He might be dying.

He might be dead.

Father needed them. But Marion's body felt like a frozen river: the inside rushing and raving, the outside unmovable.

Vivian jumped out of the cart. Looked around. Crept a few steps out.

Timothée followed her. "Come on, Mare. We have to find Father."

But Marion couldn't move. She wasn't present within her body anymore but hovered above herself. She could see the mask of panic on her own face, the rhythmic rocking of her body as she clutched her knees to her chest. There were no words, no free will.

Only fear.

Timothée and Vivian looked from one another.

"Stay with her," Vivian said. "I'll be back shortly."

"You can't go alone," Timothée said.

"I must and I will. I am the eldest." Vivian's grey eyes flashed. In that moment, she held such strength that the smallest bead of hope penetrated Marion's fear. *Everything will be alright. Vivian will take care of it.*

So Timothée crawled back in the cart, pulling the canvas over them, and Vivian disappeared into the dark.

Marion would replay this memory hundreds of times over the next three years. So many things had gone wrong. And they were all her fault. She had been the one to convince her siblings to go to the festival in the first place. She'd suggested they stay for one more snack.

And she, the coward that she was, let her sister go off alone into the night.

What a weak heart she had.

Marion had no sense of time, lost in this floating world of fear, but at some point, Timothée had grabbed her face and screamed at her: "Vivian hasn't come back. We have to find her!"

And he had led her stone-stiff body by the hand, like she was a child. Her nice boots splashed in puddles of blood and the rim of her pretty party dress stained red.

And only when they found their sister's body did Marion come back into herself. Changed forever. Just like Vivian.

For what they found was not their sister, but a screeching, scratching animal. And Marion was no longer a doting sister, but a being whose weak heart had instead turned to stone. Her only job: keep her siblings alive.

Because she'd already failed once.

The next hours, days, weeks, were a mosaic of horrors. Tying Vivian with pillaged rope so she would stop lunging at them. Finding a way down to the sewers, and spending days amidst the river of shit and piss, but at least there were no guards. Timothée limping back down to their little hiding spot, face swollen, eyes black, after getting caught trying to steal a bag of apples.

They had nothing but the things they'd brought with them on their cart: Timothée's books. And something odd had happened to their cart, which they at least could have sold for a verdallion or two. When Marion went back to retrieve it the next morning, it was nothing but a pile of driftwood, covered in seaweed.

They hadn't found their father's body that night. And it wasn't until Vivian had regained enough control that she told them what she'd seen. Father's lifeless form in the mud.

Right before the vampires had set upon her.

They made their way out of the sewers, step by step. They found work, a way to keep Vivian herself... mostly. They never returned to Seagrass, for there would be no hiding Vivian's secret from that small of a village. Better to blend in with the chaos of Wolfhelm.

And only in the quiet moments, when she was alone at the back of her leech shoppe, would Marion grieve for Father. For Seagrass. For whom Vivian used to be.

And how she had failed them all.

Now, all she managed to Kassandra was a shrug. "Nothing much to say. He was another victim in the Dark Prophet's massacre."

For the briefest moment, a thousand emotions flashed through Kassandra's pale eyes. Then her face was stoic once again. "You still hold on to this idea of him as father. You cannot accept he stole you from your rightful home."

"My home is Seagrass." Marion's voice was a breath. "And he was the dearest father one could ask for."

Kassandra tinkled down the aisle, morning light illuminating her white-blond hair. "And what did Bram tell you of your mother?"

Bram. That wasn't her father's name. His name was Henry. "My mother died in childbirth. The tragedy of carrying triplets."

Kassandra sighed. "How terrible for you to think of the blessing of your life a tragedy."

Marion never wondered about her mother. Never needed to. Their family always felt so complete with the three of them and Father, and their little home among the lavender. Sometimes Vivian pondered what it'd be like to have a mother plait your hair. So Marion plaited Vivian's hair. Or Timothée would watch the mothers in Seagrass carrying their children on their backs. So Marion would heave Timothée on her back, despite that he was taller than her.

"I've had no need for a mother," Marion said plainly. And because this was the only control she had over the most powerful woman in Thraina, she added, "And I never will."

A cold breeze blew the curtains at the back of the dais, and Marion swore she heard the echo of dark laughter.

Kassandra's lip quivered and a pang of guilt surged up Marion. She'd meant to sting the priestess, but genuine pain filled her features.

"Of course, you don't." The Archpriestess stared at the floor. "Rhaemyria's dream was stolen by that man. My biggest regret is that I lost so many years with you."

Unsure what to say but desperate to escape the silence, Marion asked: "Rhaemyria's dream?"

"Come." Kassandra held out her arm. When Marion approached, she engulfed her, sleeve wide like a wing. The Archpriestess walked them over to the wall, inlaid with a massive stained-glass mural.

Marion knew the image of Rhaemyria and Xydrious instantly. They walked upon a vibrant meadow, each holding the hand of a small child with dark hair. But their gaze was up at the stars, where sat other beings Marion did not recognize. The people in the stars reached down and wept.

"There are many legends of the gods. Some are based in truth. Others are but fanciful tales. Even our dear loremaster doesn't know the whole of them." Kassandra winked, an unnervingly normal gesture. "But I shall tell you the true tale that Rhaemyria has told me, so you may know your mother's wishes."

Mother. Marion shuddered against Kassandra's arm.

"You of course know Rhaemyria was the First Mother, the goddess of creation. She created her consort, Xydrious. From their home in the stars, they made Thraina to their liking. And they made other gods to share the stars with them. And Rhaemyria crafted her most precious creation of all: humans."

Marion stared down at the Archpriestess's robes. Each little ornament sewed upon her gown was different: little yarn dolls amidst the bells. They may have been cute if not stitched by their necks upon her garment. Now as Marion stared, the dress became more of a wasteland, like the aftermath of a battle fought by string soldiers.

"So enthralled was she by the life she had gifted Thraina, she, Xydrious, and several other gods left their home in the stars to walk among their creations. What a joy! On Thraina, the gods learned both the boons and hardships of life.

"But to feel so much for so long is such a burden. After thousands of years upon the earth, the gods grew homesick for the stars. But the problem was..." Kassandra's eyes shone. "They'd spent so long among the humans, they'd forgotten how to go home."

Marion raised a brow. This was a story not told in any liturgy or scripture she knew of.

"And so, Rhaemyria and Xydrious created something no god had ever done before: an earth-born son. Surely, a son of the First Mother and the First Father would wield such power as to guide the gods home."

They walked to the next stained-glass mural. Noctis stood among black flames, Rhaemyria and Xydrious weeping at his feet. "And their son did wield great power. But he was prideful and malcontent. He was jealous of Rhaemyria's love for the humans, so he corrupted them. What a fickle, ungrateful boy."

The windows darkened, shadows replacing sunbeams. Marion rubbed her arms against the chill.

Kassandra approached the mural, reached a hand up to Noctis. "But we know how this story ends. Noctis may have waged his war and corrupted Thraina with his vile creations. Turned Xydrious's mythical beasts to monsters. Destroyed so many of Rhaemyria's beloved humans. But he failed. His mother ripped the star from his breast. The war was over." A single tear ran down her porcelain face. "But how can a mother's heart ever recover?"

Marion scuffed a toe against the ornate floor. Her stomach growled. She wanted to find Timothée, and then some food.

Kassandra dropped her hand, turned, and held Marion's gaze. "Every legend you've heard tells you the gods returned to the sky. That they're the ones sending the starfall. But it's not true, Marion. Without Noctis, the gods could not return. They need someone to lead them."

Marion looked around. *She better not be talking about me.*

"It's you, Marion. It's you who must lead them."

Oh bother.

Kassandra crossed the space between them, gripped the side of her face. "Tomorrow night at your Celestial Rite, we will see for truth if my intuition is correct. You will catch a star, and you will not burn. You will emerge from the ashes, as Rhaemyria once did during the dawning of the world. And when you are strong enough, the gods will show themselves to you."

A great fear settled in Marion's consciousness. *She truly believes.* In all of Thraina, the Archpriestess was second in power to Darius Störmberg alone. Or perhaps even more powerful. And she truly believed Marion would lead her beloved gods to the sky...

Prophecy was a drug; people were addicted to the idea of certainty. And so they would move earth itself to ensure this. Even the Archpriestess was a victim of her faith.

What opportunities could be seized by such radical belief?

Marion blinked her eyes, her thoughts strange to her. She didn't want to exploit Kassandra's ethos. She wanted Vivian to get better, and to go back down to Thraina.

But until they'd figured out Vivian's cure, she'd have to play Kassandra's game. She'd have to catch a star and pray to whatever gods there were that Kassandra was right. She wouldn't burn.

Marion put her hand over Kassandra's. "I'll do whatever I can."

"Bless you." Tears welled in the Archpriestess's eyes.

Marion attempted a warm expression. "I should go find Timothée."

"Yes, I have business in the Academy as well." Kassandra smiled. "Please find your brother. There are things in the castle that are not safe for even godlings."

22

IN WHICH TIMOTHÉE IS SPELLBOUND BY SHADOWS

"ARE YOU SURE this is the way?"

"What?" Val crossed his arms. "Are you the only one allowed to hear things?"

Timothée followed Valentine Sun down the twisting set of stairs. He was pretty sure Setviren would say it was off-limits. But he didn't stop.

Candles dripping hot wax lit these walls instead of crystals, and soon Timothée lost count of how long they'd been walking.

He wanted to say something to Val, to ask about the school, about catching a star, but every time he was about to, he'd catch a look at Val's face, the curve of his full lips, or the brush of candlelight along his hair, and end up swallowing his words.

An urgent whisper shuddered through him, and the candles flickered in response. *This way.* Timothée stumbled and grabbed the wall.

Val whirled. "What?"

"We're going the right way." He smiled. He wasn't entirely sure why he was smiling because following the orders of a ghost—or whatever was calling him—was certainly not the best idea. Especially after his father had warned him about this school.

But he'd never ever done anything adventurous with anyone.

And certainly not with a beautiful Starling.

"Stop smiling." Val got that look again, like a rat was crawling up his arm, but this time the rat was Timothée's face. "We're exploring a *haunted* castle, not heading to the Yuletide Ball."

Timothée ran a hand through his hair. Now he was imagining Yuletide, feasts, and glowing trees, and... a ball?

Timothée barely stifled his smile. His thoughts turned to the ceremony tomorrow. All this time, he'd thought himself stuck as a poor baker boy. That he'd waste his life away in the slums of Wolfhelm, with only his books for adventures. Maybe Marion was right, and it was all nonsense. But it had given him this chance.

To wield magic would be to change his entire life. He'd never be a *nobody*, ignored or loathed by society.

He was going to be a Starling.

Pressure grew the deeper they went, and he felt dizzy with the constant spiral. Acrid moisture seeped down the side of the walls. Moss and dirt now covered the previously clean stone. They must be deep underground now.

Could it still be considered underground if you were floating above the air? Timothée wasn't sure.

"So, how was catching your star?" Timothée asked. "Tomorrow night—"

"Stop." Val held out his arm. Timothée stumbled into him.

He heard it: not whispers, but the clicking rhythm of steps. Then a different light bloomed along the walls behind them.

"Someone's coming," Val said.

"What do we—"

"Leave it to me." He slammed Timothée against the stone wall. White specks sparkled in his vision.

Val lifted one hand to the black choker around his neck. His fingers danced over the gem. It loosened and fell into his palm. He closed his eyes and tucked the choker into his pocket.

Timothée withheld a gasp. *I don't think he's supposed to do that.*

The rhythm of steps grew louder. He knew he shouldn't be down here. What if it was Setviren, and he sent him all the way back to Wolfhelm?

"Val—" Timothée hated the wavering in his voice.

Val's hand clasped over his mouth; the light ends of his hair brushed Timothée's shoulder. "Try not to scream."

Why would I...

Dark shadows spooled at Val's feet and wrapped around their legs. Timothée made a sound, muffled against Val's hand. This boy, this Dark Star...

It was all true. Dark Stars did have the power of Noctis.

The light on the walls grew brighter, the clicks of the steps louder. Shadows wrapped around their bodies.

Timothée felt the shadows and didn't feel them. It was like the brink of cold at winter and the ever-pressing heat under the Red Corn Moon.

The hard stone grated against his back. Val's chest pressed so hard into Timothée he thought his ribs might crack. Val was shorter than him, so Timothée's mouth was in line with his forehead.

Val's fingers curled on the stone wall, and he swept his gaze up, so now their faces—

Timothée swallowed.

"Don't breathe," Val hissed.

Timothée was going to pass out.

Shadows covered them entirely. The candlelight grew brighter and brighter until Archpriestess Kassandra came into view, long robes trailing, gravastarium staff held tight in her hands. Her beautiful face was fraught with worry and the tiny bells and ornaments sewn into her clothes jingled as she walked down the steps.

This hallway was too narrow. Even shrouded in Val's shadows, she would certainly see them. Val locked eyes with Timothée. The shadows wavered, pulsing along his edges. His brows knit in concentration—and the Archpriestess passed through them and continued down the stairs.

Timothée's heart flipped in his chest. She hadn't just passed around them. She'd passed *through* them.

He didn't move after one breath, or two, or three, and he thought he'd stay like that forever with Val's chest pressed against his own, both boys cloaked in darkness.

Then the shadows dripped off him with the consistency of water that didn't leave him wet.

Val didn't back up.

This was so different from dusty bakery storerooms or moldy attics. The energy between them was a living thing. Was this the spark all his stories had talked about? Because, by the Three, it felt like the air might explode if he took another breath.

A hot rush of desire pooled through him as Val breathed against his neck. So new. So different. It was immediate, demanding, *urgent*. He remembered how long it had taken with Lingrint, with Jenny, the others. But now—

He bit his lip. Being this close to Val was deliciously uncomfortable. Timothée shifted slightly, felt something against his thigh, then Val tilted his face up.

A rush of ecstasy flooded through Timothée. Maybe, maybe, this beautiful, enchanting boy wanted him. Timothée took a shallow breath. Their faces were so close that wavy strands of Timothée's brown hair fell across Val's forehead.

Timothée shuddered and closed his eyes, trying to gain some focus. But it was worse. His other senses were heightened. The scent of pomegranate, the twinkling linger of magic in the air. He sensed with sharpened clarity every place their bodies touched, the crushing pressure of Val's chest, the sharp bones of his hips, the intoxicating hard shape of him pressed against Timothée's leg.

Their breath was an uneven cadence, the only sound in the cold stairwell.

He flicked his eyes open. Val studied him with a calculating gaze. Timothée stared at Val's lips, so full on his delicate face. He wanted to grab him, to spin him around and push him against the wall and kiss him until they were both dizzy with it.

But that was something only good kissers did.

Val pushed him away and stumbled down a few stairs. His face was frozen in a snarl. Like he was furious. But it was so quick, the blink of a star, that Timothée almost thought he imagined it.

What just happened? "So you're a—"

"Indeed I am." Val reached into his pocket, pulled out the black choker and slipped it on. "Let's get this over with."

"But Archpriestess Kassandra went down there."

"Are you afraid?" Val smirked

Yes, but Timothée trailed after him anyway. Val's shadows had disappeared, but it still felt like a cloud hung over him. *What did I do wrong this time?*

Down and down they went until finally the stairs opened to a dark hallway, filled with crumbling stone. It smelled like earth and something foul Timothée couldn't quite place.

"I think we're getting close," Timothée said.

There was a fork ahead: to the left was a small metal door. To the right, the hall continued into darkness.

"This way." Val headed toward the door.

Timothée stood still at the fork, eyes trained into the darkness of the path to the right. *This way.* A slight breeze lifted his long curls. "Wait. I think it's—"

"I heard something from in here." Val opened the metal door. "After you."

Timothée shrugged and went in. They could always explore the hall after. It would make their adventure last longer. He wanted to ask Val about magic. He knew it was rare to catch a Dark Star. He had so many questions. He'd follow this boy anywhere.

The first thing he noticed when he entered the room was the smell: a reeking, heavy musk, like rotten eggs. There was a circular walkway around a pit filled with—

The door slammed shut, and the light went out.

Something terrible stuttered in Timothée's heart.

No. Please.

He took a breath, gagged. The putrid air was thick as soup. "Val?"

From the other side of the door, Val spat: "Just because you glow, it doesn't make you powerful. Or chosen. Or important to anything... or anyone." His voice was muffled through the door, but Timothée heard the venom behind his words. "You don't know what some of us have given up to be here. And you waltz in and claim the castle is talking to you?"

"Val, I didn't—" Timothée stuttered against the door.

"That's not my name," he snarled. "Have a good day, Greywick. Let's see if shining bright can help you out of this one."

"Val?"

No answer. Timothée pressed his hands against the cold metal handle and pulled.

The door was locked.

He wasn't surprised.

"Valentine," he said again, but his voice didn't carry, and it didn't matter if it had. The Starling had left.

What had he done? Why was it always like this? And damn the Three, why did it smell so bloody bad in here?

He was shaking, and he clasped his elbows to stop the frantic movement. *Damn, damn, damn.* He realized he was crying and roughly wiped his face with his sleeve until his eyes burned.

He slammed his fist against the door. Then slid down.

And waited alone in the dark.

23

IN WHICH VIVIAN PRETENDS
SHE CAN FLY

"THIS WAY." DARIUS pulled open a huge white wood door, and Vivian blinked as wind blew back her hair. "Come on."

She followed Darius out onto the grounds of the school.

"Wow." They had landed underneath the stars, when everything had been silhouetted in deep blues and the crisp white lines of moonlight. But now the Isle of Argos was painted in color. Pink splashed over the faraway fields, and the Glass Cathedral reflected puffy orange clouds. A small village was filled with brightly painted houses.

"That's Selene Crescent," Darius explained, following her gaze. "There are shoppes and a tavern. It's where we spend most of our nights off. The merchants live in homes at the end of it. But everything's closed now."

"I don't think Timothée would come here alone."

"There's a walkway around the whole school. Perhaps he wanted to have a view?"

"We might as well check," Vivian said absently as she followed him. But her mind was still stuck on the view, unable to take it all in. This isle was a whole other world.

A world her father, or the man who had called himself such, had once lived in. It had to be true. Setviren had crafted a perfect likeness of a man three years long dead.

They walked over a bridge that led outside of the circular wall around the school. A path led around the bottom of the school's wall, cresting the edge of the Isle. Only a stone railing the height of her hip lay between her and the clouds.

She stumbled to a stop, the crisp morning air sticking in her throat as she sharply inhaled.

Darius turned to her, but there was no judgment on his handsome face. "I found it quite unsettling at first. Sometimes I still do. Within the castle walls, it's easy to forget we're on a floating island."

But Vivian wasn't afraid. There was a humming in her blood as if she had seen this view before and merely forgotten. She felt as if she could reach out and scoop the clouds in her hands, taste the mist of them on her tongue.

She stepped closer to the edge, peered over: a sharp brown cliff face that tapered into nothingness. The clouds were so thick, they hid the world below.

"How is it even possible we're floating?" Vivian asked, voice full of wonder. "Can starcraft be that powerful?"

"The Celestial Church says Rhaemyria raised this Isle into the air over three hundred years ago."

Something flashed through her mind: it almost sounded like a laugh, or perhaps it was just the wind breaking against the side of the school.

"Come on." Darius held out his hand.

Keep your distance from the Prince. Marion's words echoed in her mind. She ran her fingers over the flat top of the railing. It was wider than her hand. "I'm not afraid."

A whole island that flew from the power of a god.

Because of me. A sharp voice rang in her ear, and it sounded familiar and new all at once. She shook her head, looked down the cobblestone path. Both the walkway and railing were flecked with colored gems.

Darius cast a look over his shoulder at her. Wind rustled his golden hair and splashed his cheeks pink. "What are you thinking, Vivian?"

"I was wondering if my father... if Bram Cavald ever walked this path." The name felt wrong on her tongue.

Darius slowed his steps to walk beside her. "We can look for information about him, see what he was like. I'm sure some professors knew him. They've all worked here for generations."

Generations, of course. Starlings with enough magic aged so slowly they could almost be called immortal. And to be a professor at the Celestial Academy, one must be very powerful.

How old was her father then? They'd celebrated his forty-fifth birthday several weeks before the massacre in Wolfhelm. But could that have been a lie too, like his past?

She took a deep breath. There were answers here. Maybe one of the professors knew why Bram had stolen the Greywicks away.

"We don't have to talk about it," Darius said, noting her silence.

"No, I..." She slowed, put both hands on the flat top of the railing and looked out at the horizon. "My father was a farmer. We bought our food from the local market. He tilled the soil and came home every day with dirt on his face. I can't imagine him being a professor. Being a Starling."

Darius leaned over the railing beside her, resting on his forearms. "I was six the first time I wandered into my father's war tent. I remember looking for him and not recognizing the man who stood before me. I'd only ever known him as the father who put Celeste and I on his shoulders and ran around singing ballads of my favorite heroes. But the man I came to know during the Trinity War... He was a ruthless warrior, a cunning tactician, and a king who would go to any lengths for Andúrigard."

Darius's gaze was faraway, the storm clouds swirling in his blue eyes. She wanted to reach out and clasp his hands, but instead knotted hers together. "We lived such different childhoods," she said, "you and I."

"In some ways," Darius said. "But from what I gather, even if your father was wrong in taking you, he gave you a childhood of love. Same as my own."

Vivian looked down. Was he wrong for taking them? She had so many questions about her father but did not know if she had the heart for the truth. "Tell me more of your father."

"He was proud and stern. He let nothing get between him and what was right. He overturned the ancient laws when he married my mother. She was a commoner, a flower seller in the Wolfhelm market. But when he met her, he knew she was a queen, his queen..."

Vivian glanced over at him, but he wasn't looking at her, his cheeks bright red from the cold.

"But, ah, my father... That was just one of the many ways he fought. He said the only way forward was together. My father believed the only path toward peace was uniting the three realms of Thraina. And he fought for that with blood and honor in the Trinity War."

"And you believe that too?"

"I do. We're stronger together. Think how you and your siblings held hands in the square. Not even the vampires could stand against you. And my father was brilliant. He raised Carmilla and Khalid as his own. I am closer to them than any blood family I have left. They will return to Medihsa and Kirrintsova, knowing as I do, that if we want a peaceful united land, we must stand together."

Did Khalid and Carmilla feel the same as Darius? They would return to their homes eventually, but would rule as figureheads, while the courts of Andúrigard truly reigned.

"You are right, Darius. Perhaps our childhoods are similar. We both had the love of our father, and we both lost him. Lost in the same night."

Darius straightened, ran a hand through his hair. "My father survived the war only to be killed in his bed chambers by an assassin."

"The Dark Prophet."

"Yes. I thought I killed the monster that night, but he survived."

"Do you think he's really the vampire of legend, the one that served Noctis?"

"Those are ancient myths. The Dark Prophet's probably just a fantastical zealot. As much as I hate to admit it, he is powerful. But he will die upon my blade with all the monsters in his service. And I will avenge both our fathers."

She wondered how he had gotten so far away.

A crisp wind blew in, clouds of fog circling around their feet. He rolled his shoulders. "We should keep looking."

Vivian lagged behind him, his words tumbling over in her head. She hadn't just lost her father that night. She'd lost something else, the human part of her.

Perhaps this place could help her find it again.

The walkway curved around the entire castle. Every so often, they walked beneath great shadows, where balconies and towers spilled out from the Academy above.

"I don't think Timothée came this way," Darius said.

"No." Vivian absently ran her hand along the stone railing. Hopefully Marion had found him by now. How far could he have gotten anyway?

"I suppose we should check in with your sister."

"One moment more." Vivian turned to look out at the sun-splashed sky. "I like it here, but I feel like I shouldn't like anything to do with this place. Marion says we must remember what Father told us. He was frightened of this school. But I..." Darius came up behind her. "She probably wouldn't like me telling you that."

"You can tell me anything, Vivian."

I wish that were true.

He delicately touched her arm. She wanted to lean back into his warmth. She ducked away, continued along the path.

His brows creased. "What are you thinking?"

"Marion was saying it's probably not the best idea for us to spend so much time together." She turned. "I mean, you might not want to spend time with me. My siblings and I... We're already such an oddity. Everyone is always looking at us, talking about us. If I'm with you, everyone will talk even more."

She trailed off. Her words made little sense, just a jumbled web of fear.

"Marion has always looked out for us. We lived such a simple, safe life. Now everyone thinks we're the children of the gods. And if you and I... I know I kissed you, and I can't presume... Oh, I probably shouldn't have done that and—"

Vivian let her rambling words fall away, realized her fingers were touching her lips. Darius was leaning on the stone wall of the castle, hands in his pockets, considering her.

She threw her hands out to the side. "That's it."

He rose a brow, quirked a half-smile.

"What?"

"I'm certainly hearing a lot about what Marion thinks." Darius stepped toward her. "But I don't want to know what Marion thinks. I want to know what you think."

"I..."

He stopped in front of her, chin dipped low.

She could lie, tell him she believed everything Marion said. But there was already such a lie between them, and it took up so much space, there wasn't room for any others.

"Darius, I think..." Her words trembled. "I think about you every time I close my eyes, and I can see your face in perfect clarity. The sound of your voice echoes in my mind. And I think if I cannot feel your touch, the ache of it will consume me."

The words tumbled with the morning wind, and she knew she could not take them back. But she didn't want to.

Even if they were a betrayal to Marion.

A betrayal to her father's memory.

Because she knew, if she survived the night, this was not something to run away from.

Slowly, he bent his forehead to hers. "Since the massacre, I have not felt at home at the castle in Andúrigard." His words were low and rough. "I thought perhaps the Academy would be different, but it's all so new. There has only been one time I've had the feeling of home in the last three years."

She gently ran her fingers along the sharp angle of his jaw.

He smiled, lips curving under her fingers. "Talking to you in that candle shoppe was the first time I felt like myself in so long."

"I know."

"And, just so you're aware," he leaned down, "the memory of your kiss has haunted my every waking moment since."

"Darius."

"But," he stepped back, "if it would displease your sister, I can keep my distance."

She studied the rueful expression on his face. She knew he would leave if she asked it of him, but there were things even she was not strong enough to do.

Vivian looked over the edge of the railing, at the clouds soft as pillows. She turned back, hair flying across her face. "I'm sure Marion won't object if you kept close for my safety."

He smirked. "What do you mean?"

How long had it been since she had teased someone, had them smile at her? No matter what she did, Marion and Timothée always treated her like a sick girl, fragile as glass.

But with Darius she was who she wished she could be.

She braced her hands, then lifted into a sitting position on the railing ledge.

"Vivian!" Darius lurched forward. "Be careful."

"I am being careful." She smiled back at him. "You're here."

Darius let out a long breath, then realized the placement of his hands: one wrapped around her back, the other gripped on her arm. "Very clever, Ms. Greywick."

"Don't let go," she whispered, and stretched out her hand behind her, as if she could touch the clouds beneath.

"Never."

She parted her legs, as he stepped closer between them. "But this does have me worried."

"Don't be." She leaned back even further. "If I fall, I'll just fly."

He was bent over her now, arm braced around her back, chest flush against hers. She crossed her ankles around his back and knew if she were to fall, he'd fall with her.

The clouds swirled around them, and for a moment she imagined careening through the air, the beat of wings, the whinny of a horse...

Darius straightened, pulling her up with him. "I'm sure you could. But I'd be remiss to see you part so soon."

"Darius."

"Yes?"

Every choice she'd made since meeting him had taken her on a dangerous path. But it had taken her here, and for whatever reason, this was where she was supposed to be.

Even if it was only for one day, and one night, before the starfall.

"I think," she lightly brushed her fingers on the base of his neck, "I think you should kiss me."

The words barely left her before he pressed his lips against hers. She dragged her hands up the back of his neck and tangled them in his hair.

Her mouth tingled, and she knew her fangs wanted to drop, but urged the sensation away. *Not now.*

Darius pulled her closer, and she skid along the top of the railing until their bodies were flush. Her skirt rose over her ankles, and her legs wrapped tighter around his hips. His lips trailed to her jaw, and she gasped as desire swelled within her.

Vivian skated her hands down his shoulders, then pulled back, gooseflesh scattered across his forearm. He was wearing only a thin cotton shirt. "You must be freezing."

"I'm fine." There was a low rasp to his words. "I forgot to grab a cloak."

"It's because I'm wearing yours." She started unclasping the buttons.

He covered her hands with his. "And it shall remain on you."

She followed his gaze down to her dress, now showing through the open cloak. Only a slim white shift. She realized how exposed she was, the angles of her body clearly visible underneath the fabric.

His quickening pulse thrummed in her ears. She delicately touched the tips of his fingers with her own, then led his hand to the column of her neck. The edges of his palm skimmed the lace of her dress.

"You said you ached for me to touch you," he said lowly. "Touch you where?"

Dark waves of hair fell over her shoulder as she tilted her head. "Everywhere."

His jaw clenched, and the muscles in his neck moved as he swallowed. He kept one hand firmly on her back, as if he thought she might tumble right off the isle. But with the other, he slowly drew it over her chest, gliding over her breast.

She made a small sound in the back of her throat. With his thumb, he circled around one of her nipples, the fabric sliding against her skin.

She dug her fingers into his hair, pulling herself closer. "What if someone sees us?"

Darius dragged his hand back up to her exposed collarbone. "There's no one around. It's just you, me, and the sky."

Vivian let her lips drop to kiss the hollow of his throat. He smelled of pine and cold air. Her mouth tingled; she willed the feeling away.

"May I?" His fingers hovered over the buttons of her dress.

"Yes."

Delicately, he undid the first few buttons. A sharp burst of cold rippled through her, but it was quickly replaced by the warmth of his hand slipping underneath her dress. He cupped one of her breasts, thumb skimming over the point of her nipple. She arched into the touch.

He repeated the action on the other side; her body grew tight and tense, heat building between her legs. "Darius…"

"How does this feel, darling?"

He squeezed her again, fingers firmly kneading into the soft flesh. She murmured incomprehensively into his shoulder.

His nose nudged the hair away from her ear. "Vivian?"

"It feels good. Anything with you feels good."

He gave her a soft smile, continuing to touch her. He pinched her nipple between a forefinger and thumb, pulled lightly.

She gasped, digging her fingers into his back.

"Like that?" He raised a brow. "Tell me what else you like."

Her gaze dropped. "I-I don't know. I've never kissed anyone besides you or done anything like this."

He pulled back slightly but did not take his hands off her. "Well then, we'll have to discover that together."

The thought sent a wild thrill through her, body sparking at the idea. He dropped his hand from her breast, let it trail over her stomach, down her leg to where the hem of her dress had risen. "But that means, Vivian, you'll have to let me know what you like, what you want..."

He slipped his hand under the fabric, his touch warm on her leg as he slowly moved higher.

Her whole body shivered with anticipation. "What does the Prince of Andúrigard like?" She pulled closer, legs wrapped tight, sliding to the edge of the railing. Then she felt...

She felt the long hard length of him through the thin lining of his pants. Felt it press between her legs.

He laughed softly, face flushing. "As you can tell, I like you. Everything about you."

She squeezed her eyes shut, rocking her body against his. "I like the feel of you."

And she did, she did, she did. A wave of desire coursed through her, hot and heady. His heartbeat was so loud.

"Vivian..."

The shape of him pressed against the sensitive skin between her legs, all the nerves sparked alert. The points of her breasts rubbed against the cotton of his shirt.

His hands caressed down to the base of her spine, pressing her against him. His other hand gripped tight on her thigh.

And that's when her fangs dropped. She gasped and quickly pulled him close, his face tucked into the crook of her neck, so he couldn't see.

She breathed in through her mouth so she wouldn't smell him. Squeezed her eyes shut. She had to get out of here. Marion was right.

Gently, Darius drew his hand from her legs to graze her back. "Is everything okay?"

"I—" she whispered, the teeth uncomfortable in her mouth.

Darius pulled away and helped her do up her buttons. She watched him with a close-lipped expression. Then he kissed her forehead. "We don't have to move too fast. I seem to lose all control whenever you're around."

Not in the way I do.

A screech sounded on the wind, and Vivian startled, lurching into Darius's arms. A falcon hovered in the air above them, a falcon with blue-tipped wings.

"Minerva," Darius murmured.

"Taf's falcon."

It shrieked again, loud and long, as Taf turned the corner. Minerva flew down and landed on her shoulder. "There you are," she said. "I thought we had two missing Greywicks on our hands."

Darius sheepishly ran his hand through his hair. "We thought Timothée might come down here."

"Mm-hmm." Taf raised a brow. "Setviren found your brother. He'd locked himself in the sewer."

Vivian took a deep breath of morning air. With Darius further away from her, she could force the fangs away. The same feeling as cracking knuckles or rolling stiff shoulders. "How did he manage that?"

"No idea. It locks from the outside so..." Taf shrugged. "Bet Khalid would know. He seems to know everything around here."

Taf started to walk back to the Academy.

Darius twined their fingers together as they walked back to the castle.

And all the burning heat in her body settled to an unfamiliar warmth around her heart.

A heart which only beat from leech blood.

24
IN WHICH TIMOTHÉE LEARNS
OF A DARK LEGACY

AFTER ABOUT AN hour of being trapped alone—there was no way to tell time in the dark—Timothée realized Val had never heard the whispers at all. Everything had been a scheme to lock him in here. He had been such an easy target, the new kid who knew nothing about the Academy.

But what had he done to make Valentine Sun hate him? His mind raced with a thousand possibilities. Because of everyone proclaiming him and his sisters the Lost Stars of Thraina? Because he was some idiot kid wandering the halls? It must have been his imagination feeling Val's racing heart, their bodies pressing together like two shattered edges fitting into place.

In the end, it didn't matter. Timothée knew why. It was just who he was, who he had been his whole life.

He didn't dare walk further into the room, not with the ledge he'd glimpsed earlier.

After about two hours, light poured in from high above and something sloshed down in front of him, slopping into the gaping middle hole.

And that's when Timothée realized he was locked in the waste pit.

There was really nothing for it. The next time it opened, he yelled up for help. It took three more times before someone heard him.

"We've been searching everywhere for you!" Setviren said when he unlocked the door. He was wearing silky green pajamas and a long night cap. "However did you find your way down here?"

I was tricked by an evil Starling, he thought but instead mumbled, "I got lost looking for the lavatory."

"You certainly found a part of it." Setviren wrinkled his nose. "Of all the places for a child of the stars to end up!"

The walk back to the sanatorium was awful. Daylight streamed through the windows. The Starling students should have all been asleep, but someone must have told them the new kid was covered in shit and had to be rescued by the loremaster. *Valentine, no doubt.*

By the time Setviren led Timothée through the main building, the halls were crowded with blurry-eyed students wearing nightrobes and pajamas. A crowd gathered, following him with stares and whispers. And not the wondrous kind he and his sisters had received yesterday.

The students covered their mouths and wrinkled their noses.

No wonder. He spelled like a pit.

So much for a good first impression.

Timothée shuffled behind the loremaster, despite being taller than the older man, and looked down at his untied boots. They walked past the alcove where he'd first seen Valentine, standing before the painting.

He felt drawn to approach.

He hadn't looked at the painting before, not really. But he stood in front of it now. Something clutched at his heart. The painting was of a battlefield littered with blood-laced bodies. Standing upon a mountain of dead, with a cape of shadows and black armor, was a god.

Heart racing, Timothée tracked his gaze down to the bottom of the portrait where the gold title card lay: *The Battle of Silverdrop Valley, Noctis, God of Shadows.*

"Noctis." The name was heavy on his tongue.

"Oh, Three above," a trembling voice said and Setviren scuttled behind him. "Whatever are you doing?"

When Noctis fell, it wasn't only his life that was destroyed. It was anyone who had or ever would swallow a Dark Star. People like Val, who were forced to bind their magic. "What... What did Noctis do?"

Timothée wasn't sure how one could fear a portrait, but Setviren shook as he stepped toward it. "I suppose you should know the truth."

"The truth," Timothée echoed.

Setviren touched his palm to the oil painting, and it began to move.

"Starcraft," Timothée said. "But it's daytime."

"Powerful Starling enchantments can last beyond the night." Setviren made a sound in the back of his throat. "A rather impressive lesser god gifted this portrait to Rhaemyria to memorialize the dark legacy of her son and the righteous but brutal choice she had to make."

The portrait shifted in front of him: swirls of dark magic forming an ancient castle. There was something familiar about it. "Is that Wolfhelm?"

"Wolfhelm Castle, yes, from an age ago," the loremaster said. "Noctis stole the young Störmberg prince and created the first vampire."

The image changed to a brilliant glowing silhouette backed by wings of fire. "Rhaemyria bid her son destroy his monstrous aberration. Not only did he refuse; he created an army of them. Noctis and his acolytes spread ruin across Thraina. It wasn't just the humans he corrupted, but Xydrious's mythical beasts."

A great creature with the wings of a hawk and the body of a lion flew across the portrait. Shadows spiked through its body, devouring it until it was nothing but a beastly version of itself with glowing purple eyes. One after another, more mythical creatures appeared: a winged horse, a giant snake, a dragon of sparkling scales.

Each suffered the same fate.

"Such beautiful creatures used to roam the world." Setviren wiped his eyes with his sleeve. "All of them corrupted. Rhaemyria had no choice but to make it so Noctis could not take them and use them against the fight for our celestial souls."

Shadows swirled in the oil, and an army marched in front of a mountain, running red with lava. They opened their fanged mouths in triumphant snarls. Among them marched the mythical creatures, all writhing with shadows. Above flew a glittering black dragon. At the head of the army was a figure garbed in a cape of shadow and a black helmet that covered his face. Noctis. Another figure stood beside him, one Timothée recognized.

"The Dark Prophet," Timothée said.

Setviren let out a huff of indignation. "That fool from the square? Nothing but an imposter. Xydrious killed the Prophet of Stars—the first vampire—at the end of the Blood War."

A powerful figure burst into the image, silver and blue armor riding a horse with starlit wings.

"And Noctis..." Timothée said in a dry throat. "What became of him?"

"To protect Thraina and her people, the great goddess Rhaemyria had to make a terrible sacrifice."

A cold shiver ran up Timothée's spine. It felt like he was there among the burning rocks, smoke hot in his nose. Two silhouettes faced each other in the painting, one dark, one light. Rhaemyria and Noctis. Rhaemyria struck him through the chest, and when she pulled back her hand, she held a swirling purple ball of light.

"Rhaemyria was forced to strike down her own son, to rip the star from his chest. And then she cleansed Thraina in a great fire so the people might once again know peace."

The shadow form of Noctis dissipated.

"Afterward, she tore the top off of Mount Argos and rose this isle to the sky. She created the Celestial Academy for Fallen Stars, entrusting it to Archpriestess Kassandra. It became forbidden to catch a star without the protection of the Academy and the Church."

Was that what the choker around Carmilla and Val's neck was? Protection?

Setviren moved to place a hand on Timothée's shoulder but wrinkled his nose and stuck it in the pocket of his robes instead. "You will learn this and more of the history of Thraina. Your father kept many things from you that must be righted."

"You mean Professor Bram Cavald?"

"Quite right, yes." Setviren's face paled, then he said, "Let's get you back and sorted, hmm? Your sisters are probably worried sick."

"Right," Timothée said. But he hesitated, looking deep into the painting. It was the same as it had been in the beginning, Noctis in black armor, standing on a pile of bodies.

But this time, he wasn't wearing a helmet.

Timothée knew that face: the dark brown hair, the curve of his mouth, the grey eyes. Timothée knew that face because it was *his* face. It very well could have been a portrait of him.

Is this why everyone always avoids me? Is this who I am on the inside?

This terrible destiny around him—there was no going back. Marion could say they weren't the star children. She could say their glowing was a coincidence. But she was wrong.

This was who he was. Who they were.

Noctis was their brother.

It was no wonder the Dark Prophet had called him that name. Timothée looked exactly like the fallen God of Shadows.

25

IN WHICH MARION MASQUERADES AS A STARLING

IT WAS THE dusk before the Celestial Rite, and the Greywicks were at a party.

The closest Marion had ever been to a party, that is.

Selene Crescent, the small village on the Isle, was filled with Starling students in gold and blue uniforms. Food stalls handed out drinks and sweets, and a band played delightful music that filled the air.

All to celebrate the night the Lost Stars would claim their magic. Or burn to ash.

The triplets stood awkwardly in the middle of the courtyard. Timothée's hair was still damp, curls only now forming. Marion had insisted he stay in the bath until all the stink of the sewer-pit left him, but sadly she still caught whiffs.

Honestly, she thought, *locked in the sewer room by a beautiful lilac-eyed boy.* Only Timothée could manage that, and on his first night here.

Though she would have a few choice words for that boy if their paths ever crossed. They'd spent the rest of the day in the sanatorium, and Timothée had been gloomy for all of it. The new clothes he'd received were far too big, and he kept yanking up his pants.

She cast a glance at her brother, and a chill ran through her.

After he'd taken his hours-long bath, he'd led them through the halls, all the way to a portrait of the fallen god.

"Do you still think this is all a big coincidence?" Timothée had pointed at the portrait. "He looks like me... Or I look like him. And see here? Vivian's eyes, Marion's lips. He's our brother!"

Never mind the other thing Timothée had said. A mysterious voice that seemed to be coming from within the castle. Like the voice that had called her name in Archpriestess Kassandra's office...

Was it all a trick? Something planted to spread seeds of doubt in their minds? In the end, Marion had thrown up her hands and said, "That's why we're here. We need answers."

Now, Vivian must have sensed Timothée's unease. She grabbed his hand, squeezed it three times. "Tonight, you'll catch your star."

The thought brightened his mood, and he flashed a smile. Of them all, Timothée had dreamed of this the most.

But nothing could brighten Marion's mood. She watched as the sky grew darker, heralding them closer to their destinies. Even her siblings must have tired of her foul temper. Vivian wandered off at first sight of Darius, and Timothée was swept up by an Evening Star girl named Fiona who took it upon herself to tighten the waistband of his pants with a needle and thread.

Marion sat on the edge of the fountain. There was so much commotion around her, students laughing and eating and singing shanties and worst of all: *trying to talk to her.*

Marion Greywick did not enjoy talking to strangers.

But... She did enjoy sweets. And everyone kept supplying her with goodies. When her mug of apple cider ran dry, it was replaced with a thermos of hot coco. Tins of cookies and warm croissants and sugary figs kept being passed around, and she was urged to taste everything.

When one is filled with nerves and most out of their element, eating sweets is always the best course of action.

When did I become like this? Back in Seagrass, she spent her evenings twirling around their little cabin, pretending to be at grand parties.

Now, every well-meaning greeter seemed a threat.

Prince Darius had his arm around Vivian's waist, and she looked equal parts awed and comfortable. *I will have to warn Vivian of this prince,* Marion thought. *Again.* It was all well and good to play the part of princess, but Vivian could not continue this little game any longer.

Not with how sick she was.

"The sun is setting, the stars will start falling, and I pray to the Three the most beautiful girl in Thraina will join my house!"

She was instantly washed in the smell of mint and orange. Khalid Ali Bagheeri looked every bit the dignified scoundrel, with that perfect tendril of hair falling between his brows.

Her whole body flushed. She hadn't spoken to Khalid since he'd had his hands all over her. What a stupid idea that was.

"Hey." He sat beside her. "You doing okay?"

Did he not feel the least bit awkward? They hadn't left on the best of terms. She'd denied him a kiss, and he'd threatened her with love.

"I'm... I'm—" she began. Why were words so hard to find around him?

He laughed and threw an arm around her shoulders. "Don't think twice about what happened this morning. You and I—we're going to take this Academy by storm."

"If I don't turn into kindling," she muttered.

"Not you, Mare. There's nothing to fear." Khalid gave a lop-sided smirk.

She could educate him on all the things there was to fear, but a sensation of relief flooded through her at his presence. In a sea of strangers, it was nice to have a... a...

A friend, she thought decidedly.

And besides, the glittering sugar glaze all over his face and lips distracted her.

"Look at you," she murmured. "What a mess."

With the edge of her sleeve, she rubbed at the sticky sugar on his face. Tentative fingers ran over his swollen lips. His mouth parted slightly against her touch.

"What can I say?" His warm breath drifted over her fingers. "There are cinnamon buns."

Marion dropped her hand and focused on the cobblestone before her, hoping she wasn't blushing too much. "Fair enough."

A crowd of boisterous Evening Stars approached.

You'll never be like them, a wicked voice chided in her mind. They were all here to learn starcraft, become great Starlings. She was here for answers, to cure her sister.

Khalid stood and gave a hearty laugh, embracing Prince Darius, who was at the front of the group.

Behind the Prince stood Marion's sister. Vivian looked like an actress in a stage performance, made up by the fading light, hair a romantic tumble over her shoulders, eyes rich with desire. Marion darted to her sister's side.

"Remember our Celestial Rite, Dare?" Khalid grabbed Darius's arm. "Seems like only yesterday we were out here finding our own stars. Now we must let the younger generation carry on!"

"Not yesterday." Darius laughed. "Just earlier this moon."

Despite herself, Marion felt a smile tug at the corners of her lips as they all laughed together.

"A memory I treasure deeply," a smooth voice said, and a new boy walked up behind them. He wore a dark purple cloak and moved like a cat, stalking and silent.

But what Marion noticed most about him was his hair: silvery lilac, with eyes the same color.

There could only be *one* boy like that in the school. One boy who had harassed her little brother.

Before she said anything, a new host of students appeared behind the boy, all garbed in purple and black uniforms. Carmilla stood among them, her blood-red hair bright against the night.

This could only be the Dark Star house.

Marion licked her lips. There was something hard about them, in the way they stood knitted so tightly together. And each one, from Carmilla, to this Valentine, wore a thick black choker around their neck.

Khalid turned to the newcomer. "Ah, the majestic Valentine Sun graces us with his presence! A memory we treasure together, my friend." His eyes flashed, and something unspoken passed between them.

"Good evening, Carmilla," Darius said, then turned to the lilac-haired boy. His voice deepened. "Valentine."

"What? No hello kiss?" Valentine said mockingly. "Don't dare say you didn't miss me."

Darius didn't acknowledge him, but Marion felt the sparks of tension.

"You offer him a kiss, but not me?" Khalid placed a hand on his heart and feigned an expression of offense.

Valentine gripped the taller boy's neck. "Khalid, my darling, if we began, we'd never stop."

The crowd began to chuckle. Vivian mumbled, "Are they...? Have they...?"

Carmilla stepped closer. "Have never and will never." The gorgeous Dark Star girl picked at an invisible thread on her purple jacket. "They're both so enraptured with the idea of themselves, it's manifested into this chaos whenever they're together. The whole thing is quite annoying."

Marion wanted to laugh, crack a joke with Carmilla about the size of Khalid's ego, but she was too focused on Valentine. He had hurt her brother.

Marion leaned into her sister, hissed: "Is that boy the one who locked Tim in the sewer?"

"Purple hair, purple eyes," Vivian whispered back. "Beautiful enough for Timothée to lose his wits over. A likely culprit."

Marion looked for her brother. He'd wandered over and stood awkwardly on the edge of the group. A very short Dark Star girl with faded pink hair introduced herself as Amaryllis and was trying to engage him in conversation, but Timothée looked like he may throw up.

Justice had to be served against the Dark Star boy that had hurt Marion's brother.

Presently, Darius walked stiffly over to Vivian. "I remembered I have to speak with Professor Setviren about something. If you'll excuse me."

He walked away from the group. A cluster of Evening Stars trailed after him.

Valentine worried his bottom lip. "I get the feeling he doesn't like me."

Khalid barked a laugh. "Well, yeah. Maybe you shouldn't have stolen his lover."

Valentine grabbed Carmilla's waist and drew her close. "Can you blame me?"

Alarm bells clanged in Marion's mind. What were they saying? Did that mean Darius and Carmilla had been together? Marion looked at her older sister. To anyone else, her face was perfectly nonchalant. But Marion saw it in the stuttering of breath, the slight tremble of her bottom lip.

Her sister had gone and fallen for this prince. And to know he had been with this staggering red-haired beauty—

No, no, no. She couldn't have her sister collapsing in heartbreak before the Celestial Rite.

"Khalid?" she said sweetly. "Can I borrow you?"

He gave a roguish grin. "Any time, any reason."

"Great." She grabbed his earlobe and yanked him away from the Dark Star crowd.

"A-a-ah!" he cried and stumbled after her.

"What's the story, huh?"

"What?" He rubbed at his earlobe and made a pouting face. "You want the gossip?"

Marion scowled at him.

He gave a mischievous grin in response. "You know I deal in gossip and secrets, right? Everything has a price. Even words."

Heat simmered in the bottom of Marion's feet, rose up her legs, and shot through the top of her head. And it wasn't the delicious heat Khalid had made her feel in his dorm room.

It was the heat of rage.

"I don't care about your stupid rules!" she whisper-yelled.

He snatched her wrist. "Well, you should. You're going to be a Starling, Marion. Secrets are your currency now. The more you know, the more power you have. The more power you have, the more likely you are to survive." His eyes flickered. "Remember, I know why you're at the Academy. It's not going to be so easy as just finding a cure. You're going to need to cheat, steal, barter, bargain, and eliminate to get what you want." He licked his glistening lips. "Consider this your first lesson."

Something flickered between them: mutual frustration, anger. Acceptance. Khalid was her friend, but he was also a lifeline to this terrible world she'd found herself in. As much as she didn't want to, she'd have to adapt. Or she'd be left behind.

"Alright," Marion spat out. "I want to know about Darius and Carmilla. And Valentine and Carmilla, for that matter. What's the cost?"

"A half-hour of your time. Doing an activity of my choosing." At her aghast look, he sighed. "Don't worry your little matronly heart. It will be something most chaste."

She crossed her arms, stuck up her nose. "Fine."

"Fine." He smiled. "It all began—"

Vivian wandered up, moving like a lost ghost. "What are you talking about?"

Khalid gave Marion a wry look. "An hour of your time if you want her to know too."

She threw her hands up in the air. "Yes, yes. Get on with it!"

"Are you talking about Darius?" Vivian asked sadly.

"Yes," Khalid said, "and he seems quite taken with you, so you might as well know the facts. He and Carmilla started dating—"

"Wait," Marion cut in. "Didn't you all grow up together?"

"I'm just glad she went for him and not me." Khalid shrugged. "But don't worry. They both claim the only thing between them now is politics. But there's some bad blood between Darius and Val."

"Why?" Marion asked.

"Carmilla and Darius were like lovebirds a year ago. But that summer, she went home for her recess in Kirrintsova… and came back with Val. There you have it: one heartbroken prince, a very smug former empress, and a whole lot of awkward family dinners."

Marion watched the fear play across her sister's face. Was Darius still pining over Carmilla?

"So, Valentine and Carmilla are…" Vivian said, her voice a little too nonchalant.

"That didn't last long. They're both too dramatic. And I think Carmilla is jealous that Val looks better in eyeliner."

Marion glanced back to where Valentine and Carmilla stood in front of their crowd of Dark Stars. They certainly appeared a powerful duo, both so indifferent, looking around like everything was placed before them to be judged.

The heat was back, and it needed to be expunged.

"Thank you, Khalid." Marion turned away from him and her sister. "If you excuse me, I have justice to enact."

She stormed over to Valentine. His lavender eyes were lined in thick kohl, and he smiled as she approached. "Back so soon from talking about me? I can't blame you, I supp—"

"Why did you do it?" she snarled.

Val's smile was pure wicked ecstasy. He didn't ask what she was talking about. The glimmer of delight in those evil eyes revealed his understanding. "Simple," he said. "I don't like him."

He spoke so candidly, curiosity clouded her anger. No one liked Timothée, and she and Vivian could never find out why. "It can't be because he's a Star Child. You didn't try anything with me!"

"I don't mind you, actually." He blinked. "It's his face I can't stand."

His face? Marion shook off her curiosity. This boy was a fox. "Well, next time you decide you're annoyed with my brother, remember you're not just dealing with one of us."

A presence appeared beside her, cold and tall. "You're dealing with all three of us," Vivian said.

Valentine's face held that calm, bemused smirk for a beat too long. Finally, he said, "Trust me, darlings, I'm counting on it."

Setviren appeared at the entrance of Selene Crescent. He whistled through his teeth, drawing the attention of the students. "It is time to make our way to the meadow, Starlings. The Celestial Rite is about to begin."

26
IN WHICH VIVIAN ATTENDS THE CELESTIAL RITE

VIVIAN'S FATHER NEVER spoke of the Celestial Academy for Fallen Stars. Not unless he was making a point of how horribly evil it was. But that had not stopped Vivian from hearing about the Celestial Rite.

Thraina was full of magic, but it all came from one source: falling stars. And catching falling stars was only permitted at the Celestial Academy.

A chill spread through the air as Setviren led them into the dark and murky night. Dozens of students followed behind them as they left the stone trappings of the Academy and headed toward the Meadow of Shattered Stars.

Some of the Starling students held lanterns, while others used their fingers to direct small bobbing lights in front of them. Low, murmuring voices of excitement echoed.

There had never been two Rites in a year, never an exception in all the centuries the Academy had existed. But as Setviren had repeated multiple times, they were exceptional.

Vivian certainly didn't feel exceptional, shivering beneath Darius's cloak.

A figure came into view at the horizon of the meadow. Archpriestess Kassandra.

Vivian could barely take such beauty in. With each step they drew closer, Kassandra appeared more goddess than woman. She was dressed in such ornate grandeur, any queen would pale beside her. Her gown was orange and fire-red. The colors wove together like rippling flame. A sparkling gold breast plate was bespeckled with jewels, shining every color. Her white-blond hair was piled upon her head in tiny braids and Vivian wondered at the poor soul trusted with the Archpriestess's tresses. Her headpiece was a golden tiara with a massive red ruby at the center. Layered red and orange glass spread out from the sides like wings.

"She looks so powerful," Vivian whispered, unable to hide the awe in her voice.

Marion gave a loud huff. "If she's so powerful, how come she wasn't able to find *her* three lost children? Seagrass isn't that far from Wolfhelm! She's nothing but flash and no substance."

Marion's words were dismissive, but they held a truth. If the Church really was as powerful as it seemed, how come they hadn't found the triplets?

"Welcome." Archpriestess Kassandra's voice carried like thunder on the wind. Though she smiled at them, the glinting black staff in her hand and the host of Celestial Knights kept the expression from feeling warm. "You have reached the terminus of destiny. Behold, the Meadow of Shattered Stars."

A steep hill sloped downward to a great field beyond. The meadow was sapphire in the night, like a frozen ocean, and the moonlight sparkled over white rocks, clustered together like seafoam.

"My my." Setviren's gaze trained upward. "There has not been such a night in some time."

"The stars are waiting for you," Archpriestess Kassandra said. "The gods have opened up the heavens in celebration of your arrival."

Setviren replied, "The Prince, his wards, and the missing Star Children, all starting in the same year. Ah, how the stars have aligned."

Marion's eyes flicked from the sky to the loremaster. "So, what do we do?"

Setviren said simply, "When the stars fall, you catch one."

Archpriestess Kassandra narrowed her eyes at the loremaster then stepped forward. "One of the falling stars is meant for you. Perhaps a star of the morning, blessed by the goddess Rhaemyria." Her voice lowered a pitch. "Or one of Xydrious, an Evening Star."

And what of the stars of Noctis? Vivian thought. *Dark Stars.*

Her mind turned back to Archpriestess Kassandra, whose rich and ethereal voice held captive all the watchful students. "The star will come to you and hover in your hands. That means it has chosen you. You must not let the star touch the ground, for then it dies. Once a star has chosen you, place it between your lips, and its celestial magic will bind with your heart." Her glass-bright eyes held each of them still. "Catch a falling star and the world becomes yours. Create new destinies. Change your fate. You will become Starlings and Thraina shall bow before you."

"As above," Setviren said, touching three fingers to each eyelid.

"So below," the Starlings replied.

Then with an elegant flick of her wrist, Archpriestess Kassandra bid them forth unto the field.

"I wish there wasn't an audience," Marion said.

Starlings gathered at the crest of the hill. Clumps of blue and gold and purple uniforms spread out on the cold grass. Some had brought quilted blankets and steaming thermoses. Setviren spoke with two other official-looking people, one a middle-aged woman wearing a hooded cape of gold, the other a handsome man in a purple waistcoat. Perhaps they were other professors.

Timothée too was gazing at the crowd, but his eyes were frantic, as if he was looking for someone.

"Don't worry," Marion said. "I had a word with that boy. He won't bother you anymore."

"W-what? No, I—I mean, it's fine." Timothée skittered down the hill and away from the crowd. His little black cat trailed dutifully at his heels.

"Don't go by yourself!" Marion called.

Vivian watched her sister run after their brother. Here, on the crest of the hill, the stars looked stuck in the sky. She couldn't imagine them falling like rain.

A warmth spread over her, and she knew who approached even before she turned. Darius touched her shoulder. "I wish I could help you out there." He flashed a rapturous grin. "But I don't think you'll need it."

Vivian felt conscious of the rising murmur of the crowd.

"Everyone's watching us," she whispered.

"Everyone's watching you."

She wondered if it was more than her being a Lost Star. That perhaps standing so close to the Prince of Andúrigard might be drawing the students' attention.

She looked down, then back up at him. "I'm sorry, I still have your cloak."

"Keep it." He traced a gentle hand down her arm. "Remember what I said? The stars will line up to greet you."

Something shot across the vast blue of his eyes, a single white streak. Vivian whirled so fast Darius had to catch her in his arms. There it was! A white blur across the horizon—the first fallen star of the night.

As if on a silent cue, other stars shook and rattled from the sky, dropping from the tapestry of black. They sparkled with sharp edges as they drew closer, then burst up in sparks as they hit the ground.

Vivian realized the rocks scattered across the field were not rocks at all but fallen stars—uncaught and dead.

It was forbidden to collect dead stars. Well, forbidden for anyone except Starlings. If legend held true, that was how they made their mystical weapons of stellarite.

"They're so beautiful," she whispered.

Darius still had his arms around her, and she leaned into him. "You said you've never seen a starfall. Isn't that so?"

"Glimpses of them," she whispered. "My father never let us out during one."

"The man who stole you," Darius said.

Was that who he was now, who he would always be?

What about the man who had carried her on his shoulders, laughing as he dunked them both into the cool waters of the Seagrass surf? The man that tucked them into bed at night, swearing he would keep them safe? She blinked away hot tears.

"Go get your star," Darius whispered in her ear.

"'kay." She took a deep breath. The night air was cold as she stepped away from his warmth.

Each step squelched with mud as she descended the grassy hill. Her siblings awaited her in the meadow. Stars flew down like scattered showers, bursting upon the ground in brilliant sparks.

"Does anyone remember what the instructions were?" Timothée grinned.

"Don't tell me you were daydreaming during our first lesson?" Vivian poked his arm.

Marion gazed up at the sky. She didn't appear to have heard the joke in his words. "Catch a falling star and the world becomes yours. Create new destinies. Change your fate. You will become Starlings and Thraina shall bow before you."

But it was Darius's words, not Archpriestess Kassandra's, that ran through her head. *The stars will line up to greet you.*

And one of them was made for her.

The grass was wetter here, and her boots sunk into the marshy ground. Little pools looked like portals to another universe, with white light reflecting throughout them.

She closed her eyes and tried to make herself as serene as possible. Light flashed against her lids. But when she opened her eyes, the stars still fell around her, none of them hovering nearby.

She tried to focus, but her mind wandered. She couldn't help but think of Seagrass.

Salty tears fell from her eyes. She was worlds away from there. A fear that had coiled deep in her heart slithered its way out.

What if it wouldn't work? What if she was too sick? She still glowed the same as before, still knew the warmth of the sun, and the taste of bread. But still… *What if I'm too far gone?*

"Please," she whispered. "Stars, *please.*"

She gazed up. Her hair fell loose from her bun and tumbled down her shoulders. Looking up like this… It was just her and the stars and nothing else. Misty lines streaked across the sky.

There was a storm of stars spinning, raining down in sweeping circles.

And she thought again of her father, who was not her father. But if that were so, why had he had the same wave to his hair as Timothée, the same stubborn grin as Marion, and had she only imagined the same flecks of blue in her and her father's eyes?

She didn't want to cry, but it was happening anyway, her gaze still skyward. The stars were falling so hard, and they had the most particular sound as they shimmered past, the lightest twinkle on the piano, or seashells tossing in the waves, or the smooth chime of ice breaking.

The stars were singing and dancing. And she needed to as well.

She moved until she was twirling and twirling, and water splattered her ankles and the hem of her dress. And the stars were ribbons of white light spinning 'round and 'round her. Breathless and broken, she saw above her one star, hovering over her head. An odd sort of halo.

Her feet slowed and with her vision still spinning, she shot her hand up, straining her fingertips until they brushed the glittering edge of the star. It was a ball of light, a million colors and none at all.

Slowly, it shifted into her grip. She clasped it, and it was as frozen as ice and hot as a flame.

And the moment she held her star, the ground opened beneath her, a swirling circle of galaxies. With her star in her hands, she fell through the earth.

27
IN WHICH MARION HOLDS THE UNIVERSE IN HER HANDS

A BURST OF LIGHT, a rush of wind, and a gap in the ground. That's all Marion saw before her sister was there and then she wasn't. Marion had watched the glowing star descend from the sky, circling above Vivian like a playful bird. But as soon as she'd put her hands on it…

The ground had swallowed her up.

Fear crested through Marion's chest. "Vivian? Vivian!"

Marion hauled up her skirts and ran across the meadow to where she last saw her sister. Collapsing to her knees, she clawed at the grass. But there was nothing. No evidence her sister had ever been there.

Through blurry eyes and the thickening star shower, Marion stared up at the hill where Archpriestess Kassandra stood calmly. The voice that surged forth was more beast than girl: "Where is my sister?"

Ragged breath after ragged breath tore through her chest. Archpriestess Kassandra did not respond, but the Starlings, all huddled together in their different houses, began to whisper. Darius had Loremaster Setviren by the shoulders and was shaking him like a puppet. It appeared the Isle swallowing up students as if they were stars was not the norm.

Timothée touched her shoulder. She clutched his hand as if it were an anchor and let him lift her to her feet. Together, they stared at the Archpriestess.

"What's happening?" Timothée called. "What did you do with Vivian?"

Kassandra wrang her hands over her staff. Finally, she spoke, voice magnified by Setviren's magic: "For a star to settle by your heart is for the spirit to accept the divination of the gods. You may be god-born, but you were raised by a traitor and a heretic. Rhaemyria herself carved this isle from the mountains of Thraina and rose it closer to the cosmos. There is deep magic within; it shall test you with a trial. We shall see what mettle your hearts truly hold. Carry on, Greywick children. Your sister will emerge with her star if she is worthy."

Timothée's grey eyes shone with determination. "An extra trial. Lucky us." He squeezed Marion's hand three times then kissed her cheek. "You can do this, Mare. Nothing can stop you."

Marion said nothing, though she wanted to cry after her brother as he turned away and wandered further into the field. She stood still, letting Kassandra's words take weight.

It wasn't enough to catch the star. They would face some unknown trial.

And if they were not worthy?

Marion looked to the ground where Vivian had stood moments ago. The Isle would keep them.

Marion stumbled backward, her legs suddenly too weak to hold her up. What was she doing here? The sky streaked with falling stars. They landed all around her, some immediately turning to black rock, while others flickered against the wet grass. She was supposed to catch one.

And if she did, she'd be pulled into the unknown. If the trial didn't kill her, the star could burn her from the inside out. No, no. She had to get off the field. No one could make her swallow some damned star. Father had *told* her the school was evil. Why hadn't she listened? Why hadn't she run when there was a chance?

Her body was a trembling mess. Her fingers were numb, and her legs were not her own. Where were they taking her? She ran through the meadow, but the stars were everywhere. Her vision streaked with light. They would burn her if they touched her; this she knew. But how would she get away?

It was like three years ago, when she'd been struck still in the cart, unable to go after her sister. Unable to save her father. Nowhere to run. No way to change her fate.

Marion staggered in a circle, tugging on her hair. Die within the Isle, burn under a star, or flee. Those were the only outcomes. But she couldn't think straight. Where was there even to run to? There was the meadow and the sky.

The sky. The stars swirled together like a kaleidoscope. How vast the cosmos stretched. She leaned her head back until her long hair touched her hips. Last night, when she'd first stepped upon the Isle of Argos and looked up into the sky, she'd thought the stars looked like peaches, ripe enough to pluck.

Marion took a shaky breath. *It's only the whole universe.*

She may be a coward, but she could reach her hand to the stars.

The aether of life surrounded her.

You belong among the stars. That's what Khalid had told her. No, she didn't want to be there. She wanted to be on the ground. She wanted to go *home.*

But there was no home without Vivian and Timothée.

And she'd left Vivian once before. She wouldn't do it again.

So there was only one choice. She'd have to bring the sky down to her.

The swirling stars seemed to gather. A bright line shone above, blooming like a flower in spring. Closer, closer, it grew until her skin lit up with warmth. How nice it felt, a caress of light. A strange comfort filled her chest, dispelling the fear. Like an embrace she'd been missing all her life.

"Where have you been?" Marion whispered. "I've been waiting for you."

The light bobbed in front of her face, and Marion knew she could step back and let it fall.

It wouldn't do to let it extinguish in the wet earth. This was her star, and it needed a heart.

"My heart is not strong or brave," she whispered to the light. "But it is yours, if you'll take it."

Marion held her hands up and the shimmering light settled in her palms.

And as she brought it to her lips to swallow, the ground opened beneath her.

28

IN WHICH TIMOTHÉE LOOKS TO THE WEST

MUD FILLED THE new boots Setviren had given him. The field was all sloshy muck. Timothée never knew if his next step would land on firm grass or ankle-deep in a cold puddle.

Yvaine padded unhappily behind him. For being found a street cat, she hated whenever her paws got dirty. Timothée let out an anxious breath. The heavy dark of night was fading, and a slim purple line crested the horizon.

Dawn was still a while away, but the thought of it lingered like an unwanted guest.

Marion and Vivian had caught their stars ages ago.

Where are they?

Archpriestess Kassandra stood stoic on the top of the hill, unbothered by the fact two of her adopted children had been inhaled by the very isle they were all standing on. Setviren at least seemed to have the proper response, trembling like a dozen ants were crawling up and down his body.

But maybe that wasn't because of the missing Greywick girls. Maybe it was because of Timothée, still wandering the field like an idiot.

Vivian and Marion had caught their stars so easily. *Where is mine?*

He could almost convince himself he was afraid. Afraid of what would happen if he caught a star and the Isle swallowed him.

But that wasn't it.

His sisters had gone into the unknown and he'd follow them anywhere.

There was something else. *Maybe I'm not meant to catch a star.*

Timothée cast a look at the hill. Even worse than the Archpriestess's gaze was the eyes of all the Starlings. Watching. Waiting.

It was one thing for a normal person not to catch a star. Quite another for someone who was supposed to be a god.

Timothée stood in the darkest part of the field. Stars fell lazily, as if they were as tired as the students.

He didn't want to look at the sky. It hurt to be reminded of what he'd seen when he'd gazed into its depths at the beginning of the night.

Like the depths spoke back.

Look up, a voice hissed in his mind. The same voice that had been leading him around the castle, that might have led him somewhere if Timothée hadn't gotten distracted by—

A figure stepped out from a cluster of purple uniforms. Despite all his effort, Timothée hadn't been able to stop thinking about him.

Valentine Sun. *Val.*

Timothée swallowed in a dry throat.

Then Val was standing in front of him. Despite walking through the same field, he hadn't splashed a single speck of mud on his pants. "You're doing it wrong."

"Why should I listen to anything you say?"

"You really shouldn't," Val sneered. "Normally, if you do, things will turn out poorly for you. But in this case, you need to listen. You have to stop trying to choose a star. Let one choose you."

I'm not trying to choose one, he thought. More like *not* choose one. "That's not—"

Val sighed and snatched his wrist. "You're afraid."

"I'm…"

Val looked up at him from beneath dark lashes. He was wearing a long-sleeve purple shirt, casual pants, the broken pieces of a uniform. With a tenderness that didn't match his expression, Valentine turned his wrists, so Timothée's palms opened to the stars. "You'll never catch a star if you're afraid of it."

Timothée shook his head, staring blearily down at his hands. "I am afraid," he admitted. "But I don't think it's of my star."

"Then look up," Val said.

So he did.

The sky was vast and the crest of the horizon crept pink and gold and red, all fading to a bright blue.

There are no stars there for you.

His gaze swept further to the west, a dark expanse where one star clung to the deepest part of night.

The star quivered and then fell. It crashed through the sky in a burst of sparkling light. The Starlings of the Celestial Academy cheered in excitement.

But something else latched onto his heart as the star drew ever closer. He didn't back up. He didn't move. And it didn't fall to the ground like all the rest that had passed him by.

This star was his star.

The star slowed its approach. It pulsed and wavered, tendrils of light flickering in and out.

And it wasn't until the star was hovering above his hand that he realized Val still gripped his wrist. He looked down at him through the burning brightness, saw a wide-eyed gaze, lips parted, as Val said something—

But it was too late. The very fabric of the grass and mud bended beneath them. It didn't open into a hole like he'd thought. This was something else.

A gateway through space and time.

And he didn't fall. It pulled. Pulled him, and his star, and Val, who still clutched his wrist.

29
IN WHICH VIVIAN FACES HER FEAR

SHE WAS FALLING. Stars swept past, long streaks of light bursting into flame, until the air and the stars and the galaxy caught her in its embrace. Something pushed her upward, a gentle nudge between her shoulder blades.

Then she was standing, and the world reformed around her. She recognized this place. Gilded walls faded into a star-swept expanse. Wolfhelm Castle. She had walked these halls two nights ago when she'd come across Carmilla and stared up at a portrait of Darius and his family.

But this world did not seem real. To her left was the void of space, sparkling galaxies and stars, and to her right were walls and walls of portraits. A dark blue carpet lay beneath her feet. A hall extended to a bright glowing orb.

Every inch of her trembled.

My star, she knew deep within her.

Very clever, little Greywick, a voice said.

And she knew the voice. It had talked to Timothée, and it had talked to her. Was the whole Isle of Argos alive? And why had it taken her here as soon as she'd caught her star? It wasn't enough to catch one. She had to swallow it.

Vivian walked down the hall to her star, but it seemed never-ending.

It won't be that easy, the voice said. *If you wish to claim your star, you'll need help from your true self.*

"What?" Vivian said lightly, then slowly turned to the wall with the portraits.

The first frame was empty, nothing but a blank canvas. But the rest of the paintings were of her.

Her breath caught in her throat. Moments so burned into her memory she could taste them. A portrait of her as a child, bright eyed, with a bundle of lavender tucked behind her ear and a sweet honey sucker in her mouth. She could smell the fields and the salt air and the wood smoke scent of her father's shirt.

My true self. That little girl was long lost.

She swept past the other portraits: a teenager with hair braided high atop her head, an elderly woman with wrinkled eyes. A frantic, scared girl, fangs in her mouth, tears streaking her cheeks. An image of when she'd first turned.

Vivian walked quickly past that one.

Another portrait made her stop, mesmerized. A regal woman wearing a blue fur-lined cape over her shoulders. Her face was a mask of strong conviction, and a sapphire crown laid atop her dark wavy hair. There was something familiar about the crown...

Her heart clenched. She had seen that crown on the portrait of the last Queen of Andúrigard. The scent of pine and snow and Darius swept over her, and she felt the warmth of his presence.

"That can never be my true self." But still, she could not stop herself from gently touching the portrait, pressing the queen's mouth.

The oil paint smeared beneath her fingers. It was unfinished, new—a future yet decided.

To see if you're worthy of a star, the voice in her mind began. It was a low voice, male, a haunting echo to it. *You'll have to face your fear.*

She heaved in a breath and made herself turn away. Something darkened around the next portrait and her heartbeat increased.

It was not of a girl, but of a twisted creature. Ashen skin hung off a bone-riddled body, crouched and huddled into the corner of the frame. Knobby knees and elbows jutted out like broken branches. Limp oil-slick hair hung around its face, all hollowed cheeks and buggy, milky eyes. It was all so awful she couldn't tell what the worst part was.

Perhaps it was the mouth, sharp teeth piercing the lips, two long fangs dripping with blood. Or the wings that protruded from its poking spine like a bat. The tips had sharp-edged claws. Dark purple veins riddled the leathery membranous skin.

Vivian inhaled a shaking breath, trembled. "My true self," she said. "A monster."

A weight fell upon her shoulders, as if a decision had been made.

The creature blinked. It quirked its head, then crawled out of the frame. It clambered toward her as if the very weight of its bony wings prevented it from standing. It gnashed its terrible teeth and swiped a clawed hand. Vivian cried out, the claws cutting through her leg.

Sharp pain shot through her and a gush of blood spread down her ankle. This might not be reality, but it sure felt like it. If something happened to her body in here, she didn't know if she'd be able to make it out the other side.

She didn't particularly want to test that theory.

When the monster swiped at her again, she staggered out of the way, feet falling off the other side of the hall into the void. Then she was sinking again through space and stars, the hall of portraits getting smaller and smaller.

Something leapt from the suspended hall: the monster with its spread wings and furious face. It knocked her out of the air. She plunged through the stars, desperately trying to hold onto one, hands streaking with silver light. Her fingers caught on something, a rope of braided flowers. A powerful aroma filled her nose. She tumbled through a field, dirt and petals snagging on her dress, in her hair.

She stopped, breath gone, body aching, and rose to all fours. She was in a field of purple lavender. Her field of lavender. But there was smoke in the air. She choked on it. And when she looked above the field, their cabin... It was on fire.

There was a horrible screech and the lavender rustled behind her. She first heard a vicious snarl before the sharp tips of bony wings emerged above the flowers.

The monster was coming for her.

Vivian pulled herself up and ran through the lavender. The petals blew away in shimmering stardust as she rushed past them. "Help!"

The creature's hot breath blew on the back of her neck. Great flames rushed from the windows of her cabin, black smoke trailing into the star-swept sky.

A figure came into focus, kneeling before the cabin. Long, dark hair cascaded over his broad shoulders.

But she would know him anywhere.

"Father!" She burst out of the flower field.

He stood and turned to her, blue eyes blazing. He held something in his outstretched hands.

Time seemed too slow as she approached him. The burning cabin dimmed in place of what he held in his glowing hands.

A sword. White wings wrapped around the hilt, and the blade shimmered like stardust. A brilliant sapphire emblazoned the handle.

"Take my sword and face your fear."

She hovered her palm over the sword's hilt, trembling, and said, "You're not really my father, are you?"

"I'm whatever I need to be," the man—the something—said. "Now, take my sword, change your destiny, and claim the star I sent you. I made it for you, my darling."

"Father?" Tears tumbled from her eyes, and she knew as soon as she took the sword, he would disappear.

She didn't want to lose even the ghost of him.

The lavender trembled behind her. She gripped the sword and turned. The monster leapt from the lavender field, wings spread wide.

Vivian plunged the sword into its stomach. It slipped in easily. So easily.

The creature shrieked, wings flailing as its body went limp on her blade.

Lightning flashed in the sky, then booming thunder. And when she spun, rain splattered her face. She blinked the water out of her eyes. She stood on the top of Wolfhelm Castle, the sword still in her hands.

Another lightning strike and she saw Darius upon the castle's turret, his blade crashing against the Dark Prophet.

"Darius!" She ran toward him.

He turned to her, face splattered with rain and blood. "Vivian?" His expression turned to a vicious snarl, and he stalked closer. "You lied to me!"

His gaze wasn't on her; it was behind her. She whirled, saw that monstrous creature creeping forward, claws spread, fangs out. There was no sign the sword had ever touched it.

"No," she cried. "I didn't. I wanted to—"

The Prince of Andúrigard thrust his sword at her and the monster. And it was all she could do to stumble back, then she was falling, falling again off the castle wall.

She blinked her eyes, and she was running through the burning streets of Wolfhelm, pushing water out of her eyes. Back to this night, this nightmare.

The night that had begun everything.

Around her, houses and shoppes blazed with great fire, backed by terrified screams.

A flash to her left, a blur of darkness, then pale wings spread, and the monster lunged at her. Vivian swung her sword, missed, and the creature's claws slashed across her chest.

She screamed and staggered back. Her arms ached, but she lifted the heavy sword, and when the creature lurched at her again, she caught it in its thigh.

Black sludge dripped in the place of blood. Vivian stumbled further away, but the moment she looked back at the creature, the wound had healed, like it had never been there.

"What?" How was she supposed to defeat this thing if she couldn't hurt it?

The monster jumped, flapped its wings, and slammed into her. Her head cracked on the cobblestone. Her vision blurred, this dreamworld reducing to the dirty blood-filled puddles, the smell of smoke, the drip of rain.

The sword slipped from her fingers.

The monster was tearing her apart. It clawed through her skin, then opened its jaws and sank its teeth into her neck. The wings wrapped around her, talon points puncturing her shoulders.

She thrashed and cried beneath it, but she could not push it off her.

So she stopped moving.

Why not this end for her?

The monster was always going to kill her eventually.

30
IN WHICH MARION WANDERS THE DEEP MAGIC

MARION FELL THROUGH blackness and timelessness. She was not concerned about careening headfirst through the nothing; it was her star that worried her. It flew from her hands, drifting into the dark until not even a pinprick of light emerged.

"Wait," Marion said. "You chose me."

And just like that, she stopped falling. Instead, she was standing, trapped in a room made entirely of stained glass. Even the ground was the mosaic image of a woman with long blond hair holding a yellow flower.

Is this a dream or a memory?

Ahead of her was a door. A plain brown door with a shiny gold knob.

Marion took a deep breath. "This must be my trial."

Indeed, little Greywick. A trial built to see if your heart is worthy of a god's magic.

Marion leapt at the voice. It came from within her head and from the darkness. "Who are you?"

A friend. One who has undergone my own trials of a similar ilk. Face your fear, Marion Greywick. No trial will tame you.

"Are you the voice that spoke to us in the castle?"

A dark chuckle. *I* am *the castle.*

Marion set her jaw. There was nothing else to do. She couldn't stand here on the stained glass for the rest of her days. She had to endure this ordeal, swallow her star, then find herself the biggest slice of cake the Academy had to offer.

"I suppose I'll start with the door." Tentatively, she stepped over the mosaic glasswork. The woman's face—closed eyes, slight smile—seemed too serene for this purgatory.

She stepped up to the door. There was a bronze plate at the top with the words:

The Deep Magic knows the past, present, and future. Leave the past to burn and rise from the ashes of despair.

Marion said, "I do hope that's not a riddle. Riddles are a bother."

She examined the door. A dial sat above the golden knob. It was set to a symbol of a flame. She turned the knob, and the dial switched to a pictogram of a gust of wind. Turning the knob again changed the dial to a wave. And finally, one more twist revealed an image of a leaf.

"What is this changing?" she whispered.

The past. The future. You'll find your star behind any of these doors, Marion. Find your star, face your fear, and return to the present.

"Simple enough," Marion said with as much sarcasm as she could muster. Her chest still felt too tight, her throat too dry. But there was no way but forward. "If I get a choice, then I shall choose the symbol of the leaf. It represents earth, doesn't it? And earth reminds me of Seagrass. Of the lavender fields, and the fresh tilled soil. Yes, that sounds like a good place to start."

Very well.

Marion closed her eyes and inhaled the stagnant air. She opened the door.

She did not step out to lavender fields or fresh tilled soil. She stepped out to death.

A FOREST STRETCHED before her, or the remains of one. It was night, but a full moon illuminated the destruction. White, charred trees stood as skeletons. Ash blew in the wind. Little embers caught in her hair. Smoke curled through the barren remains, filling her lungs.

Is this the past or the future?

The door remained behind her, the dark brown wood looking entirely out of place among the ash-white tree corpses.

Marion took a few tentative steps forward. *Find my star. That's all I have to do. Find my star.*

Shouts echoed up ahead. Marion's heart thudded. Should she hide? There was nowhere to conceal herself in this barren wood. *I have to find my star.*

She ran.

Smoke concealed anything more than a few steps before her, but the screams were getting louder. She ran faster, cresting over a hill. The smoke cleared and—

A volcano. Lava ran like blood down the sides. Great bursts of gas erupted outward, spewing chunks of boiling rock. And at the base of the volcano was an army. Or the remains of one. Survivors struggled to scramble away from the lava, leaving others to be swept up.

Marion cried out, falling to her knees. What was this horrific sight? Her stomach lurched, and she vomited over the charred ground.

"What do you want me to do?" she sobbed to the castle. Was the voice even with her anymore?

As if in answer, the volcano gave a mighty belch and a bright light shone above it. A light Marion knew instantly.

"My star," she growled.

But to get to it, she'd have to navigate the molten rock. And worse than that, the soldiers. Marion wiped her mouth, brushed tears from her eyes. No, she'd never make it. She'd burn before she was even halfway there.

She started down the hill anyway. What else was there to do? She'd chosen the earth door and been taken here. There must be a way to her star—

"Help me!" A black armored soldier ran up the hill toward her. In the moonlight, Marion caught the flash of fangs.

A vampire.

"Get away from me!"

"You can stop it!" the vampiric soldier cried. "Make it stop. Save them. Only you can end this!"

"Don't come any closer!" Marion shrieked and sprinted back up the hill. An ashen forest and erupting volcano. She'd read about this in Khalid's book.

This was Noctis's army. Rhaemyria had destroyed them with molten rock.

Marion raced back into the destroyed forest. *I can't be here! I'm not supposed to be here! This isn't* my *past!* Her chest ached with exertion.

The man's footsteps sounded behind her. He kept screaming: "Help me! Help me!"

That man—that vampire—was afraid. But he was a *vampire*. A part of Noctis's army. There was too much lava, too many soldiers—

The wooden door appeared out of the smoke.

Marion grabbed the golden handle. "Not this door! Not this door!" With a snap of her wrist, she turned the dial once to the wave symbol, yanked opened the door, and threw herself inside.

SHE LANDED ON a rocky beach.

With a cough, Marion sat upward, blinked the grit out of her eyes. *Where did that damned door take me now?* Wherever it was, it had to be better than before. She'd chosen the wrong door the first time, but no matter.

The voice had said her star lay behind all the doors. She could still pass this trial.

A cold salty wind and the gentle lull of waves brought her focus. And laughter. There was laughter. She looked around. It was night-time, but the starry sky revealed she was on a small island knotted with fir trees and driftwood. There was a large rock outcrop. Inside, people were cooking, talking, dancing. Children chased one another around a bonfire.

Marion breathed a sigh of relief. Surely, she could find her star here.

She stood and walked from the beach toward the rocky area. Her wooden door remained right where she'd fallen through.

The air was cold and, in the distance, there was a larger landmass. The twinkling lights of a city gleamed across the sea. Could it be Wolfhelm? Fishing boats rocked over the foamy water. The salt-spray was familiar... and yet it wasn't.

Was this the past or the future?

"Hello!" Marion called as she approached the gathered folk. "I'm looking for something bright and glowing—"

Every man, woman, and child snapped their heads toward her.

"Did we deserve it?" an old woman asked. "Did we deserve your wrath, Sun Daughter?"

"What?" Marion staggered backward.

A child clutched a little doll around its neck. "That's why you killed us. 'Cause we wished upon our stars."

"No!" What were they saying? This wasn't her memory. It couldn't be her future. She pushed away from them, darted back to the beach. The door stood right where she'd left it.

No, she couldn't go through again. Her star was here somewhere. She would stay until—

The ground shook. The tide was receding. Fast.

Marion's shoes dug into the wet sand. Where was the water going...?

"You bury us under the sea, Sun Daughter."

Marion turned to see all the people standing in a line behind her. "Will you stop it? Will you spare us?"

The water had retreated a great deal now. She had no memory of this. "There's nothing I can do."

The ocean roared.

A massive wave surged across the horizon. At the front of the wave shone a bright light. Marion's star engulfed in water.

"Tidal wave! Run!" Marion screamed and shoved a woman in line. "Don't you see? You must run!"

But the woman didn't budge. "Did we deserve it? Did we deserve it? Did we deserve it? Did we deserve it? Did we deserve it?"

"Shut up!" Marion clutched her hands over her ears to drown out the woman's voice and the roar of water.

The tidal wave thundered toward the island. Marion's body shot with fear. What was she supposed to do? Her star was trapped in that burst of water. And these people were all just standing here, waiting to die.

Leave the past to burn and rise from the ashes of despair. What did any of it *mean*?

The great expanse of sand between the beach and the tidal wave pulsated with the star's light. If she walked out to meet the wave…

Marion yanked on her hair. No, no, no, she couldn't. She'd be swept away, lost to the waves forever. It was seconds away now. Salt water sprayed over her. She would die here—

Marion scrambled past the line of people and sprinted to the door. She spun the knob and leapt through.

IMMEDIATELY, WIND WHIPPED at her hair, at her clothes. She stumbled out onto a stone floor, trying to find her bearings amidst the storm. Wind. She must have flung the knob to wind.

She *had* to find her star. Two chances were gone already.

Where was she now? Cold air, piercing rain, a torrential gale, and the sky lit by flashes of lightning. There was a stone railing before her, overlooking a dark horizon. She was high up.

Using her arm to block the wind, Marion stepped away from the door and tried to collect her bearings. She knew this place…

The white stone. The glint of glass in the flashes of lightning. The dark field in the distance.

This was the Celestial Academy for Fallen Stars.

Glass shattered and tiles flung through the wind. Lightning cracked upon a spire, splintering it in flames. Marion screamed and bucked down to avoid getting hit with shrapnel. The castle wouldn't withstand this storm. But what storm could be so strong as to destroy the Isle that had stayed afloat for hundreds of years?

This wasn't her memory, either. At least, not yet.

Marion held tight to the rail. Her star, her star, her star…

Light flickered in the dark sky. She knew it on sight. It was coming toward her.

Marion took a shuddering breath. No matter what it was—molten rock or tidal wave—she *had* to face it. There were no excuses. Her fear could not claim her this time.

But what appeared out of the murk was worse than anything earth or water could create.

It was the being that destroyed her way of existence three years ago.

On wings of darkness emerged the giant bat that had killed her father, its one yellow eye glowing with the light of her star.

"No," Marion whispered. "No. Please, no."

The wings of the great animal propelled it through the storm, the glowing eye wholly focused on her. Marion collapsed to her knees and stared up at the sky. Tears streamed down her face and flung away in the wind.

"Castle!" she cried. "Please. I can't face this. Help me!"

There was no answer.

A shadow crept over her skin. Slowly, she looked up.

The massive beast perched on the railing and peered down at her. Its fox-like face and leathery wings were all too familiar from her memories. She pictured her father's limp body hanging from its sharp claws.

She trembled away from the creature, back hitting the magical door. The bat quirked its head, the one eye glistening with celestial light.

"Get away from me. Leave me alone!"

Was she to kill the beast? She had no weapon, no magic.

The bat sniffed, wings extending. Rich brown fur covered its whole body. Then it spoke: "Hurry, Marion. The castle is lost."

Marion screamed, covered her ears. "Don't say my name!"

"Marion?" The voice was a deep baritone. "Come with me now."

Anger mingled with her fear. "You killed my father. Murderer!"

"There's no time. Whatever you're on about, *quit*." The bat beat its wings to keep its balance.

Marion shook her head back and forth. "Why did you do it? Why did you kill him?"

The bat's one gleaming eye almost appeared pleading. "Trust me."

"Never!" She surged at the bat, hitting it with all her might, and throwing it off balance. It cried out, a heart-wrenching sound, and fell over the edge. The wind whipped the creature into the wall. Unable to get its wings up in the storm, the beast careened to the ground.

Marion held her breath. "My star?"

There was the crack of lightning and the ground shook. The white stone fractured beneath her as the whole balcony gave way. Marion fell. Wind and rain whipped at her. Crumbling stone hit her face, arms, legs. But there! The door, also falling to the ground.

She heaved her whole body through the air, reaching for the doorknob. With a burst of strength, she turned the dial for a final time and pulled open the door. Holding onto the falling doorframe, she hauled herself through.

Fire. That was the last symbol. The last chance.

MARION GROANED. SHE was lying flat on her back and her whole body ached. A bone-deep exhaustion filled her. She had failed three chances so far. This was her last attempt.

She squeezed her eyes shut. What would she see when she opened them: a memory or future vision of fire? If she couldn't overcome the other three, what chance did she have here? Her only hope was her siblings had fared better—

Marion sniffed. There was a familiar scent, one of sea salt and chimney smoke and...

And lavender.

Marion sat up.

It couldn't be. She was lying in a field of lavender flowers. To the east churned a great blue sea. And before her was a small wooden cabin.

Her cabin.

Her home.

She stood. A lovely breeze caught her hair and skirts. Flower petals swirled through the air, and she held up her hand to catch one. This... this was her memory. That damned dial had finally gotten something right.

With a tentative look back at the wooden door in the middle of the field, Marion walked toward her cabin. Her throat tightened, but not from fear. It was all so real. She could practically see Timothée asleep among the flowers and hear Vivian's voice calling for him.

By all accounts, she shouldn't be smiling. But she was. Tears dripped down her face, but she didn't brush them away. She was *home*.

The cabin door opened. "There she is! My girl!"

A man leaned against the doorway, dark hair to his shoulders, face full of scruff. Blue eyes flashing with wicked humor.

"Father?"

It was just a memory…

Marion dashed toward him. He enveloped her in his arms, and she smelled the familiar smoke and lavender oil. The way he stroked her hair and laughed as she squeezed him—it was all so real.

"Father," Marion choked out, "I've missed you."

"Missed me? You've only been out in the field for an hour."

Marion squeezed her eyes shut. "Right. An hour."

"Come inside, dear. Let's have a tune." He pulled away but the look on his face was genuine love.

He's no traitor or heretic. The Church is wrong. He's just Father. He's always been Father.

Marion thought her heart might burst as she stepped within the cabin. Everything from the rosemaling on the dish set in the kitchen to the colorful quilt on the rocking chair by the fire made her long for this to be real.

"Take a seat, love. Stay a while." Father pulled out his dulcimer. A tune arose with swelling tension.

Marion sat in the rocking chair, felt the firmness of the wood beneath her hand. Out the window, she could still see the door standing in the lavender field. This was the furthest she'd ever been from it in one of these visions. But nothing could attack her here in the cabin.

Besides, where would she go? Back to the exploding volcano and vampire soldiers? To the tidal wave, about to sweep an entire island under its inky depths? Or to the giant bat who had torn this life away from her?

This was the last door, and it had led her home. The door of fire.

Marion yawned and tucked the quilt around her legs. The only fire here was the one burning in the hearth. It flickered with bright yellow light, an ethereal glow.

Marion blinked. The fire… It wasn't a fire at all. It was her star.

What? She fell to her knees, scrambled across the floor. It was no trick. The star was right there. She could pluck it from the embers and bring it to her lips right now.

The music stopped. "Are you leaving now?" Father stared down at her.

"I-I have to go back. They're waiting for me."

"What about me?" The dulcimer fell to the ground. "Are you going to leave me, love? Again?"

"No, Father!" Marion jumped up, wrapped her arms around him. "It's just... This isn't real. It's a memory."

"But what a lovely memory it is. What is for you out there?"

A chill drifted through Marion's blood. The deep magic had shown her the past and the future. If she swallowed that star and survived, what would happen to her? Was she destined to condemn the innocent to the waves? Would she face the giant bat again?

"I have to go back, Father. I wish I could stay."

Her father's grip tightened on her shoulders. His voice sounded deep and ancient: "If you swallow that star, Marion Greywick, you will burn."

"Father..."

He pulled away, stroked her chin. "Stay with me where it's safe. Nothing can hurt you here. Stay and let this be your only memory. The fear will fade away."

Marion blinked at him. She didn't want to burn. She'd known all along her heart was too weak for a star. And Father wouldn't lie to her. He wanted to protect her. He always did.

Outside of these cabin walls, there was only evil. Evil she would experience, evil she would cause. But here, she was safe.

She had the distinct feeling she was forgetting something. But it didn't matter. Father would protect her.

A bucket of water appeared beside her. What good luck!

Marion picked up the bucket and doused the hearth.

It was time for her star to extinguish once and for all.

31

IN WHICH TIMOTHÉE IS TRAPPED IN AN ECHO OF THE PAST

AND GRATED HIS cheek and stuck to his lips. Timothée rose to all fours, spat onto the ground. The wet splotch of his saliva slowly sank beneath the grains.

There was an angry groan. Val lay behind him, feet in inky water.

They were on a beach of black sand, black rolling waves, and a horizon as broad as it was close. The air was thick, smelling of salt and wet rocks.

"Val?" Timothée crawled over to him. "Val?"

Val's eyes shot open. "What the fuck did you do, Greywick?"

"I don't know what happened," Timothée said. "But I don't think you're supposed to be here. No one else fell through with Viv and Mare."

He looked around but didn't see any sign of his sisters. Wherever the Isle had taken them, it wasn't here.

A soft meow sounded, and Yvaine padded toward them, leaving little paw prints in the sand.

Val gave a long sigh. "What is this place? Why did you bring me to some creepy beach?"

"I didn't do anything." Timothée followed his gaze. He knew this place. "I grew up here." He recognized the curve of the shoreline, the sheer rocky cliff. But there wasn't a little cabin at the top of the hill like he remembered. Instead, a towering stone structure stood with a waving flag bearing the crest of a snarling wolf.

"Wolfhelm Castle," Val said.

"It kind of looks like it," Timothée said. "It has the wolf sigil, but it's missing the three stars."

Val's eyes were glossy as he stared at the flag. "The Störmbergs didn't add the stars until they officially aligned with the Celestial Church during the Blood War."

"A castle from the past," Timothée murmured, "and a beach from my childhood."

What did they have in common? Timothée's feet dragged in the sand. *What is this place? Why am I here?* Val's face was unreadable. *Why are you here?* Loose hair blew across Val's eyes in the sharp ocean breeze. It appeared almost white in the non-light of this place.

But there was a small dash of light here. Not the sun or the moon, but a shade of billowing grey on the horizon.

"Star," Timothée said.

Light skipped over the waves. It was moving closer and closer, shadows lengthening to a striking violet.

The star he had caught hovered over the water. Its light was so bright he couldn't look at it directly. Energy swirled off it: heat and magic screaming between his ears.

"That can't be my star," Timothée said softly. "It can't be. It's a…"

He looked at the swirling purple light. And he made himself say the words he had known the moment it had settled in his hands. No, before that. The moment he'd stepped onto the meadow and seen it sitting alone in the sky. As if it had waited a thousand years for him to just look up.

"A Dark Star," he said. "I caught a Dark Star."

As if it could be anything else.

Since he had glowed in the square, he had felt so close to magic. He could become a hero like Darius, live a life of greatness. The life he'd dreamed of, even as a baker boy.

But every hope of that life had ended the moment the star settled in his hands.

He blinked back tears. Val stepped beside him.

"This is *your* fault!" Timothée whirled.

"I didn't ask to be dragged down here, godling." The star lit him in sharp contrast, harsh angles of light along his cheekbones, deep shadows across his jaw and lips.

Timothée stumbled away. "This wouldn't have happened if you hadn't come down to the meadow and ruined everything!"

"You'd never have put your fear aside and caught a star—"

Of course, you're *here,* a cold but familiar voice said in his mind.

That voice… It was the castle. It had tried to lead him deep within the Isle before.

"You brought me here!" Timothée cried.

Val glanced over at him. "Who are you talking to?"

"The castle. It speaks to me," Timothée said. But only him, it would seem, given Val's blank stare.

Welcome to the beginning, Timothée Greywick. The voice echoed around him and inside him. *You've been sent a powerful gift.*

"I don't want it."

Are you worthy?

"Worthy?" Timothée stammered.

"Fuck," Val muttered under his breath. "If this is testing if you're worthy, we are dying in this place."

Timothée shook his head. "I don't want to be worthy of that!"

You who have caught a star, it is time to see if you have the power to wield it. Face your fear.

Or die.

"Face my fear," Timothée murmured. "There's nothing worse than this."

Val gave an annoyed huff. "You don't know what nothing is, Greywick."

Timothée stepped away from the star, feet catching in the sand. He didn't want to see if he was worthy. He didn't even want the star. There had to be a way out of here without swallowing it.

Yvaine swished her tail angrily, gave a yowl. She looked forlornly around at the black rocks and black sand and black water.

"I'll find a way out," Timothée said. "Just not that way."

"So you're going to condemn yourself to this purgatory because you're mad you can't be some grand hero?"

"That's not it," Timothée said. Val had used shadowcraft in the hall. Had that been evil?

But his own fate wasn't supposed to lead him here. "Do you ever wish you hadn't swallowed your star?"

Val stepped away, eyes wavering.

"If you had to go back, would you still swallow one, knowing the type of magic you'd get?"

And maybe it was this place, maybe it was the heaviness of stars and time weighing on them, but he felt something about Val melt away. Val touched the frayed edges of his lilac hair. "I—"

The choice was simple. It was so clear in Timothée's mind. He'd rather exist in this nothingness than swallow that star. But he'd dragged Val with him, and Yvaine. He had to get them all back to the surface.

Val sank to the black sand, put his head between his knees. "Whatever. Can you just fail your trial so this can all end?"

The words of the Isle came back to Timothée: *Face your fear or die.*

The world was still around him, the gentle pull and push of the waves, the castle with its waving flags.

Black fog took the form of a male figure, tall, with a cape of shadows.

Timothée Greywick, look at what has been sent to you, the darkest star in the sky.

The shadow figure gestured to the swirling star. Was this a vision of his brother, or who he was meant to become?

Timothée inhaled a sharp breath and looked over his shoulder.

"Can you see the shadows?" Timothée whispered. "Can you hear them?"

Val lifted his head from the cradle of his arms. "I already told you I can't hear the crazy voices in your head, Greywick."

The shadow figure gestured beyond to the hovering star. *Swallow the star and darken the sky so the gods have no home to return to.*

The Dark Prophet's words rang in his mind: *Noctis and I stood on the Isle of Argos as his shadows devoured your precious school.*

The way Archpriestess Kassandra had looked at him, the way Setviren had trembled at the portrait on the wall…

They'd known. They'd know what was bound for him before he had. And there was nothing he could do. Was this his destiny? To end up like his brother?

The sky crackled with lightning, and a bolt struck the shadow, breaking it apart.

"Rhaemyria ripped out his star." Timothée stumbled back, the words of Setviren's legend coming to his mind in striking clarity. "She covered Thraina in a great fire to cleanse it of his shadows."

"What did you say?" Val looked over at him, eyes wide.

Light swept across the sky. Fire swirled in a torrent before hovering above his star. Flame given shape. A bird of feathered flames.

A phoenix.

"You, Timothée Greywick, are a wicked thing." A voice boomed around him, commanding, all encompassing. "The last child of the gods almost destroyed my world with a star like that," the voice echoed. "You will not be given the chance."

A great wave of heat washed over him. He stumbled back, fell to the black sand. The firebird dove and surrounded his star in flames. Timothée stared at the star hovering above the black water. He couldn't see the purple light anymore. It was too hot, a red and orange blaze.

"You who caught a Dark Star," the voice of fire said. "You will burn."

32
IN WHICH VIVIAN CHANGES HER DESTINY

THE MONSTROUS CREATURE bore down on her, claw-like hands digging into her flesh, its pointed teeth gnashing.

She had always known this was how she would die. The monster tearing her apart piece by piece.

I did not think you would give up so easily, that voice chided in her mind.

"You don't know what it's like to have a monster inside you all the time," she whimpered helplessly.

You have no idea, little Greywick, the voice replied. *You're not going to kill this monster.*

She knew that. It wouldn't die. "I'm trying," she moaned as she felt an agonizing crack of bone in her wrist. She tried to kick her legs, loosen this monster's grip.

The Isle roared in her mind: *If you cannot beat the beast, tame it. Tame the monster within.*

It couldn't die. The thought blazed across her mind.

But perhaps it could change.

With the last of her strength, Vivian twisted her legs around the creature and rolled to straddle it. She pressed hard on its shoulders, feeling the frail bones through the skin, the weak flesh give in. It writhed beneath her, snarling, fangs showing, dark blood dripping. The monster couldn't move.

But...

But it really wasn't a monster, was it?

Vivian let out a shaking breath and forced herself to stare at it. Tears streamed down her cheeks, splattering onto the creature's body. Because those were her hands. Even beneath the clawed nails, she recognized her long fingers. Fingers that had painted the walls of her house, had made cards to label the lavender, and drawn fantastical pictures from Timothée's stories.

And slowly the claws digging into her went slack, the grey-tinged flesh fading away.

Vivian forced herself to keep looking at the monster.

To keep looking at herself.

She drew her eyes along its naked body. It didn't look human anymore, but she recognized the ribcage sticking out of the flesh, the heavy chest that couldn't seem to inhale enough air. But she tried to remember the taste of lavender cupcakes, and Marion's turnip stew. One day she would taste those things again.

And she was hungry. So hungry.

So hungry for change.

Change.

She needed to change.

She studied the face, the same way she used to study Marion or Timothée or even her Father before she would draw them. Inspecting every angle, every soft and hard edge. Limp strands of oily hair fell along this creature's face. Eyes murky, but beneath the clouds and sparse lashes, they were grey. At last, she made herself look at the mouth, the snarling lips from which beneath jutted long, grotesque fangs.

But she had kissed with those lips, kissed with those fangs safely away. Kissed a boy she loved.

And beneath her, the fangs retracted, and pink cracked lips replaced them.

The creature arched its back—one last attempt to break her—but she gripped its shoulders, slammed it down, and snarled right back, twin fangs jutting from her face.

A monster to fight herself.

Herself to fight a monster.

Then there was nothing beneath her but a puddle, her own reflection staring back.

She collapsed to the ground, panting, clutching her neck. Blood flowed beneath her fingers, and there was blood in her mouth. And the world expanded around her. There was smoke and blood and cold stone and Father's unmoving body.

Someone clutched her face.

"I'm sorry," a shadow above her spoke.

No, not a shadow.

A man.

"Who...?" She willed this moment into focus. A sweep of long dark hair covered most of his face, but not the singular yellow eye.

He might have been beautiful except for the fangs protruding from between his blood-splattered lips.

Maybe he was anyway.

"I'm sorry I can't help you anymore," the man said again, still clasping her head between his palms. "You'll have to do it all on your own. But I know you can. Do you hear that? Your heart. It's already started again, and it's as strong as you are."

The ground swallowed her, and the man swept away.

Stars rushed by, and when she landed, she was back in the portrait hall. Back with the images of her.

A slash ran through the canvas of her monstrous self.

Dare you make another choice? the voice spoke.

"I will," she said.

Her clothes were ripped and tattered, and she held the sapphire sword in hand. Vivian walked again through the hall until she found the first one. The blank canvas.

"I have not yet made my true self." She pressed her palm to the bare portrait.

Vivian Greywick, the voice said as the stars spun around her, *it's time to swallow your star.*

A glowing blue star wove itself in brushstrokes across the canvas.

She held out her palm, and the star jumped into her hand. She brought it close to her body.

"It would seem," she whispered, "we've got a great deal to live up to. If you want to jump back into that blank canvas, I won't blame you."

But she did not fear it leaving, because somehow, she knew this star was hers, and she was its. It crackled and sparkled in her hands, giving her its answer.

Slowly, she brought the cupped star to her lips and let the light press against her face. Something surged inside her chest, and it filled her with a great weight. A heaviness gripped her feet, and her blood hummed beneath her skin. And for the first time in so long, she was unafraid.

Vivian Greywick swallowed her star.

Her vision contracted until the heavens surrounded her: the black tapestry of night and pinpricks of light everywhere she looked. She seemed to move at a great pace, sailing through the cosmos. Herself, and yet more.

"Vivian," a voice said from all around her. "My Vivian. Forged on the wings of starlight."

It was her father's voice.

She kept speeding through the night sky until a bursting white light appeared ahead. She could stay here among the stars. But the light beckoned her. She must return to Thraina.

Vivian's eyes shot open, and she was again upon the meadow. But a shimmering blue glow surrounded her.

The magic of Xydrious hummed beneath her skin. But for whatever reason, all she saw was her father—who was not really her father at all.

"Evening Star," she gasped.

An applauding crowd echoed the word atop the hill, and loudest was the brilliant cheer from Prince Darius himself.

She touched a hand to her heart.

An Evening Star—their fates intertwined tighter still.

She glanced around the meadow. No sign of her siblings.

A sea of blue rushed around her, cheering and celebrating. She waded through them to clutch at Darius's shirt.

"Marion and Timothée?" she asked.

Darius pulled her close, explained Archpriestess Kassandra's words of a trial. Both her siblings had caught a star, as she had.

"They will make it," she whispered. She had to believe that, if she believed in anything.

"Of course they will," Darius said.

Beyond the crowd that gathered around her, Archpriestess Kassandra gave a small smile. Loremaster Setviren dabbed the corners of his eyes with his sleeve.

Darius drew her chin up to look at him. "You're an Evening Star."

"I'm an Evening Star."

She was, wasn't she? She'd become part of something magical. Or perhaps found a magical part of herself.

The vision had showed a glimpse of what could lie beneath. But she'd defeated the monster. Or kept it at bay, at least for the moment.

She gripped Darius's wrist, the ends of the blue ribbon curling around her own. In front of the entire crowd, she kissed the Prince of Andúrigard.

He smiled and kissed her back.

A girl. A vampire. An Evening Star.

She had pretended to be a human for so long. Pretending to be a Starling shouldn't be much harder.

33

IN WHICH MARION MAKES A FATEFUL VOW

MARION GREYWICK SAT in her childhood home. She might have been here since the first creation, and she might be here until time ceased all meaning. It didn't matter. She was with Father.

He sat in a rocking chair beside her. He'd long since stopped plucking his dulcimer. How could he play anymore? Roots and moss and grass had grown over his legs, his body, his hands. They'd grown over her too. Everything in the cabin was covered in dirt and vines.

They'd been here a very long time.

She had the distinct feeling she'd made a choice. She would stay in the ground forever.

There had been the smell of lavender here once. Now it smelled of musky soil. There was soil in her nose, she realized. The cabin was filled with it: mulch and mold and moss.

Ah, well. It was better than the alternative. She just couldn't remember what the alternative had been.

It was ever so dark in here, though. She could barely see her Father's blue eyes. The only light came from a dying ember in the hearth.

I put that fire out, she thought. *Before it even had a chance to truly burn.*

Father was smiling, though his face was barely visible amongst the roots tying him to the rocking chair. He looked happy.

Marion smiled too. *I was too weak to save him. But we can be together here. Isn't it nice?*

There it was, that annoying, tickling feeling in her mind. Something clawing for purchase in her awareness. There was something else she'd been too weak to do. Someone else she couldn't save. What was it? Who was it?

No matter.

There was nothing to fear.

Marion.

Marion blinked slowly. Oh, that was her name. Someone had said it. It wasn't Father. He was just sitting and smiling.

Marion Greywick, stand up.

Oh bother. She was too heavy to stand. Her quilt was made of moss.

Stand up!

Fine, fine. She pried a hand free of the vines gripping her to the chair. Her whole body felt sluggish. But she forced herself to stand up anyway.

You can't stay here, Marion. There are things you need to do.

Things she needed to do? Not her. She was going to sit back down now—

Marion!

That voice. It gave her that itchy feeling too. She'd heard it recently. She didn't know why, but she thought it was a friend.

Heed me, godling. Let your fear defeat you. Then rise stronger.

Fear? That wasn't why she was here. She was here to be with Father.

Your father is dead.

No, he was right here, sitting in the rocking chair. Smiling at her. Bugs crawled out of the hole in his dulcimer.

He died three years ago. Remember, Marion, remember!

Oh. Oh bother. There was blood dripping from Father's mouth. But he was still smiling at her. His eyes were white and glassy. Blood spurted from gashes over his chest: claw marks of a giant bat.

Marion staggered back, tripped over the vines crawling across the floor.

"It's alright, Marion," her father said, but his skin was drying out and tightening over the bones. A worm shot from his eye socket, his eyeball popping out and plunking into the mulch. "Stay here and everything will go away."

"Father?" Marion whispered. Roots crawled up her legs, pulling her wrists tight to the ground.

Your father is dead. But your sister and brothers still have a chance.

Sister and brother? The itchy feeling erupted in pain. Images flashed in her mind's eye: a rainy cobblestone street, water running red with blood, the inside of a cart. Her sister running into the dark. Her brother shaking her shoulders, screaming at her to do something.

"No," Marion cried. "I can't go back."

Face your fear, Marion. And rise from it stronger than before.

Her brother and sister… Timothée and Vivian. She had abandoned them. Where were they now?

"Lie down, Marion," the skeleton sitting in her father's rocking chair said. "Stay with me."

"This isn't home," Marion whispered. "If it was, Tim and Vivian would be with me."

"Stop talking," the skeleton said.

But Marion didn't like being told what to do, so she said, "I think I have to leave."

With a snarl, the skeleton tore from the chair, roots and dirt flying from its bones. "You're a fool! You think you'll survive the world out there? That star will burn you up."

"You're not my Father. Father believed in me."

"No, he didn't. He knew you'd never survive the Academy. The world's too big for you, little bird."

The roots grew tighter around her body. Dirt spilled down the side of the cabin, falling into her mouth and nose. "The world might be too big for me. But it's not too big for us." For the Greywick triplets.

She would do it.

She would rise for Vivian. For Timothée. For her father's true memory.

She would rise for herself.

With a cry, Marion ripped the weeds off her body. The hearth, the dying ember. Her star. She lunged toward the fading light.

"No!" the skeleton screamed. It swung forward, clutching her ankle with bony hands.

Marion kicked hard, shattering the bones. She knelt down into the hearth, nursed the tiny ember in her hands.

"I'm sorry I abandoned you," she whispered. "It won't happen again. Never ever, in all my life. I'll protect you. I promise."

A promise she would keep.

The little light flickered slightly, and Marion's hand felt warmer. She took a deep breath.

She brought the star to her lips and swallowed. White light radiated down her throat, through her chest, to her heart. Marion's hands flung out to the side, fingers spread wide. Her head shot up to the heavens. A brilliant golden light ignited around her.

Heat seethed within her chest. A blaze that could never be extinguished.

Leave the past to burn and rise from the ashes of despair.

Marion stood in the remnants of her home. Anger raged within her, making her heart beat with a fiery vengeance.

"Daughter!" The skeleton reached for her.

"This is not my home," she growled. "And these visions are not my fate."

All the pieces of her that had been buried in fear lit up. She cried out, voice crackling, and flames erupted from her skin. Her hair waved with orange and yellow fire, her skin flared, and every pulse of her blood was an inferno.

She placed her palms flat against the tangle of roots covering the cabin floor. They caught immediately. With a roar, she threw her body against the vine-strangled walls. It shriveled to ash, then the wood beneath ignited. The cabin was on fire.

"This is not my chair!" She grasped the rocking chair and mossy quilt. "This is not your dulcimer!" Everything was kindling.

"No, Marion. No!" The skeleton writhed within the embers.

Marion stalked over to him and took its ashen skull between her hands. "You are not my father."

The skull shifted before her, skin growing over, eyes where the empty sockets had been. Her father's face once more. He smiled sadly at her.

Marion sucked in a breath. She felt it. The prescient awareness of the life that was, the life that could have been.

Rise, firebird.

Marion clutched the face tighter, tighter, tighter, her hands growing hotter, hotter, hotter. Her father's skin melted between her fingers.

She dropped the corpse to the ground and walked from the cabin. It was completely alight now. But it couldn't hurt her. Just like her star couldn't. *I won't burn. I am stronger than the flame.*

The lavender field gave way beneath her searing fingers, stems and blooms torched with a single touch. Smoke drifted out to the sea.

She stood before the wooden door. Turned the knob. The dial clicked a final time to a new symbol that hadn't been there before: a circle. Somehow, she knew what it meant. Aether, the celestial matter.

Heat blazed behind her. She wanted to look back but knew she couldn't. Her home was gone.

She had destroyed it with fire and ash.

"Catch a falling star and the world becomes yours. Create new destinies. Change your fate. You will become Starlings and Thraina shall bow before you."

She opened the door and stepped through.

Darkness. Cold. Time and space and the stuff between the stars.

Then wet grass. The frigid chill of night. And a fading golden light surrounding her.

From the ashes.

She was back on the Meadow of Shattered Stars. Up on the hill, her sister stood surrounded by blue uniforms.

A triumphant cheer cut through the silence. A crowd of golden uniforms on the hill leapt up. Balls of fire, sprays of water, and clouds of snow erupted in the air. The Morning Stars screamed and hugged each other. The lot of them raced down the hill, a howling mob of bright yellow light. "Morning Star!" they cheered. "Hail Rhaemyria! A Star Child is a Morning Star!"

She touched her chest. Her heart beat strong and fierce. And nestled beside it was her star. A Morning Star.

Marion let herself be picked up and surrounded by the other students. They hugged her and congratulated her and cheered her name.

Through the crowd, she saw a face she recognized.

Khalid smirked. "Little leech girl no longer."

That past had died, along with the rest.

She had killed it.

Been forced to kill it.

Because of the Church.

Marion stared up to the top of the hill where Archpriestess Kassandra stood. Her face was unreadable, but in the shimmer of a falling star, Marion saw the trickle of tears.

Whatever the Church wanted with the Greywicks, Marion knew one thing.

It would never tear them apart.

Eyes blazing with fiery starlight, Marion Greywick stared at the Archpriestess and made a vow. *Try to burn my feathers. You will only ignite me. I will see the entire world feed my flame. And when I am through, I will stand upon the ashes of this Church.*

And I will rise.

34

IN WHICH TIMOTHÉE GETS LOST IN A STORMWIND OF SHADOWS

A GREAT FIRE SURROUNDED Timothée's star. Streaks cascaded into the air, bursting into fireworks of flame. Torrents broke off and shattered the rock wall beside him and smashed into Wolfhelm Castle above.

"I heard a voice that time." Val scrambled to his feet.

"That one was hard to miss," Timothée stammered. "What is that?"

"Face your fears," Val mumbled, then he looked over, eyes wide. "Is that what you said?"

"Yeah?"

"You couldn't fear something normal? Like snakes?" Val hissed. "You had to fear—"

"A goddess?"

"Rhaemyria," Val said.

And now Timothée knew what this fire was. Because the goddess Rhaemyria had killed her last son with this magic. What made Timothée any different?

This was his fear. His trial.

You who have caught a Dark Star, you will burn.

The flames encircling his star grew wider and wider and wider. Timothée's heart lurched. He scooped Yvaine into his arms. "Come on. We have to get away."

If there was any outrunning this at all.

He started sprinting up the beach when he realized Val wasn't beside him. He slowed and turned. Val was a dark silhouette against the raging fire.

Timothée dropped Yvaine to the sand. She hid behind an enclave of rocks further up the beach.

"Val!" Timothée gripped his shoulder. He was stiff beneath his palm. "Val?"

"It's pointless," Val said. "Don't think you'll be able to escape this."

Timothée forced him to turn. The air was growing warmer and sweat dripped into his eyes. "We have to try."

"Do you? Just a moment ago, you seemed content to waste your life away in this pitiful existence."

Timothée dropped his hand. "I didn't mean it."

He would have swallowed that star if it had been the only way. Catching a Dark Star hadn't taken away all his hope.

Only most of it.

Val tilted his head back. Another wave of heat washed toward them, blowing his light hair, painting it golden. He looked eerily familiar in that moment, but Timothée couldn't place how. "It doesn't matter."

Timothée dragged him back a few steps as the ocean water bubbled. "I thought you wanted to live!"

"I didn't want to be stuck in nothingness with you." Val smirked. "This isn't nothingness. This is a glorious end, of fire and flame and stardust. How it should have happened."

"What's wrong with you?"

Val gripped his face, pulled his body flush against Timothée's chest. His fingers dug into his cheeks. "You."

"W-what?"

"I haven't known a moment of peace since the first day I met you," Val said. He drew Timothée closer. "Since the moment you were sprawled out on the ground in front of me with an expression that didn't match your face."

Timothée gulped in the air. It was too hot, burning his lungs.

"You took away every hope I had, Greywick." Val collapsed against him, head on his chest, as if even the will to stand had gone out of him. "And if I die in Rhaemyria's fire, I can find joy in the fact it will take you with me."

"You're actually crazy." Timothée dragged him behind some large rocks, away from the spreading flame. Stones from the castle fell around them, and a flag blew across the black sand. The Störmberg sigil, the ancient one without the stars. But the other side was the present sigil, the one they still flew to this day in Wolfhelm.

Yvaine darted out and batted at it. "Yvaine." Timothée sighed. He grabbed her by the scruff and tossed her behind the rock just as a cinder hit the flag and the whole thing burst into flame.

Timothée peeked out at the world, the boiling ocean, the crumbling castle. "You really made it all the way to the Isle of Argos, only to die."

Val slumped against the rock like a ragdoll. "You really came all the way to sit on a beach with me for eternity instead of swallowing a star."

Timothée laughed. He couldn't help it. "Maybe we are both crazy."

Val narrowed his eyes, and there was the briefest flash of softness on his face, lit by one brilliant burst of flame. He murmured, "Maybe."

Even trapped in this place, he was beautiful.

Timothée sniffed and sat down beside him. He wasn't sure how long it would take for the flames to reach them. "Do you think my sisters made it out?"

Val gave him a sidelong glance. "Probably. They seem smarter than you."

"Yeah," Timothée said. "I know they did. Marion wouldn't let anything stop her. And Viv, well, she may not show it, but she's stronger than she looks."

A great ball of flame burst in the air, lighting the sky orange and gold. "Do you have any siblings?"

"What, do you think because we're about to die, I'm going to tell you my life story?" Val cast a glance at the burning Wolfhelm Castle. Then he hissed out, "A brother."

Timothée didn't know why, but it made him happy to learn this one thing. "Older or younger?"

"Older," Val said without looking at him. "Half-brother, actually. My mother died when I was born. I think that after losing both his wives, my father didn't have any love left for us. But with my brother, I didn't need a father. He was enough."

Timothée's heart ached. "Marion was that to me and Viv after Father died. She was all we needed too. Sometimes I wonder what she needed."

Timothée looked down at the Dark Star boy. His eyes reflected the blaze. Then Val snarled and pushed hard on Timothée's chest, standing with the momentum.

"What?"

"Damn the Three if my last moment on Thraina is swapping sad stories with you."

"I thought you wanted the flames to take you," Timothée said.

"It's too late for that. You ruined the moment," Val huffed. "So go out there and do some hero shit and prove you're worthy or whatever."

Timothée gave a small sigh. "I caught a Dark Star, remember? I don't think being a hero is in my future."

Flames were crawling up the beach now. "Let me enlighten you, Greywick. There are no such things as heroes, and someone can just as easily do monstrous things with righteous Morning or Evening starcraft. So swallow your stupid star."

"I—"

"I do," Val said suddenly.

"What?"

"You asked me if I regretted swallowing my star," Val said. "I do regret it. Maybe if I hadn't, I wouldn't have lost my brother."

Timothée opened his mouth to respond, but Val silenced him with a glare. The world was red around them, glowing across his hair, his face.

"I also know if I hadn't swallowed a star, I'd be dead. So you have to make the same choice I did, Greywick. Death or darkness." Val blinked. Maybe he was crying.

Or maybe it was stardust.

Timothée's heart pounded in his chest.

Was it a heart worthy of a star?

"Then help me," Timothée said

The heat was almost unbearable now, the air thick. The world wavered in front of him.

"Help you face a goddess?"

"I am a god," Timothée said, the words surprising even himself.

"A god without magic."

"Help me claim it." Timothée stood and gripped Val by the shoulders. "Besides, it's not really a goddess. It's just my fear."

"Well," Val sneered, averting his gaze, "your fear still burns like starcraft."

A moment flashed before his eyes: the Dark Prophet, gathering all the shadows in his hands. The sky darkening and blocking out the stars. The Prince's sword crumbling without his magic.

"Blacken the sky and steal the magic of the gods."

Val's eyes narrowed.

"Don't you see why I need you?" Timothée moved so close, their foreheads touched. "It's starcraft. Can you block it out?"

Val studied him, lilac eyes glimmering.

"You used your magic in the stairwell—"

Val smirked. "Made an impression on you?"

Timothée flushed. Hopefully his cheeks were already red from the heat. "Until you locked me in the sewer."

Val rolled his eyes. "Are you ever going to get over that?"

"Are you trying to distract me so this wall of flame devours us?"

Val looked up at him from beneath his dark lashes. "Trust me, Greywick. If I was *trying* to distract you, you would know."

Heat roared in Timothée's ears, the hiss of the inferno growing closer, chunks of this world breaking off, flowing into an expanse of space and time.

"Listen, before you change your mind, think about who we need to do this for." He picked up Yvaine, thrust the little black cat in Val's face. "She didn't ask to get stuck on some creepy beach and devoured by a god's fire because she thinks I'm going to follow in my brother's footsteps and destroy the world."

Val's face was unreadable. He looked from Timothée to Yvaine, back to Timothée.

"Every moment I'm in your presence, I despise you a little more." Val pushed away and unbuckled the black band around his neck.

"So are you going to create a little bubble around us, and then we can run on the beach to—"

"Greywick." Val pocketed the black choker. "You asked for help, so let me help."

He walked a few paces out onto the sand and faced the fire. "All right, you gigantic sun bitch," he murmured, "I thought you were done pissing me off, but apparently not."

Timothée felt the first spark of something cold in this place, saw the great dark shadows. Shadows pulled from the space around the world, the space between the stars. They drew toward Val. Darkness swirled at his feet and rose to curl around him like an embrace.

Against the angry roar, there was something beautiful about its delicate simplicity.

A storm cascaded around Val. Just as Timothée could no longer see the boy beyond the shadows, they shot upward and stuck in the great expanse. A black dome formed around them. A darkness no starlight could pierce.

The flames that wrapped around his star fell away, leaving the swirling purple glow.

Val looked over his shoulder, hair mussed. "Is this what you had in mind?"

"How did you do that?"

Val gave him a hard look. "If your fear can get that big, why not my magic?"

Free of fire, Timothée sprinted toward his star. Yvaine followed him, then leapt upon his shoulder. The star settled on the crest of a wave, like it was waiting.

Val kept his hands extended, breath heavy in his throat. "I can't keep this up forever, Greywick."

The sky swirled with inky shadows. Fireballs rained onto it, breaking apart on the outside darkness. Timothée's feet splashed in the black water. His star hovered close by.

Val backed up into the water, still holding his hands in the air. His knees buckled. "H-hurry."

Timothée stopped beneath his star. It shrank down to the size it had been when he caught it. Behind him, the world was crumbling, chunks of rock falling into the enormity of space and time.

Death by fire, or death by darkness.

Maybe there wasn't a difference.

The star settled between his palms.

Shadowcraft was waiting for him.

The type of magic that had leveled kingdoms and defied the gods.

Val let out a cry. The darkness above them crackled, then broke apart. Val wavered on his feet, and Timothée reached out with his free hand, gripping Val around the waist before he fell to the inky water.

The darkness of the sky dissipated, and a roaring tirade of fire sped toward them. Rushing to consume his star.

But it did not belong to the phoenix.

Timothée brought the star to his lips and swallowed. A great energy filled his mouth, then his throat, his chest. He cried out, doubling over. His body glowed white, and it felt like a million arrows were being fired from inside his ribcage.

Was the star burning him from the inside out? After all this?

Like the eclipse of a sun, the outward iridescent beams coiled over the ground, as if heavy and weighted by intense gravity. And the light turned black as pitch. Black as shadows.

Timothée shook his head, vision blurry. Saw the rain of fire sweeping toward them. No, no.

He threw up his hand. Shadows surrounded him and the ground opened.

TIMOTHÉE WAS FALLING.

Stars and galaxies swept around him. His mind felt foggy, distant. A strange rippling sensation funneled through him.

A boy fell alongside him, eyes closed, body limp, a black cat clutched in his arms. Shadows swirled around him. Timothée grabbed his head. "Val?"

Val blinked awake. For a moment, his face was soft, trapped in the place between sleep and waking, eyes half-closed, lips slightly parted. Timothée threaded his fingers through Val's wisping hair.

He coughed slightly, croaking a name Timothée couldn't hear. Shadows tightened around them, drawing Val closer.

"Wake up," Timothée said. "Your magic. You have to stop the shadows."

There were too many of them. They cloaked their bodies, blackened the stars with wisps of smoke. Timothée reached into Val's pocket, drew out his enchanted choker, and clumsily clasped it around the Dark Star boy's neck.

The shadows didn't dissipate.

Val shook his head, his voice rough. "It's... it's not me."

Of course it wasn't.

Timothée had swallowed his star.

And he had stopped the fire.

A terrible awareness spread through him. Every fiber of the universe came alive, and Val was right.

These were Timothée's shadows.

He felt the fabric that wove the stars into the sky and knew it was his to control.

The world rushed up to meet him: a field of dead stars and wet grass.

Timothée had returned to the Celestial Academy for Fallen Stars.

He had swallowed a star of darkness and ruin, and there was no place for that magic to go. He was a dam broken, a cup running over. Black tears fell down his face, and shadows writhed around his body, unwilled.

He saw a glimpse of Val scrambling away, Yvaine clutched to his chest, face part fear and something he couldn't name.

Shouting. Celestial Knights running down the hill. They had swords in their hands. His sisters screamed.

He couldn't stop this.

A Celestial Knight ran toward him, and his sword looked so sharp. *This isn't my fault. Don't come any closer,* Timothée tried to scream, but his throat was thick with magic. *I can't –*

A pointed shadow struck the knight. It lanced through his armor, and Timothée heard the agonized scream through the haze of his mind. The body dropped to the ground and didn't move. Shadows slithered over top, covering it like it had never been there at all.

Another wave of darkness extended out from him.

He couldn't control this. It flooded every nerve, every space of him.

He'd made the wrong choice.

He should have let the fire devour him before he devoured the school.

Darkness fell out of his body like a stormwind of shadows. It crept over the meadow, up the hill, and toward the waiting Starlings.

A realization cut through the flurry of Timothée's thoughts.

The Greywicks' father hadn't wanted to protect them from the Celestial Academy for Fallen Stars.

He had wanted to protect the Celestial Academy from them.

Thank you so much for reading Wicked Academia: Lost Stars! We hope you enjoyed the first adventure of the Greywick triplets. We would be so grateful if you would take a moment to leave a review. Reviews help indie authors like us so much!

Leave a review on Amazon:

Leave a review on Goodreads:

Here's to catching stars and kissing in the shadows.
The adventure continues in…

PREORDER NOW

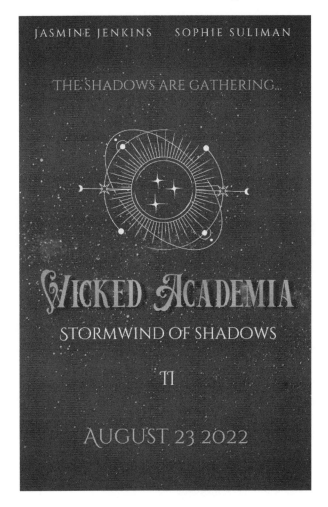

JASMINE JENKINS   SOPHIE SULIMAN

THE SHADOWS ARE GATHERING...

WICKED ACADEMIA

STORMWIND OF SHADOWS

II

AUGUST 23 2022

About Us

Jasmine Jenkins and Sophie Suliman are sisters who write new adult fantasy. They live in British Columbia, Canada. They love telling stories full of magic, adventure, and romance. When not writing, you can find them exploring the beautiful forests of their home, playing Dungeons & Dragons, or connecting with their amazing readers on social media.

DISCOVER YOUR MAGIC

What star would you catch at the Celestial Rite?

Are you curious, clever, and serene like a Morning Star?

Imaginative, determined, and resourceful like an Evening Star?

Emotional, passionate, and feared like a Dark Star?

Scan the QR code or visit

https://www.wickedacademia.com/discover-your-magic and take
the quiz to find out!

ACKNOWLEDGMENT

Building the world of Wicked Academia—from its first serialized version to the illustrated copy you hold in your hands—has been both the hardest thing we have ever done and the most rewarding.

It has been such a joy to create our magical school, the wicked students who inhabit it, and to foster a community of strange folk like us.

There is no way we could have done this alone.

Firstly, we want to thank our mother and father. They were the first ones to read our odd little book, and the first to love it. Thank you for always being our biggest fans, supporting us through every endeavor, no matter how strange, and believing in our dreams. We love you.

To Graeme, whose ideas, encouragement, and love have been a guiding bolt during this adventure and all the ones before. You are both sword and shield, a boundless supporter, and an endless advocate. The stars are closer when you are here.

To Auntie Jo, who has fed us through every book we've ever written. This book was fueled by your vegan chocolate chip cookies!

To Melanie G., Kendra S., Lisa D., and Taylor I. From the very first month we shared Wicked Academia and beyond, you have supported and believed in us. Having friends like you supporting us from the get-go gave us the courage and resilience to continue onward. Thank you.

To Zara S., who, despite never reading a fantasy book in her life, decided to create a character and join our world. Our walks, talks, and your boundless enthusiasm and encouragement bring joy to our lives. Thank you for caring.

To Ambrose, Emily, Lindsay, Solis, and Taylor: the dream team! Your friendship has been a gift. From fun bots, to role-play inspiration, to hyping the book, you five are a ray of sunshine. The publishing world is dark and scary, but knowing we have a team of brilliant, kind, and fun people behind us makes the dream all the more possible.

To the Wicked Academia community. Whether you're on Discord, Instagram, TikTok, or elsewhere... Thank you. Every "like", "share", or comment has meant the world. Every time you opened one of our newsletters or read a Friday chapter. Every time you posted fanart and loved our characters the way we love them. Every time you joined us for a movie night, shared a relevant meme, or just said hello. You are a part of the Wicked Academia family.

And finally, to our Patrons. We cannot say this enough: Wicked Academia would not be possible without you. You believe in us. You allow us to take time to pursue our wildest dream. You literally made the book in your hands possible. Thank you.

This thanks extends to the following Starlings and the others shining around the world:

Paige B., Laia H.Z., Kellie W., Bethany R., Lindsay K., Chelsea O., Samantha S., Siobhan CK., Kiara B-M., Glory S., Shyanne T., Nikki F., Loren H., Ambli A., Hannah W., Adi F., Bailey M., Emily Elizabeth K., Madeline B., Lea T., Louisa., Flossy Z., Emily B., Lena F., Emily S., Clarissa M., Mari Frances L., Ashley F., Carrieann Z., Ada B., Alison B., Kate M., CJ Nash., Lisa McF., Ally Z., Courtney R., Kayleigh P., Mack B., Jana K., Erica B., Naomi R., L Callaghan., Amaryllis W., Melanie G., Angel L., Bailey M., Marielle S., Lisa McF., Kellie W., Mysti L., Alison S., Jaime D., Symphony A., Skylar., Laeti G., Erin D., Lauren M., Kendra S., Yacine N., Winter A., Melissa W., Ada B., Alisa D., Siobhan CK., Freya G., Katie D., Lea T., Emily B., Kendal W., Victoria G., Irma N., Nicole T., Emily Elizabeth K., Hannah W., Alison B., Raegan L., Matt M., Nikki H., Madeline B., Lindsay K., Dianna L., Joya, and Sara N.

Here's to wishing on falling stars, kissing in the shadows, and all your dreams coming true.

Love and Starlight,
Jasmine and Sophie

Bonus Chapter
In Which Darius Meets a Girl With a Blue Ribbon in Her Hair

GREY CLOUDS PARTED and Wolfhelm spread out beneath him. Darius Störmberg leaned over the wicker basket as the large hot-air balloon carried him closer and closer to his city. *My home, my people.*

He cast another glance up, hoping to catch one last look at the Academy. The clouds had swallowed it again.

The nerves in his stomach confused him. Shouldn't he be joyful to return to Wolfhelm, to return home? It wasn't that he hadn't missed the familiar streets, or the tall towers of the castle, or the hard-working staff. It was just… As soon as he stepped off this air balloon and onto the ground, he wasn't a student of the Celestial Academy for Fallen Stars anymore. He was Prince Darius, heir to the throne and last of the Störmberg line. He had decisions to make, responsibilities amounting to much more than passing a class. His decisions as Prince affected all of Thraina.

His stewards handled the day-to-day of running the kingdom, though there were still some matters that required his attention. And some festivals he simply could not get out of attending, no matter how much he detested the day.

At least there was someone who was looking forward to the party. "And not to mention the sugar sticks," Khalid said. "I'm going to stuff my face with those! And the plays, the dancing… It's going to be amazing. Especially without Setviren nagging at me to listen to his lectures every spare moment."

"Oh, I'm sure you'll get enough of his nagging during the allegiance ceremony," Carmilla groaned.

"My favorite part," Khalid said flatly.

"Speaking of," Darius nodded out the side of the balloon where Setviren passed them on his sky skiff.

"Oh stars," Carmilla said. "Those goggles make him look ridiculous."

"He always looks ridiculous." Khalid impersonated Setviren's ever-frowning face.

The three of them burst out laughing, and Darius was grateful they decided to take the balloon together. Grateful that he had his two best friends beside him, and they could find the happy moments in the hardness of the day.

"FOCUS!" Setviren yelled at them.

Darius steadied his breath. They were drawing close to the castle now. Orange light crested over the horizon. The old loremaster had been wrong in assuming they couldn't get the balloon down before sunrise.

Darius centered himself and felt the magic of Xydrious flow through him. Felt the fire of his star ignite beside his heart. The gases in the air felt like an extension of his fingers. He concentrated, changing their composition. The flame powering the balloon shrank as he manipulated the air around it. Slowly, he guided the balloon down to an open space in the castle courtyard.

As soon as they landed, they were surrounded by court officials, guards, and Setviren, red goggle lines around his eyes.

Setviren scrunched his nose up at a pad of paper. "Your Highness, I have you scheduled to meet with Duchess Leesa this morning, but it seems her carriage has been delayed on the road."

Lines furrowed on Setviren's brow. There was only one thing the loremaster hated more than someone talking during his lectures: an upset schedule.

"I suppose," Setviren's thin lips quivered, "we can break our fast in the dining room and hope that—"

"Or," Khalid stepped forward, "we could get breakfast in town. I'm sure the vendors are already opening their shoppes. It would be educational for us to see the beginning of the festival."

"But what of—" Setviren started.

"We'll be back before His Highness's next appointment." Khalid's voice dripped with charm. "The guards can escort us."

"I'd rather sleep," Carmilla mumbled. She looked put together as always, her short red hair pinned back with golden clasps. But Darius could tell she was tired. All three of them had already adjusted to the Celestial Academy's routine of sleeping during the day.

"Come on, Mills. This is a once-a-year event." Khalid flashed his cunning smile at Darius. "What do you say, Your Highness?"

"Well," Darius said, "it may be good for me to spend some time among the people."

Setviren couldn't argue with that, as much as the veins in his head pulsed. "Alright, alright." He threw his hands out. "But take the royal guard and keep your hoods up!"

Khalid gave a mocking bow to Setviren then yanked Darius and Carmilla toward town.

Celestial Knights trailed them discreetly, and Darius took in a deep breath of morning fresh air. He nudged Khalid. "I am once again grateful for your quick thinking, my friend."

Khalid smirked and put a hand behind his head. "Nothing but self-preservation, Dare. A breakfast with Setviren would have put me right to sleep."

"Speaking of sleeping," Carmilla yawned, "if you two do not find me a coffee and some food, you will have to carry me back."

"Then breakfast it is." A smile broke across Darius's face. He threw his arms over Khalid and Carmilla's shoulders.

Dusty pink light spread over Wolfhelm, turning black shadows deep purple. The capital had awoken in a fervor, delighted energy radiating out of every shoppe. Today was for celebration. Bright banners of blue and gold hung between shoppe windows, and gates and pillars had been decorated with garlands and flowers.

"I keep hearing about a bakery around here," Khalid said. "The cinnamon buns are supposed to be better than the taste of starlight."

"I don't care what they taste like," Carmilla said. "I need them now."

Khalid led them through the streets, packed with stalls full of smoked meat, spices, fruit, and vegetables. Some sold books and pottery. There was even an entire stall selling busts and paintings of the Prince.

Darius's cheeks reddened and he pulled his hood lower. He mused on Khalid's words as they walked. *Better than the taste of starlight.* He remembered it clearly: catching his own falling star. The burning sensation as he'd placed that living star in his mouth, how it felt like he'd filled a hole inside himself he hadn't even known was there. Now he always felt it, a burning ember right beside his heart, ready to ignite at the first sign of night.

He glanced at his two friends. Under their cloaks, they wore their uniforms, each the color that represented the star magic the gods had blessed them with. All three of them had swallowed different stars.

Carmilla cast a disdainful glance at Khalid. "People are going to confuse you for a beggar wearing that old thing."

Khalid clutched his ratty brown cloak. "I'll have you know that this belonged to my great uncle. It's a family heirloom. That, and it's terribly comfortable." He gave a twirl as if to prove the point.

"You're hopeless," Carmilla groaned.

Khalid wrapped an arm over her shoulder. "We'll get you breakfast soon enough. Or is there another reason you're so grumpy today, Mills? Not used to all this sunlight? Or do you miss your bonny lad?"

Carmilla shoved him. "We haven't been a couple in forever, you moron. He was far too obsessed with his last paramour."

"And yet you still spend every waking moment with him." Khalid turned to Darius. "She says that's the reason they're not together, but I think she just couldn't handle dating someone prettier than her."

Darius didn't respond. He was quite over any romantic feelings he'd had for Carmilla, but that didn't mean he wanted to talk about her romantic exploits. He especially didn't want to think about Valentine and Carmilla.

He'd been young and foolish. They both had been. But he'd truly believed she'd loved him. Until she'd spent a summer in Kirrintsova and returned with a boy she'd met there, telling Darius, in that blunt and unapologetic way of hers, that it was over between them.

Darius didn't think he would have liked Valentine Sun even if they'd met in different circumstances. The boy had a calculating gaze about him, as if he was dissecting every word. His eyes prodded for weakness. He reminded Darius of a line from one of the old texts his tutors had made him read: *Trust not the fairest smelling flower, for it often bares the deadliest poison.* Of course, Valentine had followed Carmilla to the Academy, swallowed a star of his own, and even if it was a—

"Tease me all you like, Ali Bagheeri." Carmilla smiled darkly. "For all your flirting, who have you been with? Ghosts in the night?"

"Darling," Khalid smirked, "I'd rather bed a thousand ghosts then wake up to those purple eyes of Valentine's."

Carmilla slapped Khalid's cheek playfully. "And that is why you are a coward, and I am not."

Khalid whispered something to Carmilla, and they laughed together, and Darius was sure it was at his expense, because the next moment they were both walking on either side of him. He vowed to think no more on it, grateful for the friendship he still shared with Carmilla.

Carmilla leaned her head against his arm. "Ignore Khalid. He's a fly, constantly buzzing for your attention."

"A fly, really?" Khalid laughed. "What about a bee, or better yet, a beautiful butterfly?"

Darius smiled. "You certainly do like to stand out, my friend."

Just in the short time they had been in town, the streets had grown busier. People wandered arm in arm, dressed in heavy layers against Wolfhelm's autumn chill.

Khalid tilted his head and pointed up. "Ahh, even down here, she finds us!"

Darius followed his gaze. Above them, just breaking through the clouds, emerged the Isle of Argos. Atop it: the Celestial Academy for Fallen Stars.

I'll be back soon, he thought with fondness in his heart.

Khalid walked backward in front of them. "Professor Kunuk!" he called up.

"Stop it," Carmilla scolded, but there was laughter beneath her words. "You're making a fool of yourself."

Khalid gave a rueful smile and spread his arms wide. "If you can hear me, I promise my paper isn't late! It just needed a little extra love and—"

There was a crash and Khalid bumped into a crowd gathered outside a shoppe.

Darius quickly pulled him back before his friend toppled over completely.

"Whoops." Khalid gave a sheepish grin and backed behind Darius.

They stood in front of an old candle shoppe. *The Wonderous Wick* was written in curling painted letters above the old building. Khalid had knocked a candle out of a customer's hand. The owner was up in arms over it and was taking it out on a young woman. *Poor girl must be an employee.*

"Always with your head in the clouds." The owner smacked the girl on the side of the skull.

Darius stepped forward, but Khalid tugged him back. "We should go."

Something fluttered from the girl's hair. A blue ribbon. He caught it before it hit the ground.

The owner kept berating the girl, but Darius's gaze was caught on the blue silken ribbon in his hand. Such a simple thing. He looked up just as the girl turned around, clutching a broom.

Her dark brown hair blew across her eyes. They were big and blue... or grey. He was too far away to tell, and he had the sudden urge to step closer. She bent down, her dress blowing in the light morning breeze. Something burned beneath those eyes as she glared back at the shoppe owner.

But the shoppe owner didn't notice. She'd already turned away, speaking to the customer with the broken candle. "Now, let's get you a new candle. My clumsy worker won't mind paying for a replacement."

"A harsh punishment," Khalid muttered under his breath.

The fire in the girl's gaze wavered at the shoppe owner's words. Darius gripped the ribbon tighter in his hand and stepped forward.

"Excuse me," he said to the owner. "Let me pay for the candle. It was my party that knocked the girl."

The owner turned to him, and a false smile appeared on her face, as if she had been looking forward to reprimanding the girl. She thanked him nonetheless as he placed a handful of coins in her hands.

"Of course, he did that," Carmilla said.

"What did you expect, Mills?" Khalid laughed. "He sees a pretty girl in need and must save the day."

Darius turned back to them. "I needn't interfere if you hadn't been so clumsy, friend."

Khalid just shrugged.

The girl didn't seem pleased with him helping her, her face fixed in a scowl.

"You dropped this." He knelt before her and held out the ribbon.

She flicked her gaze up at him, and her expression immediately softened.

She had a wild sort of beauty. Like a half-finished painting, with bold lines of unblended color, like a sculpture with only one part rendered.

"Thank you." She reached for the ribbon and their fingers touched. The star in his heart burst to life, and he felt a shiver of celestial magic course through his body.

How odd. It was the same feeling as when he drew on the light of the stars to use his magic. But the dawn now ruled, and the stars slept.

She studied him, the same way he was studying her, but there wasn't any recognition in her gaze. *She does not know who I am,* he realized. There was no long stare of reverence that he often felt trapped under. No, she…

"You didn't need to do that." She stood and tied her hair up, revealing the elegant curve of her neck, the sharp cheek bones, and a spattering of freckles across her nose.

"No one should be punished for watching the wonders of the sky," he said, standing. "It wasn't your fault."

"And it wasn't yours." She looked up at him and smirked. "We can blame the ruddy Prince and his stupid festival for drawing all the crowds."

Darius felt his cheeks flush. If he had any lingering doubts that this girl knew who he was, they were instantly dashed.

Carmilla and Khalid laughed behind him. "It *is* a stupid festival, isn't it?" Carmilla said.

"Don't the people love it, though?" Darius asked, though he was more inclined to agree with Carmilla. But surely it was not all such a waste. "Exciting games and food and music? The sweep of a dance?"

The girl smiled, and it was so enchanting, Darius thought he would pretend to be a commoner forever if he could continue staring at that smile.

She held up her broom. "Well, first I'll sweep the candle shoppe, then I'll surely owe the Prince a dance for all the loveliness he has brought me today."